COME
JERICHO

COME JERICHO

a novel by
GEORGE BELLAK

WILLIAM MORROW AND COMPANY, INC.
New York   1981

Library of Congress Cataloging in Publication Data

Bellak, George J.
    Come Jericho.

        I. Title.
PS3552.E5317C6   813'.54   81-4858
ISBN 0-688-00125- 4   AACR2

Printed in the United States of America

First Edition

1   2   3   4   5   6   7   8   9   10

BOOK DESIGN BY MICHAEL MAUCERI

This book is for S.W.B. whose insistence and belief brought it to life, and for Nina who was there and made me a part of it.

THERE

The heat at noon was unusually intense. Polished aluminum stands burned the fingers. Broad-brimmed hats protected only so much. The Americans swore and slurped endless cans of soda provided by the commissary truck's frigid guts. The others, drab in black pajamas and conical hats, proceeded slowly toward the rough wooden benches and tables waiting for them. On the way, passing a mountain of cardboard boxes, they each selected one before settling down for the midday meal.

The bearded man and the auburn-haired woman were walking toward the blue van when the first shriek burst from a female throat, ululating in horror. Almost instantly, the screams of other women joined, one igniting the other until the sounds of loathing and disgust rose like a wall.

Shocked, the bearded man whirled and saw the pajamaed men leap up in shouting rage, grab boxes and hurl them to the ground, at trees, at the tables themselves, smashing the squares anywhere and everywhere they could. A blur of pasteboard sailed by his face, splatting to earth at the woman's feet, spewing its contents. She recoiled, jumping back, sickened, her right foot crunching a box lunch, once chicken and cheese, now a writhing mass of six-inch worms fighting for life, heaving, desperate invertebrate strands covering everything and staining all with their brown mucus.

As his companion added her screams to the cacophony, the bearded man snapped his head toward the table where every box held hordes of the repulsive, weaving feeders, bodies half-cut and oozing. As though on signal, the women fled in all directions, hopping and dodging to avoid the glop being sprayed like live rain. Moments later the men followed, and the Americans, dazed, were left to stare at the mess of twisted and broken chicken wings, flat

7

pulped breasts, bleeding thighs and great puslike gobs of yellow, all infested by the undulating blanket.

The bearded man reached out to steady the auburn-haired woman, who turned from him, retching. A man in dark glasses came up. He held a side of cardboard upon which red crayoned letters made themselves into a command.

The bearded man snatched the message, gripped it angrily in his fist, crushed it and dropped it amid the worms.

CHAPTER

1

When the call came, Paul had just returned from a weekend at Stella's place on the island. It had been another despairing episode replete, on both their parts, with awkward silences, with restaurant meals providing a welcome break, with shared misgivings of impending nightfall and the double bed. He left Sunday at six. The spring air was like silk and the earth was greening over. Speeding along the parkway back to the city, he had no idea how he felt. He was, he supposed, numb—in sensory limbo—and it troubled him.

It was still troubling him when he flipped his telephone answering machine to "Playback" and unpacked his bag. The tape reproduced his lawyer's voice with depressing accuracy.

"Paul—Carl Becker. These damn machines give me a pain in the ass—really. Anyway, I'm calling Saturday. Three o'clock. Get back to me as soon as you can. Mike De Luca's people tracked me down and made you an offer. *Mike De Luca.* They called just like that."

In his surprise, Paul dropped the hairbrush. Quickly, he phoned Carl, but the housekeeper said the Beckers were out for the evening. He left his name; he would have to wait. It would take doing.

In Paul's ten years as a film editor, he had done six features. He had earned a respectable living as a dedicated assembler of those bits and pieces of dormant nitrate protoplasm that eventually become the completed movie, jumping to life as the individual frames pass the projector lens, lapsing again to death on the other side.

He loved movies the way others might jewelry, reveling over a setting, a camera placement, a shade of light. He was enraptured by the very act of threading reels onto an editing table. When the frozen images transcended their quietude to become, on the ground-glass viewer, animated acts, moving objects and bodies, he felt magic at work. Even after all these years and all those reels. Now he had been called by a master.

9

Much later, he was to try to puzzle out why he had been called, how Michael De Luca could have known that he would be what he wished him to be. They had never met. There was no way of De Luca's knowing what Paul wanted or needed, no way at all. Yet, from thousands of miles away, from a hundred names, all possibly unknown to him, De Luca had reached into some secret hat and picked his.

"He's shooting this picture someplace in Mexico," Carl told him on Monday morning, consulting his yellow legal-sized notepad, "someplace called—what . . . Oac . . . Oacala? Ever heard of it?"

Paul had not.

"Well, he's been there for almost ten months now with that monster war picture of his. He's chewing up money by the millions, actors by the hundreds, and he's giving the studio executives shingles because he won't even talk to them. I'm told he's spent over twenty million dollars, and he's barely into it."

"His last picture made, what—fifty million?" Paul countered.

"It was one of those freaks. No one had confidence in the property, no one." The phone rang. The lawyer told his secretary to hold the calls for the next ten minutes, thereby demonstrating how important Paul was to him.

He talked on about De Luca, his excesses, his secrecy, his mistresses. He talked about everything except that De Luca was, by any measure, a driven, dedicated artist.

"Who told him about me?" Paul asked.

"His office didn't say. Just said he told them to get hold of Paul Gordon. You know those tight-mouthed bastards."

"When would he want me?"

"In an hour—you know. He has his pick. Now the money's very good, but I've heard that some kind of funny stuff is going on down there."

"What do you mean, funny stuff?"

Within the hour, Paul was in touch with a west coast friend who normally knew every esoteric shred of gossip.

"Paul, the guy is in some crazy place. I've met people who've come back from there but they just clam up when you ask them anything. But you know De Luca operates like some Borgia. He's got secrets on secrets, and he burns money like confetti to keep it that way. You never know the truth. But some kind of unusual mysterioso is going down there. I get that vibration. If you go, check with your astrologer first."

On Tuesday, Paul phoned Stella. They met for a drink at the Algonquin, a hard place to be silent. He told her of the offer. She fingered her curls—those tight Grecian ringlets he had been breathless over at first sight.

"Really funny for that man to call *you* to work on his picture. You're about as unalike as dynamite and porridge, from what I've heard about him. And he likes people on his own wavelength."

"It could be a chance to work with someone terrific," Paul said patiently. "I want to do that for once in my life." He leaned forward for emphasis. "Most of the pictures I've worked on have been crap —directors who caved in under money pressures, ruined the story, put in theme songs. This man puts it on the line. He takes risks."

"Umm." Stella sipped the Campari. Paul hated her resistance.

In silence they observed the action. Enough denim in the lobby of this cultural watering place to make the proper political statement and enough hacking jacket to make the proper class identification. Paul felt awkward in khakis and his old seersucker single-breasted. Stella, in a blue silk blouse and rust-colored slacks, was in harmony. He had always harbored a vague feeling of discomfort at how easily she was comfortable anywhere while he felt protrusions and angles all over. She ascribed her sense of "in place" to what she did at the Public Broadcasting station where she met and dealt with so many idiots and incompetents at all levels that she was rarely thrown by anyone, anyplace, anymore. They had met at that very station, two years ago when he had put together a documentary on strip mining. He had seen in her someone firm and sure. She had seen a somewhat shy, attractive, talented man. They had gone to bed almost immediately, and the act, to their surprise, drew them together. They seemed to fit, key in lock, bump to hollow. For over a year Stella felt she had encountered a rare man, giving, compassionate, appreciative of her own gifts, and saw them coming together as equals, no matter the flaws in each. What Paul saw he did not say; Stella was more effusive, more given to projection and dream.

It was midway in the second year that the flow of energy between them became, first, subtly altered, then not so subtle.

"Well," Stella said finally, "you're going to work with the wunderkind then."

"I think so."

"How long will you be gone?"

"I really don't know." Oddly, as he looked at Stella, Sylvie came

11

to mind. They looked nothing alike, were nothing alike, and yet Sylvie, willowy, uncertain, constantly tremulous, was evoked full-blown. Separations? He wondered what she was doing now, five years after the divorce. His mind went from Sylvie to his Volvo; he'd have to store the car.

"Look at us"—Stella interrupted his reverie—"breaking up amicably."

"You surprised?" he asked, surprised himself.

"I'm pleased we're able to talk about it. There's been a lot of silence these last months."

He thought of the explosions that had led to the silence.

"If you had simply disappeared and faded away into the Mexican sunset, it would have been hateful," she added.

He was not totally sure of that.

"So many people get ugly with each other when they split," Stella said intensely, "and the memories get all twisted. I don't think I could bear it if we did that."

She seemed so reasonable and uncritical, so loving, almost, that shards of his original attraction speared him. Stella possessed the intelligent good looks he had always admired. Her high cheekbones and gently flaring nostrils (courtesy of Slavic genes), the deep-set dark eyes under her curly blond helmet, might have been, in some other woman, too exotic; in Stella they became almost wholesome. There was, too, a tempered grace about her rounded body that made her complete. She was smart and capable and energetic.

"I'll get the check," he mumbled.

She covered his hand with hers and said, quietly, "It's all right, Paul, it's really all right."

That night Paul told Becker to accept De Luca's offer; he would be on a plane within seventy-two hours.

"Fine," the lawyer said. "You go to Mexico City and check in with De Luca's guy there. He'll arrange the work permit and all the other papers. Take a couple of days, they say. Then you'll fly out. Remember to get pills and don't drink the water."

From Mexico City it is fifty minutes by air to Oacala in the south of the country, just above the place where the Isthmus of Tehuantepec begins, to end, finally, near Guatemala. The 737 is scheduled to depart at ten-thirty every morning. It departs sometimes at eleven, sometimes at twelve, overlapping the scheduled twelve-fifty-five which fails, mysteriously, to take off now and then. Sometimes even the ten-thirty does not leave, and any reasonable explanation will not be forthcoming. These departures seem not to be dictated by timetables or wind and weather so much as by whim and prior pilot romantic involvement. Once the passengers are aboard, however, this Latin laxity becomes flying madness. The aircraft starts its taxi even before the doors can be secured and is moving while the last safety handle is being snapped down. The plane then races along the asphalt as though in a speedway competition. It hurls itself into the air at a seventy-five-degree angle as the taped clarion of the mariachi band pours into the cabin, smothering the gasps and cries of the passengers.

Eventually the plane heads south, past Mount Popocatépetl, serene and ancient, its cratered peak lost in the heavy clouds. Below, burning mesquite bushes appear amid grayish-green rock-strewn farm plots. As the passengers begin to unwind from the takeoff, the plane's shadow leaves Mexico City's high-rises and glides over glaring desert where adobe huts stand nakedly vulnerable, yet defiant. Wisps of smoke ascend from their dried mud chimneys. On occasion, a small boy can be seen to cease scolding his five goats, clutch his serape, put a cupped hand to his sombrero and gaze skyward at the familiar miracle passing overhead.

This day the plane had taken off at a quarter of twelve—not too bad, all things considered, the passengers agreed. Because of some quirk in the weather, the pilot had swung toward the coast, and Paul, sitting in row F, at the window, stared down as Acapulco came into sight.

From this height the bay appeared a perfect unmarred crescent gently slicing into the shore, small waves breaking foam upon iridescent sands. Golden bodies graced that sand—oiled, petted, dieted, well cared-for, few of them Mexican. Beyond the bodies rose the solid phalanx of hotel structures blocking the avenida from view. Stone bulk on stone bulk, they rose twenty, thirty stories into the air, like mauve fortresses concealing the sight of the real town, the old town, the native quarter whose inhabitants had almost nothing at all to do with the cliff dwellers save to sell them souvenirs on the beach, clean out their toilets or service them sexually. Other than that, the two populations seldom met. To the Guerrero Indians of Acapulco, the *norteamericanos*, Hawaiian-shirted and flower-skirted, were like a race from outer space.

Minutes later, the plane banked left. The coast dropped away. Villages disappeared, and suddenly the vaguely forbidding Sierra Madre rose up underneath. Thrusting fifteen thousand feet, veiled

13

in mist, wreathed in snow, the mountains did not welcome. Their tight-branched trees, mottled and rust-colored, were a scabrous and threatening skin. To be lost there, even simply to *be* there, was a defiance of nature. And yet, on the lower reaches where the tree line broke, there were yellow-green corn patches and a few of the inevitable mud-walled huts. Paul wondered how the hell they survived there, those skinny people with their even skinnier animals and their threadbare clothes.

He watched, half in a daze, as the 737 flew over the sierra for for some twenty-five minutes. Abruptly—this pilot did everything abruptly—the nose tilted down and the descent began. In a few minutes the mountains became less threatening. The glisten on the peaks became water. The mountain fur became trees. Now and then Paul could spot a trail winding through the brush. Then he became aware, with some surprise, that there were walls reaching up above the aircraft, as it dove through a canyon. Vibrating, the plane slewed and yawed as thermal winds swept by. In an instant the plane dropped twenty feet, leaving Paul's stomach behind. The forty passengers gasped at once. A child wailed. The stewardesses busied themselves. The steward looked out the window.

The invisible currents battled for ten long minutes and then, gradually, eased their hold. Paul's stomach contracted less. The aircraft's shuddering ceased, and the aluminum skin became solid and reassuring once more.

Down below, Paul could clearly see the Oacala valley. In the center was the city of Oacala itself, nestled snugly as a nut in a bowl of what were now verdant foothills. The sierra had turned lush, adorned itself with rivulets, graced itself with grasses and flowers, with fruit trees and avocados. The earth was black and rich in this valley. As the plane swooped in, speedily, and most of the passengers braced themselves for the landing, Paul felt a sense of remove from the other side of the mountains, that sense which had kept this valley relatively intact for so many centuries, had kept the old Indian ways from disappearing and the Zapotec mysteries alive.

When the plane rolled to a halt to the applause of its riders, and he stood in the open doorway ready to move down the steps, a powerful fragrance entered his nostrils. The air, laced with strong orange and mimosa and lemon verbena, was unlike any other he had ever breathed, though he had one flash of a summer long, long

14

ago, in the mountains, with his mother, picking blackberries. Beyond the airfield, his eye, searching the valley plain, was drawn to the ring of circling hills which created a gentle shade, while up above the sun shone, it seemed, in some especially beneficent fashion.

Instantly, he felt in the grip of some other world, some saved graceful remnant. He shook his head in admiration for De Luca. How did he ferret out this place to make a movie? Only fifty minutes from Mexico City, it seemed as remote as the Australian outback. Trust De Luca to come up with something like this. Trust him to discover the harmony.

In the middle of May with the thermometer hovering between sixty-five and seventy-five—perfection for anyone else—Stella couldn't get warm. The feeling of strange chill started the day after the Algonquin drink and lingered like a hangover. She would awaken before the alarm went off and be wide-eyed in seconds, jangling with images sensual, commercial, trivial. Her mind raced to make connections she had no real interest in making. Outside, on New York's East Sixty-fifth Street, the light had barely slanted over the parked cars and she lay under the flowered percale, eyes open blankly, staring at the blue ceiling, brain unable to shut off.

To soothe herself, she would brush her thighs together in gentle movement, the generated excitement obliterating conscious cerebration. She would push herself to the edge of climax, hips undulating, hands pressing on the bed; but it was flat, unrelieving. And the figure in her mind was Paul, always surprising and disturbing to her, the more so since in the last months their sexual connections had had little force.

What the hell, Stella would muse, as the light in the room grew stronger, what the damn hell? What is going on? What do I want? Is it ego? Because *he* was the one to finally break? And what would have happened if De Luca hadn't called him to work, anyway?

Making the Melitta coffee and eating her grapefruit in the east-facing kitchenette, Stella probed the innocent fruit viciously. If, at thirty-six, she wasn't mature enough to deal with nostalgic memories of an ex-lover, then something was very wrong.

The grapefruit tasted bitter and she hurled it into the garbage can. Had she already forgotten her irritation with so much of what Paul was?

15

"Are all only children like you?" she had asked him once. "Do they always feel that something is missing and they don't know what to do about it?"

He had turned away then and she had been, instantly, contrite, for she had affection for his vulnerability, though she disliked it at the same time.

After she had seen one of his films, she remarked that he was as good a film editor as there was in the business—better; but he always seemed to need someone to look up to, to lead him.

"It's as though you abdicate your own judgment, as though you're uncertain of your own talent."

He had replied, with frustrated annoyance, "What do you want of me, really? Just what do you want me to be for you?"

She had not been able to answer and felt the lack in herself as well as in him. On the day Paul had left for Mexico City he had called to say good-bye. She had felt, inexplicably, like crying. The conversation had been pleasant, but it left her feeling limp afterward.

At work Stella carried on as always, which, this week, meant maneuvering a venal oil company into funding a documentary on environmental pollution. Public Broadcasting had struck again.

She had her hair done, kept her two big lunch dates, went with her homosexual friend, Robert, to a new musical, bought some Christmas gifts at Saks, stayed for a time at a publishing cocktail party where she met a Los Angeles movie executive remarkably unlike what he should have been. He was urbane and fairly sensitive and without a heavy tan. When he asked her to dinner, she accepted.

After dinner she took him home to the inevitable bed. His name was Mark and he had a firm, taut body which she admired. He stroked her flanks and told her she was enormously stimulating and exciting to be with.

"Umm," she said, not wishing to talk at all, just wishing he would mount her, enter her. She wanted to push and pull and move and throw herself about. With someone she hardly knew, might never see again, it was possible.

When he did enter her, expertly, she closed her eyes, clasped him to her with expectation of the carnal rush, waiting for the lubricity to occur, for the very sounds of wetness alone to stimulate. All she felt, though, were his movements, sure and deep and unmoving to her. In despair, she lifted her legs, locked them be-

16

hind his back, straining to him. He pierced her deeper, making soft, endearing sounds, but she experienced only a dull friction. In a panic that all sensation was gone forever, she turned her body, heaving up and reversing the man in bed with her so that she was mounting him now. He accommodated himself, muttering, "Yes . . . yes . . . yes . . ." and continued thrusting. She thrust against him, grinding her pelvis, feeling the dampness on her throat and forehead, determined to finish.

He thrust more violently in response. She felt the jabs not as pleasure but as pain. Her back began to ache and her movements slackened. As they did, he climaxed. She was hardly aware of it, only became so when his movements lessened and ceased. When she felt it was decent to do so, she rolled off and lay beside him. Turning her face away, she wished very hard that he wouldn't want to spend the night. She loathed herself for not being able to respond and was amazed by it.

The next day, a fever burning in her, Stella counted the days that Paul had been gone, determined that, from what he had told her of his plans, he was still at the Castillo Hilton in Mexico City. At twelve o'clock she called the hotel and asked to speak to Señor Gordon.

"Who?"

"Gordon." She enunciated very clearly. "Señor Paul *Gorrdon.*"

"Ah, Señor Gorrdon."

"Yes."

"*Momentito.* One moment, please."

She heard shuffling then, and voices. The clerk came back on the line.

"Señor Gorrdon has out-checked, madame."

"No," she said, "he won't check out till tomorrow."

"I am sorry, señorita, but Señor Paul Gorrdon, from room *veinte y tres*—twenty-three—he has out-checked and left for the south."

Unsettled, she asked, "Are you sure?"

The clerk was sure. "Oh, yes. He has taken the flight for Oacala. We made the arrangements for him."

"Damn. Oh, damn."

"Excuse?"

"There's no excuse," Stella said. "None." And she hung up, softly.

CHAPTER
2
:=×=×≡×≡×≡×≡×≡ 2 ≡×≡×≡×≡×≡×=×

The Oacala air terminal was small and modern, precast white-washed concrete emblazoned with a gigantic mural depicting "*La Revolución*." Peasants in white, ocher faces somber, stood shoulder to hip like rhythmic waves of grain. Bandoliers crossed their chests; raised rifles and machetes howled defiance. Beside them, idealized raven-haired women in the colorful Oacala *huipils*, the native over-blouses and skirts, raised fists against the Spanish grandees in blinding armor on rearing horses.

Before then and since, time had mingled the seeds of the invaders and the invaded, but here, in the Oacala valley, the old Indian blood was strong and often very pure, with deep connections to their ancestors, the Zapotecs, great forebears of the Aztecs in this valley, the constructors of a great civilization destroyed in mystery. The language the people spoke best was the ancient Nahuatl, though they all knew Spanish. The dignity and independence of the old ways were kept almost uneroded. In the foothills of the Sierra Madre the secret rituals of their fathers were still practiced in defiance of the priests who knew but said little. The government frowned but issued only "educational advice." On Sunday mornings the churches were filled; on Sunday nights the same people filled the hill caves.

These small, dark, fine-boned people had managed to survive remarkably intact. They scratched their plots of earth, raised their chickens and corn; some worked in the blanket and ornament factories, and—in the fastnesses of the mountains—they found hidden recesses in which to grow the damp-leafed marijuana plant. They sold the pickings to the smugglers, the dopers who came down from the States looking for a "score," finding it difficult to believe that the plant, useful to their people for so many hundreds of years in sacramental ways, was worth what the Americans would pay. They

18

accepted the fact, however, without question. As they accepted the danger of the police, who, upon discovering a tract, would imprison them, beat them senseless or even take their lives "accidentally."

The mural on the terminal wall said nothing of this, however. It said BIENVENIDOS. In some fashion, Paul actually felt welcome.

A broad-chested man in a T-shirt, long-haired and clean-shaven, Lee Riders low on his hips, blue-and-white track shoes completing his ensemble, approached. He appeared to be in his late twenties. A bad case of peel had attacked his prominent nose. His well-developed upper arms were solid mahogany. When he spoke, his voice came from New York.

"Hi—you're Gordon, right?"

"Right."

"I'm Steve Kruger—with the company. I'll drive you in."

He held out a large hand, which Paul dutifully shook.

"How'd you like the flight?"

"Few surprises."

"Yeah. Bumptidy-bump. It's always like that." He scrutinized Paul closely. The look asked how long this one would last.

After the bags came, Kruger led the way to a fire-engine red jeep and they swung aboard. He reached over to insert the starting key but hesitated, swiveling his head to the right, where a stoop-shouldered man in a serape hunkered down, a yard away, his large, mournful eyes staring at them.

"Hey, Chico," Kruger called, frowning, "*qué pasa?*"

The hunkering man snapped his eyes closed.

"That son of a bitch ain't sleeping," Kruger muttered, and called again, "Hey . . . *oiga!*"

Wordlessly, the man uncoiled like a creaky spring and walked away, his shoulders bobbing.

"What's happening?" Paul asked.

"I don't like them hanging around my jeep."

Kruger was obviously bothered and took time to cool down. He unlocked the glove compartment and rummaged for his cigarettes. As he did so, Paul was startled by the dull gloss of an ugly black pistol snout among the matchbooks and spare fuses. Before a second look was possible, Kruger slammed the compartment shut and nimbly raced off, saying nothing, leaving Paul vaguely disquieted.

The paved road, new blacktop, drew an absolutely straight line from the airport to a large, vegetation-covered mound, perhaps a hundred feet high, which stood squarely in its path. It then pro-

19

ceeded to curve serenely around, continuing dead straight again. As they passed the hill, Paul craned his head around.

The driver chuckled. "Yup. The highway goes around that thing. Know why? Because that's an old Indian pyramid. Burial hill or some such, covered over by all that stuff, but it's in there, somewhere. So no one goofs with it. They leave it—and go around."

They went *around*. Paul stared as the hillock receded. Impressive. The pyramid and the blacktop coexisted; one wasn't sacrificed for the other.

Twenty minutes on the blacktop and they were inching along the cobblestone streets, competing with burros for space. Life flowed around them. Ancient, wheezing Austins, new Toyotas and Fiats, pre-sixties Detroit monoliths raced in place as fragile-boned, impassive-faced Indian women picked their way through, bearing enormous loads of fruits, vegetables, electrical wire, pottery, on their heads. How did they achieve that balance? Paul wondered. Perhaps that walk, that steady swaying movement. And perhaps they were balanced by the sleeping infants they carried on their backs knotted in the shawls.

"Got you a room at the Jaime." Kruger threated patiently through. "Pretty old, but classy. They put air conditioning in a year ago, they say. Damn thing even works about half the time. Not bad."

"How long have you been here?"

"Old hand. Came in with Mike almost a year ago for preproduction. Been here ever since."

Paul was impressed. "You never left?"

"I had a week's R and R in L.A. Saw my girl friend. She'd changed a lot. I came back."

"How far along is the shooting?"

"Got me. Mike's the only one who knows anything. Sometimes everything just sits, you know, till Mike figures out the next move. Last month we didn't hardly shoot a goddamn thing for over three weeks, then we did a Cong torture scene."

"I know the picture's about Vietnam," Paul said, "but that's all I know."

"That's almost all *I* know," Kruger said. "Anyway, Mike has this Green Beret unit in the story, see, and in the sequence we shot, the tough major looks the other way when some of his guys work over a Viet with their lighters. I wasn't there, but I heard the scene was terrific."

20

He laughed. "The Cong guy was a Mex actor and he was giving a little trouble, reacting. So the guys just, like, singed him a little, for real. Accidentally, you know. He just went apeshit, screaming like hell, and Mike kept the cameras running. We're here."

The Jaime was an elderly five-story structure in the colonial style, but the architects had gone Oacala in some places with strange parapets and mounds reminiscent of pyramids. The mural splashed onto a side wall was of a puissant industrial Mexico holding out a friendly hand to its neighbors of the south. The room assigned to Paul by the smiling desk clerk was very pleasant. Handcrafted wooden furniture set the tone. A small balcony faced the Sierra Madre. A blue-tiled bathroom exhibited an enormous bathtub and shower with impressive lion-headed handles.

"Can I grab a shower?" Paul asked.

"Mike said to bring you right over."

Paul accepted the dictum. Back into the jeep they went. Kruger wheeled across the central square with its raised bandstand, cafés on the four sides, masses of orange and yellow and blue flowers everywhere.

"This is the Zócalo. Everybody comes out to do their thing here. Siesta's getting over so it's jumping a little."

The seats and benches were filling with Oacalan men, some in stiff suits, some in white trousers and Mexican shirts. They ate small tortillas or sweet rolls. They drank strong coffee or small tequilas. The air was brisk with chatter and bustle. Here and there, obvious foreigners rested their sightseeing legs, cameras on the table alongside the bottles of flavored Tehuacán water.

Turning a corner on two wheels, Kruger went through a series of alleys, the last of which opened onto a large center square flanked by four brick and corrugated metal buildings. American occupation was immediately evident in the grouping of trucks and jeeps, in the signs indicating SOUND DEPARTMENT, CAMERA DEPT., ADMIN., CASTING, in the bustle of loading, in a truck piloted by a bare-chested, ham-handed car jockey, his cassette speaker blaring out heavy rock as he took off with a screech of rubber. Here, too, were the small, thin Indian bodies working under Yankee direction, fetching and carrying patently unfamiliar objects, handling them gingerly and awkwardly to the outraged yells of the brawny supervisors.

"Christ, you chili chompers are gonna drive me outta my mind.

I do another picture outta God's country, you can put me in the goddamn booby hatch!"

Kruger shook his head disapprovingly. "That's the key grip. He's letting it get to him. There's no bowling here, see." He tugged at Paul's arm. "Come on, Mike's got an office on the first floor. Welcome to the crazy house. I'll see you later."

Paul took a deep breath as Kruger left him. The flight, the new sights and sounds, had been exciting, masked any anxiety. But now a small ache began to form in his stomach. He waved good-bye and walked across to the largest building.

The converted warehouse, as he entered, proved to be a cavernous floor divided into many partitioned areas and rooms. Four men and two women were gathered about a huge bulletin board. Obviously film crew members, they checked typed schedules against other schedules posted on the board. The men were uniformly in jeans. The two women wore cutoffs and Mexican tops. All had walkie-talkies strapped to their belts.

"Excuse me," Paul interrupted, "where could I find Mr. De Luca?"

Instantly, they turned to examine him. There was interest and tension in the looks, querying and evaluation, the sniffing out by the pack. On of the men, lean-faced, eyes shaded by tinted aviator glasses, was frank in his open examination. He wore a flowered polyester shirt, and a gold medallion nestled among his graying chest hairs. Two rings of keys hung from a wide leather belt clasped by an intricately welded brass belt buckle. He appeared to be the oldest of the group, in his early forties, every year crowded with experience.

"Gordon?" he said.

"Got me." Paul smiled. "How'd you know?"

"He knows. He knows," one of the women said. She had long braided hair and efficient shoulders. In her early twenties, she was one of the new generation of female crew members, beneficiaries of the feminist movement.

"I try to know. I'm Sal Sieberling." He produced a formal smile and held out his hand. "I sent the wire that got you hired."

Paul shook the hand, not knowing what to say.

"Mike's waiting to see you," Sieberling said quickly. "He's in that office, the one without any name on it."

"Thanks." Paul felt Sieberling's eyes still searching him. It was an efficient stare.

He walked down the hall and knocked on the unmarked door. It opened, and Mike De Luca was there.

Paul's first impression was one of delicate bulk. Despite the paunchy middle and the swelling hips, despite the fleshy white chest revealed beneath the open *camisa* as well as the somewhat puffy face beneath the jet-black beard, De Luca's eyes filter-soft, his handshake firm and secure, his smile wary yet warm, put him into a kind of balance. He was not as tall as Paul had expected, but the impression was one of largeness all the same and, instantly, Paul could see what they meant about Michael's "thing."

"There is this thing about Michael," a writer once told him. "When he's with you, he's with *you*. No one else exists. He and you. In this business, that's rare."

"So," De Luca said in a soft and musical voice at once confident and pleading, "sit down. Have some wine? A beer? I'm glad you've come. I need all the help I can get. I'm in over my head with this picture." He grinned like a small boy, shrugged, sipped from a glass of iced wine.

"Your office made an offer I couldn't refuse," Paul said.

"Good. Good. Very good."

Paul told him he admired most of the pictures the director had made, more than admired, wished he'd worked on some of them with him, thought them quite courageous.

As he talked, the director grimaced and looked away. Paul immediately understood that De Luca was embarrassed. Later, he came to know that Michael could not take compliments; they agonized him somehow; that wasn't what he was in the game for.

"Hell," De Luca said, "I decided to try stuff. My old man was a grocer in the Bronx. He ran this teeny joint where he made the best heroes. He used to tell me you had to try stuff or it was no good." He laughed in affectionate memory. "He himself never tried anything—except more anchovies. He had a fine tenor voice. 'Hey, Luigi,' people used to say, 'you shoulda be in the opera. Go try. You be-a good-a. You be-a first-a-class. You beat-a them all.'"

With an economy of movement, De Luca re-created the moment, filling it with tenderness, and Paul saw the springs that fed the humanity of his films, the need to tell stories of sweet people frustrated, generally, by the overwhelming power of institutions. De Luca sipped again.

"Great guy. He came down, last month, to bring lasagna."

"Brought lasagna from New York?"

23

Paul shook his head in unabashed admiration. De Luca reached down to his Adidas and said, looking at the floor, "I think maybe it's going to be all right with you."

Paul didn't quite know what that meant, but he felt the shyness in De Luca's voice and marveled that this dedicated and imaginative artist should still retain the reserve and delicate instincts of someone not so celebrated.

"I saw the picture you cut about prisons," De Luca continued. "You got the most out of the footage, I happen to know."

That was pleasing. Some directors never acknowledged an editor's contributions; everything had to be theirs.

"As a matter of fact," De Luca said, "when I needed someone here, I told my office to get me whoever it was who cut that movie." His eyes rolled up sheepishly. "I didn't even know your name, but I do now." He laughed and asked if Paul had ever tried directing a film.

"I directed, if you can call it that, a little nuts-and-bolts short for an auto company."

"Gosh," De Luca said, leaning forward, attention totally on Paul, "I never did any of that. I went right from film school to the coast and started scrambling for a foothold. I was lucky, very, very lucky."

"Talented helps."

"I was lucky," De Luca insisted.

"I got my first job as an assistant when I was in L.A. only a year. That was because someone had faith in me. He was a producer dying of television. I mean he was a fifty-five-year-old Hollywood kill case, some important movies in the past and then nothing. But he could make a living in television, so he did. But he couldn't hack it. He still had dreams, visions, and they haunted him night and day. When I met him, he had just been told by his doctor he had cancer. It astonished him. He hired me and died eight months later. I learned a little then. Don't let the bastards give you cancer. Don't give them an inch. I told myself I had to do things my way, or I'd never be anything . . . to myself, that is. I don't give a shit what I am to other people."

The door opened after a single knock, revealing Sieberling.

"Hi. I just wanted to make sure you found the boss."

The phone rang. De Luca picked it up, listening intently. Sieberling stood by quietly, his back to Paul, but in some mysterious

24

fashion, his attention seemed to be directed *behind* him. Suddenly, De Luca's voice rose up in sputtering anger.

"Damn it, fuck the siesta. I want that sequence shot, Allan. *Now.* You hang in there."

Slamming the phone down, he turned to Sieberling.

"Marcus, at the jungle location. He's set up to do second-unit at the helicopter base and somebody goofed. No one called Denny's pilots. He was going to reschedule for the afternoon, after siesta. Christ!"

"I'll get out there," Sieberling said swiftly, and left. With the close of the door, De Luca's anger dropped away.

"That's why we're here so long, see. The most disorganized location ever. Hard to get things centralized, but it's perfection here for what I'm trying to do—and"—he grinned impishly and his teeth shone whitely through the beard—"it keeps the studio idiots away. It's uncomfortable here and they don't like to be uncomfortable. They have to take that bouncing plane down here from Mexico City. I put it around that two people were badly hurt when it crashed once. Sheer fabrication."

Paul laughed with him. "So that's what's going around."

De Luca stopped laughing. "What's going around?"

"Some more of your invented rumors, I think. Something mysterious is supposed to be happening here."

De Luca sipped his wine in silence, his mood changing, then he said, "Paul—I'm going to confide in you, can I? Can I do that?"

Surprised, Paul nodded, and De Luca took a deep breath.

"Something *is* happening. It started months ago when a load of important costumes coming from the cleaner's disappeared. They never turned up. We lost a lot of time over that."

Was he serious? Paul wondered.

"After that, other things started to happen. Thefts, foul-ups. Once a whole location meal for two hundred people had worms in every box. The extras went crazy, ran away saying it was a bad sign. And there was a note telling me to stop making my movie."

Paul found it difficult to keep the slight skeptical edge from his voice. "But why is this happening? You're just making a film."

"Just a film?" De Luca brooded. "Maybe, but some people don't want me to make this movie. They'd like to stop me. They'll go very far to stop us, Paul."

It was still a mystery.

25

"Why would they want to stop you?"

De Luca's voice, calm, took on the tone of a teacher enlightening a student.

"Reactionary forces would love to stop me, Paul. Right-wing forces. Local fascists, landowners, industrialists. These entrenched bastards run this country like a fiefdom. And Vietnam represents a deep defeat for them, a bitter defeat. And they hate what I'm trying to do."

Paul looked up at De Luca in bewildered surprise. The director continued.

"I heard it first when I asked to come down here to shoot. A lot of big shots were leery. They asked me what I was going to make. I was smarter than they—a love story, I told them. But I had to tell them the setting. When they heard Vietnam, well, the shit really started to hit the fan. One objection after another—all phony. I got the real reason from someone who knows the moves here. They felt I'd come in and somehow ruffle the waters. The little people, the peasants, would be making some good money, for one thing, and might get uppity. Then also, they might get the message of the movie about how little people all over the world get shafted by the powers that be—and they'd make trouble, become terrorists, take to the hills, for God's sake. They told me, almost point-blank, that if I came down here to expect trouble." He clenched a fist. "But I'll be damned if I'm going to let them run me out. I stay here and I make my movie!" A sigh escaped. "And the last thing I want is for the studio to latch onto this; they'll use it as a whipping post."

Cautiously, Paul agreed.

"Meanwhile, we go right on working; we don't let the problems get us down." He smiled ruefully. "Still want the job?"

The smile broke the tension and Paul gurgled, "Are you kidding?"

De Luca cackled. "All right. Your first assignment is to get acquainted with the material. There are seven screenplays so far." He gestured, with distaste, toward a stack of folders. "But don't take any of them seriously. Who knows how many more I'll do before we're through here?"

The office door opened again to admit a young woman whom Paul judged to be in her late twenties. Her hazel eyes were extraordinarily large and luminous. Her hair, cut in bangs, was almost the color of her eyes. She was lean-framed and very tan. The French jeans and Indian moccasins she wore did not conflict with the intricately embroidered Mexican blouse that blazed green and

26

orange on her shoulders. In one hand she held a can of film and in the other a logbook. Her fingers, on the left hand, carried two small and beautiful silver rings. She was devoid of any other jewelry or makeup. There was a naturalness about her, a lack of artifice, that he instantly liked.

"Oops," the woman said, in a strong voice, "just wanted to talk to you about that girl's test, Michael. She looks no more like a Vietnamese than my mother in Connecticut does."

"Rack it up." De Luca leaned over, took the orange shoulders in his hands and kissed the back of the woman's head as she put the reel of film on the Moviola. She turned, smiled at the director with a calm, assured air, kissed him on the lips and turned back to the reel. It was a sweetly intimate moment, and yet, in some way, Paul felt he was not intruding; he was simply there.

"You see our rapport," De Luca said. "You see how well we work together, director and editor." He laughed happily, sipped his wine. "Rennie, this is Paul Gordon."

She was Rennie Loomis and volunteered that this was her first job as a full assistant editor. Up till then she had been an apprentice.

After the hellos, she nudged the toggle, moving the film through the sprockets. Flapping gently, the frames entered the harsh white light. Flickering images appeared on the small ground-glass viewer, resolved themselves into a jungle scene, a bamboo forest.

Paul arched to see. The camera panned right toward an opening in the brush. A small female figure emerged, dressed in black pajamas and conical Vietnamese peasant hat. The figure approached the camera, stared at it self-consciously for a moment, turned right, turned left. For almost thirty seconds the frames moved into and under the rapidly moving shutter, producing a fluttery face—a girl, young, fragile, almond eyes frightened—or seemingly so. Her face was delicately high-cheekboned. Her long, jet-black hair streamed down her back. Her eyes, however, were sky blue. They startled in that face, jarred.

"See . . . shows up too much."

"Umm."

The frames flapped clear. The viewer turned white. Rennie flipped the switch, stopping the movement.

"She doesn't really look Vietnamese, no," De Luca said. "But there's something about her."

The door came open once more. This time it was a man. Tall,

heavily mustached, straw hair matted slightly, he wore a half-zipped-up flying suit and a crooked smile.

"Call me, boss man?"

"Denny . . . damn it, they're waiting at the location. What happened? Where the hell are you guys?"

The flier didn't answer. He lit a cigarette and leaned against the wall. De Luca approached and zipped his jacket, affectionately.

"God, you really must have had a time last night, you old cock, but will you get those monkeys of yours into their machines so we can get the shots we need?"

The flier winked at Paul and saluted smartly.

"Watch out for this sumbitch; have your balls every time."

He went out, still saluting.

"Denny heads up our air force," De Luca explained. Before he could elaborate, the phone interrupted with a production problem.

"Tell it to Sal," he screeched. An assistant came in with a star problem. Another broke in with location pictures. The phone rang again, continued ringing. The production designer appeared, needing urgent decisions. Taking his entourage with him, De Luca vanished, leaving Paul alone with Rennie.

He realized that his turn had come and gone; De Luca was on to other things. Smiling supportively, Rennie urged him outside.

"He's all over the place. People tear him apart. He's the one with the vision about all this. If we can help him bring it off, we will have been part of something very important, I know that."

Outside the building there was a new clutter. Generators, cables, crewmen urging broad-hatted peons to drag a truck from a huge rut. Mexican women in braids and long dresses carried sacks of laundry, of food, stepping nimbly with their unshod feet over camera boxes and crates marked "Explosives." There was the smell of maguey in the air and some boy, on his break, was in the shade of a wall picking at a guitar. A quiet-faced woman, obviously not Mexican, in expensive blue slacks and immaculate white silk shirt, came toward Rennie and Paul. She had long golden hair and her eyes were hidden by large-framed sunglasses.

She saw them, waved and turned into a doorway. Rennie waved. They walked on.

"That's Michael's wife," she said.

CHAPTER

3

When the film company first arrived in Oacala, the tiny Cantina Uribe had been a shabby local café catering to those who worked nearby, around the Zócalo. Now, the Oacalans, with the exception of a few stubborn mestizos, the mixed bloods, who sat stolidly and drank their beer, were gone. The patrons were the American film crew—to the delight of the Mexican couple who owned the place. The delight was based upon solid economic fact, for with a generous advance from De Luca, a huge new lemon-yellow refrigerator, with an extensive ice-making capacity, had been flown in from Mexico City and fitted out to work with bottled Tehuacán water. This machine, it was discovered, required more powerful electrical arrangements than had been expected. Once again, Michael provided. Thus connected, the refrigerator became the beloved centerpiece, petted and cleaned constantly by Señora Uribe. It manufactured the ice demanded by the Americans in all their drinks, cooled the favored San Miguel beer and did miracles of conservation for the guacamole. Nightly, stout Señora Uribe lit a candle and whispered to her patron saint that he must keep an eye on the health and welfare of blessed Michael De Luca.

There were four crewmen with the map of California on their faces in the cantina when Rennie took Paul in, ordered iced coffee and launched into an account of the problems faced by the editing team—gargantuan problems. Michael loved to shoot and shoot. He opened the camera lens to any and all kinds of sequences that came to him. He made endless notes, but no one could see them except himself. He had ten ways to end the picture, twenty ways to open it. He had used up half a dozen chief editors; Paul was the seventh. Some had lasted only two days. He had used up three cinematographers. The fourth, who had been here three months already, was the Hungarian Laszlo Kodály.

"He's done terrific work, but he's a loon," Rennie pronounced. "He'll do anything to get moody pictures on the screen. And he has cute little perversions—some kind of compulsion that he holds in check with pills, apparently. God, he's weird. He yells and screams too, but Michael thinks he's brilliant."

Outside, in the street beyond the open door, there was a sudden clamor of hoarse shouts and pounding feet. Paul looked there and held his breath as two men, in peasant clothing, came running into view, chests heaving with exertion, holding pistols in their hands. They slowed for a moment in the opening, then sped past. In seconds, three policemen appeared in the vacated space, darted looks into the cantina and raced after their prey, disappearing. Paul felt he had been watching frames of a film.

Señor Uribe, unperturbed, went to the door and shouted a question. From someplace down the street came an answer. He grunted and turned back to his clients.

"Is no thing. Somebody tries to make a robbery of the bank. They say is Aguillar, the *terrorista*. But they say everything is him. No can believe *policía*." He went back behind the counter and the crewmen went back to their beer, laughing at the madness of this country.

Rennie saw the color come back slowly into Paul's face and said, "It's all right. Mexican cops and robbers."

"When I saw those men," Paul said, "the first thing that came into my head was—"

He broke off, and Rennie, looking searchingly at him, asked, "What?"

"Well," he said, uncertain of how far to go with this, "De Luca told me some . . . funny things have been happening."

"Did he?" She sipped her coffee and he wondered if she would, somehow, indicate to him that the director had a first-class imagination. Instead she said simply, "I'm glad Michael confided in you. He's funny. He operates a lot on chemistry. Either he likes you on first sight or he never looks at you again. He likes you, I can tell."

She had neither confirmed nor denied anything, he noted, and it probably wasn't important at all—maybe.

The editing rooms were in a small, separate building. Entering, Paul felt immediately at home. The sight of the film-filled metal barrels, the racks of circular cans, the spindles, the rewinds, the Moviolas, all soothed whatever anxieties he had. Rennie introduced him to the two other assistants. One was a taut man in his twenties, all slim hips and pouter-pigeon chest. A razor-edge beard drew a line from his cropped head to the hard cleft of his chin. Rennie called him Rick, but his name was Richard. The other assistant was a woman in her early thirties who was introduced as Flo Ankrum. She had extraordinarily fine features, which, Paul had the impression, she did what she could to disguise. She looked at the world through gold-rimmed glasses over which a wonderfully tousled mop of semi-brown hair went in six directions at once. She had some heft to her and wore a covering loose blouse. Her eyes behind the glasses were challenging. Rennie told Paul she was a strong feminist who felt that Michael should have made herself, Rennie, the chief editor. Paul noted that there would be enough problems without that particular one surfacing. Rennie giggled and agreed. She showed him to a small partitioned area.

"This is you."

"Grand luxe it's not."

"The air conditioner conks out all the time. The last editor worked in a trailer that had its own generator."

"I'll try it here," Paul said. He sat down at a small desk, ancient and battered.

Rennie opened a small file cabinet, exhibiting a variety of fat colored folders.

"Read, but don't go blind. Some of these have been so overtyped, you can't make sense."

She pulled the scripts from the file and put them on the desk. Paul reached out for the topmost, in a green cover. His hand brushed Rennie's and he could feel the edges of moisture on the delicate hairs. She looked at him warmly and said she'd be back. Then she left him alone with the screenplays.

The first page of the first script read: "The following is a narrative synopsis of this as yet untitled film. It has been written so that the screenplay reader will be able to follow the story line despite scenes missing from this version, scenes still to be written and/or revised."

He settled down in the uncomfortable chair, turned the page and read on.

> This film's locale is Vietnam. The time is the sixties. The film concerns a small army and air force unit about to launch a preemptive attack upon a corner of that world, focusing on a native village in the lowlands called LOC BINH.

31

American Intelligence has shown that an important gathering of Viet Cong forces is to take place at some undetermined time hence. These forces would then move to hit an American highway link, vital to the war. A preemptive attack, a strike with ground forces, artillery and helicopter gunships has to be planned in utmost secrecy. This strike is called OPERATION JERICHO.

One of the Intelligence officers is Captain Sam Ryan. Ryan is a man of fairly decent instincts who is not totally certain the estimates are sound. He has become, after some years, more and more uncertain of the war itself, but believes his country is not venal, is honest, is trying to do its best in a terrible situation.

In contrast is Ryan's commanding officer, Colonel Clarence B. Muller. Muller is a by-the-book Army man. He believes in doing your duty and leaving the rest to the politicians whom he despises. He also distrusts Ryan, sensing his feelings. He tries to work around Ryan but cannot wholly do that. Still, he feels that Ryan will be an ultimate danger to him.

The story is made more complex by Ryan's relationship with the wife he left behind whom he knows does not love him and by Muller's brutal liaison with a young Vietnamese girl. The suspense of the film is maintained by the question of whether the Cong will discover the attack plans. If so, what will they do? What will Ryan do with his growing uncertainties?

In fact, Ryan comes to believe absolutely that Intelligence is in error. There is no need for OPERATION JERICHO. He is too late to do anything about it, however, for plans, once made, must be acted upon. The machine is rolling. Besides, Muller believes Ryan is wrong and the Cong will gather. Ryan, however, is correct. There is no meeting of the Viet Cong. Despite this, the entire village is destroyed, needlessly, villagers and all. Ryan, almost deliberately, steps on a mine and dies.

The screenplay itself began on the following page. Paul read it through, found it filled with gaps but tense and interesting. He picked up the next script.

In this version he found that Ryan confronted Muller, who put him into the stockade on the eve of Jericho. Ryan escaped, went to warn the villagers, but was cut down by a lone Cong who happened to wander through. On this version De Luca had scrawled: "Too heroic by half. A lot of bullshit here."

In other versions of the story, Ryan had an affair with Muller's Vietnamese girl. Becoming suspicious of her and feeling he might, in some way, be betraying his own men who are decent, Ryan vacillates until it is too late. Jericho begins. Ryan has helped bring it about, sees its horrifying end and does not die, but is forced to live. Ryan will have to exist with what he has done.

In the seventh and last draft of the story, De Luca had invented an order from headquarters which confirmed Ryan's suspicions that Intelligence had been lying, for their own purposes. Confronted with the order, Muller believes it comes from men who know nothing about the field. He orders Jericho advanced in time to thwart them. Ryan confronts him with the order. Muller directs him to continue, nonetheless. Ryan tells his men about the order from HQ. When he does so, they are convinced he has gone somewhat mad. With Ryan almost raving, Jericho begins and the village is wiped out. On the last page of this script De Luca had written: "Has some things in it. We'll see."

It took Paul five hours to read the seven scripts, scamping some passages. When he put the last folder down, his eyes burned, his bones ached and he wanted a shower badly. Suddenly, he realized that it was almost eight P.M. New York time, that he had been in Mexico City earlier that day. The door opened and Flo Ankrum came in to ask if he would start looking at the footage later that night.

"Early tomorrow," he pleaded. "I'm bushed."

"I'll set it for nine. Okay?"

"Sure. How long have you been here?"

"Almost three months."

"Having fun?"

"Some of the time." She nodded toward the pile of scripts. "What do you think?"

"What do *you* think?"

"I'd like to see stronger female characters."

He laughed; it was so predictable.

"What's funny?"

"I'm sorry. I was thinking about something else. Maybe by the time Mike has a finished script he'll do what you ask," he covered lamely.

"Never," she said.

33

Once in his room, Paul unpacked and, with anticipation, moved to the bathroom and the shower. He undressed, turned the faucets and was rewarded with a slow trickle of water. He opened the taps all the way. Some spitting from the ornate shower head ensued. The Hotel Jaime had not yet conquered shower technology.

Later, as he stepped from the bath, he heard the telephone ring. He answered and found an affable Sal Sieberling, who proceeded to inform him that De Luca would like them to have dinner together in about an hour; a driver would be waiting.

The driver was a tall, muscular Angeleno who drove as though he were on the Hollywood Freeway and who could not understand how Paul could live in dirty, dangerous, decrepit New York. It wasn't easy, Paul told him.

The private "road" leading to the De Luca establishment was a quarter-mile of new asphalt strip bordered by dripping acacias, by lemon and olive trees shimmering lightly so that their silver undersides caught the light. The house was a huge glow of pink stone with a large open court at whose center a marble fountain sprayed a panoply of stone fish and deer. Behind the court, arched porticos led to a tiled terrace and opened french doors. The plantings here were profoundly beautiful. Ancient and profuse, tended by many generations of hands, the roses massed so that their reds and pinks melded into almost solid color while the orchids, sultry and graceful, looped their necks toward each other and the jonquils. Here and there Paul saw peach and plum trees and graceful fruit he did not recognize. At this hour the sun, lingering, was a fading mist of hot orange. Soon the soft and fragrant twilight would begin.

The Angeleno drove past the two Mercedes, the Lincoln, the BMW and the pickup truck. Two gardeners, who were still pruning, doffed their hats in respect as the Fiat passed.

The blonde Paul had seen in the morning appeared. She wore beautifully cut silk lounging pajamas, deep purple and subtle red, and was younger than he had thought. Her alabaster complexion and crystal-blue eyes spoke of health and skin care. Her mouth was luscious—perfect strawberry lips over gleaming white enamel. She moved fluidly, almost languidly, within a serene and well-ordered aura. In contrast to the shoeless, rumpled De Luca, Paul saw her as from another planet.

The director, smiling as though he knew exactly what Paul was thinking, said proudly, "This is my wife, Catherine."

34

"I'm pleased to meet you," Paul said.

"I'm happy to meet you," she answered in a reedy voice that did not go with her face. "Michael's told me how happy he is you came to be here with us."

"I told her," De Luca affirmed, "I told her that. Listen, I believe in first impressions, and my impression of this collaboration is that it's going to work. Now let's have some dinner."

"Yes." A vague smile crossed Catherine's face.

She was incredibly neutral, Paul decided, and it was very difficult to think of De Luca with her.

The center hall was immense, baronial; the dining room to the right was formal and imposing. A refectory table had been set with heavy napery and silver for four. A huge ten-branched gold-inlaid candelabra illuminated the splendid Spanish plates. It was hard to resist gawking.

A small, swarthy man in his late fifties, hair jet black and curly, with eyes moist as the Adriatic, came in. He wore black trousers and a deep-blue shirt. Everything about him was dark and soulful. He was introduced as De Luca's father. The two of them greeted each other with affectionate cries and a warm hug. The elder De Luca sat down and the dinner began. The meal was served by a sweet-faced Mexican girl who, shyly, looked away from everyone as she served them, first, the cold soup, then the salad and finally the chicken with hot sauce. The food was remarkably good—local ingredients handled with care by an imported Italian in the kitchen. The wine, too, was not local.

"Mikey ask me to send him something he can drink in this place," the elder De Luca explained, "so I send him a couple of cases of Barolo." He kissed his fingers. "How you like?"

"Very good," Paul said. "Really good."

"Americans. They think all we got in Italy is Chianti. But Barolo —like blood from the grape."

"My wine steward." De Luca laughed with affection.

The father leaned toward Paul and swished the wine in his goblet.

"So, you come to help my Mikey, eh? Good. Nice." Before Paul could respond, he added, "My Mikey is a genius, you know—like Michelangelo, like Leonardo."

Michael guffawed. "He's also my press agent."

"I know what I speak, eh, Caterina, what you say?"

35

He leaned closer to Catherine and affectionately pulled at her cheek. Michael chuckled and pulled at the other one. Catherine squealed.

"Stop it, you two."

The two men broke out into laughter, pounded each other's shoulders. Paul watched them, fascinated.

De Luca looked at his watch. "Hell, we've got to hurry." Answering Paul's unasked question, he said, "We're shooting some night stuff at Ixtepan. One dialogue scene with principals and some action stuff. You're coming, of course."

He was already slipping on a pair of desert boots, so Paul rose and said formally, "Thank you for dinner, Mrs. De Luca."

"There'll be a hundred dinners," De Luca said. He kissed his wife good-bye, waved to his father, grabbed Paul by the arm and rushed him outside. A Mexican driver waited beside one of the Mercedes. Michael stuffed Paul into the backseat and they were off.

"*Ciao—ciao . . .*" the elder De Luca shouted. Catherine De Luca stood silently. Oddly, all grace was gone from her body. She almost slumped.

CHAPTER

4

Once inside the beige Mercedes, the sweet fragrance of nature was replaced by the smell of glove leather. Paul fitted his body into the thick cushions, hardly hearing the engine, for the windows were turned up and the air conditioning whispered to them.

They drove, in brooding silence, along the asphalt, which changed soon to a pebbled road. Through the tinted windows Paul saw they were passing tar-paper and tin shacks outside which big-bellied, naked children stared at them with large eyes. On dull red coals tortillas were being cooked by old, stringy women with rags for clothes as small silent men hunkered down around the fire.

"Look at them," De Luca said soberly, "poor bastards. They made a revolution and what did it get them? And how many will even get to see my picture, which is about people like them?"

He turned to look out the rear window, studying the road behind them. Turning back after thirty seconds' observation, he muttered, "I thought I saw a headlight reflected, but it's nothing."

He fell silent again. The Mercedes purred along, smoothing out the rough stones. In the shadows Paul stared, surreptitiously, at De Luca's profile. The eyes looked blankly inward, but he knew that the brain behind those eyes was working furiously upon the night's scenes.

He remembered a critic once writing of De Luca that he had thirty-five-millimeter cells—the size of movie film—in his bloodstream and that was why it all came to him so organically. Sometimes he felt that was true of himself.

"Paul." De Luca's eyes shifted to him. "This will be your first time with the company. Watch everything tonight."

"Right," he answered automatically.

"You don't understand," De Luca said with a trace of irritation. "Every one of the crew gets between me and what I'm trying to do simply by being a group of people, and a collective will rises from them that can be opposite to mine, even though they are supposed to be my instruments. The job is to work that will so they do what I want as I want it and when I want it."

Did that include him? Paul wondered. Almost in answer, De Luca looked at him with challenge. Then he looked away and said nothing more until they reached the outskirts of Ixtepan village.

Ixtepan was the current incarnation of an ancient Zapotec Indian village. It had been carved out of the jungle in pre-Columbian times and now survived mostly because it was the village nearest Monte Tecla, an important archaeological site.

Monte Tecla was a two-thousand-year-old miracle. A two-hundred-foot-high manmade pyramid of stone, slate and crumbling plaster, it defied time. Though dusty and overgrown, it rose in lone majesty from the valley floor, its 312 steps intact, its shape unmistakable, its legend powerful to all in Oacala.

Upon Tecla's acre-square plateau the ancients had built a religious complex whose meaning had, long since, been lost but whose echoes could be heard in the voices of the *brujos*, the medicine men, as they conducted secret rituals in the mountain caves. The site, a mecca for those studying the Zapotecs, was impressive even to the casual tourist. At one end were odd-shaped burial vaults; nearby were hollowed-out chambers thought to have been priestly residences for those who oversaw the living sacrifices, hearts pulled from writhing bodies. Some distance away were bizarre stone constructions designed to hold those victims at the exact angle for their blood to drain into the channels cut through the center section.

At the opposite end were labyrinthic tunnels where entangled heaps of bones had been found, some with skulls cloven in two. This was the refuse pile, the garbage heap, of those sacrificed. Above these caverns were numerous weather-blasted sculptures, gods half-animal, half-human, eating, supplicating, fornicating. There were four small, circular temples with intricately patterned carvings at the base and open roofs. Scholars suggested these were astronomical stations and that those primitive people, long before the birth of Christ, knew of the galaxy and the solar system and measured time and space.

There was a weed-strewn empty area surrounded by contoured

stone benches, which was a game-playing ball court where players had once pushed a baseball-sized pellet with shoulder, hip, groin, leg, toward a small wicket goal. It was thought that the losers were instantly beheaded, creating winning incentive in the next team.

The centerpiece of Monte Tecla was a still quite well-preserved large temple raised above all else. This temple was octagonal in design and had eight onyx pillars, one at each corner. The massive floor blocks were rose marble. A hemispheric niche, empty and cracked now, once obviously held some holy of holies—an image of great meaning. Into every pillar were carved mysterious and undeciphered inscriptions.

The Monte Tecla booklet, sold by the Oacala Museo Arqueologico, talked of the pyramid's being shrouded in mysterious origins, of the wisdom of the ancients, of the theories of the eight perfect pillars as representing eight forces of life for the old Zapotecs. It spoke, vaguely, of certain primitive Indians who believed in its mysterious power, even today, and there left the subject.

The Monte was the first thing Paul saw of the village, and it startled him. It looked otherworldly in the clear moonlight, ghostly, the white onyx pillars gleaming.

"Hey . . ."

De Luca told him what it was. "Isn't it great, brooding over the village the way it does?"

"It looks magical."

"The Indians around here use it that way. It's part of their on-going old religion. They come up here for secret ceremonies, I'm told."

By now the Mercedes had entered the small village. It was typical. It had three porticoed colonial administration buildings and a collection of mean dirt-floor huts built on two dozen dirt streets. One paved street, cobbled and rutted, led to a small square, at the end of which, in Roman magnificence, stood the massive village church, twin towers reaching skyward, blessing the miserable shacks below.

The church took pride in its reliquary containing a finger bone of St. Sebastian in an emerald case and exhibited it every year on his saint's day. The altar held a twelve-branched solid gold candelabra donated by a Oacala merchant in memory of his beloved mother. One wall of the church, the south, was decorated with a mother-of-pearl Christ figure. The other three walls were aglow with gold-leaf filigree from top to bottom. The pews and benches were shiny with the prayerful sweat of generations of devoted, kneeling peasants.

The Mercedes moved through the square, past the church, and emerged at the other end of the darkened, ill-lit village. Here, however, electric light blazed, boiled and steamed. This was the location.

In this section of the location, the construction crew had built the Vietnamese village of Loc Binh. It was perfect in every detail. Thatched roofs, pole construction, bamboo jungle beyond. Here also the Hollywood builders had dug in with their buses and trailers, had set up prefab sheet-metal shacks to hold lumber, machinery, explosives for battle scenes, replacement parts for the cranes and dollies needed to hoist the camera at any angle required. The bulky seventy-millimeter Panavision cameras themselves were not trusted to sheds. They were stored in a special camera van, kept locked and supervised.

A short distance from the Vietnamese village, a series of winding Saigon streets had been constructed, complete with bars and shops. Abutting it was a facsimile of an American airstrip with hangars and repair depots. Beyond that, an American command complex had been built, a headquarters building in the field, weathered and sandbagged, constructed to U.S. Army specifications —with the exception of swinging walls that revealed all to the camera. It was this area which was bathed in a hot white blaze now. That light was being directed by the cinematographer, Laszlo Kodály, an intense, stocky refugee from the Budapest film studios. He wore a baseball cap on his balding head and had the inevitable light meter around his neck.

"More there," he shouted. "Heavy there. Give me light, damn it. More five thousands."

The electricians, complying, climbed wooden rigging like monkeys as Kodály roared at them, lapsing into incomprehensible mother tongue every so often. The men clamped huge lights onto steel poles, wrestled thick cables to a rumbling generator truck which provided the power.

"Better, better," Kodály shouted.

Sal Sieberling came over to the Mercedes as it stopped, and opened the door.

"Looking good, chief."

Emerging, De Luca said, "There's going to be trouble with one of the assholes over the scene, watch."

Paul followed. He had been on many sets in his life, but coming upon this panorama fresh, this make-believe of lights and excitement, he felt again the grip of intense anticipation. The night-shooting mood took its hold, quickened his blood.

"Looks pretty real," Sieberling told him. "I never was in Nam, of course, but Denny and some of the boys he flew with say this is how it was."

He looked up and shouted to an assistant, "Teddy—get those people back, will you? Get them back."

At the edge of the clearing, huddled in shadow, Paul saw half a dozen serape-clad figures watching, motionless. Sieberling was unhappy at their presence.

"Sons of bitches will steal you blind. I hate to have them around, but what are you going to do?"

A lean, tense man in the uniform of a U.S. Army colonel stepped forward. He looked in every way the officer he was depicting, except that a layer of Kleenex was secured under his chin and over his shirt, keeping the collar clean of the deep tan makeup that had been freshly applied. He waved the pages of script he held and said, "Can we talk about this scene, Michael? As the colonel I ought to dig his doubts, but that isn't in here."

Rennie clutched Paul's arm and whispered, "Damned ego-ridden actor—all he wants is more lines."

A compact, khaki-shirted actor with captain's bars ambled over, scratching his crotch.

"Can't we just shoot," he asked plaintively. "I'm getting hungry."

The colonel-actor glared.

"I'm trying to put some subtext in this, get inside the character."

"I want to get inside the chiquita who's waiting for me in the trailer," the captain-actor mumbled. The crew guffawed.

"Jesus," the colonel exploded, ripping the Kleenex from his shirt.

"Watch Michael," Rennie whispered.

With great patience, De Luca soothed the waters. He assured the colonel-actor he would welcome his every invention, he wanted the scene played to its fullest. Then, retreating to Paul, he said tersely, "I'm shooting around him. He can act his way into heaven but it won't be on the screen. Make notes."

"I see what you mean," Paul told Rennie.

41

"I hate actors," she responded grimly. "They always give Michael trouble."

The scene went well, but De Luca shot it four more times for the master angle and then went into fifteen more variations and close-ups. By then almost three hours had passed. When Paul looked up next, the Mexicans, with the exception of one figure at the tree, had gone.

Another hour went by. As a new angle was to be shot, one of the huge arc lamps flared blindingly and winked out, to the groans of the electricians.

"Son of a bitch," Kodály shouted.

"Let's take five," De Luca ordered.

The first assistant shouted the break, and the crew fell into conversation as the lamp was changed. Rennie walked to De Luca, who sat slumped in his chair, and Paul went with her. She took a stance behind the director and massaged the back of his neck.

"That," De Luca said, eyes closed in bliss, "is wonderful."

Unneeded, Paul wandered away, traversing cables and connection boxes. At the edge of the forest he heard a soft, polite voice behind him say, *"Buenas noches."*

He turned, startled. The voice belonged to the man near the tree, who moved forward now, gingerly, into the slight rim of light. He did not look like other Oacalans, not Indian at all. He had too much conquistador blood in him, the Western eyes, the height, the features, all attested to that. He wore denims and boots. A red woolen shirt and a nondescript serape kept away the night chill. He looked steadily and confidently at Paul, displaying a gentle smile.

"Buenas noches," Paul answered.

"You are a player—an actor? You must excuse me for knowing so little of this but I am much interested."

The sound of his English was so unexpectedly good that Paul looked at him more closely.

"No, I do technical work."

"Yes, of course. The cinema is very technical, much engineering is needed."

De Luca shot the scene again and the Mexican fell silent. Paul noted that his attention was not on the shooting but beyond and to the right. He looked but could see nothing except two local policemen who had ceased their patrolling and were now leaning against trees, yawning.

"Okay, cut," De Luca called. "Wrap it up for tonight."

Quickly the practiced breaking down and storing of equipment began. The precious camera loads were removed and handed to Rennie. Within the hour a pilot would have them on their way to the waiting processing lab in Mexico City. Feeling his responsibility, Paul was about to join Rennie when the Mexican put a soft hand on his arm.

"Excuse, please, I would like, if it is possible, to speak to the man there. He is the *jefe*, no?" His eyes moved toward De Luca.

"Maybe some other time," Paul said, surprised, "but he's busy right now."

"*Sí, naturalmente*, but if it can be possible . . ."

"I don't think so."

"*Por favor*," the Mexican persisted in a gentle voice. "I am told he is a good man, a true artist. I have something to say to him."

Astonished, Paul realized the man was serious and quickly said, "I'll tell him."

"I thank you; I be here."

The Mexican took a few steps and was swallowed up by the blackness, leaving Paul nonplussed. Uncertain, making his way back to where De Luca was conferring with Sieberling about the next day's shooting schedule, Paul decided to interrupt.

"Michael, it's crazy, but there's a Mexican out there who says he wants to meet you."

Sieberling's suspicious eyes instantly swept the jungle edge. "Where is this guy? I don't see anybody."

"Back in there." Paul indicated the darkness.

"I'll send some guys in after him," Sieberling growled, but something had gripped De Luca's imagination.

"Wait a minute. What did he say?"

"That he had something to tell you."

"Mike, be sensible," Sieberling pleaded.

De Luca turned away from him and whispered to Paul, "Maybe it's information for sale." Turning back, he ordered, "Sal, keep an eye out. Paul, come with me."

"Damn it," Sieberling called after him, watching nervously. Reluctantly, Paul followed, and in seconds both he and De Luca were lost to the work lights; only the clouded moon shone where they were, and the trees formed grotesque shapes.

In the thicket De Luca asked, "Where is he?"

"Someplace here."

Paul peered into the shadows and a sudden whoosh of branches revealed a tiny center of orange light. As he recoiled, the man who had accosted him stepped out from behind a tree, a cigarette cupped in his palm. At his back was another man, stocky, face wide as a melon, tiny eyes watchful; in one hand he held a rifle quite casually.

The tall Mexican broke into a gap-toothed smile.

"Ah, sí—I know you will come. I have never before seen how the cinema is made. It is so interesting—the players, the lights, so many people. When I sit in the *teatro,* I never think of all this."

When De Luca's face went tight with disappointment, the Mexican seemed to understand. Quickly, he extended his hand and said, *"Buenas noches.* I am Luis Aguillar."

He said it as though expecting to be recognized, but De Luca looked puzzled. In the next second, however, he sucked in a surprised breath and murmured, "Aguillar?"

"Sí. Aguillar."

The Mexican smiled warmly. He shook De Luca's hand and then Paul's. His grip was firm and sure; Paul's was sweaty.

"I have much interest in the cinema," the Mexican said, "and I have business in the village tonight, so I stop here and watch, but also, I wish to tell you, señor, that you have much courage, much *cojones,* to make this story about the wickedness of Vietnam and the guilt of your country."

In this jungle clearing, coming from this tall, grave man, the words were very surprising.

"Isn't it dangerous for you to be here?" De Luca asked.

"It can be always dangerous when I come down from the sierra," Aguillar answered calmly.

Paul found the moon-faced man locking eyes with him. As he turned away, uncomfortably, it came to him in a burst. Aguillar. This was Aguillar, the terrorist. He looked at him with a new curiosity.

"You speak English so well," De Luca said. "I mean, I'm just surprised."

"I study English—and German, too," Aguillar said, "at the university in Mexico City. It was while the war goes on. We made, there, demonstrations against that war, against America and against our own government, too. They sent the federal troops against us with machine guns. And they open fire, too. Many of my friends are wounded—some are killed. The government says it never happens,

44

that we make it up—like the cinema."

He had not spoken angrily, but in sorrowful, measured and moving tones.

"Some of us heard about that," De Luca said.

"And that is how the stupid federal government makes opposition, eh? The government itself becomes the best teacher."

"Always," De Luca declared. "Always."

"You take this valley, señores, here in Oacala. There is so much beauty but also much suffering and poorness. Whoever fights against this, the *policía* try to catch and put in prison. So the government teaches again. I have been up in the Sierra Madre for a few years now. From there we try to fight, to organize, but it is hard."

He acknowledged Paul's attention by turning to him directly, with a sigh.

"Señor, I give you a question. How does God choose who does this, eh?"

"Too big a question," Michael interposed. "Some of us simply feel these things."

"I wish," Aguillar said wistfully, "He chooses someone else. For myself, I like to eat well, sleep in a bed every night, and that does not happen in the sierra, oh, no. And women—" He paused, musing. "Most of us are young, you understand, and hot all the time—and there are no women in the sierra—the balls ache."

He broke into laughter, and Paul was struck by the humanity of the man which did not detract from his dark dignity and calmly resolute air.

"Listen," Michael said, "I would like to help your movement." His body straightened, his shoulders pulled back, and Paul saw, with surprise, that he was as tall as Aguillar, who was startled by the proposal.

"I mean it," Michael persisted. "I'm talking about money."

"Always, we need money," Aguillar said slowly. "The merchants charge us twice as much for a pair of boots. Can we take food from the farmers? No—so we buy what we must have. And some of *them* charge us more." Again he smiled with an air of rueful resignation. "It is hard to force politics on people, eh? Sometimes you must buy them."

"That's reality," Michael agreed, and Paul heard the note of admiration.

"If you have something for us," Aguillar said quietly, "you go

45

to the shop of Isac Ismena on the Calle Diaz. From there they will know how to find me."

"Will he trust me?"

Aguillar thought a moment. "He will trust you if you say to him that you wish to buy a disk of the Deer Dance music."

"Deer Dance music," Michael repeated. "Okay."

The moon came out from behind a cloud. Pale light filtered down upon the four men. Moon-Face touched Aguillar's shoulder. He nodded and said, "Now we must go, Paco and I. *Adiós.* For me it is very good to have taken you by the hand."

Without warning, he turned and plunged into the brush. Moon-Face threw a slightly worried glance at Paul and followed. In seconds both men disappeared. Michael grabbed Paul's shoulder excitedly.

"Fantastic. He's beautiful. All dignity. And brave. He risked his life to speak to us. The police would give an arm and a leg to get him."

"I thought he was just some kind of a movie buff," Paul said as they walked quickly back toward the lights.

"In a way," Michael said, "we're both fighting the same people. I wonder if he knows that." He looked at Paul, his eyes filled with momentary speculation, then they emerged from the jungle into the clearing. Instantly, Sieberling approached, frowning.

"What happened?"

De Luca did not reply. He walked away, looking for Rennie.

Sieberling looked at Paul, who shrugged and walked away as well. It had been an eerie episode, and he was not totally certain, at that moment, which was the reality, the movie set or the jungle and the two Mexicans. And at this point weariness attacked his bones. He had been inundated with sensation and data; it was overload and his circuits jangled. He closed his eyes as everything before him shimmered. In the darkness whirling behind his eyeballs he saw—Stella. She frowned at him from close by. He wished her away but she wouldn't go.

He opened his eyes in time to see Michael and Rennie walking off, hand in hand, toward a large trailer parked nearby. It was painted blue and the shutters on the window were closed. Before they went inside, Michael turned on the top step, saw Paul looking at him and raised his right fist in revolutionary signal.

Then the door closed behind them.

CHAPTER
5

Paul regretted not taking a sleeping pill. The night, a succession of jagged dreams and spatial displacements, was a damp excursion into unpleasant levels of his unconscious. The odd minutes of fitful slumber were performed to the distant echoes of marimbas and guitars, which proved to be not so far away since they were being manufactured by the Zócalo mariachis outside the Jaime.

During the night his right leg began to ache, throwing him back to the nights of his childhood when he would wake in the dark feeling a tired strain in his thigh. Usually, it would happen after the recurring, frightening dream in which his mother died and there was, now, no one to take care of him. How would he survive? Who was there to save him from his dumb aunt, his dumber uncle and their family of gross children of whom he would now become a part? He would jerk awake in terror and stare dazedly at the ceiling until he realized that his mother was in the next room breathing heavily and moaning slightly in the embrace of her own dreams.

When he was two, his father had died of cancer. His mother had been reluctant to talk about that with him, and it was only his persistent curiosity that had unearthed the facts. She said little of his father at all, and hearing the other boys on the block complain about parental discipline, he had cautiously concluded that his condition wasn't so bad.

He rubbed his leg and the ache began to drain from it. That recalled the track team at college. He had joined feeling the need for some physical activity, something that would get him away from books, away from the hours on end he spent in movie houses of all sizes and descriptions. He had run the half-mile and looked forward to the massage, at the end of practice, by the elderly black trainer who called him Pauli and had wonderful tales about an

47

endless store of relatives. That had been in the early sixties. His friend Tom had been on that team as well. They had sought each other out, spouted reams of profound garbage at one another. Then, suddenly, Tom dropped out of school and disappeared. Paul was told that he had gone into the Army, but he was never sure if that was true. The team wasn't fun after that, and Paul stopped going to practice.

Thin threads of dawn appeared in the Oacala sky. The urgent crowing of roosters rose to mingle with the rasping of the shutters. Eyes wide, Paul was carried back to his own two years in the Army before his medical discharge for the hernia inflicted by a foolish attempt to lift a jeep out of the mud at Greenville, South Carolina, where the roosters had sounded exactly like this. He was grateful to the Army, however. That vast, impersonal entity had sent him to the Signal Corps and Motion Picture School to learn, by the numbers, how movies were made. He had jumped into that endeavor as into a warm, welcoming bath; worked day and night, ate, slept and dreamed movies, movies, movies, in concert with other twenty-two-year-olds who envisioned becoming the Truffauts, the Capras, the Fords of their generation.

Only one of the group came near. He and Paul had become very close. As a team, they made a training film which became an underground Army classic. It was no small feat to take the subject of tank maintenance and construct something of beauty and utility, but everyone agreed that they had. The supervising officers had not been exactly certain it *was* utilitarian, but they recognized craft verging onto something else and let the film be circulated. The Tank Corps loathed it and twice tried to destroy the negative. Washington loved it and referred to it, privately, as their Ingmar Bergman tank movie. With some glee, Paul recalled the reams of official correspondence the project had produced, the good times, the laughter and the vows to go on and make films together.

Though the Ingmar Bergman tank movie had been jointly done, somehow Paul had ended up with the editing credit while his friend was credited as the director. It hadn't mattered; what had mattered was the experience—and the closeness.

Paul rose from the bed, his throat very dry. He poured himself a glass of water from the ceramic bottle. It was tepid and flat-tasting. He fingered the stubble on his chin. His whole face felt lumpy, a derelict's mattress. He looked in the mirror. There were puff bulbs beneath his eyes, disturbing the flat planes of his face,

48

distorting the full mouth and the solid chin. He leaned in, pulled up the lid of his right eye and stared at the pulsing, tiny veins around the brown center. Very cloudy.

He went to the window, pried the shutters apart and winced. The Sierra Madre del Sur, in the distance, reflected more light than he had expected. Not wishing to, he heard Sylvie's voice the week after they had been married and were at Stowe, skiing.

"Look at it! Look how magnificent the mountains are!"

She had clung to him, almost weeping with insane joy. Their life together must always be like this, always in intense, perfervid happiness. He winced at the memory. "Always" had been a year and a half—eighteen months of smothering, drowning, reaching for straws.

The telephone tinkled behind him. Dazedly, he picked it up.

"Hello."

"Paul?"

He made no connection to the voice.

"Hello."

"Paul, it's Stella."

"What?"

"It's me, Stella. I'm just calling to say hello."

"Where are you?"

"In New York."

"Oh . . . what time is it there?"

"Nine in the morning. It's eight where you are, isn't it?"

He reached for his watch.

"It's ten after eight here."

"You sound throaty. Did I wake you up?"

"No."

"Are things going well?"

"I've just about arrived."

"How's De Luca? Does he fit the stories?"

"He's not like the stories. He's what he is."

"Aren't we all?"

He didn't know what to say next, so he said nothing.

"Paul?"

"I'm here, Stella."

"Paul, I don't really know why I called, except that I had an impulse and I followed it."

He didn't answer again and she said, "Oh, Paul," but caught hold quickly. "I'll hang up now."

49

"Stella . . ."

"Listen, I don't expect you'll have a similar impulse, but should it attack you, follow it too. I won't mind."

"I will," he said. "I promise."

"Good-bye, Paul."

"Good-bye."

When Paul hung up, he stared out at the mountains again. Tufts of layered clouds moved gently across the lower reaches. Reedy music from a clay Aztec pipe came from somewhere out there. After a few minutes' reverie, he was not certain the telephone conversation had actually taken place; it seemed to be part of the night's events. He staggered into the bathroom to shave.

The next 110 hours were spent examining the tens of thousands of feet of film that had already been shot. Some footages had been edited into rough sequences; others were masses of disconnected close-ups, long shots, action, dialogue. Almost nothing checked against any of the scripts. Flo, who was helping, explained that only after the film had been totally edited did Michael have a script set down of what had been done.

There was little time for meals or sleep at this point in the feverish catching-up process. Paul grew red-eyed and dry-mouthed. He ate cantina sandwiches and dozed on the goat-leather couch in his tiny office. He made note after note to himself, trying to absorb the material, put it into his bones. He grappled with where every foot of film might fit into the story De Luca was trying to tell. His drive and his ideas won grudging admiration from Flo.

"Nice notion," she'd say. Or "Good way to go. Stylish."

In these hours, with the whir of machinery and the constant flickering of light, in his enthusiasm for and exhaustion with the film, Paul had grown to like Flo. There was a certain gawky over-reaching about her, a defiance, a dare to knock her feminine block off, that was curiously endearing. If she had not come to trust him, she would not have opened up about Sieberling.

"He's the anti-Michael, you know, the flip side. If Michael wants it, Sal does it. He hires and fires while Michael evades and avoids. He knows all the politics where Michael pretends to be innocent. He knows where all the bodies are buried, who's doing what to whom in the company—all that stuff, all the stuff Michael keeps away from."

"Michael has to make a film," Paul responded. "If he involved himself in all the junk around him . . ."

"Some of it's not junk." She didn't explain.

Paul rubbed his eyes, flipped the toggle and watched the colonel-actor explain Operation Jericho to the captain for the tenth time in the same take, blowing his lines finally and screaming, "Shit, shit, shit!"

At four in the morning, in his hotel suite in town, De Luca took his fingers from the typewriter keys and decided that this version of the end of the film might work. He pushed his chair back and padded about the room. The flush of writing excitement, as always, reddened his forehead. If only he could go from the written page to the film exactly as he saw it. A dream. To have no one shape what he did but himself. Never happen. With the best of intentions few really ever understood the totality of what he was after. He had a feeling that Gordon might, though. What a plus that would be, to have a really talented ally.

Two sharp reports crackled through the night. He looked out the window toward the avenida but could see nothing. The valley looked peaceful, but much went on beneath the surface. Some of his crew, he knew, went about with handguns concealed in locally made holsters. Those damn police. Either they were totally impotent or had been bought off by the harassing forces. Mingled with his anger was a tide of frustration at having to keep what was happening as quiet as possible lest the waves reach the shores of Studioland. Sons of bitches—always a struggle.

He walked back to the desk, fingered his new pages, put them down and found himself staring at a Polaroid picture of the young, blue-eyed Mexican girl whose test he had seen. There was something mysterious about her face—not simply the blue eyes. There was a decidedly erotic look about her. Hooded, yet innocent; knowing, yet open—and very ancient. He walked away from the picture, energy still restless in him, and came into the bedroom. He looked at Rennie sleeping, the sheet at her waist, her small breasts, round as oranges, rising and falling. He leaned over on impulse and kissed the pink nipple nearest him. When she stirred, he sat down on the bed's edge and cupped his hands over the breast, squeezing gently. Slowly, her eyes opened, blinked.

"What time is it?"

"About four."

She yawned. "You coming to bed?"

He rose and started to pace.

51

"You know something—Paul Gordon has a handle on this story. I've read his notes."

She yawned again.

"I know he's going to be helpful. I'm going to talk to him, in the morning, about the end sequences. He's on my wavelength, Rennie. That's goddamn rare."

"Yes." Awake now, Rennie watched him pace.

"And he's sympathetic. He's not trying to compete with me."

He approached the bed again and stood over her, almost vibrating with excitement.

"God, if we can pull this off, if we could just pull this off . . . All I want is to make it the best way I know how. If I can keep it together long enough to do that—"

"Come to bed, Michael."

"I've got to do *something*. The studio people are screaming about my budget figures. That *cafóne*, Lufkin, with his accountant's mind may be coming down. If he does . . ."

"You'll handle it," Rennie said.

"Got to. Got to."

She sat up, rubbing her shoulders, watching him, filling herself with every move he made, every expression that crossed his face. These moments, when he shared with her his creative leaps and fears, made her part of his innermost processes. As a child, in Connecticut, when she sat her flying pony bareback, feeling cool air in her face and the thump of her pelvis on the hard backbone, her daydreams had included being found by some wild, roaring poet with whom she would run away, to become his inspiration, his interpreter to the world, midwife to his visions.

"Come here," she said, gesturing. "I'll help you."

"Yes," he said, "yes." He fumbled with the zipper on his jeans. "I'll do that."

He took his hands away, stood there absolutely passive, but his heart beat strongly.

"Maybe Paul can help me with Lufkin."

Rennie had the zipper open. She pulled down the jeans and his teal-blue shorts. His legs, like stenciled tree trunks, glistened thickly with black hairs. His sex rose up, springing clublike from his center. Rennie leaned toward it, touched it with her tongue. Michael's eyes were far away. He stood over her as she gently took him into her mouth, but he seemed not to be there except for the energy, the tension, which emanated from him and which she would now assuage, drain, so that he might sleep, might rest his body against hers.

He pressed her closer to him. Her eyes turned up to his face and saw his teeth catch his lower lip. Then her eyes closed in satisfaction.

Between the hours of one and three in the afternoon, Oacala takes its siesta. Streets empty. The vendors move into the shade and lie down on their mats. The children play quietly in the dirt. Even the burros doze.

On the Avenida Primero Mayo, hardware store on one side, rebozo factory on the other, stands the Palacio Cinema. In fact, it tilts, for an underground stream has dislodged the foundation, and the shell, built of thirties concrete and stainless steel (which time has stained to refute the claims of its builders), has shifted. Inside that greasy, onyx-walled palace, at the siesta hour, De Luca gathered his chosen to view the results of the previous day's shooting.

Slumped on a lumpy, horsehair-oozing, velvet chair, Paul watched the meticulous re-creation of the village of Loc Binh become flesh on the screen. The scenes involved an American patrol scouting the village and avoiding discovery. The shots, raw as they were, held a tension and a beauty that Paul knew would make a fascinating sequence. The use of the camera, its point of view, was unique. The choice of important detail was unerring. The acting was utterly convincing.

Not to De Luca. He kept grimacing, shaking his head and muttering to Paul.

"Look at that. He walked out of the shot when he should have stayed in. Look at that. He looks like he's pissing, not standing over a punji trap. Damn."

"That's nothing," Paul whispered back, "a couple of frames. We'll get them out; the rest is terrific."

De Luca examined his face for lies. Finding none, he said, "I've written a new ending I'd like to show you later."

Paul wondered if he had heard correctly. De Luca's pages were always kept secret. They were doled out only as the necessity of production arose. No one ever saw even a partially completed script in advance. But De Luca had, just now, undeniably, singled him out for an incredible confidence. He had, Paul realized with an exhilarating rush, been drawn confidently closer.

53

Before he could respond, the screen filled with violence. An air action was in progress. Three Cobra gunships, every inch of them decorated with death—rockets, machine guns, automatic cannons—swooped and swirled, dived and strafed. Close-ups showed Denny Burns flipping buttons, peering through sights, looking down at wreckage, communicating with his flying companions. Eerily, without sound, bullets struck flesh, cannons flamed, rockets slammed into houses, sending earth and bodies sky-high. From a seat in the rear Denny Burns's voice drawled.

"Man, am I goin' to get the Silver Star for bein' a badass hero like that? I sure as hell deserve it. Look at me. I'm knockin' everyone outta the game. I oughta be mentioned in dispatches, at least, don't you think, Mike?"

He drawled laughter, and someone sitting with him chuckled as well. De Luca called back.

"You're going to get the D.F.C. for this picture, Denny."

Paul heard a deep rumble from an uncertain row.

"The Distinguished Fucking Cross!"

He turned to the voice and saw a tall, gaunt man sitting almost doubled in his seat, a haze of cigarette smoke around his head. His deep-set black eyes stared dead ahead of him. Beside him sat Flo Ankrum, and she tightened her lips, shaking her head slightly in what seemed to Paul to be a despairing movement. From Denny came a laughing hoot in response.

When the lights came on and everyone rose, Burns came over to De Luca.

"I'll tell you this, kiddo, it doesn't look too phony. No one who was ever flyin' around there is gonna get fooled, but you sure might fool a lot of other people that it happened like that."

"How *else* did it happen?"

The tall man rose, and Paul was able to see he was silver-haired and unshaven. He spoke, over the cigarette at the side of his mouth, with no difficulty and with flat eloquence.

"You got up there in the air, you pointed your guns at those poor schmucks, you pressed the right buttons and you blew them up. That's what I shot you doing. Just that. So what's the big deal about how it really happened?"

"No big deal," Burns said. "No big deal. Except you don't know shit about what went down there, that's all, Marcus. You sat in your nice Hollywood house and you talked to your nice Hollywood friends about all that killin' goin' on, and you played all that ten-

54

nis on Sunday mornings at that private court. Ain't that right? Hell . . ." He laughed good-naturedly.

"Right," the tall man said, taking a deep lungful of smoke. "I don't know a goddamn thing anymore, except how to make movies."

De Luca burst into laughter. He seemed to have enjoyed the exchange between the two men, almost fostered it. When Burns and his semi-crew-cut flying-fatigued companion left, he said, "That's our sideshow. Do you know Allan?"

The tall man turned out to be the second-unit director, Allan Marcus. Paul had heard of him, vaguely. At thirty he had been a Hollywood promise; had made two crackling thrillers which earned him great praise. Then, something happened. Two wives and three pictures later, he had no career, no woman and no prospects. A moderate amount of drugs and Scotch had kept him shuffling about, wondering where it had gone and what to do about it. An occasional second-unit job had kept him afloat. A producer, taking a chance, had hired him for an important film. Instantly, he proceeded to quarrel with the star and the screenwriter. It ended as it had to—with Marcus being fired. It was then that De Luca had found him, remembering his two films. Needing a second-unit director, he had taken him on, given him action sequences to direct, fed him small, unimportant scenes that he himself was too busy to do. Marcus always worked well for Michael. It was as though he could never be on his own, anymore; freedom was too worrisome. But with Michael taking the responsibility, he could shoot well, and Michael appreciated what he did.

As Paul rose to leave, he saw Sieberling put a hand on Flo Ankrum's shoulder and say, "I hear you're organizing some kind of women's thing on company time."

Flo jerked her shoulder away, flashing back, "You haven't heard right. Some of us rap during our break time. That's it."

"Lay off," Sieberling said. "We don't need any more trouble around here. You bitch enough as it is."

He glanced fleetingly at Marcus, who stood back and walked off after De Luca.

"Oh," Rennie whispered, catching up to Paul. "Just location nerves."

Outside the theater, as Flo Ankrum, clutching Allan Marcus's arm, walked past the corrugated gates of the closed shops, she shook her head despairingly.

"I wish," she said, "that when that creep opened his mouth and put me down, you'd said something to him."

Allan looked at her, bewildered.

"What could I have said that would make any difference?"

"It's the saying that's important."

"You are so young it hurts, do you know that?"

She glared at him. "I'm twenty-seven."

"Young."

She walked in silence for a moment, but the silence was too much for her.

"Do you ever differ with Sal or Michael—ever?"

"Nope."

It was said mildly, with no emphasis. The very placidity of expression was a rebuke, and Flo swept her hand away from his arm. Allan looked at her with puzzled compassion.

"Do you know what the hell you're doing? Here you are into this women's movement and you're screwing around with some guy old enough to be your father. That's not the way it's supposed to be, is it?"

"No," she answered slowly.

"Then . . . ?"

"I don't know. I'm attracted to you."

He said nothing as they walked on. She started again.

"What are *you* doing with *me*?"

He laughed. "I get horny—like anybody else. And the Mex women aren't clean."

Her face tightened with anger. He took her hand in his, gently.

"Okay. I like you. And we are in this goddamn place which is giving me the willies. But you don't really understand the first thing about my life."

"And you don't understand the first thing about mine."

"Probably not. So?"

"So," she said slowly, "it doesn't seem to matter, does it? For now. Except . . ."

"Yeah." Allan squinted at the sun. "Except. Well, you take what you can get, don't you?"

A wizened Indian woman offered them a blue-and-red blanket at a good price. Allan moved on without response. Flo refused politely and gave the woman ten pesos.

Entering his office, De Luca felt buoyant despite the problems.

Considering everything, the dailies had been damn good.

He looked at the scenes to be shot at the end of the week and wondered when the studio emissary would pop up to spy on him and bring back tales. Certainly, though, with all those millions invested, the studio had to go forward with the picture, but they might try to remove him, replace him, change everything. If they tried that gambit, what would his response be?

He checked his watch, resolving to call his lawyers and talk about that nagging question once again. The brutal truth was, if he allowed it to stare him in the face, that the studio *could* do something to wrest the film from his control. He had made many concessions in the financing contract to get the project going; if they discovered the harassment and its dollar costs, they might find a clause somewhere and his five-year vision would go down the drain. Despite the fact that he had earned tens of millions for them, some of the ex-agents in the front office hated his guts.

He riffled through the script again, but a sudden scratching noise, from a corner of the room, broke his train of thought, forcing him to look in that direction.

A small figure was seated on the rust-colored couch. Surprised, De Luca saw that it was a young woman—almost a child. Her black Indian hair fell in braids, and she had delicate features, soberly composed. She wore blue jeans and a vivid purple Mexican wedding shirt. Seeing the startling blue eyes, he realized who she was.

"Oh," he said.

The girl smiled gravely. It was a smile heart-affecting in its simple dignity, and Michael perceived a strong sense of self about her.

"*Buenos días*," she said. Her voice was extremely musical, the liquidity of Nahuatl in her throat. "I walk in. I apologize. But I say to myself, I must to see you, I must."

She stood as she spoke, and he saw that she had a small but full frame, was not slim, bird-boned, like most Oacalan women, but rounder.

"How did you get in here?" he asked severely.

"I wait till no one sees and then I come in. Not hard. Policeman always to fall asleep."

"I know."

She laughed softly.

"Where did you learn your English? It's pretty good."

"In school. I learn some things. But, every summer at the *casa*,

57

there comes American girls to stay with Señora Ríos, girls of an age—fourteen or so. I work for Señora Ríos, in the kitchen. I speak to the girls for many years. I learn what they do not teach me at the school."

"I'll bet." He laughed now, coming out from behind the desk to sit, relaxing, on an edge, enjoying the girl.

"What are you doing here?"

"I take for you a . . . test . . . a test, yes," she said, carefully, "for the cinema, you make."

"I know. I saw it."

"But you do not like me?"

"Hold it," he said, "I might like you very much but still not think you should be in my cinema."

"Oh, that is very bad, then."

"You want to be an actress, is that it? Go to Hollywood, meet the stars?" He mocked her and knew it. "You want to make love to Roberto Redford on the silver screen?"

He knew she did not catch everything he said, but she understood enough. To his surprise, she shook her head.

"No, I am not actress."

"Then what?"

Her eyes opened wide then, as though she were talking to the village fool.

"I like to have the money. I like to meet American people. I like . . ." She did not finish, just stared at him boldly.

"You want to help your family?"

"No." Her head shook. "My family is Indio—up in the Sierra Madre del Sur. I am here in Oacala City since I am ten, alone."

"What's your name?"

"Elvira. Elvira Talapan."

"How old are you?" He came closer.

"I have almost eighteen years."

He stood quite close to her, looking down. She looked up at him, her arms holding each other across her breasts, and he could see her chest pumping despite the look of extreme calm on her face.

"You're a brave girl, to have come to the city at ten."

"I die in the mountains," she said simply. "I be slave to my father and my brothers and only make the tortillas from morning to night and never go to school, never."

As she said this, there was a flash of iridescence from her eyes.

"Jesus," he said, startled. "Blue ice."

"What?"

"Where do you get those blue eyes with your Indian father and mother?"

"No one can to say." She smiled again but it was not the grave smile; it was almost merry. "No one will to say."

He laughed with her at that. "Some blue-eyed Spaniard in the woodwork."

"What?"

"Listen," he said carefully, "can you come back here, say—tomorrow night—to talk?"

"In the night?"

"Yes."

"I can come, yes," she said with no hesitation.

"You're sure?"

"I come," she said. She waited for him to say something more, but when he did not, she walked slowly to the door, her huaraches making a very soft noise. Without looking back, she opened the door and left. When she did, De Luca turned to his desk, rummaged through the pile of photos until he found hers. Staring fixedly at it, he held it at arm's length. Then, slowly, he put it down.

CHAPTER

6

Working steadily, intensely, that afternoon, Paul found Rennie to be a fine assistant. When he told her he felt very lucky that she was there, she said, "I think Michael is lucky that *you're* here. Everyone has this feeling about Michael that he's a loner, that he doesn't need anybody. God, how untrue that is."

Covertly, he observed as she bent her finely shaped head over a reel of film, arching her slender neck, her smooth round shoulders catching the light. From the corner of his eye he saw tanned flesh between the top of her slacks and the short vest she wore and felt a sensual stirring, which he quelled by working swiftly and smiling at himself.

The hours went by in a blur of reeling film. He and Rennie did the correct, formal feeling-out dance of new colleagues. By near seven, when they broke for a drink, they trusted each other enough for serious conversation.

Walking outside, still film-engrossed, they saw Sieberling, his tanned face undercoated by a shocked pallor, pulling De Luca toward the parking area where all eight of the company's huge trucks, loaded with equipment, had their engine hoods up, like so many huge open snouts, and the drivers huddled about the bodies in a tight, anxious knot.

"What happened?" De Luca was shouting. "What has happened?"

"We've been hit," they heard Sieberling say. "Sons of bitches. The trucks won't start, none of them."

The commotion brought all activity to a halt. The Mexican helpers averted their eyes. The passing crew members stopped in their tracks. Rennie, however, started toward the trucks like a startled doe and, automatically, Paul followed. He reached them in time to hear Steve Kruger stutter his explanation.

"Mike, it took us half the day to get loaded. Then when I got

60

into the cab, the mother wouldn't turn over. I almost ran the friggin' battery down tryin'."

A short driver, bald, pug-nosed as a chow, joined in.

"Nothin'. Not a tick. None of them. We called José to look."

From underneath an open hood a lithe mechanic in coveralls showed himself. He held a couple of box wrenches in greasy, practiced hands and seemed either embarrassed or frightened—it was hard to tell.

"What's wrong?" De Luca demanded grimly. "Why won't they start?"

"In the petrol tanks, *jefe*"—the mechanic's voice sank to a whisper—"is much sand."

De Luca stared at him, shocked. The mechanic swallowed hard and continued. "In all of them. I check the carb of one and is much dirty. *Madre de Dios*, I say, what is pulling here? So I open the fuel *tubería* and I see white sand. Is all no good, *jefe*, no good." He looked down, humbly assuming the guilt.

"Are you sure?" De Luca demanded, "are you damn sure of what you're saying?"

"Is so, *jefe*. I put stick in petrol tank, comes up *mucho* sand." He averted his eyes as De Luca exploded.

"Jesus Christ!"

The drivers looked down, scratching cheeks and noses. Whoever was near moved away as though on command. Rennie reached out a hand to De Luca, who shrugged it off. Sieberling, trying to keep his voice calm, asked how long it would take to clean the tanks out.

"Don' know. Big job. Got to take them down, blow them out, blow out carbs, *tuberías*. Take two days, maybe more."

"Impossible," De Luca cried out. "We have dusk shots scheduled." He wheeled on Sieberling. "Can't we rent trucks? Unload these and load them?"

"Mike, it's going to be tough getting hold of trucks like these in Oacala."

"Do it. I don't care what it takes to get them but get them. I will not waste two days now."

"Mike, I'll try." Sieberling stepped closer to De Luca. "I'll go to see Quesedo, too."

"What is he going to do?" De Luca was contemptuous. "Police pigs. They're bought and paid for."

"Yeah, but—"

"Don't give me *but*'s. I don't make pictures with *but*'s." He glared

61

at the crippled mastodons in frustrated rage.

Dusk streamed into night before three small trucks were located. De Luca was forced to cancel all shooting. He had Sieberling issue orders that no company vehicle was ever to be left unguarded in the future and that everyone was to be alert against future sabotage.

"Furthermore," Sieberling commanded, "no talk about this is to get around. It's our business and nobody else's."

Directly after the meeting, De Luca locked himself into his office with Rennie. Paul, somewhat shaken, went back to his strips of film. He finally tumbled into bed at three A.M., exhausted and pursued by visions of Viet Cong and GIs and, somewhere, Stella, in a paratrooper uniform.

Sal Sieberling was having a tequila with Police Captain Quesedo at the cantina.

At a corner table, he removed his tinted glasses, blinking his eyes rapidly. He was sensitive to light. The tinted glasses were necessary, and though aware that most of the company felt the shades were a deliberate manipulation of his image, he did nothing to correct that idea.

He scorned popularity contests. Being well liked had not provided his house at the beach or his BMW or his glider which sat at the Santa Monica airport; that glider which took him aloft, swooped him, dipped him softly on warm currents, cradled him gently in the fluidlike airstream, rocked him soothingly, made him feel free and disembodied, released all the tightness, unlocked him from the vise he carried, almost constantly, in his chest. Not even women could do that for him. The release he felt with them was tempered by the knowledge of his dependency. Almost immediately afterward, that depressed him.

He had not always had the BMW and the glider. He had done his time, paid his dues. He had scuffled and scrounged, been a lackey for a dozen producers and directors. He had had cars repossessed and begged a month's rent extension, shopped in May's and even taken buses. Until he had met Michael De Luca and known, *known*, that De Luca was his destiny; that being with him, anticipating his needs, knowing the buttons he wanted pressed, moving any heaven and any earth to help him, would get him off the beach forever, transport him to another plane. He had been right.

The police captain was drinking Cuervo Gold with a coffee chaser. His round face, in which his small eyes appeared as black buttons, was screwed up appreciatively as he sipped the tequila and smoked his cigarillo.

His uniform was well tailored upon his solidly made and thickening body, for he believed strongly that much power resided in appearance; to be important, you must look important. When he was twenty years old and in the army base at Guadalajara, it had been borne in upon him that all enlisted men wore shapeless bags, all officers wore smartly epauleted, sharply pressed jackets. The lesson had not been lost.

Now, nineteen years later, he was fond of recalling those days and an American girl who had been at the university.

"She come from Chic-a-go. She was *hebrea*. Dark, like us." He laughed at the memory. "She burns like a fire, my friend, like a fire. 'Injoostice,' she says. 'Injoostice here in Mexico. We must to do some-t'ing here—the workers of the world.'"

"A Red?" Sieberling was less than interested but pushed the sincere button in his voice. The captain shrugged, shifted his seat to move the weight of his gun around on the belt. He raised his hand for another Gold, and Señora Uribe came hurrying over, a smile pasted to her face.

"*Mucho gusto, capitán. A sus ordenes.*"

Quesedo paid her no attention. In the corner, Señor Uribe, having paid his share of bribes to the police, looked away.

"*Comunista*, I don' know." Quesedo stroked some tequila drops from his mustache. "She talk to me 'bout the God of the Judíos—angry God, always need the sacrifice, *comprende*? I oonderstand that very good. Is like the God of the Azteca—joost." He started on a new tequila.

"She makes me to go fuck-fuck with her. I very scared then. I come from Jalisco. She comes from Chic-a-go. I t'ink I get into bad trouble. She tells me all people be brothers. I tell her she be *loco*."

He waved his hand in dismissal.

"She be too *loco* for me. I don' see her no more after that. She go to Guatemala to find real Indio." He guffawed, then quieted somewhat and said plaintively, "I dunno why I t'ink of her so much times."

"Okay." Sieberling had endured the recital and wanted it over. "What about what happened—the trucks?"

"Umm." Quesedo's small eyes came back to the present. "Maybe is *mordida*. Somebody comes to you, asks *mordida*?"

"No, nobody comes for that."

"Umm." The policeman reflected. "Maybe now they come."

"Maybe," Sieberling said, "but my boss thinks that some big shots don't want this picture made here."

"We are *policía*," Quesedo objected weakly. "We don' have to do with politics."

"I'm trying not to laugh."

The policeman grinned.

"Just remember, we have a deal with you for protection. What good is that deal if you're getting slipped more pesos *not* to protect?"

"No, no," Quesedo protested, "we don' do that."

"Look," Sieberling persisted, "if somebody is paying you to look the other way, why don't you level with me? It might be to your advantage."

"I am honest man, señor; I don' do like you say. We make a good deal. I take care."

"Except we're getting hit and our shooting schedule is delayed and it costs us a bundle."

"I see what to do," Quesedo said. "I all the time co-op-er-ate, no? I don' bother nobody of you when you go to the hills to buy mari-juana?"

"Look," Sieberling muttered, "we've got a lot of people; we can't control them all."

Quesedo leaned over and punched Sieberling on the arm, delighted. "Joost so, joost so," he crowed. "I cannot to control all too." He swigged the rest of the Gold and bit the lemon with teeth as yellow as the rind. "Maybe is good I have talk with the *jefe* to show him that—"

"No, no," Sieberling broke in anxiously. "You talk to *me*."

"Umm." Quesedo squinted at Sieberling. A crewman had fed the jukebox and it broke into life, the green, red and blue neon pulsating and Frank Sinatra's voice singing, "Chicago . . . Chicago . . ."

"Sí," Quesedo said, fondly, puffing on his cigarillo, "the hebrea sings *canciones*." His brows knit and, over Sinatra, he ground out a counterpoint, uncertainly: "Arise, you—you—" He shook his head. "I forget. Is a long time ago." His eyes dreamed to Sinatra's scratchy tones.

All the next day, there was tension in the company enclave. The tougher grips and gaffers kept hitching their pistols up. The camera crew kept busy with make-work, loading film into magazines, checking camera motors—and avoiding their chief, if they could. The Mexican laborers stared, big-eyed, as José and two other mechanics pulled the fuel tanks from the trucks. Four machine-pistoled police walked about, eyes darting, fingers on triggers as though the revolution were about to start.

As the day wore on, it became clear that the sand had injured the carburetors and they had to be taken down. Repair would take at least another twenty-four hours, and night shooting was postponed again. Instead a crew would be sent out for background shots which would be cut into the picture later. At five o'clock Paul was informed that De Luca wished to see him. Coming into the office, he was confronted by an excited director waving a copy of the local newspaper.

"We're in a fight with these reactionary forces, Paul. They're out to crush the picture. This business with the trucks shows me how far they're willing to go. That's how things are done in this country, force, brutal force. Remember what Luis told us about the police and university students? Shot them down like dogs. We didn't even do that—except at Kent State."

He jackknifed up on the couch and held open the paper. There, on the front page, murky with ink but recognizable, was a picture of Luis Aguillar. Above his head flared an equally murky "TERRO-RISTA ATAQUE."

"His guys ambushed a government tax collection office and destroyed all the records." De Luca's voice rose, gathering emotion. "You know what I'd like to do? I'd like to go see that man he told us about on Calle Diaz and make that contribution."

As he spoke, his skin seemed to give off an electric glow. His back straightened with conviction. The mission was taking possession of him. The idea, the drama of it, the conspiratorial aspect combined with the *righteousness* was overwhelming. Paul could see the development taking place under his eyes.

"Look," he said, "I'll go with you, of course; what the hell."

"I'll get some money from Sal. Maybe five thousand pesos? What do you think? Is five thousand chintzy?"

"It's fine," he said, having no idea whether it was.

"No—ten is better. Meet me outside."

He waited ten uneasy minutes for De Luca to join him at the Mercedes. When, finally, he appeared, he held a black leather briefcase raised in silent, significant signal. The chauffeur held open the door. They clambered into the backseat and De Luca ordered them driven to the Calle Diaz.

"Diaz?" The driver was plainly surprised.

"Calle Diaz. Let's go."

"Calle Diaz. Sí."

His face was impassive; Calle Diaz was in the Indian quarter of the city.

De Luca thought a moment, looked out the rear window and said, "But don't go there directly—move around a few streets first."

"Sí, señor."

He turned right at the Zócalo. De Luca whispered to Paul, "In case we're being followed."

They did not seem to be followed by anyone. The streets held a few mopeds and burros and a stalled taxi, steaming. De Luca sank deeply into his seat as the car snaked through street after street, his hands clutching the briefcase to his lap. After a few minutes of silence, he whispered, "I got twenty thousand pesos. That's less than five hundred dollars—little enough." He fell silent again, Paul keeping the silence with him. Finally, after twenty more minutes, the driver announced, "Calle Diaz."

"Okay." De Luca came alive. "We're looking for some kind of shop, a small shop, run by an Isac—"

"Ismena," the driver said, pointing. "Is there. I stop here. Cannot go down street. *Demasiado* small."

"Right. Pull up here." De Luca looked at Paul, his eyes gleaming. "Let's go."

They left the car and went toward an unpaved cul-de-sac. The few shops here were grubby, most with hanging streamers of fly-paper exhibiting dozens of trapped victims swinging in the light breeze. One of the shops, small, dark, with an earth-packed floor, sold a variety of cheap pots and pans with a sprinkling of exotic plastic ware. The name, neatly lettered, was ISMENA. They stopped in front of the braided rope doorway; then they crossed the threshold.

In the cool and shadowed shop, a mahogany-colored man in Indian white quarreled angrily with two teenage boys. Incomprehensible Nahuatl, the Indian tongue, raged from his lips. The boys in torn pants and T-shirts giggled and mocked him. He pointed to the doorway. They pointed at the doorway. He slammed his hand down on the rough wooden counter. They chopped the air in parody. Their eyes were slightly glazed and they suddenly became aware of the intruders. The smaller, pinch-faced and knock-kneed, pranced up to them.

"How you doin', man?" he said in perfect imitation American.

The other, long matted hair swinging wildly, made smoking gestures. At this the shopkeeper picked up a reed broom and advanced upon the boys with it. They hooted in derision, said loud words and, laughing, ran from the shop.

The shopkeeper stood there for a long moment, unmoving. He had a broad face for an Indian, but the long-boned nose was Mayan, as were the full lips and the almond-shaped black eyes. His splayed feet were gray with dust and he appeared to be in his forties, but it was almost impossible to tell. His face held absolutely no expression. De Luca greeted him.

"*Buenos días.*"

"*Buenas tardes,*" the shopkeeper answered. He put the broom back in its corner and moved, slowly, behind the counter which held an abacus and a cigar box.

"Let's go closer," De Luca murmured, and they moved to the counter. The Indian did not move.

"Señor Ismena?" De Luca asked.

"Sí. Ismena."

"*Habla inglés?* English, speak?"

The shopkeeper hesitated, then nodded.

"Speak *inglés*, little."

"Good," De Luca said. "We want to buy a record and we are told that you have it. A record. A *disk*. A disk of the Deer Dance music."

A bare flicker crossed the shopkeeper's face.

"Deer Dance?"

"Yes, Deer Dance."

"Who tells you I have this disk?"

"A friend, a very good friend."

De Luca turned to Paul. "Maybe you ought to stand near the doorway. If anyone starts to come in, call something."

Feeling like an inexperienced actor in a spy sequence, Paul stationed himself, nervously, at the doorway. It was silly, and yet he knew it was all very real; police here shot—all too casually.

At the counter Ismena's gaze was unblinking still, and De Luca looked back at the shopkeeper in open admiration.

"I have," he said softly, "something for . . . a certain person . . . who lives in the hills."

He saw another flicker.

"I am told you can get . . . this . . . to him."

He lifted the briefcase to the counter, undid the straps, reached in and scooped out five bundles of bills in tight rubber bands.

The shopkeeper looked at the exposed pesos with surprise and quickly reached out, pushing them back into the security of the briefcase.

"No show," he said. "No show." And his voice had abandoned neutrality.

Hastily, De Luca restrapped the case. As he did, the curtain at the doorway parted and Paul called out, explosively.

"Mike!"

De Luca turned quickly, trying to hide the case. Ismena took a step backward as two figures darted in through the ropes. It was the two giggling boys returning. They held sheets of bundled newspaper in their hands which they hurled at the shopkeeper. He retreated, instinctively, as the load of concealed dung flew through the air, spotting the counter with brown, smelly lumps, flecking his clothes and hair, settling on the pots and pans.

Paul felt relieved and horrified at the same time. The act was mad, seemed even madder as the boys took a split moment to enjoy the results, then danced around in glee and sped out, leaving a frozen De Luca clutching his case with a grip of iron.

Silent, a tight bitterness pulling at his lips, Ismena brushed the dung from his white shirt.

"Who the hell are those kids?" De Luca asked.

Ismena shrugged.

"I mean why?"

Ismena looked De Luca straight in the eyes then and said, "Marijuana."

He reached out suddenly and took the briefcase. "I see this be all right. You go now."

"Right," De Luca said. "*Hasta la vista.*"

Paul nodded his good-bye. They brushed through the curtain to the street. Behind them, the Indian had already disappeared into a back room.

The Americans walked rapidly toward the waiting car, past the shabby shops and the few curious Mexicans. One man appeared to glare hard at them, but when they passed a foot from him, they saw that he was staring vacantly into space.

Seeing them, the driver yanked the car door open. Once they

were in, he ran to his seat, started the engine quickly and pulled away, his face betraying his relief. He backed and filled swiftly, turning finally toward the leafy avenue blocks away. Thumping over a boulder, in his haste, he apologized. "No good here."

"That man, Ismena," De Luca said appreciatively, settling back, "is one of your natural Mexican folk heroes."

"Aren't the police sure to get him, sooner or later?" Paul wanted to know.

Before De Luca could answer, an ancient truck darted from a cul-de-sac with surprising speed and bore down upon the Mercedes. De Luca's driver jerked erect, shouting, "Ai!" and frantically hauled his wheel to the left, slamming on the brakes. The Mercedes juddered, its frame wrenching. Burning rubber, it skidded slowly, majestically, to the right and then came to a skittering stop. Inside, De Luca and Paul were thrown forward and down, grabbing for handholds. Outside, the truck brushed the car and roared across the street, disappearing into an alley.

The driver, the blood drained from his face, his hands frozen to the steering wheel, turned around in shock and kept calling, "Is okay? Is okay? Is okay?"

De Luca nodded grimly. He hauled himself back into the seat, flexing his right arm at the shoulder. Paul rubbed his left knee, which had slammed into the door. He sat down again, gingerly. The driver started the engine and backed up, slowly, his eyes checking every inch of street. Paul leaned against the leather and looked questioningly at De Luca.

"Maybe," De Luca answered.

CHAPTER
7

Upon his return from Ismena's, Paul worked with Flo Ankrum until almost nine o'clock. She told him there was a lot of talk about "revenge" and "kicking ass"; exactly whose hind parts were to be punished was unclear—though they had to be Mexican, that was sure.

At nine Rennie came in and Flo left to have dinner with Allan Marcus, who claimed that being denied access to a corned-beef sandwich for so many months was unbalancing him.

After Flo's departure, Paul and Rennie worked together for another hour. When he told her of the near collision, she was upset; if it had been a deliberate act coming upon the heels of the truck sabotage, it was a disturbing escalation. Still, Mexican drivers being what they were . . .

Paul decided that he was free to tell her something about the "mission," feeling that Michael probably would, and it did not surprise her. Michael had these deep feelings about ordinary people; she knew Paul understood and appreciated that. Not too many men would get involved with a terrorist. But Michael was extraordinary. Told about the stoned boys and the dung flinging, she expressed surprise. Certainly, there was much traffic in drugs in Oacala, for export. The state police were always sending in undercover agents to break the chain from grower to buyer to shipper or dealer. Still, when she had first arrived at Oacala, she could not recall seeing any skulled-out natives; that was not their way. Now, it seemed to be happening more and more.

"You know, they use all kinds of stuff in their rituals here, mescaline, peyote, grass—things we don't even know about. But it's supposed to be sacred, not for the ordinary guy. Speaking of which . . ." She produced two hand-rolleds, offering him one.

70

"This is sensational stuff, the best. You know who the connection is? That mousy assistant hairdresser."

They sat there, in the midst of the film clutter, she seated on a cleared spot on the floor, her legs drawn up under her, he on his desk. The herb was sweet and slowed their talk. They spoke of films and Vietnam and disillusion and ambition. He fleetingly mentioned Stella. She talked of the college debating-team champion who had deflowered her and followed that act with his contest-winning piece about "Caesar in Gaul." Startling him, she asked suddenly, "And what *did* you think of Catherine?"

"I knew you were going to ask that, at some point."

"Well?"

"Look"—he passed the joint—"I have no way of telling anything about the woman."

"Come on, Gordon, don't fudge. If you're smoking with me, be honest with me."

"I mean that. She doesn't give too many clues." His head was buzzing and he felt his eyes getting red.

"She's a steady one." She took a deep final toke. "She's in for the long pull. She knows almost nothing about what Michael does, you know. It's like she lives in some other world. She's not *interested* in what he does, couldn't care less. Isn't that incredible? Because Michael *is* what he does. He's built to make wonderful movies. And if she doesn't care about that, how can she care about him at all? How can she?" Her voice, which had been somewhat languid, now took on urgency.

"I don't know," Paul answered, not being able to follow, exactly.

"I know. Because I know what Michael is all about. There are very few Michaels in the world, very few. My father would hate him if he knew him."

She leaned forward for emphasis.

"My father claims that the proper business of America is business —everything else is unimportant." A shudder shook her. "Can you imagine?"

Her unbound breasts quivered beneath her blouse, and he felt himself reacting again. She lurched forward.

"You trying to get up?"

"I *am* getting up," she answered tartly, but somehow couldn't get the leverage right. He helped. She clung to his fingers and giggled.

"Isn't this fun?"

"Terrific."

"You're okay, Gordon," she announced, "and I am very hungry. What about you?"

"Yes," he answered solemnly, "hungry."

"I," she said, in an equally solemn fashion, "will go pee, fetch Michael, and then maybe the three of us will go to the Jardín Juarez for a super dinner. Excuse, please."

Slowly, gracefully, she made her way out the door, and Paul, looking after her, thought she was perhaps ten years old and laughed aloud.

Emerging from the toilet, Rennie gave her blouse a final smoothing tug and meandered out into the night to cross over toward the administration building and Michael's office. The area was deserted. The trucks had been hauled away. Dimly lit by one street lamp, there was only the sound of a leaking water pipe somewhere and the shuffling of feet from the Zócalo where the nightly *pasada*, the circle walk, was already taking place. She hummed a bit of the "Mexican Hat Dance" music and tapped her feet.

Crossing to the admin building, she passed the single police guardian on his wooden chair tilted back against the wall. He was sound asleep. She went by him quickly, almost skipping over to De Luca's office, and knocked, calling, "Michael, it's me."

In a moment the door opened and De Luca stood there, frowning.

"What's up?"

She pulled his head toward her lips and kissed him on the mouth.

"What's going on?"

"I'm collecting you. You and Paul and I are going to have chicken *mole* at the Jardín."

"Not tonight," Michael said. "I'm working on some plans for the Jericho sequence and there are a million problems. Go without me."

"Oh," she said forlornly. "Oh."

She blew him a kiss and started back down the hall as De Luca closed the door. She hurried outside, past the sleeping guard once more, and was heading in the direction of the editing rooms when she heard the padding of feet from the opposite direction. It took her eyes moments of strain to locate and focus upon someone moving toward the administration building.

The figure moved toward her and she moved toward it. They passed each other almost directly under the single yellow street bulb, and only then did Rennie completely make out the small long-skirted form with the splash of orange rebozo around her shoulders and a blood-red flower in her hair. Even then she was puzzled until, catching her breath, she saw the girl's blue eyes and knew who she was, knew where she was going, knew why, knew everything about this moment. Then the girl moved out of the light and toward the place where Michael was. Her body limp, Rennie walked toward where Paul sat, waiting.

Of course, she said to herself over and over again, as she walked, of course, of course, of course.

In his office De Luca paced, considering ways and means to side-track the negative, worrisome talk that would, inevitably, spill out and cause yet more trouble.

A good face; it was important to put on a good face. Perhaps he ought to give the company a little something extra for loyalty. A party—they always liked parties. Dancing, music, food—but not Mexican food. He could fly everything he wanted in from the States. Why not? He would fly in all the things everyone loved and missed, all the goodies he himself coveted. He made a note to himself. But even as he made the note, he caught sight of his opened script and the problems he had been considering. He needed marshland, rice paddies. Three important sequences took place there and none of Sieberling's scouts had found anything in the valley that could be used. He groaned, threw down his pen and went to the refrigerator. Those were key sequences, establishing much of the feeling of Vietnam. He sighed, found a tin of chocolate cookies, munched one. He could rewrite for another location but it would not have the sense of authenticity, the feel. It would be like—a movie. He rejected the notion. But where would he shoot? He slammed the refrigerator door closed.

Absorbed in questions, he was annoyed at the second knock. When he opened the door and saw the blue-eyed Indian girl standing in the doorway, smiling shyly at him, he took a moment to remember he had asked her to return and wasn't at all sure he wanted her there.

"*Buenas noches*," the girl said. "I come—like you say."

His eyes swept over her. The orange rebozo and red flower were perfect. The long black skirt brushed the floor, and her violet top revealed a scoop of warm brown skin. She was like some exotic fruit. He reached out to her arm, guiding her inside.

"I am glad you came." He motioned toward the couch. "Do you want something to drink? Some *vino*? I have some good white *vino*."

"Sí," the girl said, sitting easily, "I have."

He fetched the wine and glasses, filled them, gave her one, sat on the edge of his desk and sipped, watching his visitor sip from the good Baccarat. She was so—childlike, and yet round, gently swelling, it seemed, everywhere. And her eyes watched always, never left his face.

"You're watching me."

"Sí."

"Why?"

"*No sé*. Do not know."

"I don't mind," he told her, and he didn't. Then he said, "Listen, I'm going to ask you something—don't get angry. Have you been with many men?"

She shook her head slowly.

"I'm not sure I believe that. You don't seem like other Mexican women. You're too bold."

She nodded proudly. "Sí. I will not be like them."

That was interesting. He sat on the couch with her—at the opposite end. She had returned, knowing exactly what would happen, of course, but there was something unsettling about her candor.

"Do you have a lover?"

"No man, no."

He smiled at her emphatic tone. "Are you going to tell me next that you're a virgin?"

"Sí."

"You don't really have to play this kind of game with me."

"What is—play?"

"Make-believe. Little white lies. *Mentiras*."

Her blue eyes opened wide with fire. "*No mentira!*" She sat up stiffly and her anger appeared genuine. "I am *vir-gin*. I never know a man. Since ten I am careful, I watch. Oh, yes, many times men, they pull at me—*borracho* men—too much mescal. But always I run away. Three times the *patrón*, where I work, he tries to put me on the table in the *cocina*. He tells me he will make, for me, the *casa elegante*, if I let him do to me. I cry. I run to my room. Once he follows me and tears my clothes and hurts me here." She touched her breasts.

74

He listened, skeptically. With mock sympathy he said, "Here?" and touched her breasts as well.

"No!"

She recoiled from him and rose to her feet. She was trembling, and whether it was from fear or wounded pride he couldn't tell. He did not believe she would leave, but she started to do that, her slim yet rounded back facing him like a sculpture.

Uncertainly he rose too and called, "Hold it—please."

She hesitated at the door and then turned, wary as a slapped-at bird, her eyes distrusting.

"What you said," he fumbled, "sounds so familiar—like a story."

"For you is a story," she answered angrily. "For me is my life."

It was a declaration, and it stabbed him with remorse—deserved, he thought.

"Do you still work there?"

She said nothing and he felt she was still debating whether to bolt or not. "I really want to know," he added.

"Sí," she said, "and the señora tells him nothing. If I stay, one day he will hurt me, this I know." Her voice took on a deep, pride-filled tone. "But I stay the way I am birthed till I wish."

She touched the flower in her hair, and the movement took his breath away with its strength and sensuality.

"Listen," he asked, "why did you come back here?"

"You ask me to come," she answered simply. —

"Yes, but I'm a man and I looked at you in a certain way—and you came here to me."

"Sí."

"I don't understand."

"Because, you are good, I think. You are kind, and I must to leave that house so *I* choose. I see you and I know you will see me. Maybe, I think, I will please you. If I please you then I choose. You do not to understand?"

"Yes," he said, "I do. You're incredible. Please come back."

He reached his hand out again, and this time she did not move away but came toward him, sinking with him to the couch. Gently, the rebozo falling from her shoulders, she put her arms about his thick waist and cradled her head upon his chest like a child finding home. He hesitated, then his arms went about her and he leaned down to kiss the top of her head. His fingers went to the skin of her shoulders and he felt her settling, pleasurably, into his hand. Her face turned up and her lips were parted, her eyes closed. His hand

75

dropped to her thigh, where he felt the flesh warm beneath the long skirt and he experienced again, after a long time, a tightening in his chest, an anticipatory excitement.

"You're something else," he said, "you are really something else."

She did not answer, but simply pulled toward him until she became a small, round ball of softness burrowing into his bulk and forcing through him a surge of very surprising emotion.

All the way to the restaurant, Paul sensed the change in Rennie. The giggling, the ebullience, was gone, replaced by a hollow silence. Finally, he felt compelled to ask if she felt all right.

"I'm okay," she told him, and then she said, "You're really quite a lovely man."

"What," Paul asked, taken aback, "is that all about?"

She patted him on the cheek. "I'm drawn to types like you, that's all."

The cab stopped and they got out, but she held his hand, tightly, and wouldn't let it go. As they were about to pass through the whitewashed arches of the Jardín Juarez, Denny Burns and two of his fliers emerged onto the street. They were tequila-happy and Denny squinted at Rennie and Paul, theatrically.

"Where's the head honcho? Where's the big man?"

"He's working," Rennie said.

"He damn well better figure out who's hittin' us."

"Damn straight," mumbled Denny's wingman, a brush-cut six-footer called Gimper since he acquired a limp when two bullets sliced his calf tendon over the Mekong Delta.

"Just leave it to Michael." Rennie forced a bright smile and pulled Paul into the restaurant.

Gimper looked after her and gravel-throated, "Private stock. The rest of us have to make do with these Mex whores who don't like the smell of soap, and De Luca has his private stock."

"Make a tape and send it home for Christmas," Denny jeered.

"There's the crew chicks," the other flier said. He was called simply Jonesy and was younger. He had not been in Vietnam and, secretly, felt that lack of experience keenly.

"Gawd," the wingman groaned, "those uptight bleeding hearts. Boat-assed dykes, all of 'em." He shook his head sadly.

"Jesus, you're getting such a bundle to be here and just fly that dumb crate of yours every couple of days or so, you oughta stop yapping and kiss my ass for getting you this detail," Denny jeered.

76

"I'll kiss your ass—with this." The flier laughed and half-pulled a thirty-two automatic from a concealed holster. The younger flier mock-ducked and shouted, "Flak . . . flak . . . Coming in hard at six o'clock. Take evasive action."

"Let 'er roll!" the wingman shouted. "Kick ass!"

"Je-sus," Denny said, "I'm not with you guys."

He walked away. The two others followed, prancing along. From around the corner two barefoot peasants in white came into view and found themselves entrapped by the scampering men.

"Look out. Look out. Hellcat express comin'!" the Gimper shouted as he and his companion charged headlong into the peasants. One of the men fell to the ground; the other was hurled against the wall. The man on the ground was up, instantly, trembling with anger. His voice shook in his throat.

"*Gringo puerco.*"

The wingman drew himself up and glared.

"What are you sayin'? What the hell are you sayin', you monkey?" He reached out, drunkenly, for the Mexican.

"Cool it," Denny called.

The younger American swayed, befuddled. Gimper, however, gripped the collar of the peasant's cotton shirt and, with one downward ripping motion, tore half of it off.

Unhesitating in his anger, the Mexican reached for the short machete in its scabbard at his waist, pulled the thick curved blade into the open and slashed at Gimper, barely missing his face.

"Jesus!" Denny yelled, reaching for the Mexican's arm. The wingman stumbled back, groping for his automatic pistol. At this the second peasant charged forward, and Denny hurled himself at the man, shoving him back.

From around the corner a police jeep suddenly appeared, rocking to a halt as three armed policemen jumped out. They were over to the battlers in moments, and seeing them, the peasants simply went limp. Their hands went down; their eyes looked sullenly at the ground.

The police took no notice that they were not being resisted. They lashed out at both peasants with their rifle butts, drawing blood. They jerked the men to their feet, hauled them into the jeep and sped away without saying a word to the Americans.

Gimper pocketed his pistol, straightening his clothing, while Jonesy fingered his reddened and swelling nose.

"Hell," he muttered, "that chili chomper's got a hard head."

"Damn," Denny said angrily. "you can't go around fuckin' everybody over, here. This ain't Nam."

The wingman shrugged uneasily. "I was just havin' some fun."

"Okay," Denny said. "Let's go over to the Red House. I don't know if I'm still in the mood to get laid but I'm damn sure gonna try."

"Denny," the wingman asked plaintively, "when are we gonna get finished with this goddamned picture?"

"When we win." Denny grinned. "When we win."

CHAPTER

8

✕══✕══✕══✕══✕══ **8** ══✕══✕══✕══✕══✕

The grapevine, that jungle growth which leaps over oceans and deserts, told Stella that Michael De Luca had taken a new mistress, a full-blooded Indian girl with whom he had become totally infatuated. He was starring her in his movie. He was setting her up in a mansion. He was buying her all of the Mexican National Treasury's solid gold bangles.

"I also hear," her lunch date, an angular woman who ate up coast-to-coast airspace as though it were yogurt, said, "that there's trouble on the set."

"What kind of trouble?"

"No one will talk about it."

"Is it anything about a man called Gordon?"

The lunch date craned her neck forward anxiously, her splendidly firm hair bobbing with anticipation.

"What have *you* heard? Are you saying that De Luca is gay and is having it on with this man Gordon?"

The lunch was upsetting to Stella. Hearing even slightly possible details about the production brought Paul back to her, strongly. She found herself looking at old photographs. Worse, she found herself looking at Paul's face through a magnifying lens she kept in a desk drawer. She knew it was ridiculous but she did it anyway, trying to fathom something in that face that would provide a clue to her own feelings.

She broke a weekend date with an architect she thought she liked and went to her house on the island. She mooned about, and every time she tripped over some object that Paul had bought for the place—the Chinese vase or the Italian fruit plate—she experienced a sentimental pang.

On Sunday she went to the local movie house, which was showing a horror film about a bewitched girl who turned her parents

79

into huge ants because they didn't like her boyfriend, but she didn't have one single satisfying thrill of fear. On Monday she went to a Feminist Media meeting—subject: "The Love Hype"—and cheered madly. On Tuesday the architect called again. She agreed to a SoHo dinner.

At dinner, she kept looking at the architect's darkly handsome features and, silently, debated the extent of her attraction to him. He was an intense man, knowledgeable and quite successful. He looked upon Stella with great interest. She could, he had told her, admiringly, in the past, listen—and she could talk. She was gracefully a woman and a woman full of grace. In short, he was coming on to her very strongly and very acceptably, with taste and class and not without some depth. Not too opinionated, yet sure of himself, not a man, it seemed, who pulled back from engagement. She contrasted him with Paul and declared him, easily, the winner.

Over the cheese and espresso, Stella became very fond of him, thought about his longish brown hair looking so silken and fine, wondered what his body was like beneath the patterned shirt. It would, obviously, be muscular. He skied and swam and looked marvelously fit. He seemed oblivious to her appraisal, but of course he could not be. It was a nonegotistical performance, and she liked it very much indeed.

In his loft it all started out well. They had slipped onto the extremely wide Italian leather sofa in an absolutely natural progression of events. There was no pretense, but it was not without a certain romantic ambience, a sense of feeling and caring. He had shown her drawings for a new, revolutionary building he was doing in the Midwest. He listened, raptly, as she told him of the film on African village life she had screened that morning. He declared he wanted, someday, to go to Africa and design simple, inexpensive housing for villages, give back to the world for what the world had given him. Her heart had leaped at that and she kissed his cheek, impulsively. He took her hand, kissed it, and said maybe, one day, they could go to Africa together. She said she would like that and, finally, touched his hair. It was, indeed, silken and smooth and very erotic. He touched her hair, in turn pleased. Then they had embraced and gently fallen to the couch's soft belly.

Once out of her clothes, however, and with the architect's strong body all over hers, with his lips on her breasts and thighs, with his hands, sensuous and gentle, moving over her back, Stella be-

80

came horrifyingly objective. What she liked about this man, she thought, was not the man himself but the *idea* of the man. With that perception, all heat vanished.

Why? she railed at herself. Why? He's lovely. He's wonderful. He cares. And she began to weep, inexplicably.

Instantly, the architect ceased his movements. Concerned, he leaned down to wipe away her tears. It wasn't him, she moaned over and over again, not him. Apprehensive, puzzled, the architect sat back on his haunches. Stella continued to sob. He sat there, somewhat stunned, hands over his groin. Finally, she controlled herself. She told him she was sorry, very sorry. He said he understood, though he didn't at all.

"It's just me," she said, getting up to put her clothes on, "it's just me, that's all. It has nothing to do with you."

The architect nodded.

"Really, it's me," she repeated, "just me."

She felt herself about to go into tears again and, losing her balance, sat down on the couch as the flow started. She tried to stop it but it came anyway, and she sat there, one leg in her blue bikini underpants and the other leg out, crying like a lost and lonely child.

For the next five days she was irritable and depressed. At her office the twenty-year-olds began muttering meaningfully about early menopause. Stella bought two hours from Dr. Markell and found herself unable to go through it all again: the childhood brightness, the father who loved her so much and who told her she could never fail at anything, the mother who smiled and was sweetly complaisant, all in the framework of a Chicago suburban life with the university beckoning the cleverest sons and daughters to its bosom, those sons and daughters generally springing from Hamtramck steelworkers.

"I think this is a futile exercise," she finally told Dr. Markell. "There's something very wrong if I have these kinds of reactions, if I keep thinking about a man I had an affair with for two years and was always critical of."

"Always?"

"Oh—nothing is *always*, you know that."

"Ah."

"There are things about him *you* would say are like my father."

"I would?"

"Warmth. Depth. Honesty. Decency. Gentleness."

81

"Ah."

"Physically . . ."

"Yes?"

"Ridiculous. He wasn't the greatest lover in the world, believe me, but I had this sense of—well—this sense of trust—and I could let myself go with him, somehow."

"Umm. Yet critical."

"Because I always had this feeling he was on an edge—teetering, afraid to assert or commit. He doesn't even like to work alone; he's always looked for partners, men to lean on. I wanted him to be on his own two feet."

"Like you."

She ignored that and went to the heart of the matter.

"I must be sick not to be able to respond to other perfectly loving and wonderful men."

"Sick is just a word."

"And another thing, love is a shuck and a myth and a hype—romantic love, that is. How can you deny that?"

"I didn't deny."

"You *looked* as though you were going to."

She decided, after the two hours, not to come back. They would just rehash her inability to find someone just like her father, the real reason for her never having married, etc., etc., and all the rest.

"I am so *bored* with it all," Stella told Dr. Markell as she said good-bye. The man didn't appear concerned; he almost smiled.

The next day, instead of making out her departmental budget first thing, she wrote a letter to Paul. It was a cool, breezy letter filled with chatter. She hoped he was having a good time South of the Border. She would love it, for laughs, if he could find the time to knock off a letter to her, reporting all the fun and games that must be going on, reports of some of which were surfacing right here. She was about to sign her name when a strange giddiness came over her, for she had looked at her desk calendar and the idea occurred. It occurred at the exact second she had thought about what kind of ending the letter should have—"Yours truly"? "Warm regards"? "As ever"? "Yours truly" was the way you sent in a job application; "Warm regards" conjured up images of coals still glowing; "As ever" was a statement of eternal fealty. She settled for her name. And the idea settled at the same time, took root and made her giggle.

Once she sent the letter off, she started humming an old Beatles tune and did her budget in record time. Her staff and the entire office found her in great form for the rest of the day, and fresh mutterings were heard about Stella's new, and as yet unseen, lover.

CHAPTER
9

For ten days following the truck sabotage the Jericho company behaved like a military outpost under siege. Vehicles moved only in groups. Locks on equipment vans were inspected daily for breakage. Denny Burns organized his fliers into making surprise sorties over company areas to spot suspicious actions from the air. On one such tour Jonesy, zooming down on a Mexican woman squatting suspiciously near an untended camera, was prepared to radio an alarm when he realized she was simply relieving her bladder. Whether vigilance was paying off or the enemy was holding his hand, there was no follow-up to disturb the picture making, and, inevitably, the state of alert slackened into grumbling confusion.

Throwing himself headlong into work, Paul tried to ignore the other currents that swirled about outside his cutting rooms. He knew that Rennie no longer stayed in the blue trailer. He knew that Sieberling had taken a lease on a small villa in a good section of Oacala and that Michael's Indian girl was installed there. He knew that Michael, determined to cast the girl in the role of the Vietnamese, had sent to Mexico City for tinted contact lenses to disguise her blue eyes; but the lenses didn't fit, gave her extreme pain, looked strange in the tests, and her attempts at acting looked even stranger. The scheme had to be abandoned.

Paul liked the girl the one time he met her. She was very direct, almost innocently so. He would not have imagined that she could engage De Luca's sophisticated mind or physical tastes, but she obviously did. Curiously, he felt stirrings of a certain loyalty to Rennie. He had arrived on the scene when there was a pleasantly settled air about their affair. Now that had been shattered. Yet, while working every day with him, Rennie divulged almost nothing at all about her feelings. If she felt wounded, it did not show.

The truth was that Rennie had been unable or unwilling to confront Michael about his coolness toward her. She had been perfectly prepared to share him with the Indian girl as she shared him with his wife, feeling that there was some secret essence of Michael that she alone fathomed, some unique gift she brought him which, through the alchemy of their relationship, he transmuted into visions on the screen. She had not been prepared for being closed off from that part of him. But faced with the reality, she knew she had no choice.

The change, however, created a more than subtle alteration between Rennie and Paul. He felt it strongly in the brush of her body, in the way she spoke to him, even in the way she sometimes touched his arm. He felt slightly uncomfortable with it all, vaguely disloyal. Then one evening Michael pulled him into the Mercedes on the way back to Oacala from Ixtepan, ostensibly to discuss production problems.

"We have to find some marshy, rice-paddy-type location or go to the other side of the country, or maybe even to California, to shoot second-unit. God, I hate that."

Paul thought there must be land like that in the Oacala area.

"You find it," Michael said testily. "Go ahead. Oh, like to have some dinner with us?"

Paul was agreeable. He had expected the driver to take the road to the De Luca hacienda, but instead the Mercedes stopped in front of a small restaurant on the outskirts of the city. They were led to a pleasant table in the garden, where De Luca ordered margaritas, continued talking about the problems, but broke off, suddenly, eyes lighting up, to say, "Here she is."

Paul looked up and saw Elvira. He blinked. She wore a long dress cunningly made in the Indian fashion but of an exquisite shimmering blue and tailored with the flair of a Parisian gown. Around her throat were coiled two heavy golden strands supporting a blazing, leaping leopard wrought of gold and emeralds. Intricate yellow hoops hung from her ears, and a snow-white flower in her hair made her deep saffron-colored skin glow with a gold of its own.

Michael was amused at his surprise. "Isn't she something else?"

"*Buenas noches*," Elvira said softly.

"Hello."

"You have been long? I am late?" She sat in one graceful movement.

"No, no." Michael's eyes kept sweeping over her. "Want a margarita?"

"*No, gracias.*" The demureness of her response was absolutely unforced.

During the meal Elvira said very little. She did not appear to even listen to the two men. But from time to time Paul could see her glance up at him. When Michael excused himself, there was a momentary heaviness which she, surprisingly, tried to fill.

"You like Mexican food?"

"Yes, I do."

"Maybe one day, Miguel brings you to my *casa* and I cook for you *real* Mexican food, Oacala Indio food."

"That'd be nice."

His eyes kept going to her necklace, and she said, with some pride, "Is Azteca, much old; Miguel buys it for me."

"Really impressive."

"You are his good friend, he says."

"Oh . . . well, sure. I am."

"They talk much of me—his friends?"

"I don't know," he said, confused at the question.

"They wish to know about—the Indio girl?"

"Nobody asks *me* anything."

"*You* wish to know?"

"Never." He tried to laugh. "I never get into these things."

He felt even more awkward when he found himself at the De Luca dinner table forty-eight hours later and engaged in polite, domestic conversation with Catherine De Luca. He imagined himself on a yo-yo, manipulated by an unseen giant thumb and forefinger.

"Since you've come," she was saying, "Michael is much cheerier. He's relying a lot on you." She tinkled her little bell, and the two maids scurried to remove the dishes.

Michael forked a last mouthful of rice and said, "I hate that bell. I detest it."

His wife ignored him.

"*Café,*" she ordered, "*por favor.*"

Later, after the coffee, the De Lucas, father and son, went to the piano to play and laugh. Paul was left alone with Catherine near the fountain. She wore her hair in a bun this evening, smoothed down along the sides of her face with slight wisps of hair escaping the discipline and caressing her cheeks. She looked very much like a Renaissance portrait Paul had once seen in the Uffizi in Florence.

"Well," she said, "there are lots of things going on at the set, I hear."

"Always problems," he responded with a slight sense of discomfort.

"Yes, there are always problems, I know that very well. That's how Michael prefers it—filled with problems."

"Really?" What was she getting at?

"Oh, yes, Michael always does his best work when there are problems." She said this with emphasis. "But as for me, I don't care at all for what is . . . temporary, whatever is here today and gone tomorrow. That's not important, so I take no notice of those things."

"Good idea," Paul told her, his palms moist despite the dryness of the night.

When she wandered away, he decided that the best way to handle it all was to float over it with the aid of the offered snifters of brandy. It worked well.

He went back to his hotel, wobbly and woozy, to find Stella's letter in his box, forwarded and returned four times over, by the Mexican post office. Upstairs, sitting heavily on the bed, his head buzzing, he read the lighthearted correspondence and became enraged at the tone.

What the hell was she writing all this junk for? He read it again. Hi—hello there! How are things? Keep in touch. It was disgusting. The woman sounded like an idiot. He dropped the letter to the floor, lifted his legs to the bed and began, almost instantly, to snore.

At eight in the morning, sleeping with an arm around his wife, De Luca was awakened by a call from Sal Sieberling.

"You'd better come down. There was a ruckus last night and a couple of our guys have been arrested. The police are talking about deportation."

"Shit," he groaned. "I'll be right there."

When he arrived at the concrete *comandancia*, Captain Quesedo was behind his desk listening, with pained eyes, to someone on the other end of the telephone.

"Is bad," the policeman said. "The state *policía* are much *en calor* by this, señor."

Quesedo looked at Sieberling and leaned back in his chair. The production manager pulled off his dark glasses and wiped the sweat from his ears.

"Okay. Two of the special-effects guys got a little high last night."
De Luca waited.

"Out on the street, that is. And they smoked a lot, it looks like."

"No good to do this in Oacala, no good," Quesedo muttered.

Sieberling picked up the story. "So about six guys, and a couple of women too, were running around the Zócalo, stoned out of their gourds. A cop sees them and tries to grab them, but they crack him in the chops and run."

De Luca winced.

"So the whole party gets into some cabs, and they drive over to the Muraga district where they figure there won't be any cops. They climb the hill there and smoke a lot more dope and maybe some action starts with the women."

"For sure," Quesedo said.

"All of a sudden," Sieberling continued, "farmers from the district, a bunch of them, come charging up. This is three o'clock in the morning, Mike. They start beating the hell out of everybody."

"Why?"

Quesedo explained, "Señor, the hill at Muraga is much old. It is Hill of the Dead."

"The Muraga people," Sieberling amplified, "—they didn't like carrying on like that on this . . . Hill of the Dead, or whatever the damn thing is. Meanwhile, the state police at Puerto Bayan get word that something crazy is happening at Muraga and they come zapping over in an army half-track, loaded for bear."

"God."

"They come up the hill, kick some ass, grab everybody and throw them into a truck."

"They take all of them," Quesedo concluded, "to the station at Bayan and they lock them up. When I hear of all this, I call my good friend Señor Sieberling and I say there is much trouble now. Is serious t'ing, mari-juana, to the gover'ment. How it look to United States? Everyone say much best-quality mari-juana grow in hills, cross the border, cost *mucho dólares* in your country. Okay. Is true. So we try to burn, poison all the crop to stop the *traficantes*. Marijuana is not for *campesinos* in the street, you oonderstand, is too dangerous. Now comes the cinema here, and there is much trouble."

De Luca looked away from the sighing policeman. Of course his apes went to the mountains to score dope. Some even tried to ship a kilo home disguised as gifts or offered Oacalan girls a snort of coke.

"Which of our people are involved?"

"Mike"—Sieberling cleared his throat—"it's the explosives team."

"Oh, Christ!" De Luca slammed his hand against the concrete wall, startling Quesedo, who sat up instantly.

Sieberling put the dark glasses over his eyes. "Yeah, I know."

"Listen"—De Luca turned to Quesedo, his face contorting—"I need those men. I can't do this picture without them. Those men are key, do you understand? They're key men for me."

"Señor, the *federales*—the *inmigración*. They will say this is no good for Mexico, the men must to be deported, go back home."

De Luca glared at him. "They'll say that because they're *told* to, because the people who are trying to stop me will pay them off to give those orders."

Quesedo looked over to Sieberling for comfort. De Luca jumped from his chair. "Those men are the best explosives team in the business, the absolute best. There are no men like them. As rotten and dumb and stinking as they are, they are the best."

"Sí . . . sí . . . the best, sí." Quesedo's face was ashen.

"This picture is filled with scenes that only *they* can make work. The final attack—the Jericho. No, goddamn it, I will not allow them to be sent out of the country."

"*Jefe, jefe . . .*" Quesedo implored.

"No," De Luca thundered. "It is political, corrupt, and you know it damn well."

"Captain," Sieberling interjected soothingly, "there are always ways to do things, you follow me? There are always ways to work things out."

Quesedo turned pensive. "Maybe is possible to speak to the *inmigración.*"

"Right," Sieberling urged. "Let's go to whoever's in charge. No matter what . . . pressure they get, we can do business with them."

"Sí, but must be . . . must be . . ." Quesedo struggled to push a path through his reasoning. Slowly, he found one. "Happens this in Muraga, no? *I* command in Muraga. The Muragans are always to make trouble. I go to *inmigración* and I tell to them that, eh? I say your men do nothing bad, is all the Muragans." He saw the look on De Luca's face and said, "Is true. Sí. Hurts them not a little taste of the *cárcel.*"

De Luca knew that meant the jail, a little taste of jail for the Muraga people.

Sieberling quickly said, "Mike, he has to have a talking point, particularly if there's going to be a power play. The important thing is getting our guys back."

De Luca made no answer.

Sieberling said, "Mike, you've got better things to do than hang around here; the captain and I will take care of business."

"Sí, we try, *jefe*. Who can tell?" Quesedo turned momentary cheery philosopher. "Joostice is funny t'ing, so much funny. Sí."

Driving away from the police station as the morning mists hung in the air, De Luca was enraged at the idiotic explosives men: this too was sabotage, in its own way.

In light of the real sabotage going on, Paul refused to accept the event as anything more than a mini-crisis. Gradually, he converted De Luca to grudging laughter. What a place to have a binge—the Hill of the Dead! It was all actually ludicrous.

De Luca agreed and, like a black-bearded Santa, offered the present he had been thinking about for some time, knowing, of course, the effect it would have. How would Paul like a chance to direct the scene Allan Marcus was scheduled to do the next morning?

Paul thought he had misheard. "What do you mean—me shoot the scene?"

"Just what I said—take over from Allan."

"Wait a minute—you're saying you want me to direct that scene? I mean, really put it on film?"

"Don't you want to?"

Paul's mind raced to the scene. An action scene, yet with elements of emotion. And it included one of the principals, the Chinese actress they had imported from San Francisco to play the Vietnamese girl instead of Elvira. Did Michael have this much confidence in him?

"You can do it with your left hand," De Luca was saying. "I know from your work that we look at things the same way. I have another idea too. . . ." He hesitated. "But that's for the future, after Jericho."

"Michael, I'd love to do it."

De Luca smiled. "It's only a beginning. When people help each other, trust each other . . ." He winked and strode to the door. "Right now our problems include getting those asshole explosives people back."

"Don't worry about it," Paul said, euphorically. "They'll come back and blow up half the valley on cue."

He was amazed at what was happening and aware that this was, possibly, a pivotal moment in his life. Quickly, he took up the script and searched out the three green pages that would, through him, become part of the film.

When Rennie was told of the plan, she squealed with pleasure, rubbed the nape of his tense neck and told him that he did, in fact, have eyes like Michael's. She fetched him iced tea and said that she knew—absolutely knew—that he would go on to become a fine movie director.

Later, they had Señora Uribe's latest concoction, a construction of chili-laced ground pork shaped like a hot dog and tasting somewhat like a moldy sausage. The taste was not important, however, since the chili incinerated the palate and anaesthetized the taste buds. Fanning their gasping, flaming mouths, they alternately choked and laughed.

Still later, at half-past ten in the evening, when they ended work and locked the editing rooms, Paul felt somewhat more reassured about his assignment.

"Take my word," Rennie said, linking arms with him, "this is the beginning. For yourself, I mean. You'll see how good you are."

"I hope."

"I know. I can see what's in you. And I'll help in any way I can. You deserve it."

They had dinner in a small restaurant near the Zócalo, and when they emerged into the soft night, they found themselves delightfully entrapped in the *paseo*.

Every night, in Oacala, the *paseo* ritual took place. As the uniformed brass band blared, open-toned, from the bandstand, the Oacalan men and women strolled along, making two large circles around the small park, each circle going counter to the other and composed of people of the same sex. Men walked to the right, women to the left, the circles inches away from each other, the comments clearly audible, the eyes darting from face to face, the hands clearly limning descriptions and fantasies. It was a nightly event, never varying. It was the church-permitted outlet for blood daily heated to the boiling point. It lasted as long as the band played, which was well near midnight. With the participants came the bench-seated elderly, spectators and commentators of authority. Alongside, children as young as two or three played in the grass or dozed under the benches. At midnight the circles dispersed. With appetites whetted and unfulfilled, with sighs pressed from aching bodies, the chains broke. Here and there a daring couple, managing to signal an actual connection, disappeared, together, down a darkened street. But for the most part, the celebrants crept home to solitude, thrashing dreams and the hope that the following night would bring some astounding event—some incredible act of courage which would free them from the confines of their tradition-bound lives, those traditions which had come only a few hundred years ago, imposed by the Spanish conquerors and sealed by the Church.

The foreigners found themselves walking in opposite directions, stepping smartly to the music of the Mexican folk tunes. The Oacalans, amused, shook their heads at the funny *norteamericanos*. They were offered sweet cakes, and someone was daring enough to say *"Buenas noches"* to Rennie. When the *paseo* ended, they fell together and moved, still in step, to Paul's hotel. There were no questions, no uncertainties.

In his room, when Paul saw Stella's letter on the bureau, he felt compelled to put it into a drawer before he could take his shirt off. Apart from that, he felt very good about what was happening. Rennie used the bathroom, leaving the door half-ajar. He heard the gentle stream on the porcelain and was brought up short. All the women he had ever known turned on the tap to obscure the tinkle. When it became his turn to use the bathroom, he hesitated, then closing the door, he turned on the tap and berated himself for not being able to be looser, simpler, more natural—as Rennie was.

"Where *are* you?" she complained, and when he came out of the bathroom, she was already in bed, hands behind her head, smiling contentedly, the sheet to her waist.

Looking at her, Paul was struck by the notion that Michael must have seen her like this many times; that, in fact, he would be, to a degree, reproducing Michael's performance.

"Paul," she said. "Paulus . . ." She stretched her arms out to him. "Come on over here. I'll make all those aches go away. Come on."

He went to her, lay down beside her, touched her skin.

"You feel terrific," he murmured.

She touched his groin and laughed.

"So do you."

The single touch was enough. He felt, as she wound her legs around him, that he was certain and sure with her, very certain and very sure.

92

CHAPTER
10

At six A.M., with the valley wreathed in cloudy green, Flo Ankrum joined the crew at the location. In U.S. Army fatigue pants, a "People Power"–emblazoned T-shirt and a floppy jungle hat perched atop her brisk hair, she presented a certain chic image. Meeting her, in his own well-cut blue jeans and Izod tennis shirt, Allan Marcus thought she seemed more set for a demonstration than a day's movie work but speculated that maybe it was the same thing.

Flo had just discovered that Paul had been assigned to film the scene. Annoyed, she asked Marcus if he did not think it unfair of De Luca to ignore him when there was a sequence requiring some degree of sensitivity to be shot. The tall director smoothed back his silver thatch and said, sleepily, that Michael was the boss. That hardly satisfied her.

"But you're the second-unit director; doesn't it gall you a little?"

"Not when I get my check."

"There are other things, damn it," she said fiercely.

"Tell me what."

"It's like a slap in the face, Allan."

She was so earnest that he sighed and touched her face tenderly, making certain no one saw him in the act.

"Don't patronize me," she gritted. "I have more respect for you than you have for yourself."

"Could be," he said. "Probably."

She felt like crying with frustration then and wanted very much to shake him physically in an attempt to make him understand the chance she had taken, the investment she had made in him, on the basis of mysterious movements in the region of her heart. She had always been attracted to near-lost causes, to underdogs, to the oppressed. Black struggles and Vietnam found her on the picket line.

For years grapes never passed her lips. Strip mining, asbestos making, oil spillage, all the consumer causes were the locus of her life. Her father, an English Jew from Hammersmith and still a gray-flanneled, middle-level executive in the wool trade, was at a loss to understand why she did the things she did. When she wore workman's boots, he pretended not to notice. When she talked of "the need to struggle," he pretended not to hear. Better to ignore; perhaps it would go away. It didn't. When she became convinced that women were an "oppressed minority" and took the matter up with her father, Leslie Ankrum had not the slightest notion of what she was talking about. He himself had always respected women, always. He opened doors for them, gave up seats in the bus, carried their packages. Now here was his own Florence going on in these wild ways. What did she want? *What the devil did she want?*

Sieberling, observing, knew what was going on. Of course Flo was steaming Marcus up; she could never keep her mouth shut. He regretted the day she had come onto the picture. And here she was, approaching him with that shifty look in her eye that spelled trouble.

"Hi," she said. "We got a call from the lab this morning that only half the dailies will be coming in today. There's a holdup on the rest."

"What do you mean, a holdup?"

"That's what they said."

"Yeah—but didn't you ask what's going on?"

"I did—but they were in a hurry and—"

"Damn it." Sieberling felt his gut flooding with anger. "You're responsible for all that stuff, now you come and give me some kind of a story . . ."

"It's what they told me, Sal." Her voice shook, though she tried to keep it level.

"*I'm telling you.* Me. I'm telling you, sweetie, there's been enough of this crap around here, now you just take some responsibility . . ."

"Don't," she said, "call me 'sweetie.' "

"Oh, shit. You just watch your ass."

He stepped away from her rapidly. It took him ten minutes to calm down enough to focus on something else.

On the edge of the set, tense, checking and rechecking the pages to be shot, anxious for the actors to appear so that he could rehearse them, arrange the scene as he played and replayed it in his mind,

Paul looked about him at the camera and crew, at the hair stylist, the makeup people, at the wardrobe lady, the grips and gaffers and prop people ready to make the slightest adjustment, ready to respond to whatever fancy swam into his consciousness. He had been on many sets in his professional life—all the paraphernalia of make-believe was familiar to him; dozens of times he had seen these lights, these lenses, these wind machines; scores of times he had watched the routine, boring filming of a scene—so much effort for one small result, often discarded. Observing, however, was vastly different from doing, from *directing*. It was fashionable, he knew, for many directors to decry the actual filming experience, to make weighty statements about their haste to leave the set behind and enter the quiet precincts of the editing rooms, there, with quiet contemplation, to create their works of art from the already invented images.

Half-truths. Or half-lies. Michael and some others lived, at bottom, for the imperial power that allowed them to construct the frames from their dreams. And today, Paul knew, all these people, all the objects, even the elements themselves, were subject to his vision. For this brief time he had been given the key.

"Okay." He alerted his assistant. "Let's go."

From the makeup trailer, the three actors in the scene approached. Paul felt a tightening of his stomach muscles. From its placement, some distance away, the rumbling electric generator provided the bass drone for the morning chirps and flutterings of the hummingbirds.

"Good morning," Paul called. "Good morning, folks. Let's get over here and I'll tell you what I had in mind."

The actors started to move toward him, but as they did a sudden showering arc of intense blue sparks shot up from the shadows beyond the Vietnamese hut, and with a tortured crackling and sputtering, the main electrical cable, thick as a man's wrist, whipped about. All the lamps flared at once and then plunged into darkness. The generator went from a drone to a scream and then silence. Though the day held light of its own, the removal of fifty thousand watts appeared to blacken the entire area.

There was instant and almost total quiet at this. Actors, crew, Mexican helpers, all froze in their places. Then a hoarse shout roared out from the jungle edge.

"Son of a bitch!"

Paul stood riveted to the spot. Sieberling and two grips raced toward the silent generator truck where its operator, a bare-chested, startled vision, stood as taut as one of his own wires.

"Some son of a bitch cut the cable. Jumped me from behind, knocked me down and beat at it with a machete. I saw him run. He's near those trees."

Sieberling looked down at the thick cable. It was slashed almost in two, the copper strands blackened at the cut, the rubber edges burned and smoking. The two grips were already on their way toward the clump of cypress to the right, one of them holding a pistol.

The two policemen assigned to the set appeared at the truck, looking uncertain and bewildered.

"*Qué pasa, señor?*"

Ignoring them, Sieberling moved carefully toward the trees. Abruptly the leaves shuddered. The grips charged, broke into the brush. Sieberling followed immediately but held up, seeing no one. He whirled to his right and left. The grips whirled as well.

"Shit," one of them said. "He had to be here."

Sieberling looked for leaf movement but saw none.

"Spread out and move back to the set."

Immediately, they moved six feet apart and walked slowly back toward the set area through the brush, alert for any alien motion.

Near the camera, in the eerie stillness, Kodály whispered, "Never. I never know this before. This is dangerous." Hearing him and frozen in place with Sieberling beating the bush, Paul felt like a fool. Deciding he must do something, he stepped, carefully, toward the shadowed jungle.

As he reached the edge, he saw someone standing rock-still in the shadow of a cypress tree and halted, crouching low to the ground. From this vantage point he could make out the figure and saw that it was a Mexican man standing against the tree and doing —what? Urinating? Huddling? It was unclear.

As he watched, the seraped figure moved. Stepping carefully, and almost soundlessly, it came away from the shadows and, surprisingly, came straight at him.

Paul straightened quickly. The man, unalarmed, took his hat off, respectfully. Muttering "*Buenos días,*" he passed by.

Before he could take another step, the two grips had stepped from the jungle and Sieberling was shouting, "You! Chico!"

The Mexican turned. As he did, the grips brought him down.

The generator man came crashing out, breathing raucously. Sieberling called to him, "This the guy you saw running?"

The electrician looked at the Mexican pinned between the grips. He appeared to be in his fifties, graying, and a cut showed red on his temple.

"Yeah."

He said it hesitantly, however.

"Which direction did he come from, Paul?" Sieberling asked.

Paul pointed to the cypress. "He was standing at the tree."

"Hiding, like?"

"I don't know; he was just standing."

Sieberling pulled the Mexican's machete from its scabbard. The man stood by, impassive, not a face muscle moving. Examining the blade for a blackened area that might indicate electrical discoloration, Sieberling found the blade only pitted and rusted. The handle was solid ironwood and bound with leather; it told nothing. He glared at the Mexican.

"*Habla inglés?*"

The Mexican shook his head.

"You're a liar."

There was a slight flicker from the man's eyes. Fear, Paul thought, but allowed to surface for only a second.

Sieberling pointed an accusing finger. "What were you doing near that tree?"

"*No sé inglés,*" the Mexican muttered.

"I'll *sé* you," the generator man roared. "You mother—"

He reached for the man's throat, but there was more crashing from the jungle then, and as everyone jerked his head up the two policemen came on quickly, driving another Mexican man forward. This one was much younger, a machete at his waist as well, his face bruised where a rifle butt had struck him. The policemen prodded him directly in front of Sieberling. He stood there, eyes somewhat glazed, thick black hair falling down over his gaunt cheeks, his abundant mustache flecked with crimson where the bruise had leaked some blood.

"Find man, señor. Other side. Find *him.*" Proudly, the policeman poked at his captive.

Sieberling looked, perplexed, from one Mexican to the other. He turned to the generator man. "You see two guys or one?"

"One."

"This guy—or the young guy?"

The generator man shrugged. "Jesus, Sal . . ."

"Okay," Sieberling said to the policeman. "Take both of them to the *comandancia* . . . to the *capitán*. Understand? *Comprende?* To the *capitán*. I be there soon."

"*Sí, señor. Los dos hombres. Sí.*"

As the Mexicans were marched off, the uncompleted scene returned to Paul's consciousness with sickening force, and he accosted the generator man. "How long would it take to get started up again?"

The electrician looked at him with surprise. "It ain't just the cable. The short kicked out the lamps because he smashed up the fuse box; he just cracked it all to hell, that bastard. We'll have to bring another rig in from Oacala. I'll get on the radio right now."

"But that kills the morning and the light."

"I'm doing the goddamn best I can," the generator man shouted.

"Right," Paul agreed quickly. "You are."

He watched the police put their prisoners into a jeep, feeling totally powerless and that, somehow, he alone was responsible for the morning's failure.

Within the hour, De Luca stormed into the *comandancia* flanked by Sieberling and Paul. The sight of the grim-faced trio set off tremors of worry in Captain Quesedo's heart, and, playing for time, he offered them a little tequila. Refused, sad-eyed, jowls drooping, he knew what was coming.

"I stood still for the trucks," De Luca said in a steely voice, "but now I can't be quiet any longer. My next move, you understand, is to report active and criminal sabotage not just to your superiors but to the U.S. authorities."

He had been having breakfast in the small patio of Elvira's house, barefoot and open-shirted, reveling in the new sun, in the smell of Elvira fresh from the bed, when the phone call had come. Hearing the news, he had become so enraged he had almost upset the table.

"You can tell the fascist-minded sons of bitches who did this that they may own half of Mexico but they won't stop me from making my picture no matter what they do."

"*Jefe*," Quesedo said, humble-voiced, "I am a policeman and you must to believe I do not know from *política*. But we have the men who do this and we ask them questions. We will get from them important informations."

"I think the two guys were in cahoots," Sieberling contributed. "One did it and the other was standing guard."

"Sí," Quesedo readily agreed, "is much possible." He fixed Paul with his sleepy eyes. "You, señor, when you see this old man he looks like he tries to be so nobody sees him?"

"I don't know." He strained to reconstruct, to be fair. "I thought maybe he was pissing against the tree at first."

"This man is called Ibarri." Quesedo called something to his corporal in Spanish and the man left.

"What was he doing at our location?" De Luca asked stiffly.

"He says he is on his way to where a friend keeps three goats for him, half a kilometer away. I send somebody to look. This Ibarri has three goats where he says."

"The other one," De Luca pursued. "What about *him*?"

"This man's name is Paco Coyopan; he is a burro driver." Quesedo took a deep breath as though what was to follow was the troublesome part. "He says that he has a friend at the cinema and this friend says to him to see, sometime, how it is done and he says that today he goes. This is what he says he does there. But he says he does not do this bad t'ing."

"Who's his friend?" Sieberling challenged. "That's a first-class crock."

"His friend, yes." Quesedo heaved another sigh. "This friend is a woman."

"What woman?" De Luca asked. "Does she have a name or is she just *amante*?"

Quesedo consulted a dirty slip of brown paper. "Florenza. Si, Florenza."

De Luca pulled at his beard and shook his head. "Florenza?" His eyes crinkled. "Florenza." Suddenly, he exploded. "Florence!"

Sieberling jumped. "Ankrum! Jesus, that one. I'll bet anything." He glared at Paul with mingled accusation and triumph.

The door opened and the corporal brought in both prisoners. Their hands were tied in front of them with rawhide thongs, but otherwise they looked unhurt. The soldier herded them in front of the interrogators, young man on the right, older man on the left. Seeing them, Paul felt an initial burst of anger, but it quickly evaporated, turned almost to pity as they both stood there shuffling in fright, eyes on the concrete floor. Quesedo spoke first to the old man, in Spanish, his tone deceptively sympathetic. The man replied in a soft voice, after which Quesedo turned to the Americans. "I ask him if he makes water against the tree in the forest. He says no, he just rests there."

"I don't believe him," Sieberling exclaimed. He swung to Paul. "When he saw you he probably tried to make some kind of a move, right?"

Paul looked at the older Mexican and saw the flicker again. "He tipped his hat, that's what he did."

"Ask the young one about Florenza," De Luca called to Quesedo. "Ask him to describe her."

Quesedo spoke to the younger man in accusatory, angry tones. The prisoner replied at some length, after which the captain turned back to his visitors. "This Coyopan says this Florenza is . . . how I am to say . . ." He struggled with the translation. "He says she is . . ." His hands hefted the air, made a solid body. "And on her eyes she wears the glasses and her hair sticks up."

"Ankrum." Sieberling gritted. "Son of a bitch."

The younger man muttered a few words to the older and Quesedo became livid. "¡No habla!" he shouted. "¡Silencio!"

He gave swift orders to the corporal, who jerked the men by their ropes, pulling them from the room like haltered animals. Paul felt a protest welling up in his throat, but by the time it might have reached his lips, the men were gone and the door was closed. De Luca whispered for him to take it easy.

Quesedo picked up the thread. "This Coyopan, he says his wife makes for this Florenza the . . . cleaning of the clo-thing.'

"Laundry," De Luca prompted.

"Sí—the laundry. This is how he knows her. And she tells him where you are making the cinema today and he comes and hears the noise. He t'inks it is part of the cinema so he is mucho surprise when he sees the guns in his face."

"He's lying," Sieberling said. "The son of a bitch is absolutely lying. He's got shifty eyes."

"We find this out," Quesedo said calmly. "He will tell us what is true. Both men will to say what is true. We know these t'ings."

"Get hold of Ankrum," De Luca ordered. "I want to speak to her right away."

Sieberling went to the telephone.

"Jefe," Quesedo said tactfully, "you go to do what you must. I take care."

De Luca shook his head stubbornly. "I want to know what this is about."

From somewhere beyond the office came the faint but unmistakable sound of an explosive, gasping cry. Paul looked up, startled.

100

De Luca's eyes opened wide. Sieberling continued to talk into the phone.

"*Jefe, jefe*—go to have a coffee," Quesedo urged. "I find you in the cantina and we talk later, yes?"

"Got Ankrum," Sieberling called. "She's on."

"Florence?" De Luca took the phone. "I want to ask you something, something very grave."

"Yes?"

"You know the disaster we had this morning?"

"Yes, of course."

"The police have picked someone up. We're at the station house now."

A hoarse, choked-off scream pierced the room, echoing from the plaster walls. Paul jerked erect. It was the old man. Something in the voice, the thick-lunged hoarseness; certainly the old man.

"They're beating the old man," he said loudly, looking over toward Michael.

A shriek burst through the door, starting high and going higher, pained and shocked. At its apex it was suddenly cut, chopped as though the windpipe had been seized.

Paul jumped to his feet, shouting, "Michael. Damn it!"

"Take it easy," Sieberling said. "Relax."

Quesedo rose from his chair in a frustrated thrust of his booted feet. "Why you stay here?" he demanded. "Is better you go." Impatiently, he reached for the door, pulled it open and disappeared, slamming it shut behind him.

"Michael," Flo called, "are you there?"

"Yes," De Luca said, "yes." But he fell silent again.

Paul stared at the door. Beyond, in one of the dark, infested cells, something unimaginable was happening. Sieberling hitched his belt up and said matter-of-factly, "It's their country. They know their customers. Let's just be cool."

Paul turned away from him, and De Luca's face was expressionless as Florence's tinny tones broke in again.

"Hello? Hello?"

"Florence, this man the police have says he knows you. His wife does your laundry."

"There is this lady who does my laundry, sure," Flo answered, "and she has a husband. I guess he's her husband."

"This man says you told him to come to the location. Is that true?"

"What?" She did not understand the question.

"Did you tell this man to come to the location?" De Luca shouted into the phone.

"I might have. I could have."

"Damn it, did you or didn't you?"

"I guess I did. I guess," she answered, confused and somewhat frightened by his harsh tone.

"She told him to come," De Luca told Sieberling. "He didn't lie about that."

"Ask her *why* she told him—why she did that."

"Why did you do it?" De Luca demanded.

"I just did," Flo answered. "I thought it would be okay."

Frustrated, De Luca slammed the receiver back onto its cradle. Paul slumped against a wall. Sieberling sat in Quesedo's chair and leaned back.

It was twenty minutes before they heard shuffling sounds from the hallway outside. It was twenty minutes of silence, during which Paul waited, nerves taut, for screams that did not come. The silence was more unnerving.

As the shuffling grew louder, Quesedo's voice could be heard, admonishing. Then the door opened. The captain entered first, a smile on his lips. Two policemen in dirty undershirts followed, pushing Coyopan into the room. His hair was matted with sweat; his face beet red. His eyes were large, almost bulging in his head. A circlet of braided rope was around his neck and the marks of the twisting were evident. His body sagged and his knees were together as though protecting, still, his center. An enormous blackened welt had puffed up his left cheek, and his upper lip had been split almost exactly in two. Paul stared, horrified.

"You've got something out of him," Sieberling said, triumphantly. "I knew it."

"This man tells us the truth," Quesedo said. "Does not take so long. He is not *mucho valiente*."

"What did he tell you?" De Luca asked quickly.

"He tells me that he does this t'ing of the wires. He comes to do this t'ing, to make much hurt to you."

De Luca expelled his breath, stared at the man.

"Okay," Sieberling said, "okay. Now we're getting someplace."

As Paul watched, he saw that Coyopan's tongue was thick, almost filling his opened mouth, moving with evident pain.

"Mike," he whispered, "maybe he said that just to get them to stop."

102

Quesedo looked up sharply. "He tells the truth. I have experience, señores, to know the truth."

De Luca left the desk, moved to Quesedo's side and spoke with his eyes directly on Coyopan.

"Who is paying him? Can we find that out, at least?"

"Ah," Quesedo said, "is *mucho* interesting, this. Is no pay. He gets nothing."

"No pay?" De Luca looked at Quesedo with incredulity.

"What did he do it for—love?" Sieberling called angrily. "He's taking you, man."

"No," Quesedo said. He shifted his eyes from De Luca. "Here, in Oacala, he tells, is some who do not like what you do."

"Is that news?" De Luca exploded. "We know that."

"Sí, but *jefe*, is not like you say before—is not men of power who do this." He halted, almost, it appeared, embarrassed, then went on. "Coyopan tells it is other people who say you do the bad t'ings."

"What other people?" De Luca demanded. "What is he talking about?"

Quesedo said, "Is *campesinos*—farmers—and there is others, the *trabajadores*, the . . . factory workers—some of them. Foolish ones, *jefe*, believe me. They do not like what you do, they say is bad for Oacala."

De Luca stared, open-mouthed, at the policeman. Paul wasn't sure he'd heard correctly. Sieberling said, with venom, "Those dumb bastards."

"Sí—*estúpido*," Quesedo agreed swiftly. "But they are the ones who make the *agitación*."

"Are you telling me that this whole mess is caused by people, plain people?" De Luca's voice quivered with rage and disbelief.

Quesedo hung his head. "Sí."

"I don't believe it!" The words burst from De Luca in a cry that sent chills through Paul and terrified Quesedo. Obviously shaken, De Luca fought for control as the others waited. Finally, he said, calm returning, "We do nothing but good. We bring jobs. We bring money. We fix things. We made Ixtepan live again when half the people were starving."

Quesedo nodded eagerly. "I believe, sí. But the *agitadores*, they say only the *patróns* of the land, only the *jefes* of the business, get all the money. They get rich on you, but nobody else."

"That's not our problem," Sieberling growled, glaring at the bound prisoner.

"You believe," De Luca asked, "he's telling you the truth?"

"You must to know that here in Oacala, is big fight between *campesinos* and *propietarios*—the owners of the land. The *campesinos* make the *cooperativas* to work some land someplace and the *patrón* must to get us to chase them away because they do not have the right to do this."

"I don't give a damn about politics," Sieberling said. "We're making a picture, that's all."

Quesedo fell silent. It was very difficult to talk openly to these people; one had to be very delicate. Generally, they wished to hear only what was simple, uncomplicated, and what pleased them.

De Luca was more complex—a little foolish perhaps, but he was an artist and all artists were crazy. Of the other, he could tell little save that he was a Jew, a race for which he had a soft spot in his heart. De Luca seemed to depend upon him and for this alone he was to be deferred to. He addressed him now, cautiously.

"The *agitadores* say—I only tell you what this miserable Coyopan tells me, señor—I do not t'ink this; I would put everyone who t'inks this in my jail."

"What do they say?" De Luca asked sharply.

"Well, they say that also because of you, the mari-juana comes to the young people here and because of you, much bad t'ings happen with the women, because of you the men do bad t'ings for the *dinero* and the old Oacala ways maybe don' stay no more."

"We have a perfect right to be here," Sieberling said. "Every permit, every license is in order."

"I say yes, but is like, here . . . *un bajo tierra en secreto.*" He struggled with a possible translation and finally said, "A . . . *under-the-ground*, you *comprende?* To make you go away from here. This Coyopan is one of them."

It was Paul's turn to be astonished. He stared, surprised, at Coyopan, who looked away immediately.

De Luca muttered, despairingly, "Do you believe this?" He looked from one to the other, then said to Quesedo, "It's ridiculous. Everyone here knows I feel so sympathetic toward these people and—" He broke off, his distress palpably genuine. After a moment he continued. "They don't understand what I'm trying to do, damn it. I'm *for* them. This picture is *for* them. How do I get that through to them?"

Sieberling was more pragmatic. "What's been going on, the gas tanks and stuff—that's part of this underground thing?"

104

"Sí."

"Who runs the show? Who gives him his orders?"

Quesedo raised his hands, helplessly, toward heaven. "He says he does not know this. A friend goes away from Oacala and tells him to do this t'ing. Florenza tells him where you are and he does it. It is the first t'ing he does, he says."

"He's lying," Sieberling insisted. "Can't you get him to—"

"Believe me, señores, he tells us this but no more."

"Captain," De Luca said, urgently, "ask him how we can meet with anyone from this underground . . . to talk . . . to explain myself. I will go anywhere, anytime. Ask him."

Reluctantly, Quesedo queried Coyopan, whose vacant expression never changed even when he responded with a short sentence.

"He says again, he does not know anyone, *jefe*, no one at all."

De Luca turned away, eyes desperately unhappy. Sieberling murmured, "If the studio gets told any of this stuff, it's more muscle on their side."

"There's got to be some way to get to the leaders," Paul insisted.

"What about the old man?" Sieberling suddenly asked.

"Ibarri? Oh, he knows nothing of this."

"How can you be so sure?"

"Because, señor, he does not even know what happened, the wires. He t'inks it is somet'ing for the cinema. He t'inks we catch him because he comes to steal from the *comida*, the food you have." He broke into a relieved giggle. "He makes to us this confession."

"He's the one who screamed, wasn't he?" Paul asked.

"We must to find the truth." Quesedo shrugged. "How else? He be okay. We fix his head and—"

"What do you mean his head?"

"He hits his head on the floor—*accidente*."

"Jesus."

"Little t'ing," Quesedo added hastily.

"Don't be such a bleeding heart," Sieberling complained. "It's their country, they know what to do."

"But he didn't do anything," Paul muttered, walking away.

"Let's get out of here," De Luca said, tiredly. "I want to sort things out." He looked at the prisoner once more and then, as though to put him out of his mind, looked quickly away and hastened to the door.

"*Adiós, jefe*," Quesedo called.

Following Michael out, Paul felt Coyopan's eyes on him and decided to look dead ahead. Quesedo walked with him and said rue-fully, "Funny t'ing, señor, when is only question of *dinero* . . . is okay . . . then is control. Everybody behave like they should, speak reasonable, make good deal. But when is not *dinero*, is some-t'ing else, like the *terroristas* in the sierra, or this t'ing now, then there is no control." He shook his head in despair. "Everbody like *loco*."

The last thing Paul saw as he sneaked a look behind him was Quesedo offering the prisoner a glass of tequila. Then the door closed.

CHAPTER
11
:=:==:==:==:==:== **11** ==:==:==:==:==:

At this hour, as the Jericho company car moved through the Oacala streets, a half-dozen ancient buses were transporting, in flat-springed discomfort, almost three hundred international tourists toward the dusty wonders of Monte Tecla, where there would be audible gasps as the tour guide reeled off the number and method of human sacrifices. The Germans, particularly, would be heard to murmur about the primitive brutality of it all.

Caught behind one such bus, Paul glanced from the eager tourist faces to the stream of peasants walking by, sun glinting from their worn faces, from the sheen on the women's braids. How many of these people locked away in this valley had even heard of Vietnam? And yet, Michael was doing this film for them too.

Sieberling's voice interrupted his reverie. "What about Ankrum?"

"What do you mean?" Paul turned to him.

"She told this guy where we'd be."

"So?"

"She's into funny things. She might even be in cahoots with him."

"Hmm." The idea did not seem to surprise De Luca, but Paul thought never, no; Flo would not do that, it was unfair.

"She has this big mouth on her," Sieberling said. "You know—capitalist pigs. I'm telling you, Mike, we ought to get rid of her."

De Luca probed his beard. "I have to admit I have never been comfortable with her . . ." He trailed off.

"She's snotty. She bitches. Let's not take any chances, Mike."

Paul weighed a defense, but Michael had already made his judgment.

"I think Sal is right. Until we straighten things out, we've got to tighten up. She'll have to go. Tell her as soon as possible, will you? Preferably today. Get her out of town by tomorrow."

Paul saw that Michael was addressing him and said, "Mike, I'm not the production manager."

"But she's in your department; you're her boss."

Pulled up short, he asked, unhappily, "Why don't we at least wait until we have someone to replace her?"

"Don't worry about that," Sieberling said.

De Luca had already dismissed the subject. Rubbing his eyes wearily, he said, "The real problem is, how do we handle what's happening? How do we get to these people and make them understand I'm on their side?"

It wasn't until Sieberling had left them and they were walking toward the office complex that Paul said, from the depths of his unconscious, "Aguillar."

De Luca stopped walking.

"It just flashed on me. He has to know everything that's going on, Mike. He could put out the word to stop the trouble. He could tell them who you are, what we're doing."

"He could, but . . ." De Luca hesitated. "Why didn't he know when he came to the set?"

"I don't know, but it's worth a shot."

"Yes. Absolutely. He risked his neck to see me." De Luca's words sprayed out as his excitement grew. "He could be our link. And they'd listen to him, they'd have to. Let's get to that shopkeeper and set up a meeting."

At the "little house" De Luca asked Elvira what she had heard about an "underground." She told him she had heard nothing but was not surprised. The townspeople were ignorant and disgusting. Not to recognize what Michael was doing for them was simply stupid; he was a benefactor.

De Luca lingered to eat the chicken *mole* she had prepared in authentic Indian style and thought she had the gift of clarity. It came from the struggle she had made to survive intact.

He watched her face as she touched the first beautiful cooking vessels she had ever owned. He had already seen the joy in her eyes at the sight of the heavy Spanish chests and tables, at the hand-carved fruitwood oversized bed with its intricately worked spread from Seville. Her deep pleasure in the possessions stirred him every time, and the sight of her small brown body outlined upon the unwrinkled white sheets never failed to excite him.

He wondered, idly, if she would go back to the States with him. But if that happened, inevitably, she would be lost to herself. Could

108

he see her shopping in a supermarket, buried amid the mountains of junk food, the double rolls of toilet paper and the fifty-pound sacks of kitty litter?

Her purity—her virginity—was special. When he had married Catherine, he had never been certain that she was innocent of penetration, nor had it been important to him—he thought. But the fact that Elvira had been a virgin, that he was her first and only lover, took on an importance that reached back somewhere to his bloodline, stubbornly making the connection no matter the intelligence, no matter the experience.

"Fools, they are, this *bajo* thing," she said disdainfully.

"Yes, but how do you deal with fools?" De Luca asked darkly.

The requirement that he be the one to fire Flo set off tremors in Paul's stomach. When he told Rennie, she did not have to think before defending the decision.

"It's not being mean, Paul, but Michael just can't work when he feels too many disturbing elements. I think you're the same way but you won't admit it."

When he looked at her quizzically, she kissed him, feeling warm and soft, and her perfume made his nose twitch. Last night had not been a one-night stand. With no conversation about the progression, their further intimacy had been taken for granted. Though charmed and gratified, Paul felt a little uncomfortable that he was taking over Michael's ex-mistress. It bothered him, somewhat, that Michael knew the sounds she uttered when they made love and the texture of the small red mole on her right buttock.

Rennie, however, simply took what was happening as a matter of course. "I will help you in every way I can," she had declared early that morning, patting his stomach.

Now she said, "Just tell Flo it has to be this way. She'll understand."

Paul found her in the cantina with Allan Marcus. He debated delaying the act until he could speak to her in private surroundings, but it was coming to siesta, he and Michael had planned to leave for Ismena's and he determined to get the distasteful job over with.

"Flo," he said, "I have to talk to you."

Flo cocked her head to one side and asked whether it was about the police business.

"I think we should be alone."

"Why can't we talk here?"

Miffed at her unreasonableness, he glanced over to Marcus, who uncrossed his long legs and ambled over to the tiny bar. Paul sat quickly, deciding to be simple and direct.

"Flo, they want you off the picture."

She took five seconds to absorb that. "I'm fired."

He nodded.

"Who wants that—Michael or that bastard Sal?"

"It comes from the top." That was safe enough, and true.

Flo leaned forward, her shoulders very taut. "Do they really think I had anything to do with what happened?"

"No," he lied, "but just for . . . the good of things, it seems better that someone else come in."

"I see," she said, pushing her glasses back on her nose. "They want me off the picture because, like, Sal doesn't love me a lot."

He said nothing.

"It's true, isn't it?"

"Whatever it is."

"Pigs, both of them." Her face twisted as she tried to contain the tears. "Damn them. I've broken my back for this picture."

"I'm sure you have."

The glasses came off. Stubby fingers pawed fiercely at her eyes. He reached out to her.

"I'm really sorry, Flo."

She jerked away from him.

"Okay, okay. You're just doing your job—like Adolf Eichmann."

As Flo's voice had risen, the noise in the cantina had abated. Señora Uribe, walking by with a beer, looked at Paul with worry. Two girls from wardrobe glared at him. Various crew members held their forks in the air.

He hoped that she would not go on this way. Desperate for help, he looked over to the bar. Marcus rescued him, returning to loom over the table.

"I've just been canned," Flo said defiantly, making Marcus instantly uncomfortable.

"It's not my decision," Paul said in defense.

"It's God's." Flo rose to her feet, and Paul came up with her.

"There will be two months' bonus pay."

She collected her shoulder bag and shawl. "Allan, will you take me back to my room, please?"

Marcus looked at Paul. "What's this all about?"

110

"We've all been taken off pictures before. It's part of the risk." He knew he wasn't convincing, however.

Flo put the green rebozo about her shoulders. Paul plunged in deeper.

"There's one more thing. They want to give you another month's bonus pay."

"Why?" She waited for the other shoe to drop.

Uneasily, he dropped it. "If you could possibly get on a plane within twenty-four hours, say, and go home . . . and promise not to hurt the company by talking about anything that's happened."

The girl's eyes fired like spark plugs. "And if I don't do exactly that?"

"Flo, be reasonable." Paul's voice broke a bit.

"Let them take their money and their implied threats and shove it!" She shook a fist in his face. "I'll damn well go when I'm ready and do what I want. Do they think they own the world?"

She walked away swiftly. He looked for help at Marcus, who muttered that she'd be all right and hastily followed her out. Paul dropped into a chair to be less conspicuous. Slowly, conversation returned to the cantina. Señora Uribe asked him if he wanted a beer. He said he did, but when it came he found his throat locked whenever he tried to swig.

All the way back to her pink stone motel, Flo slumped into the VW vinyl, her eyes staring but not seeing, her chin on her chest. Marcus thought she ought to be more reasonable.

"Reasonable?" she responded bitterly. "Are they? Even Gordon. They made him the gofer and he went and got me for them."

Marcus left her, and when his taxi disappeared, she slumped under the shadowed loggia, leaning against the flower-covered wall. As she did, the short-bodied, black-clad Señora Coyopan emerged from a doorway, arms laden with sheets. Seeing Flo, the woman's eyes widened with apprehension and she tried to slump past, but Flo reached out to her. When the Mexican woman winced away from the touch, Flo said, "Señora. Please. *Por favor!*"

The woman froze in place, clutching the laundry to her for protection.

"I do nothing," Flo stammered, searching for Spanish. "Not me. *Otros.* Others. Me, *nada contra su esposo.*"

The woman pulled the sheets closer to her breast.

"Believe me. Please." Flo's tears started to come out in her desperate need to let this woman know that she was not responsible for what had happened to her husband. "I'm so sorry. *Mucho doloroso. Otros* very bad. Men, *hombres, mucho malo.*"

The woman looked at her searchingly, then sighed and said, "*Sí, mucho malo.*" She half-reached out a comforting hand but withdrew it quickly and moved past.

The woman padded away rapidly and Flo's tears came freely. She felt like sitting down on the cool floor tiles, but she forced herself to move, stiff-legged, toward her room.

Late that afternoon, as the sun hung over the western rim of the sierra, creating a golden blaze, Paul and De Luca drove to Ismena's dark shop. They found the Indian alone and uncomfortable at their return. De Luca explained to the small, edgy man that there had been much sabotage of his work. He had discovered that there was an underground of misunderstanding people who were trying to drive him away, kill his film. Things had come to a dangerous point; had Ismena heard anything of what was going on?

"I have heard there has been bad things." Ismena nodded. "Yes, I have heard this."

"We need help," De Luca said. "We must get to the leaders of this *bajo tierra* and make them understand my true feelings, make them know we are all brothers."

"Luis Aguillar can tell them," Paul took up. "He knows what this cinema is about."

"Yes, and we would like to talk to him. How do we do that? Where?"

Ismena's words came out slowly, drawn with reluctance. "Is . . . possible. But by myself I can do nothing."

"We want to see *him*," De Luca said eagerly. "You tell us how."

Once again there was silence. De Luca looked despairingly at Paul. Finally the storekeeper spoke.

"Is much danger for him to come down from the Sierra Madre."

"We'll go to him," De Luca said.

Ismena shook his head. "Is more bad of anyone to know where he makes his camp. I do not even know this. For if I know and the *policía* find me, is possible I will not be very strong and tell them."

Paul remembered, with revulsion, the strangling sounds coming from the cell in the *comandancia*.

"I understand," De Luca said, respectfully. "But there must be some way we can see him."

"I try to see what can be to do. You wait and I will send you something—something which tells you it can be done or not. Now please, you will to go. Because it is not every day that two *norte-americanos* come here and some coyote maybe works for the *policía* and tells them. I am sorry to be not polite to you but is better." He looked away from them and his fingers went to the abacus; the meeting was, indisputably, over.

As they emerged to the still sun-warm street, only two Mexicans walked by, paying the Americans no attention. Still, De Luca's palms were moist and Paul's eyes searched the shadows between the adobe walls. Within minutes, pulses pounding, they were in the car driving back, excited if uncertain of the results of the encounter.

Twenty-four hours passed with the company once again alerted and poised for a follow-up of the generator attack. None came. Four more days went by in expectant tension, but there was no incident. But the uncertainty of when the *bajo tierra* might hit again kept nerves jangling.

Meanwhile, De Luca anxiously awaited some sign from Ismena that Aguillar would parley but was given none. One source of anxiety was alleviated, however, when the two explosives experts were released by the federal police and returned to their jobs.

Captain Quesedo proudly confided that top men were reached for this, men with whom he exerted considerable influence. When Paul asked about the people of the Muraga, Quesedo told him that because of the same influence, the men had received only one-year sentences on a labor gang, the women, six months.

Paul was shocked at the severity of the sentence, but when he learned that the man who cut the cable had been shot, he was horrified.

"He tries to run away from the soldiers, señor," Quesedo explained, "and they must shoot to stop him. But they do not kill him. He takes a few bullets in his back and he falls. You don't worry 'bout him. Maybe he don' walk so good no more, that be all."

Shaken, Paul stared at Michael. "And what about . . . what about the old man who did nothing; the one I saw?"

"He okay." Quesedo smiled. "He get only thirty days to do little work."

113

"But he did nothing." Paul's voice rose. "The man did nothing."

"Paul, take it easy," De Luca urged. "Calm down."

"He not supposed to be where he is, I t'ink," Quesedo said, then he shrugged, giving up altogether. "I not be the judge anyway."

"And what about any further information?" De Luca demanded. "It's been five days now."

"We work, *jefe*," Quesedo apologized, "but takes time."

On the drive back, with the mood grim, Paul said, "I've heard stories of police forcing a prisoner to run and then cutting him down when he does."

"I've heard the stories too," De Luca said, "but we asked the police for protection and they're trying to provide it. They just do it their own way. You and I can't be held responsible."

"I know, but still . . ."

"He came to hurt us," De Luca said sadly; "we didn't come to hurt him."

There was no quarreling with that.

In bed that night, Paul was still depressed. Rennie's therapy was to produce two joints filled with *sin semilla*, the valued seedless marijuana, crown jewel of the Sierra Madre crop. With the joints lit, they lay back, listening to the band sounds drifting in from the Zócalo.

"Paul—the Indian girl . . ."

"What about her?"

"What's the house like that Mike got for her?"

"Nice."

"He never got me a house." She giggled. "All I had was his blue bus."

His eyes began watering and he rubbed them.

"He gives her gold things, Paul; everybody says he does."

"He does."

"He gave me a pearl necklace once. Would you like to see it?"

"No."

"Are you jealous of him?"

"I don't think so."

"Are you still getting letters from that lady in New York?"

"Stella?" He laughed in puzzled wonder. That was another person in what seemed to him now to have been another life.

"Paul, oh, Paul," Rennie said suddenly, "I'm so glad you're here." She threw an arm over him and buried her face in his shoulder.

"Yes," Paul said, but he felt a curious chasm not bridged by the

114

smooth globes of her breasts moving gently on his skin. When he felt her lips on his nipples, on his flesh below the navel and along the cords of his groin, he tightened, involuntarily.

"Lie back," she whispered, "just lie back. You're so tense."

"Hey, come here," Paul said, reaching for her, but she continued to glide down his body. "Rennie," he finally called, softly.

"Sh. I know. I know."

But she did not know and he was unable to tell her.

After Flo Ankrum picked up her last salary check, she told Allan Marcus she had decided to stay in Oacala for a while and give herself a vacation. He thought she was totally crazy. In her room, dressed only in an ancient pink peignoir purchased in some Santa Monica thrift shop, she baited him.

"Doesn't it please you that you can get free sex without worrying about the clap?"

"Flo, you're a fruitcake. Why the hell would you want to stay in this dumb place?"

"There's struggle here, Allan. People are oppressed."

He groaned. "Christ, it's Mexican oppression, leave it to them, will you, kid?"

"I'm staying," she said flatly. "I'm staying because I won't give those bastards the satisfaction of seeing me go like a whipped dog. Besides," she added mysteriously, "I've been snooping around talking to a few people and I've learned a few things."

"What do you mean—things?"

"Things," Flo said, sitting on the bed.

"Flo," Marcus warned, "this is serious stuff. The company's going around on tiptoe. Every time someone sneezes, they swing around with guns. You're talking about a twenty-million-dollar investment, baby."

"I'm staying till I damn well want to leave."

Sal Sieberling, seething with frustration at Flo's presence, cornered her lover and hammered at him to get her out of town.

"I am not her father, her brother or her husband," Marcus protested nervously. "I have no control over her."

"You ball her."

"That's control?"

"I'm telling you, Marcus, if she doesn't go on her own, she's going to be in big trouble."

"I've told her that, Sal."

"Tell her again. Tell her that if she doesn't get her ass out of town, pronto, Mike will blackball her so hard in the union that she'll never work again."

With Flo out of the picture, Paul appointed the discreet assistant, Rick, to a more senior status. He deserved it. He was competent, but more important, he never gave any trouble. He did not drink, and when he got high it was only in private. Best of all, no one ever heard a whisper of the young Mexican boys he undoubtedly bought, those fourteen- and fifteen-year-old bare-chested youths who hung out on the edges of the Mercado where the tourists, if they were so inclined, were bound to find them. Rick was such a quiet shadow that Denny Burns said of him, in admiration, "That sumbitch is invisible. He stands sideways and you don't even know he's there."

On the morning of the sixth day after the visit to Ismena, Laszlo Kodály's driver was cut off by a motorcyclist, forced to brake hard and skidded into a brick wall, damaging the radiator. Kodály was badly shaken up and, with his usual edge of hysteria, claimed a deliberate attempt to make the car crash, saying he had noted the cycle following from the moment they left the hotel. The company driver, with a finely honed contempt for the Mexican driving ability, was not at all convinced.

The incident cast a further pall over the company. Kodály developed a mini-migraine, complete with loss of peripheral vision, and was forced to lie down. Quesedo kept phoning with word of a vague stolen motorcycle which he, personally, was investigating. De Luca paced the floor of his blue van and cast about for another avenue to Aguillar. Crew members quarreled for no apparent reason, and a costume department girl claimed her menstrual cycle had stopped as a result of tension.

By the end of that day, Paul's nerves were so jangled that when a Moviola went out with a flash of light and a protesting whir, his first impulse was to take cover under a table. It was a faulty electrical cord, but the discovery did not dissolve the knot in his stomach.

"Where's the sign?" De Luca hammered at him. "Where the hell is Ismena's sign?"

CHAPTER
12

For the next two days De Luca was unavailable, turning inward as he almost always did when pressure he could not control was exerted. He stayed in the blue van working on script revisions, sketching camera angles and scrutinizing mountains of actors' photos, seeking the perfect faces for every frame of his movie. He slept alone in the bus and took some of his meals with Paul, meals that were silent but somehow comforting.

On the morning of the ninth day, Elvira, walking in the morning sunshine toward the butcher's stall, was accosted roughly by a tall man with a pitted face who blocked her way and hissed at her in Spanish.

"You—woman. You listen to me."

She tried to edge past him, but he took her arm hard.

"I speak to you."

"Here," Elvira said contemptuously. She pulled her arm free with effort, opened the bag slung over her shoulder and found five pesos. This only angered the man, who took hold of her arm again, this time hurting her with his blunt fingers.

"Did I beg? Did I beg for money, you fine lady?"

"What do you want?" Elvira demanded. She had handled men like this since she was ten and before. They did not intimidate her.

"Listen, woman," the man said, moving so close that his breath, fouled by rotting teeth, came at her with heat, "you must tell this gringo to come to you, tomorrow, when the day ends."

"What gringo?" She tried to pull away again, but he clutched her like a vise.

"What gringo?" Suddenly, the accoster looked perplexed. "I am told to tell you only this gringo who is your man. I do not know this man but you will know him."

Elvira hesitated. "Who sent you to find me?"

"Someone I do not know."

"You know very little."

"I know a whore when I see one." As he said that he gave her arm a cruel twist, shooting pain up her shoulder. Seeing the look on her face, he grinned, one side of his mouth going up lopsidedly. "This man must be at your house when the clock strikes twelve tomorrow. You tell him that, woman. You hear me?"

"I hear," she murmured.

"You—have respect. Whore." He moved away from her rapidly and turned a corner.

Elvira's call came to De Luca in Paul's cutting room. When he heard her message, he gripped Paul's shoulder tightly and announced, "Tomorrow; we see him tomorrow!" He poured two glasses of wine, drinking half of his in one excited gulp. "Finally."

Paul was surprised that Aguillar knew about Elvira.

"He knows everything that goes on around here; if he didn't, he'd be dead by now," De Luca said.

He wandered about, waving his glass.

"These poor dumb bastard peasants, they're like the people in my father's town in Italy, earthy, simple, brave. But they're also ignorant and unthinking. They have to respect Luis though." He poured more wine. "Once we get it straight with him, I want to really get going. I think I have a fix, finally, on how this picture should work. You've been very helpful that way."

Paul shrugged but De Luca insisted. "No, it's true. And if we can move full speed ahead, I know we can wrap in nine or ten weeks. What do you think?"

Paul agreed. De Luca opened another bottle of wine.

"Listen, don't think I've forgotten about what happened with the scene you were going to shoot. There'll be other chances, I promise you. I swear to you, as a matter of fact."

"You don't have to say that," Paul muttered.

"I want to." De Luca's voice held a weight of feeling. "I get this sense that we're a good team. I don't have the slightest reservation about trusting you. I know you don't have a credit except as an editor, but believe me, after Jericho it all changes."

Paul wrinkled his brow in question.

"I've always worked alone," De Luca went on, his voice turning husky with intensity, "but the truth is I've never liked it that way. Still, who could I trust . . . except Sal? And he's good for what

118

he's good for. But I think we have a unique kind of creative combination, you and I. I want it to stay that way. I don't know exactly how, but I want us to keep working together."

He stopped talking. Both men sat for a long moment, saying nothing, until, with a spontaneous explosion, they burst into laughter. After which De Luca tossed off the rest of the wine in his glass and Paul followed suit.

Sal Sieberling came in, soon after, to report that he had found a rice-paddy location for De Luca and it was perfect.

"Sixty kilometers south of here. In the lowlands area. Flat as a pancake. Four or five acres which only have scrub on them right now. We can flood any part we want and it'll look terrific; it'll be a mass of mud, Mike, just what you want."

Denny Burns piloted the small plane that had been repainted to resemble a U.S. Army spotter.

"There it is." Sieberling, occupying the rear of the four-seater, pointed straight down.

De Luca studied the earth, barely stippled by vegetation. It was, indeed, flat—a broad stretch of brown flat land, very rare here, in the valley which undulated in gentle curves.

"Not bad, eh?" The unit manager preened.

"I'm hoping—I'm praying," De Luca intoned, containing his excitement, but it was evident, nonetheless. "Let's go down. If we can shoot here without seeing the mountains in the background, we'll really have it."

"Here we go." Burns turned the nose down at such an angle that Sieberling screamed at him to be careful, but he set the aircraft down like a feather, turned to De Luca and winked.

Outside, Paul examined the horizon excitedly. By some accident of topography, from this spot, the sierra was totally invisible. It appeared, indeed, as a thousand-mile lowland, and he burst out, "It's going to work, Mike, it's going to work."

De Luca bent over to pick up a handful of parched soil. "It's a great location, but it's dry as a bone. How do we get water on it, Sal?" Stretching his arm out, he let the crumbled dust fall from his hand. "We need all this land ankle-deep in water and mud so we get a real rice-paddy feeling. Otherwise, if we can only flood a hundred feet or so, my camera angles are limited and the audience *knows* we're faking."

"How much water can we get out here by truck?" Paul asked. "Not enough, I suppose."

"Take it easy." Sieberling grinned. "It's all arranged. Mother Nature's on the job." He pointed to a small rise. "Just down below there is a pretty good-sized fast-running creek. Comes in all the way from the ocean by way of Punta Mesa, and this time of the year it's running nice and deep. We'll get pumps in here and hoses, flood this place as much as you want. In a couple of days' operation we'll have enough mush around here to really plant rice."

"Hey!" De Luca shouted, clapping Sieberling on the back. "Did you hear that, Paul?"

"Terrific," Paul exclaimed, "just terrific!"

Across the field, an ancient Studebaker wheezed its way toward them.

"That's going to be the land agent," Sieberling explained. "He takes care of all this land for the owner."

De Luca turned to Paul, his hands forming an invisible lens and moving slowly to his left. "We can start about here, wide, then we can move in on one single strand of rice—as tight as we can get. That's the thing, that's life you see; that's what this picture is all about, really. Life, living. And that's rice to all the Viets, no matter what their politics are." He dropped his hands and grinned. "Found the place, didn't we? We didn't settle. We found the perfect goddamn place."

The Studebaker stopped very near them, and a tubby jelly roll of a man pushed himself out. "Ah—Señor Sieberling," he said, the jelly oozing from him, "what a pleasure to see you, what a pleasure."

"The big damn pleasure," Denny Burns said to Paul in a loud whisper, "is in getting all that gringo cash."

After the location scouting, as Paul was changing shirts in his room, the phone rang. He answered it, annoyed; he had planned to work on an important sequence and the day was slipping by.

"Hello."

"Paul? Hello."

The connection was buzzed over and vague, far away and fading. He could hardly hear the voice.

"Hello. I can hardly hear you. Would you please speak slowly?"

"Is this better?"

Cautiously, he asked, "Stella?"

The voice, still faint, laughed. "Yes, it's me."

120

"You sound . . . so . . . so far away," he finished lamely.

"Do I? That's odd, isn't it? Because I'm right up here, on the floor above you."

He dropped the shirt and almost dropped the telephone as well. "You're here?"

"Yes," Stella said. "Isn't that funny? I called your office and they said you were on a location trip."

"When did you get here?" Slowly, he picked the shirt off the floor.

"Two hours ago. Isn't this silly, talking on the phone when I'm just upstairs?"

"I'll meet you in the lobby in five minutes," he suggested uncertainly. When Stella agreed, he replaced the phone and got on with his shirt. His fingers felt very thick with the buttons.

As he walked down the marble staircase, he held a tight grip on the balustrade. His pulse pounded in his ears like a loudspeaker's deep bass, and he tried to reason himself into a less extreme reaction. At the top of the lobby landing, he heard steps behind him and knew, instantly, whose they were.

He turned and saw Stella behind him. She wore a very well-cut green velvet pants suit, and her hair, he noted, was no longer in the tight Grecian ringlets. It was now cut softly across her forehead, feathering out and shading her luminous eyes. She smiled, somewhat impishly, a shade of apology indicated, and came toward him.

"You've changed your hair," he said, feeling foolish.

"That's the easy part. You're wonderfully tan."

"It's the sun," he said weakly. His right hand clutched the marble; his left was frozen somewhere near his trouser pocket, and he looked at her as though she were from outer space. They fumbled for each other, avoiding lips in the kiss. After that it was somewhat easier, and he took her arm as they walked the last few steps down, feeling himself calming.

"Now," he said, "what are you doing here, what's the assignment?"

"None," she answered simply. "I'm on vacation, that's all."

"Here in Oacala?"

She ignored his disbelief.

"I wanted to go to Europe, to France, but it's become incredibly expensive, the dollar and all."

"Yes," he murmured, "so they say."

121

"So"—Stella put herself into a plush armchair in the bar—"I've never been to Mexico, and when the travel agent said it was still cheap, I said why not."

"Of course," Paul said quickly, not knowing what he was saying, and ordered margaritas.

"And I thought," Stella went on, "that I shouldn't stay away from here simply because you were here."

"No, that would be silly, very foolish. I mean, why should you?"

"Exactly."

He looked different. Healthier than she remembered. His hair was a bit more attractively shaggy, and she had the impossible impulse to comb through some of the graying streaks. Suddenly, she was quite warm in her jacket and squirmed about, removing it. He reached over to help her, and when she felt his fingers on her shoulders she felt the slightest of tremors. The waiter brought the margaritas.

"*Salud.*"

She nodded and gulped. It had taken much more resolve to do all this than she had imagined it might. She had run through all sorts of motivations for coming and all sorts of scenarios for the results; the momentary trembling surprised her.

"How long are you going to be around?" Paul tried to make the question appear casual.

"Oh . . . long enough to see the sights and stuff. How's it going?"

"Okay."

"Are you getting along with the maestro?"

"I think so."

"And do you like it down here? I mean, are you enjoying it?" She kept her tone light, but some urgency betrayed itself, for he looked at her sharply.

"I'm learning a lot, Stella."

"Really."

He decided to try candor. "We're in sync. We're on a similar wavelength. I may get to direct some sequences, and when this picture breaks, it's going to be very important for me."

"That's wonderful," she said, surprised at the sureness of his tones.

"And if I can take this chance and run with it, Stel, for the first time in my life, I feel . . ."

As he searched for the words, Stella finished: "You feel some kind of real fulfillment possible."

He sat back in his chair and nodded. The margarita started to do its work, and subliminal memories switched on, moments of lying next to Stella as the sounds of the bay licking the beach came up in the night and they took chances telling about each other . . . but that had been early on. He looked at his watch.

"I suppose," Stella apologized, "that I'm breaking into your work day. I'm sorry."

"I was just on my way back. Come on," he said on sudden impulse, "I'll give you a quick tour if you'd like."

Walking to the company compound, Paul told Stella a little of what was happening. In turn, she told him word had reached the good restaurants in New York that De Luca now had an Indian mistress; was it so? Defensively, Paul affirmed the rumor but angrily insisted that no one was qualified to make judgments because no one in those restaurants knew what Michael was about; for them, he was simply one more exotic topic—on a par with where you might go to get the best caviar.

At the edge of the compound a VW was parked. Two crew women were climbing in, and Flo Ankrum was behind the wheel. All the women looked tense, and when Flo caught sight of Paul, she gunned off with the door not yet closed.

What was that all about? Paul wondered, and distracted, trying to decide if he should avoid his editing rooms—and Rennie—he saw Michael on the path. He had an impulse to avoid him but it was too late; Michael had seen them and was waving. When he came near, Paul saw instant recognition in Stella's eyes and she murmured, "Here's the honey bear himself."

Nervously, Paul introduced them, characterizing Stella as a good friend with whom he had worked, down here to sightsee Mexico. De Luca knew better; his acute eye and ear picked up the unspoken.

"There *is* a lot to see around this place," he assured Stella. "This is a center of old Indian culture, you know."

Stella told him that she did, indeed, know—which was why she was here. She smiled sweetly, and as De Luca beamed back at her Paul sensed some strange connection being made.

De Luca swept his arm under Stella's. "We have dailies in ten minutes. Please come."

123

Paul held his breath and hoped she'd refuse. Stella clutched De Luca's arm and said she'd love it, just love it.

When Stella first put her eyes on the crumbling, ornate, lopsided theater, she adored it. Inside, the audience had already gathered. De Luca took charge of her, introduced her to Marcus, to Kodály, to Sieberling and then, when she came in, to Rennie. There was a palpable air of expectation as this happened. Somehow, everyone had divined that the visitor had been—might still be—more than a friend and was waiting to see what the scene would be like. Kodály sniffed and twitched. Sieberling sat upright in his seat; Denny Burns, sliding down in his, grinned.

De Luca played it straight. He simply introduced Stella as Paul's old friend and Rennie as Paul's assistant. He need not have done any more to fulfill the company's expectations. Unspoken messages crackled in the air like unseen radar waves rebounding from solid objects to impinge back upon the source with increased agitation. Stella, instantly aware that this clear-eyed girl was the one De Luca had dropped as a mistress, felt all the vibrations but mistakenly assumed *that* was the source of the excitement she felt rippling through the group.

Rennie, examining Stella, was not antagonistic. This bright, obviously smart and successful woman had been close to Paul; that she knew. But it had been bad between them. Everything Paul mentioned, from time to time, indicated that she had no appreciation of the *real* Paul, of his capabilities, of what—given the right road—he might become. She was more a curiosity than anything else. So, Rennie smiled, shook hands and settled in her seat.

Paul, feeling his skin clutch his body like a suit too small, searched desperately for something to say that might bring him back to the normal world.

"I guess," he finally said, "Flo Ankrum still isn't out of town. I just saw her a little while ago."

"You mean she came into our area?" Michael asked, surprised.

"Just outside. She was picking up a couple of people."

"A couple of our people?"

"I . . . think so," Paul said, pulling back. "I'm not sure."

Sieberling, overhearing, leaned forward from the row behind. "Gordon, who did she go off with?"

"I don't know," Paul said, unhappily.

"Try to remember."

"All right, I'll try." He turned away from the production manager, eager to end the conversation.

Sieberling glanced at a clipboard in his hand and spoke to De Luca's ear. "Mike, we've rescheduled sequence two eighty-six, that moonlight screwing stuff. We'll do it tomorrow night. Kodály says—"

"I don't care what Kodály says." De Luca shook his head. "It's impossible tomorrow night."

"Mike, we've got to shoot it tomorrow night because—"

"Damn it, Sal," De Luca whispered to him, "I told you I'm doing something tomorrow night that will affect the whole picture, so change the schedule."

The screen began to fill with images. As it did, De Luca leaned toward Stella. "I want you to come to dinner, tonight, to my house. My wife would kill me if she didn't get a chance to query you about what the 'beautiful people' are doing."

"But you're the beautiful people," Stella said.

De Luca laughed. Rennie concentrated on the screen. Paul looked at Stella limned by the projector light. Her profile was almost delicate, the light enhancing a softness of line, a shadowed depth of eye, he did not remember. Her hair, gleaming gold and flowing down carelessly over her ear, faded off gently into the darkness.

He wished heartily that she hadn't come.

CHAPTER

13

⁚═⁚═⁚═⁚═⁚═⁚═ **13** ═⁚═⁚═⁚═⁚═⁚

That afternoon, Stella took a sightseeing tour around Oacala, ending at the open-air Mercado where she bought an ugly black pottery mug and instantly regretted it. Jet-lagged, she walked back to her room and lay down, falling into a restless sleep from which she kicked awake, disoriented. The room was dark, shuttered. Was it day or night? As she lay there, dazed, she became slowly aware of floor-level noises that rose from the room below—rhythmic squeaking noises, plunging and heaving, plunging and heaving.

She struggled to a sitting position. Was Paul's room directly below hers? As she contemplated, the rhythm sped up perceptibly and she swore to get out within the hour, go to another hotel, stay one more day perhaps, in Oacala—for appearance's sake—and then she would leave. As she picked her way through the decision, the sounds became more and more feverish. The pitch rose. She heard thumps, bumps, knocks and gurgles. Suddenly, there was an orgasmic rush of water. The sounds ceased and Stella fell back, clutching a pillow to her face, stifling her laughter, as she realized she had been listening to the Mexican plumbing work its magic. The laughter released her and she floated off to sleep again.

All afternoon Paul worked like a maniac, hurling reels about and ripping film up from barrels with mounting agitation. Near six, Sieberling came in with Allan Marcus and a map of the land area to be flooded. Marcus was to shoot some sequences there, but De Luca had asked that plans be checked out with Paul. The tall second-unit man took it in good humor. Squinting through his inevitable haze of cigarette smoke, he observed that he'd never known Mike De Luca to trust anyone else before. Paul plunged into the discussion, suggesting physical changes in the setting and causing Marcus, when he left, to laugh and say that Paul was beginning to talk like De Luca.

126

Sieberling stayed on, watching Paul work. The silent scrutiny became so uncomfortable that Paul finally made conversation, asking how things were going, this day.

"The whole company's tense," Sieberling complained. "This sabotage business has them shook up. None of the gaffers will let a Mex near a piece of equipment. There were two fights this morning. Nothing's getting done. It stinks." He waited a moment, then asked, "What about those women?"

Paul looked up, puzzled. "What women?"

"The ones Ankrum was driving around."

"Oh." Paul felt uncomfortable with the question.

"Who were they?"

"I didn't see them very well."

"Try to remember. Try hard."

"Damn it, what's so important about them?"

Sieberling removed his dark glasses, probing the corners of his eyes with delicate fingers.

"Gordon, that girl is a bummer. She's not out to do us any good. Who knows what she's into?"

"Come on, Sal."

"Gordon, she knows how we operate. So does anyone she hangs out with, and I want to know who they are."

His first impulse was to shout at Sieberling, but he fought the seething. There had to be a balance struck. Michael had a perfect right to protect himself. This was not some skin flick. This was, already, two years of his life and could be two years more. And the production was in trouble. In that light, there was no question but that Michael had weight on his side; one made the hard choices and one kept to them. Still, a certain degree of caution was called for with Sieberling.

"I think," he finally said, "that one of them was in Kodály's department—a girl with dark hair."

"Uh-huh. And the other one?"

"I'm not sure."

Sieberling replaced his glasses. "Give me a break, Gordon, will you? I'm trying to do my job."

"Sal, I'm not sure."

He turned back to the editing table and ran a reel through. Sieberling nodded.

"Okay. See you later. Mike wants me; I'm going out to the rice-paddy location. We're taking another pump unit out there."

When Sieberling had left him alone, Paul stopped the reel and stared at the milky viewing screen in silence.

For the rest of the afternoon, Stella was wrapped in languor. The Oacala softness soothed her nerve endings, powdered her mind. The twilight perfume opened her senses, so that when two mariachis paused beneath her window to rehearse an aching ballad, harmonizing with their blend of sweet, high-pitched yearning, she surprised herself and the musicians by dropping thirty pesos on them, like tin manna from heaven.

When she had her first glimpse of the De Luca establishment Stella found, after all the rumors of venery and lechery, of wild, petulant indulgence, only unquestioned domesticity, a model for the magazines, a dream for the interviews. Exactly as it should be.

Photos of the two enchanting De Luca children, who were in the States for a visit, were very much in evidence. The master's affection for Catherine was impossible to feign. The warm bantering with his father spoke of deep familial feelings. The director inhabited the rooms of the hacienda with solidly bourgeois ease. And he was unstinting in his praise of Paul, talking of his untapped talents, his sure-to-be-productive future, earnestly describing him as one of those rarities, a loyal and gifted colleague.

The elder De Luca, wineglass in hand, developed moist eyes as he told Stella of the respect these two men felt for each other after so short a time and how happy he, personally, was, for he had come to look upon Pauli as a son and hoped that when he was laid to rest in the cemetery, with the big carved stone over his head, both Mikey and Pauli would come to visit together and share those moments.

Stella was astonished.

Catherine De Luca, stunning in a belted orange caftan, was more beautiful than Stella had expected. It was a very cool beauty, however, reflected in those calm eyes, and Stella suspected that Catherine De Luca cared very little which bed her husband inhabited on any particular night, knowing hers was the bed of longevity.

Paul arrived shortly after she did, and after perfunctory greetings he always seemed to be on the other side of the room. Twenty minutes later, Burns, the flier, showed up, chauffeuring Rennie Loomis, and Stella noticed a slight, puzzling flush glaze over Paul's face. When table places were assigned, she found Paul sitting between herself and his assistant, which seemed to her quite a reasonable arrangement except that Paul's strain was obviously increasing. She ascribed it to general nervousness at her presence and continued with the asparagus, observing that everyone, wife, ex-mistress, father, was very "civilized."

Catherine De Luca orchestrated the evening smoothly, course following course, wines opened on schedule—everything moving well on its neat, undisturbed track. It remained for Denny Burns, working on his fourth glass of Burgundy after two Chivas charges, to say, "Funny things sure go on around here," and laugh at his private joke.

It was also Burns who produced the only cloud by making reference to the sabotage and the apprehension it had produced among his fliers. When Stella asked *what* sabotage, the elder De Luca broke in, his olive face purpling.

"*Stùpido! Stùpido!* My Mikey give these donkeys everything. I see one donkey who hurts my Mikey, I give him this." He jabbed two fingers forward, grinding the tips into the invisible eyeballs of his son's enemies.

"We're taking care of it, Pop," Michael said with a significant look at Paul.

"Absolutely," Paul added.

Catherine, not too happy with this turn, tinkled her little bell, commanding the salad to be brought.

Later, as the espresso was served in the baronial parlor, Burns talked to Stella about flying. He was so remarkably poetic in his descriptions that Stella asked him if he had flown anywhere besides in Vietnam.

"Just there. Just in Nam."

"But all the other things—the things you had to do while flying— the fighting, I mean—didn't they change your feelings about the 'beauty' of it?"

Burns looked at Stella in astonishment. "If you'll excuse me, lady, you don't know shit from Shinola about it."

"You're probably right," Stella acknowledged.

Catherine passed her another Amaretto cookie. Stella remarked that her husband seemed to enjoy making films away from Hollywood.

"Well, yes," Catherine agreed, "Michael does like to make pictures in faraway places, like this. He can be in total control then— the pope."

Stella was startled by the suggestion of bite in her voice. She saw her gaze wander to light on Rennie.

"That's what Michael has to be to do his work—the pope. And people understand that. They know their job is to help him. And that's the important thing."

She swung back to Stella, an unnatural gleam burning in her eye, a shaft of inner energy she had not before exhibited.

It was almost midnight when, the coffee and Galliano drunk, Denny Burns complained about the necessity of rising at sunup "so that jive-ass Hunkie crazy man can catch the six-thirty light." He prepared to leave. Alone, Stella assumed, and the waiting Mercedes would transport the other three.

She looked forward to going. It was not at all impossible that, in the bar of the hotel, she and Paul would have a nightcap and talk. The more she thought about the prospect, the more attractive it became. So much had happened to him, it was clear, in the short time he was here. And, equally, a lot had happened to her that she did not fully comprehend, knowing only that it involved him in some way.

Meanwhile, the moon had come up full, hanging in the sky like a bone-china plate.

"Later," De Luca said to Stella, "it will turn amber and mysterious."

"Just your kind of moon," she replied, and was about to say something else when, behind them, she heard Rennie say, "Denny, will you take us? You go right near my place."

She turned to see Rennie link arms intimately with Paul and instantly felt her stomach knot and her ankles grow weak. Paul's eyes caught hers for a furtive second, and then his head turned away. She saw Rennie glance at her with a certain calculation and with painful clarity recalled the buzzing in the theater. Understanding now, she felt shamed and superfluous.

"Come on," Burns cried, "I've got to get my Z's."

She saw Paul move toward her as though underwater and was aware of a sanguine rush of bloom to her cheeks, which must have signaled to him, for his tone, as he wished her good night and mumbled something about calling her tomorrow, was apologetic and aggressive at the same time.

"I may leave early," she said quickly. "I'm not sure."

"Oh" was all he could muster.

"Good night," Rennie called. "Have a super holiday."

130

After Rennie, Paul and Burns left, Catherine disappeared into the kitchen. The elder De Luca sat at the piano to play and sing for himself. Stella took a deep swig of her *agua mineral* and called blithely, "Well, this was a wonderful evening, a splendid introduction to the wonders of Mexico, which I had been led to believe was a primitive country, only to find it has everything one could wish for."

"Didn't you know? I thought you knew," Michael said gently, "about Rennie and Paul."

"Now," Stella said, "if I could get back to the hotel, please—"

"I would like to show you an extraordinary sight."

"Now?"

"It's now that makes it extraordinary. I'd like to show you Monte Tecla by moonlight."

She looked up at him in surprise. He laughed at her look. "It's the sacred mountain, and in this light, it is unbelievable. You can understand why they made it sacred."

Without thinking, she swiveled her head toward the kitchen. De Luca turned her face back to him.

Stella stepped back a pace. "Wait a minute. Your wife and I haven't said good night."

At that, he shouted toward the kitchen. "Catherine . . . Stella is saying good night." He took her arm. "Come on."

"I don't think I want to do this." But already he was propelling her gently toward the door. From the piano the elder De Luca waved his glass and called, "*Buona notte*, Stellita, *buona notte*."

Outside, they stopped, De Luca's thick body close to hers. "You'll find I'm direct. I think you're an interesting woman."

Power, Stella thought, power allows you to be direct.

"All right," she said. "Why not? Let's see the view." He smiled, took her arm and guided her to the little Porsche, dismissing the Mercedes. Within minutes they were on their way to Ixtepan.

He was an expert driver, and the car held steady as he heeled it onto the main road. Moments after reaching it, Stella noticed him keeping a wary eye on the rearview mirror, where a light reflected dimly.

"That's a motorcycle," he said. "Funny."

He depressed the accelerator and the Porsche responded instantly, straining Stella against the seat. She grabbed at the hand bar.

"Who are we racing?"

He didn't answer but made a sharp right turn to a dirt patch,

131

hugging the inside, screeching and bumping. She dug her feet in for balance.

"What is going on?"

"I'm sorry." He slowed, checking behind him. The light was still there, keeping distance. Abruptly, he pulled to the side, braked to a dead stop and snapped off his lights. Despite the moon, it seemed frighteningly dark, and Stella demanded, "Will you tell me what is happening?"

"This is Mexico. Sometimes funny things happen on the roads at night." He looked to the rear, his eyes glued to the oncoming head-lights, and she heard the motorcycle putt-putt. To her surprise, as she too watched, the light cut out, vanished and with it the engine sound, leaving only darkness and silence.

"That cycle . . ." Eyes to the rear, he switched on the lights and waited. Nothing broke the darkness behind them. He fired up his ignition and idled. No light appeared. Slowly, he turned about, thumping over the dirt toward the paved road, smiling sheepishly at her.

"I'm sorry. I may be getting a little paranoid."

Within a half-hour they were at the village. Using the tourist bus route, De Luca wheeled to the top of the pyramid, giving the yawning, elderly guard with the uniform cap inscribed TECLA, like an ad slogan, fifty pesos to go back to his slumbers. Helping Stella out, he gestured to the stones, the pocked sculptures, the octagonal temple bathed now in unearthly amber.

"Isn't it incredible?"

In this light Tecla looked menacing; sinister secrets seemed hidden in every blue-shadowed tomb, and every stone serpent seemed poised to leap.

"It's very scary," Stella said.

"Right. It was meant to be."

He toured her for twenty minutes, impressing her with his knowledge of the past and his respect for the present. Finally, he pointed down below. "Look at that."

She peered down from Tecla to the ridged land where the moon illuminated the outlines of grass huts, of deep concrete-lined bunkers, of roughly carpentered buildings only half-completed.

"That's going to be the Vietnam plains. That's where we're going to shoot the key scene, the Operation Jericho. That's the village the air force hits and blasts to bits. I am going to shoot the hell out of that sequence and then Paul and I are going to sit down and edit it, like a piece of music, note by note and chord by chord, until the effect of this futile destruction, this barrage, this absolutely unthinking hail of death, totally unnecessary, is going to make an audience scream and have bad dreams for a week."

She smiled wryly. "Well—that's entertainment."

De Luca laughed. "You bet." He looked at his watch. "Now, just about five kilometers from here, we have a major location. I have a big blue mobile home there I use when I'm shooting. And I have some incredible Cuervo Gold which would be the perfect thing right now."

Stella leaned back against a broken pediment. Straining to strike a calm, relaxed note, she said, "I think I should tell you that this isn't going to happen the way you'd like it to."

Surprisingly, he seemed not so much offended as amused, so she continued.

"Yes, I feel a little awkward, for one thing, eating a lady's dinner and then going to bed with her husband, even apart from whether or not I would really like you to make love to me. It may be provincial, I grant you, but I still haven't worked these kinks out."

"Fair enough, but I want you to know that I consider you a very special person, really rare."

"I understand you have another really rare new friend," she said, with just a touch of mischief, "a lovely Indian girl."

"She is lovely." He laughed. "But you know that has nothing to do with you." He leaned back, examining her face with deliberation, roaming from hair to chin. "Listen," he said finally, "in my picture there is a very small part—an officer's wife, an American officer. It's about two days' shooting. I imagine her looking just like you. Would you do it?"

"What?"

"I'm serious. I want a new face, an unknown."

"I've never acted in my life."

"It doesn't take acting; it will simply take being yourself."

"It's one of the craziest ideas I've ever heard."

"Not at all. I use unknowns all the time." He laughed. "Maybe I'll launch a new star."

"God forbid."

"It's not a favor. Would five thousand dollars do it?"

She looked at him, astounded. "Why are you doing this?"

"I like your face."

"No," she said. "Oh, no."

"Think about it."

"I am exhausted. Could we go now?"

At the car he suddenly asked, "Are you still in love with Paul?"

Startled, she could only respond with a feeble "You *are* crazy."

Slowly, they wound down the Monte. At the bottom they turned onto the road back to Oacala and sped off. As they shot away from Tecla, a dim headlamp flickered into life at the base and a motorcycle wheeled swiftly from the brush, its sputter fading under the harsh caw of a crow which had taken off from Tecla stone and come swooping down in search of night carrion.

CHAPTER

14

Paul's night passed in restless gymnastics—rolling, curling, arm flinging—but sleep eluded him. He could not replace the Stella in his mind with the Rennie on the other side of the bed peacefully unaware, presumably, of the visions shooting through his brain like film gone mad.

Returning from Michael's, he had felt knobs of resentment at Rennie's obvious flaunting of the situation. This had been tempered by stabs of anger at Stella's unsettling appearance in Oacala. In the same hotel. On the floor above. First letters, now an appearance. He sat up in Rennie's bed worriedly.

On the drive back, Denny had slyly popped the subject open, declaring Stella to be a good-looking woman even if she harbored jokey ideas about Vietnam. Neither Rennie nor he had taken the bait. Once alone, Rennie made no mention at all of the visitor. It remained for him, unable to repress, to say that it was very surprising to see her here. To which Rennie had simply responded, "Yes, I can imagine." After which she washed her face, leaving him with an interior monologue to perform. He performed it till early dawn felled him.

At breakfast in the garden, at a table overlooking the jacaranda tree still dewy with night breath, Stella munched sugary pineapple and decided it would be best to leave before another day passed. Undeniably, staying around presented risks of humiliation and loss of self-respect. The De Luca incident she dismissed, with the sun, as more amusing than anything else. Thus, she was unprepared when the waitress called her to the telephone in the lobby. It was Sal Sieberling, who invited her, on behalf of De Luca, to watch the morning's shooting and to stay for lunch. If she agreed, a car would pick her up very soon.

"Oh," she said, surprised.

135

"Do I send the car?"

"Well . . ." Stella hedged, her earlier resolve melting and a new resolve beginning to clarify itself. One more day would make little difference, and she had come all this distance . . .

The Fiat arrived thirty minutes later, driven by Steve Kruger. As they walked back to the car, through the loggia, he told her they would be driving twenty kilometers to a hotel location that had been dressed to be an Army headquarters.

"It's a broken-down place, used to be a great old hotel once, and it looks just like pictures of a hotel the French built in Tay Minh Province, and—"

He stopped in mid-sentence, his teeth clamping shut, and he charged forward on the dead run, arms pumping in a fury. Stunned, Stella stood planted to the tile floor. Kruger reached the sedan just as a frail Mexican boy appeared from behind it. The driver's large hand shot out like a piston, grabbed the boy by the collar and shook him violently.

"What were you doing? Huh? Huh? What were you doing?" Holding the boy tightly, Kruger marched him around the Fiat. The teenage boy, eyes filled with fear, throat filled with phlegm, began to protest in Spanish. Ignoring him, Kruger bent over to examine the rear of the car. As he did, his captive jerked away, running off wildly down the street, leaving his shirt collar in the American's grip. Kruger took a tentative step after him, but already the boy had disappeared behind a building.

"What happened?" Stella asked.

"I'm not sure," Kruger answered sheepishly, opening his hand to drop the handful of frayed, dirty cotton.

"You're not sure?"

He straightened up, pulling the door open. "Let's go." When Stella eased in, he slammed the door shut, swearing beneath his breath, and moved forward through the Zócalo traffic.

"Did he steal something?"

"No, but . . ." The young driver cut toward a side street. "There are some things going down around here. Maybe I got him before he could do anything."

He slowed to turn out of the Zócalo. As he did, two fist-sized chunks of concrete came flying at the Fiat. Kruger saw them coming and pushed on Stella's shoulder, muscling her down as one chunk arced through the open window into the front seat and smashed against the dashboard. There was a sharp *thwonk* as the other chunk slammed into the front door and rebounded, breaking into sharp stones and dust at the impact.

"Goddamn."

Kruger stopped the car in time to look back and see the thin boy shake a fist at him in fury before running off for the second time, then he leaned over Stella anxiously.

"You okay?"

"I'm okay." She sat up and pushed her hair back from her eyes. "That boy is furious."

"Yeah—they get furious down here over a cockroach race."

On the set Stella was aware that electricians, moving lights and cables, stepped very carefully. Prop men, normally loud-voiced, whispered to each other. The Mexican helpers, avoiding all gringo eyes, knew those eyes were darkened by suspicion. Five uniformed police, more alert than the usual brace of guards, kept on the move, automatic rifles slung over their shoulders. At every unexpected noise, they stopped moving and their fingers went to the triggers.

She overheard Kodály telling his camera operator how intolerable this all was; he could not work this way, his eye was disappearing. Whatever was happening, she concluded, had set plenty of teeth on edge. She began, herself, to look about warily, not even knowing what there was to fear.

Paul walked onto the set, and she saw him stumble in obvious surprise at her presence. She waved a greeting. He waved back, awkwardly, and the assistant called for silence.

The camera started to record the scene—a confrontation between the colonel and the captain over the proposed execution of a Vietnamese found to be a Cong spy. Stella watched. The captain was not so subtly ironic.

"Okay, let's kill him. What the hell is an army all about if it's not killing, inflicting damage, forcing its will on the enemy? The more killing an army does, the more medals it gets. And the army's medals become its traditions. So let's kill the poor mother and get it over with."

As the rugged blond actor spoke his lines, mumbling them almost incoherently, De Luca halted the shooting to suggest that he speak up a bit more or he would drive the sound man into a lather of frustration. The actor spat on the floor and shook his head.

"I'm gettin' a sore throat, Mike. This place is givin' me a sore throat and a sore belly and a sore ass and that's the best I can do, and if you don't like my work . . ."

137

"I love your work," De Luca soothed. "That's why I want everyone to hear it."

He called for a break to ease things and said quietly to Paul, "He's up to his old tricks. I'm never going to get that scene out of him. He hates the words. He hates any words. He simply wants to grunt. Let's figure out a move. I'll be in the production trailer."

He acknowledged Stella with a distracted nod before he hurried away. Stella started to move toward Paul, but suddenly Rennie was there with a technical question. Even after it was answered, she did not leave but lingered.

"Why the police?" Stella asked. "Are we in the midst of a revolution *The New York Times* isn't aware of?"

"It's complicated," Paul said. "We've got to protect ourselves against some people who are causing trouble. See you." He walked away briskly.

There was, Stella noted, a certain decisive crispness in his voice she was not used to hearing. She smoothed out the wrinkles in her gray slacks and mumbled something about climate seeming to make a difference—people were one way in a temperate zone and another in a torrid.

"Do you think Paul is different?" Rennie asked instantly.

"Do *you* think so?" Stella countered.

"Yes, I do. Paul is starting to think positively about what he is and how he can succeed. Michael thinks he can be a fine director —and so do I."

There was an edgy, open defiance in her tone. Her arms uncrossed, then crossed again.

"What he needs are people who believe in him passionately, believe in what he might accomplish."

"Well, yes," Stella said weakly, "passionate belief is always good."

"You're making a joke out of it."

"A failing," she confessed.

"He's learning. He's learning about what he has to do to be what he wants."

Stella frowned, in concentration. "Could you say that again?"

"What he has to do to be what he wants," Rennie insisted. "We all have to do certain things to be certain things."

"What does he have to do? I know it sounds like a dumb question—maybe, but—"

138

"He has this marvelous chance to learn from Michael. After that . . ."

"I see."

"Do you?" Rennie's voice flared with annoyance. "I hope you do." She uncrossed her arms and strode off, moving with energy, a slim figure in well-fitting jeans.

Stella felt weak in the knees and decided it was time to go. Definitely. This breathless young woman had made the transition from the professor's bed to the pupil's with no hitches. Gifted probably. Good luck to them all.

She looked for the driver who had brought her here but could not see him. She asked for a taxi, but that was nonexistent in this world of motor pools. The urgent need to leave spawned a small panic and hearing, still, Rennie's proprietary tone did not help. Anger added to her state, she shouted at someone, "How am I going to get back?"

"In that jeep," he answered placidly, indicating one.

As she swiveled toward it, she saw Rennie standing in the shadow of a corrugated metal shed staring at her intently. Their eyes made contact and Rennie held the link tightly. Then, slowly, almost contemptuously, she turned her back and was lost to sight.

Stella looked at the empty doorway for a moment.

"Changed my mind," she called, and walked, stubbornly, back to where she had been.

In the production trailer De Luca, using Paul as a sounding board, altered the interrupted scene. His concentration, however, was not on the work.

"Tonight, when we go to meet Aguillar, I'll pick you up at half-past eleven."

He sagged into a canvas chair, his eyes closing tiredly. Paul felt a wave of empathy and assured him it would work out; they would make it work out.

Sieberling interrupted with a disturbing piece of news. He had just received a Telex from a source at the studio. A secret board meeting had been convened with Jericho as the subject. The costs were becoming astronomical and they had not seen a foot of film; they were going to demand to see footage.

"Is that a fact?" De Luca fumed. "They want to see footage? They couldn't understand my footage if it were held up to them, frame by frame, and explained by Laurence Olivier."

"Yeah," Sieberling acknowledged, "but they brought the New York people in for the meeting."

"I don't care who they brought. I've never let anybody see a foot of film until I thought they should and I'm not going to start now."

"My contact says Lufkin is deciding when to come down here to see what's going on. He could be here tomorrow."

As Michael lapsed into frustrated silence, Paul realized that the production manager was warning against exposure of the obstruction and its cost.

"Wait a minute," he found himself saying. "There are some really good assembled sequences from the early part of the picture . . ."

"I've thrown all that out already," De Luca objected. "They have nothing to do with my picture."

"I know. But if you sent them to the studio *before* this . . . Lufkin . . . comes down, it might stop him from coming."

"If you give them a finger—" Michael started, but Paul interrupted, "*I'll* send it to them, as though it were a mistake or something. They won't care so long as they see something."

Sieberling looked at him with surprise. Paul was somewhat surprised himself at what he had suggested, but it seemed to him a rather honorable deception, a good choice.

"Let's do that," Sieberling urged, "and hope."

"Okay," Michael agreed, grudgingly.

Sieberling left and shortly afterward, Paul followed. Walking from the trailer, he saw Stella and had simultaneous impulses— to skulk away and to go over. He followed the former.

At lunch break, when Stella entered the blue van, De Luca was already opening a bottle of good white wine. Greeted and seated, with the chef in white jacket buzzing about his already prepared cartons, Stella remarked that, willy-nilly, De Luca had managed to show her the inside of his famous blue vehicle.

"I want to know a little of what you're all about," he explained, pouring the Meursault, "and it has to be quiet and contemplative for that. Now, have you thought about the part?"

"Not for a minute; it's ridiculous."

"But will you do it?"

"No, of course not."

He sipped from his glass and pronounced the wine fine. She

sipped and hardly tasted it. The chef, unobtrusively, presented a pâté. De Luca held it out to her.

"Please have some. He's terrific at this."

She knifed a small wedge to a cracker and hardly tasted that either. De Luca munched his wedge happily.

"Listen, I have a notion which has nothing to do with acting." He leaned forward excitedly. "I need someone down here to handle public relations for a couple of weeks. I need a sensitivity, an intelligence like yours."

"What kind of publicity could I do down here?" She decided to play it all extremely straight.

"Oh—things come to mind. Articles for stateside magazines and papers. A visitor or two may come down and you could handle them. Things come to mind."

"You're incredible. You're a very devious man."

"I'm not, no . . ."

"I have only a few weeks' vacation. Do you really think I'd want to spend them all here, in this place, watching you make a movie, for God's sake?"

"Let's deal with that—the time factor." He urged the platter of eggplant Parmesan at her. "I've always needed someone in New York to do the publicity side and I've never had anyone. When you leave Mexico and go back, you could take that assignment on —part-time if you like. I think I have, oh—a thousand or fifteen hundred a week in the budget for someone—more is possible. Things might be stretched."

She sat back, the Parmesan steaming in front of her, at a loss for words.

"You don't dare let this get cool," De Luca insisted. "Hot, it's a feather poem; cold, it's a leaden disaster." He forked some food into his mouth with appreciative sounds. "*Mangia, mangia.*"

"You go incredibly far for what you want."

"I do, yes," he answered brightly.

"The problem is"—she managed to get a bit of eggplant to her lips—"I don't know what you really want—or maybe I just can't believe the obvious."

He laughed and spooned another helping onto his plate. Stella chewed, found it delicious, looked up and saw the chef bow politely to her.

"Ciao, Guido," De Luca called.

When the chef emerged on the other side of the blue door, two girls from makeup and a refugee from Kodály's torture chamber were passing a joint around. The chef raised his impressive eyebrows and kissed the air softly.

At eight o'clock Paul took his trickle shower. All afternoon he had been bothered, alternately, by Stella's presence and by anxiety over the approaching midnight meeting. With the tepid water sprinkling down over his shoulders like dew, he wondered if he ought to call her. Simply as a courtesy, he quickly reassured himself. He left the spray and dialed her room. The moment she answered he knew something was wrong.

"Oh . . . *mucho* goings-on in my poor stomach, Paul."

"The *turista*. You've got the bug."

"It's dancing in my colon, I swear. Colon disco. Ouch."

"I have something special for it. Stay put. I'll bring it right up."

"Where," she groaned, "am I going to go?"

When he saw her, Stella's face was as green as the medicine the Mexican doctor had once given him. She lay back on the bed in a violet robe that seemed, suddenly, too big for her and said that she wanted to die, and if that was too radical, could someone knock her on the head for forty-eight hours? Did Paul know anyone who could arrange that? He produced bottle and spoon and medicated. She swallowed and huddled into herself. On second thought, she said, maybe it would be best to die after all, and did Paul know someone who might arrange *that?* He assured her she would recover —a good night's sleep would take care of everything. Had she eaten carefully?

"Typical Mexican meal," she moaned. "Eggplant Parmesan."

"Oh." The company whispers about lunch in the blue bus with the king-sized bed at one end had caught up with him, but he had ignored them.

"Yes," Stella said, "the chef is very discreet. He serves and leaves."

"So they say."

She looked up at him. "He needn't have—oooh." And squirmed. "I suppose you simply must get this once. Everybody, I mean. It's probably in the small print of the visa if you look carefully."

The sweat beads on her forehead picked up the light, and automatically Paul reached out to the box of tissues on the end table and handed her one. She sniffled.

"The chili must come out this way—through the skin."

He laughed outright, started to sit on the edge of the bed, but caught himself.

She said, "If I'm upsetting your life by being here, I'm sorry."

"You're not doing that," he lied.

Her eyes became even more moist, and when her lips tightened, he leaned over anxiously.

"Stel, are you all right?"

In her weakened state, sentimental connections she would not ordinarily allow to be made were leaping along her synapses—flashbacks to other times; his being in bed with one of his endlessly dripping colds for which her X-rated soup was the only remedy (X-rated because of all the unspeakable elements it contained), the hip dislocation that had kept her subdued and quietly askew on the sheets for a week as he fetched her two meals a day and even sang in the kitchen. Trees, snow-brushed, rushing past the car window, flesh in the shower . . . She wanted to pull him down gently beside her. Instead, she sighed and sat up.

"I do feel better. That must be powerful medicine."

"Well, good," he said. "I'll let you rest."

He stood over her, awkwardly. She would not quite let him leave yet.

"Your assistant really thinks a lot of you."

"She's an enthusiastic type."

"She says you are—let's see if I get it right—learning what you have to do to be what you want to be."

"Whatever that means."

"She was a little cryptic, but I supposed that was about what you were *learning.*"

"I'm learning," he burst out in irritation, "about doing it, Stella."

"Doing it?"

"Yes." He moved away. "That's what I'm learning, okay?"

"Making movies, you mean?"

"Doing it," he repeated. "Seeing what has to be done and doing it. I've got to go now, Stella."

"Yes." As he moved back, she said, "De Luca offered me a job."

He stared at her.

"Isn't that crazy?"

Incredulity took him over. "Are you sure you heard him right?"

"Yes—a job down here and then back in New York."

He held on to the carved foot of the bed.

"You're not going to take it?"

"Probably not. Probably."

"It's ridiculous. What would be the point?"

"What would be the point?" Stella agreed, feeling well enough to smooth the covers. "Your medicine is working wonders."

"Keep it."

"Thank you."

Paul walked to the door. Once there, he turned around. "Stella, how long are you going to stay in Oacala?"

She looked directly at him. "Not long."

"See you," he said, and went out.

Slouching back to his room, head whirling, Paul was confused. What were the games now? Why would Michael offer her a job? Why would she want to stay on? And her crack about Rennie? He groaned, wishing she would go away and let his life continue.

CHAPTER
15

That evening, as the Oacalan shopkeepers were lowering their iron shutters and Flo Ankrum was making entries in her leather-bound journal, she heard the lion's-head door knocker rap twice. When she found Captain Quesedo standing at the door, her mouth went slightly dry.

Quesedo, who had decided that afternoon to do something to appease the Americans, examined the pink-peignoired, barefoot, buzz-haired young woman in front of him and was impressed with her . . . roundness. He blinked at the way her cushioned hips flowed beneath the flimsy robe and at the generous cleft between her breasts, which she made no attempt to conceal. There was something familiar about her intense face that reached him, too—nostrils flaring slightly, the eyes wide and startled behind the glasses, full lips, though pressed together at the moment. He told her who he was and asked to come in.

Flo jerked open the door and stood aside. Entering, Quesedo removed his uniform cap and was patting down his waves when Flo said she knew he had come at Sieberling's instigation, but that all of her documents were in order; if he wished, he could see for himself. She was a tourist, she repeated stubbornly.

"Sí. I know. I know," Quesedo pleasantly agreed. "Oh, yes—you have good visa, good *estampas*. No question. Is no question."

As he spoke he quickly eyed the room. A stack of books, batches of letters and notepaper, a small portable typewriter on a carved table lent a scholarly air. A half-opened closet revealed a ball of soiled underclothing on the floor. Two peasant blouses flopped over a pair of carelessly thrown jeans whose bottoms were frayed. A small suitcase, lid opened, carried a miscellany of more books, a hair drier, an orange juice squeezer and various medicinal items.

145

"What's this visit about then?" Flo stood in the center of the room like a guardian lioness.

Quesedo sighed. "Señorita, you must to oonderstand that a policeman, he does not do only the t'ings he wishes. He has duty—sí— duty to be sure that there is peace, that life goes smooth—sí, smooth like . . . the best tequila."

He chuckled at his comparison but Flo was not amused. What was not smooth? she insisted upon knowing—what was she doing that was not smooth?

Quesedo clucked his tongue at her, avuncularly. "I can see you be *estudiante*. You be person *mucho intelectual*. You t'ink 'bout *mucho problemas*. So, is very ea-sy for you to oonderstand that is best you be *turista* someplace else. Maybe Chapala, Lake Chapala. Oh, yes. In Chapala is many *escritores*, many writers, *intelectuales*. They all day make the *discusión*. All day, all night, they drink the tequila and make the *discusión*. You like there." He could not keep the disdain from his voice, however.

"I don't want to go to Chapala." Flo, reassured by the policeman's reasonable tone, perched on the arm of a chair, removed her glasses and began to clean them with an edge of her robe.

Quesedo laughed and shrugged. If she did not like Chapala, how about San Miguel d'Allende? Now there was a beautiful town. It had many artists and a university. She must, certainly, enjoy that *ambiente*.

Almost amused by now, Flo shook her head. "No. I like it here in Oacala. I like the Indians. I like to see the old ways. The people are real. Even when they don't have enough to eat, they're sweet."

"Ah," Quesedo said, eyebrows lifting, "you be *comunista!*"

"Oh, no. No." She thought it best to be emphatic. "I detest the Communist party. Working-class sellouts when they get to power."

"Señorita"—Quesedo came toward her—"we speak open, sí?"

"Okay," she said, watching him carefully.

"Is bad t'ings happen here to *jefe* De Luca. We must to try and find who does this. You be see in Mercado talking to people. Why you talk to people in the Mercado?"

She put her glasses on for self-defense. "I'm interested in how people live. Is that illegal?"

"You be the one who tell Coyopan to go to where they make the cinema and he does this bad t'ing."

"I spoke to him once," she objected. "His wife . . ."

"Sí, his wife is *trabajadora* here. She is joost *campesina* from the

146

mountains but he makes the sab-o-tage. You know. Oh, yes, you know."

He sighed and looked at her with reproach. "I try to be gentle man, señorita. I don' like to be hard man with womens."

"I appreciate that."

"Is better for you to go from Oacala. I ask you, please—*por favor* —to go."

Flo said nothing. She riffled the journal pages, nervously uncertain.

Quesedo continued, "You know, I can to find some law you break, Señorita Ank-room."

"That would be unfair," she muttered.

"Injoostice. Sí." He smiled. "What we can do? Is everywhere . . ."

"Yes, oh, yes." She slid over into the chair, disconsolate, her peignoir opening slightly. She pulled it closed around her knees.

Quesedo leaned back against the small chest of drawers. "Señorita, you know University of Chi-ca-go?"

"I know where it is," she answered, surprised. "Why?"

"You go to there, maybe?" He asked the question almost shyly.

Flo shook her head. "No. Considered it but didn't."

"Ah—" There was a note of disappointment in his voice.

"I have friends who went there, though—and I visited."

"Ah?" That seemed to please him. He looked down to his cap and adjusted the sweatband. Finally, he looked up. "Señorita, Señor Sieberling be not like me. He t'ink you be big trouble. I come here to make sure you go away by morning, but . . ." He hesitated, shrugged. "I don' t'ink you so bad like he says."

She sat up, surprised.

Quesedo stepped closer. "Listen, you make me promise you don' do not'ing bad, you can to stay in Oacala little while—and we be friends, okay?"

"I'm not friendly with too many policemen." But she allowed a smile to creep over her face.

"You say me okay?"

"Okay." She nodded. "But I haven't done anything wrong to begin with."

"For sure." Quesedo put his cap over his waves and tapped it expertly over his eyes. "Now we be friends, we can to have a drink sometime and make the *discusión*, no?"

"Maybe," Flo replied, relieved at the way things had gone.

"So, we see, eh? *Hasta la vista, señorita.*"

She stood up and extended her hand. "Good-bye."

Quesedo shook her hand in very formal fashion. "Sí. Good-bye." He turned smartly and marched out.

Walking toward the jeep, he decided to tell Sieberling he had thrown a good scare into the girl; she would go soon. "Injoostice," he whispered to himself, and looked back, almost fondly, at Flo's door.

Watching the jeep disappear through a square of window, Flo clutched the robe to her throat and exhaled. He could have taken a very tough line with her, and then what? Her eyes traveled to the loggia and she saw Señora Coyopan in the shadows of the utility room. As the jeep's dust settled, the small woman stepped out, a mop and pail in hand. She looked directly back to Flo's window. Flo positioned herself to catch the woman's look. They stared at each other for ten seconds, then Flo shook her head slowly, from side to side. Señora Coyopan nodded in response and walked away.

At his house De Luca awoke groggily from a nap. Catherine was still watching Televisa Mexico which broadcast the subtitled American sitcoms. Archie Bunker was beloved by the locals, who thought his ideas represented the best of American thinking. Laverne and Shirley were recognized as neighborhood types but perceived, however, as young men dressed as young women.

He looked at his watch. Almost eleven-thirty. Quickly he threw on his clothes. Downstairs his father was reading *Playboy* and listening to *Tosca*. Seeing his son pass, the elder De Luca called, "Mikey—you all right? You got a funny look on your face."

De Luca waved without reply, hurried to his car, raced to the compound with anxiety, where he routed Paul from his machines, and finally they turned toward Elvira's.

The night was untypically cloudy as the Porsche droned along, steel top up. The Sierra Madre, brooding in shadow, ringed the valley with a gray wall. Paul slumped in his seat and stared at the new asphalt flying by, illuminated by the powerful halogen driving lights. He glanced over to De Luca and wondered, with a measure of resentment, why he would offer Stella a job that would keep her in Oacala.

De Luca, catching the look, asked, "Nervous?"

"A little."

"Me too."

On the right, a ramshackle hut, dark and boarded up, swept into view. A crudely lettered sign identified it as a *"Restaurante."*

"Right in the middle of nowhere," Paul marveled.

"Mexican version of Howard Johnson's."

They drove the next swift ten kilometers in silence, Paul looking dead ahead. The night, the rushing air and the rhythm of the wheels induced lazy speculation. What if Aguillar could not help? What happened with the undeclared war then? Could it actually cause a halt in the production? If that happened, what would become of the newly opened door?

From the road behind, two pinpoints of light became visible. Turning to look through the rear window, Paul called in alarm, "Mike, there's a car behind us."

De Luca stared intently into the rearview mirror. He slowed deliberately, and the points of light grew brighter. His hands tightened on the wheel.

"You think they're following us?"

"I don't know."

Paul kept his head turned, watching the lights grow larger, more haloed. He began to feel his pulse thrum in time with the wheels. Michael said, "Let's just keep going and see. If we have to, we can outrun them in this."

He kept his speed steady, and the oncoming headlamps signaled a rapid closing. Paul watched with rising apprehension until he could bear it no longer and gripped Michael's arm.

"They're coming right up."

The headlights behind him glared fiercely, creating a blaze of circular spokes, but he was able to see, through the blaze, the huge American sedan to which the lights were attached. De Luca, tense, moved his hand to the gearshift. Peering at the approaching car, Paul made out two swarthy men in the front seat who, it seemed, were staring at him. Not checking speed as it overtook the little sports car, the sedan hung on the bumper, inches away, and Paul shouted, "Mike!"

De Luca was about to jam his foot down on the accelerator when the sedan's high beams flashed and flashed again in warning. A raucous blast from its horn split the night. De Luca twisted to the right. His car wrenched to the dirt shoulder. With that, the American sedan shot through the space and raced on, its rear red flashes fading and disappearing, rapidly.

"Wow," Paul said. "Jesus." He slumped back in his seat.

149

"You can say that again." The Porsche moved back onto the road, picking up speed. "Just your normal Mexican driver passing someone."

"How many do they kill a year?"

"A lot."

After that they ate up the highway until the new asphalt changed to old asphalt and narrowed, with no warning, to a bone-jouncing single-lane narrow roadway which made De Luca slow down. As he geared to third he glanced, automatically, behind him. A single, feeble headlamp bounced erratically in the rearview mirror. Paul saw the look on his face and turned to the small window.

"That's a motorcycle," De Luca said grimly, "and it's following us."

"We thought the car—" Paul objected, but the single light was low and unmistakably in motion.

"No." De Luca was angry. "That thing *is* following us, I know it is." He rammed the gas pedal all the way to the floorboards. The Porsche jerked violently forward, roaring in complaint, the tires squealing and smoking with sudden acceleration. Paul fell against the door heavily.

"Hold on," De Luca gritted, "tight."

He kept the pedal down as Paul grabbed for the steadying bar. The Porsche, recovering traction, fled like a miniature speed car on a toy track, engine buzzing, pulling even this road under its wheels. In seconds the single light had vanished completely. De Luca slowed, guided the Porsche along the last four kilometers to Elvira's.

Paul, shaken, looked at him inquiringly. "What makes you think that whatever it was was following us?"

"Because it happened the other night," he answered grimly. "I was showing Tecla to Stella and there it was. Somebody is trying to track us." He shook his head.

It took Paul a full minute, as they negotiated the last hundred yards to Elvira's house, twisting through a grove of powerfully scented lemon trees, to absorb what De Luca had said, to understand that Stella had gone with him to the Monte, at night. By that time they were out of the car and near the house. De Luca's digital watch read twelve-ten and there was no parked car in sight, but neither of the men acknowledged their fears. They continued on, hurriedly, through the small garden and onto the patio. With-

150

out warning, the front door opened. Elvira stood haloed by back-light, her hair braided, her blue *huipil* blending with the shadows.

"Not yet," she said softly.

Both men looked at each other in relief, and De Luca led the way into the house, going quickly to the parlor. There, he went directly to a window, lifted the curtain, parted the shutter and peeked out.

"You wish something?" Elvira asked. "I make you coffee?"

Paul, feeling like a stump in the middle of the room, shook his head. De Luca dropped the curtain and walked about anxiously, hoping that nothing had gone wrong. He stopped pacing finally, looked at his mistress and thought that a little Cuervo Gold wouldn't hurt. Elvira nodded and went to the kitchen. He started walking again, pulling on his beard. Paul sat down in an over-stuffed armchair and looked at the room. It was as cozy here, in its own fashion as domestic as De Luca's big house. Somehow, Paul noted, wherever he lived, he *lived*.

There was silence until Elvira returned with the tequila and glasses. De Luca, pouring, frowned at the girl's solemn mask and said, "Take it easy. The man we're meeting is a friend. He is not coming to hurt us."

"If you say."

She had just moved away from the sideboard when they heard footsteps in the hall. Paul rose tautly from the chair. De Luca sucked in his breath. The steps hesitated, then started again, faster. The hall was only six paces long but Paul felt it stretch out end-lessly. Finally, there was the thump of a boot, and Luis Aguillar appeared in the arched entranceway, alone.

"*Buenas noches,*" he said, coming over quickly to the men. "I am happy to see you again."

He wrapped De Luca in an embrace, then shook hands with Paul. He turned to Elvira and nodded. She bowed her head, lowered her eyes and left the room. He moved easily to the tequila. "Ah . . . very good, very good." He poured a glass, held it up. "*Salud.*"

De Luca repeated the toast and Paul, feeling uncomfortable, pronounced the word.

"So." The Mexican removed his rolled-brim straw hat and sank into the chair Paul had vacated. "I have heard about what is happening to you. I have much *simpatía.*"

151

"Luis"—De Luca seated himself next to Aguillar and leaned forward intensely—"we need help. We are suffering badly. This must stop."

"Absolutely."

"Can you explain my position to these people? Can you tell them all my life I've tried to help ordinary people, not hurt them?"

"Can you tell them," Paul added, "that if they keep on doing what they're doing, it will be very bad for all of us?"

"Ah—" Aguillar slapped the arm of the chair with his hat and jerked up. "The problem is that the people who do this are ignorant politically. They do not think as we do. It is hard to explain revolutionary politics to them. You understand?"

"Yes." De Luca spoke with force. "But they must know their real friends from their enemies. Or where will your movement be?"

"It is true, they must." The Mexican was vehement. "All the forces must become one for success."

"Can you get to the leaders, the ones who give the orders?"

Aguillar pondered. "I do not know these men myself, but believe me, I will find them. And I will speak to them and make them understand."

"They must respect you," Paul ventured.

"Sí." Aguillar leaned back, suddenly morose. "But I have so many problems to do even little things to help conditions—to escape the *policía,* to get people to come with me to the Sierra Madre. We have need of so much and we have so little." He fell into a musing silence.

De Luca looked at Paul questioningly, and Paul felt the answer come to him. He leaned forward. "If there's anything we can do . . ."

Aguillar looked up and said, quietly, "You have already given us from your heart."

De Luca jumped in. "Not enough. Whatever I gave the other time, I'll double that. More, but the money comes from what I do, the cinema I make, and if I'm prevented from making that cinema . . ."

"Of course," Aguillar said strongly. "This must be explained. I will have a meeting with those responsible. It will be understood, believe me."

From somewhere outside an automobile engine throttled loudly up and then down. Instantly the Mexican rose from the chair, his hand going fluidly to a place inside his zipper jacket and emerging

152

with a forty-five automatic. He waved Paul and De Luca down, moving quickly to the window. Elvira came into the archway, wide-eyed, but disappeared almost instantly.

At the window Aguillar waited, pistol in hand. The night sounds, soft breeze, crickets and a horned owl's hoot topped by coughing cylinders seemed incredibly loud to Paul as he crouched by a chair. With a high ping, the engine stopped, and Aguillar's body tensed appreciably. Abruptly, the engine fired up again, the sound of a faulty gear plain in its high, clipped whine. There was a screech of tires, and the engine cough began to lessen until it was almost inaudible. Then there were only natural sounds again.

Aguillar turned back from the window, replacing his pistol. As the Americans rose up from the floor, he shook his head sadly.

"Forgive me, *amigos*. Please. I worry much for the *federales*. They have their spies everywhere." He rubbed two fingers together. "They buy everyone."

"Luis," De Luca whispered, unhappily, "I'm being followed. For sure at night. But maybe in the daytime too. And it wouldn't be the police."

Aguillar's face creased with despair. "Stupid *idiotas*. When I have so much already, when there are so many worries about my own people—" His eyes snapped open and he said, almost breathless with his idea, "Miguel, it is possible that you can be much help to us, to someone, a friend, who is important, someone who does much for the movement."

"What kind of help?" De Luca took on Aguillar's hushed yet excited tones.

"Listen to me." Aguillar moved closer to his listeners. "With us is a fighter, a man who is called Jesus. He is almost killed two times by the *policía*." His eyes settled on Paul. "He is a little like you, like your age. He leaves his wife and two children to come with me to the sierra." Paul saw that Elvira had returned and was standing in the archway, listening.

"Jesus makes an action for us. He goes to bring money to one of our men the *policía* arrest. This money is for *mordida*, bribes, so maybe our man can get away. But the *policía* discover Jesus is coming and they set a trap to catch him. It is only with the help of God that he runs away from them with two bullets in him. But they see him and know who he is, so he must hide. We send him to a little hut in the mountains. But he is very sick now and must come out, go to a doctor, or . . ." He shook his head in despair.

"What can we do?" De Luca asked. Paul, glimpsing Elvira, saw that her lips were taut.

"I have this idea." Aguillar gripped De Luca's knee, intensely. "Jesus cannot walk. And it is dangerous to take him out by burro because the *policía* look everywhere on the trails. Now hear me; all the *policía* know you use the helicopters from Vietnam. You fly here, you fly there, you fly all over; everyone says there goes the cinema people. So, if one of your machines flies, sometime, to where Jesus is, no one thinks to have a suspicion of you. Then the machine goes down, takes him up. It flies away again, quick, goes with him to another spot where our people wait to take him to a village far away, safe." The Mexican stopped his flow. "You think this is *loco?*"

De Luca swung toward Paul, excitement in his eyes. "What do you think?"

"It's . . . quite a scheme," Paul said, but instant pictures whirled in his head—federal spotter planes tracking the helicopter . . . a missed rendezvous and police alert . . . a mechanical malfunction and exposure.

"It's a contribution. A real contribution and not just money." De Luca's voice was huskily emotional.

"The whole movement will give you thanks," Aguillar said quietly.

"It'll take planning, coordination." De Luca rose from the chair, unable to contain his ferment.

"Yes, much."

De Luca took a moment, then decided. "But it can be done." He swung toward Paul. "Denny. He can land a helicopter on a dime." Astonished into numbness by what he was hearing, Paul contributed a nod.

"This man flew in Vietnam," De Luca explained to Aguillar.

"I will arrange it. We will make a time. Your man will go to a spot on the map. Jesus makes a smoke fire for signal." The Mexican's excitement, rising to match De Luca's, pulled him from his chair as well.

"Denny comes down, swoops him up."

"Jesus will know where to go. He will tell your flier and they will go there. When they get to the spot, a car will wait."

"Jesus goes off. Denny hits the air again and comes home."

De Luca and Aguillar complemented each other line for line, developing the scenario. Like a story conference, Paul thought, exactly. Only this was real. And, probably, precisely the way the CIA invented its schemes.

Visibly moved by De Luca's response, Aguillar said, "I tell you that we never forget this. And I make sure that the ignorant fools who hurt you stop their actions so you can make your cinema as you should. But now for the sake of Jesus, we must do this plan soon."

"I'm ready whenever you are," De Luca said.

"*Bueno. Bueno.*"

"How do we get the information for Denny Burns?"

Paul drew himself into the conspiracy, into the circle. De Luca flashed the Mexican a questioning look. He responded by glancing toward Elvira, who had not moved.

"We will use this house. We send here the information you must know. We send it soon." He continued as though she were ignorant of English. "She will help us, I know."

Paul saw the merest change come over the girl's eyes, though her expression remained as composed as ever. "Of course she'll help," De Luca said.

"So." The Mexican placed his hat on his head and stretched out a firm hand for Paul. "I go now." Paul shook the hand and said, "Good-bye, good luck." To De Luca, the Mexican raised a clenched fist in silent salute, then disappeared through the archway, the outside door opening and closing with the softest of sounds.

"What a man—what balls!" De Luca called out. Paul felt less euphoric, but there was no denying the impressive presence. And he had agreed to help; that was the all-important key. As for the price—

"What are you going to tell Denny?"

De Luca laughed. "The truth. He couldn't care less about politics; he'll do what's needed because it might be dangerous and he hasn't had that for a long time now."

Paul laughed with him; he was right. Elvira stepped carefully into the parlor and over to the sideboard. De Luca pulled her braids playfully.

"Elvirita, *mi paloma*, Luis Aguillar—*that* is an *hombre.*"

"Sí," the girl said, "he is an *hombre.*"

It was a simple agreement, but as she bent over to refill the glasses with tequila, Paul saw a shade of worry come into her eyes.

He didn't blame her.

CHAPTER

16

═╳═══╳═══╳═══╳═══╳═══ **16** ═══╳═══╳═══╳═══╳═══╳═

At half-past two, as an errant rooster opened its throat somewhere on Oacala's back streets and competing boasts rose to shatter the night silence, Manuel Quesedo was drinking California
champagne in the Red House on Calle Libertad. He had not come
to enjoy any of the girls—a courtesy Señora Revueltas accorded him
from time to time; he was there on business—although a new girl
from the north attracted his eye. In this house each girl had her
costumed specialty. One dressed as an American teen in bobby
socks, short skirts and pigtails; another enveloped herself totally in
duenna black, a tortoiseshell comb in her tightly bunned smoothed
hair; another in a man's suit and bow tie, her hair cropped, appealed to gamier tastes. In this house that catered to respectable
fantasies, the new girl had long, curled, dazzlingly blond hair. She
wore high-cut black satin shorts and a red leather mask over part of
her face. A small whip protruded from her scarlet coachman's
boots, and she sat at the bar staring at the room in the smoked
mirror.

Quesedo amused himself, while he waited for the girl in the
orange room to finish with her customer, by speculating which of
the dozen prosperous men in the large red-and-gilt salon would
choose the masked blonde. He thought it would be the thin, effete
son of a wealthy landowner, but it turned out to be the heavyset
garage proprietor, pitter of champion fighting cocks, who approached her.

Very soon after the couple went upstairs, Señora Revueltas,
heavy-bodied and sparkling from hundreds of rhinestoned nooks
and crannies, told him the girl he wished to speak with had finished
with her client and was washing up. She was a good girl, the señora
chided, and never in any trouble. The captain assured her it was

a friendly chat he was after, finished his champagne and mounted the curving staircase to the second floor and the orange room.

The girl was tall with violently dyed vermilion hair. In the salon she dressed as a movie star in a long black dress slit to the waist, stiletto-heeled ankle-strapped shoes and a chiffon scarf wound around her throat. Here, she wore a faded purple wrapper and sat on the rumpled brass bed, arms folded against her thin chest, her small round face showing a peasant coarseness and a degree of worry.

Quesedo closed the door and, hands in his pockets, stood over her, rocking on his heels. She was frightened, he gauged, which was good.

"Maria," he began familiarly, "you know who I am?"

The girl nodded.

"Good. Good. Now, Maria, you have family in the Muraga district, eh?"

"My mother." She barely breathed the words.

"Speak to me," Quesedo ordered. "Louder."

"My mother."

"Good. You go to see her, eh, Maria?"

"She is my mother."

"Of course. You went two days ago."

The girl nodded again. Quesedo continued rocking.

"It has come to my attention, Maria, that while you visit, a man comes there, a man who does not walk well." He saw the shadow come over the girl's eyes and stopped rocking. "No lies. Tell me no lies."

The shadow left. "No."

"You must tell me only true things, for this is serious." Quesedo rocked again. "What does this man call himself?"

"He calls himself Carlos."

"And what does this Carlos talk about?"

"Just . . . talk."

He took a step toward the girl, who pulled back. Leaning down so that his face was an inch from hers, he could see how dry her lips were and the forehead already damp.

"Tell me the talk." He locked her eyes in place.

She swallowed, licked her lips. "He talks of . . . the maize."

"And?"

"And of his uncle in the mountains."

"And?"

"And his friend who is hurt when he cuts down a tree."

"And?"

The girl stopped talking.

"And?" Quesedo asked implacably. "And what does he say of the people who make the cinema?"

"He says—" The girl opened her mouth soundlessly and shut it again. Once more her mouth gaped, but no sound emerged. She shut it. Still staring deeply into the girl's eyes, Quesedo pushed his face forward slowly, hypnotically. Suddenly, *his* mouth opened and his teeth clamped onto the girl's cheek, held the flesh warningly in a steel-jacketed grip. The girl froze, closing her eyes in terror. For half a minute he held her that way, then gently released her and rose up, waiting. The girl spoke quickly, her eyes still closed, her voice quavering.

"He says . . . he says the cinema people are bad. They do bad things."

"Ah . . ." Quesedo nodded. "So he is against them. What else does he say?"

The girl opened her eyes but looked beyond Quesedo. "He says something very bad will happen to them soon."

"How soon? How soon?"

"He says very soon." The girl's hand went to her cheek, fingered the marks.

Quesedo, in his excitement, leaned down again. "And what will happen?"

"He does not say."

He repeated the question, louder.

The girl's eyes began to water. "He does not say more. Please."

"You are sure?"

"That is all he says," the girl cried out. "For the love of God . . ."

Quesedo stood up and considered. He let the girl sob for a moment, then he asked, "When do you see this Carlos before?"

"Never. I never see him before."

"Why does he come to your mother's hut?"

"He brings charcoal." The girl wiped the water from her eyes with an edge of the wrapper. "The man who comes always is sick and does not come, so this man comes."

Quesedo nodded, turning away from the limp girl, satisfied. He had been led to this man with one leg shorter than the other but had been unsure. This was confirmation. They would find him now and see. But what the girl reported was disturbing.

"Something happens very soon that is bad, eh?"

Another nod.

He reached out a hand. With a reflexive cry the girl jerked her head back, the breath going out of her. She gulped air rapidly, almost hysterically, wheezing and coughing. He waited until she had recovered and was looking at him with cowering, blotched eyes. Then he patted the cheek he had taken into his mouth.

"You are a good girl, Maria. We will speak again."

Leaving the girl stunned on the bed, Quesedo walked out to the corridor, his mind occupied with what he must do to prevent blame to himself for whatever happened. Passing a door, he heard a slight whimpering and, for a moment, it diverted him to picture the masked girl ministering to her client, the bulldog garage owner, his moment of ecstasy. But as he descended the brothel steps to his jeep, a nagging depression attacked him, a depression that not even his bed and the ample though lumpy body of his wife could shake off.

At one point during the night in bed, alone, at the hotel, Paul leaped from sleep, his body sweaty. Eyes wide, he tried vainly to recall what fear had thrust him awake. He fell asleep again, but in those lucid moments between the rigidity of fright and the enveloping surrender he heard some unidentifiable voice and had some undefined premonition.

At the compound Paul found, everywhere, a buzz of worried conversation. During the night, three transport drivers had made their own sweep of the area, during which they had spotted two Mexicans near a locked camera van. They had charged but the Mexicans had run off, eluding their pursuers, while the police guards, sitting under a tree around the corner, were listening to American rock-'n'-roll tapes on a cassette machine. Kodály, in fear that his stock of raw film had been tampered with, was checking and rechecking. Everything seemed in proper order, but the incident, after the lull, triggered a renewed sense of insecurity and frustration.

In his cutting room, Paul learned that his assistant, Rick, had been involved in a frightening incident a few nights earlier while cruising in the hitherto congenial erogenous zone of the Zócalo's north side. At one point he had noted two heavily macho men following him. Assuming *he* was being cruised, he slowed, at which point the men sped at him. One of them had whirled him around

159

as the other slapped him hard, shouting, *"Gringo degenerado,"* a phrase Rick was not unfamiliar with. He had managed to pull away from the attackers and return home safe but trembling. That had never happened before. He was convinced it was connected to the company, to what was happening; they had picked him out, knew who he was. From now on it could be intolerable. Panicked, he talked of quitting, getting out before he ended up in a back alley, not so much a martyr to Gay as to De Luca's movie. Paul managed to calm him, but hurrying to the morning production meeting, he thought Rick was right to be frightened. He hoped Aguillar's contacts would extend to the Zócalo's north streets.

The meeting, he discovered, had been delayed; Michael was closeted with the police captain, and Paul was to join them. When he entered the office, Quesedo's voice was deeply serious. He had private information he had to relay—a warning to give. Something very bad was going to happen and very soon. He had been told this by the most reliable of sources. De Luca, however, was not impressed.

"It's all changed, captain. As of last night. It's all going to be taken care of."

"You t'ink?" Quesedo looked skeptical.

"Oh, yes."

"But last night comes here two *hombres*—"

"While your men were laid back. But the message just hadn't been sent yet, you see."

"The man we saw last night," Paul added, "has to make *his* contacts."

"Who is this man you see who knows so much?"

"It doesn't matter."

"It is joost interesting that you can to find such a man and I cannot—yet."

The policeman was still fishing, but Michael wasn't likely to give him an inch. "Not everybody loves the police," he threw in. Michael grinned and even Quesedo smiled politely, but plodded on.

"Such a man who can to take care of such bad t'ings . . ."

"He's a friend." De Luca drummed on his desk, impatiently. "Let's leave it at that."

As the door closed behind the policeman, Paul said, "Cat and mouse."

"He's the cat," Michael said, "and he'd like to eat Luis whole.

160

Oh—" He drew a thick manuscript from the center drawer of his desk. "Remember when I talked about something I had in mind?" He shook the pages. "This is a screenplay I wrote two years ago. It's not something I want to direct myself anymore. Maybe after we finish Jericho you'd want to take a crack at it . . . if you like it, that is."

Paul's mouth opened and stayed that way.

De Luca laughed. "I love big reactions. Now, you could make it for my company, under my umbrella. I'd be executive producer, that kind of thing, but it would really be your picture—if you like the script."

"Are you serious?" He came back to earth. "You could sell that thing to a studio for God knows how much."

"You will like it, I think." He slid the screenplay back into the drawer. "You can read it sometime."

"Michael . . ." It was impossible to know what to say.

De Luca smiled and closed the drawer. "Now, let's try to keep everybody cool at the meeting."

Sal Sieberling had spent the last twenty-four hours tracking down the identities of the two women Paul had seen with Flo Ankrum. One was, as Paul remembered her, a camera apprentice, a twenty-four-year-old dark-haired wraith of a woman who was infatuated with light and described emotional states in prismatic terms. The other was a thirty-eight-year-old wardrobe woman, barren, unmarried and achingly maternal. She had spent many nights mulling over the possibilities of going back home with one of the limpideyed, grave-faced four-year-olds who held out their hands to her, palms up, in silent beggars' reproof.

Sieberling had fired both women on the spot, given them one day to pack and pick up their air tickets to Los Angeles. Shocked and bewildered, faced with unstated charges and veiled threats, feeling the ground cut out from under them, the women agreed to go and never speak of company affairs. At twelve-thirty Sieberling was at the Oacala airport making certain both women were on the flight to Mexico City. Only after the plane swept up, giddily, to clear the sierra, did he start back.

After returning from a visit to a native weaver, Flo learned what had occurred from messages left by the already departed women. Enraged to the point of tears, exploding with frustration, she called

161

her lover to rail at this latest display, by Sieberling, of his vileness.

"And I know why he fired them," she said. "Oh, Allan, it's so unfair."

Nothing Allan Marcus could say would console her. When he suggested lunch, she slammed the phone down, checked the time, ran back outside to her Volkswagen and ground her way through the traffic to the movie theater. Parking down the street, slumping low, she captured her frizzed hair in a rebozo in an attempt to make herself less distinct and waited. Usually, near this time, Rennie would come by to make certain the daily films had been delivered to the projectionist. Flo hoped this would be a day like all others and she might have ten minutes with her before anyone showed up. When Rennie arrived, Flo raced to intercept her before she could enter the theater. Swerving to a stop, she leaned out and called her name. Rennie looked up, startled. Flo swung the car door open.

"Please, I can't stay here, you know that, but I have to talk to you."

"Call me later."

Flo jerked the rebozo loose and hurled it to the floor. "Yvonne and Thelma have been fired, Rennie. Not only that, they're already gone. That bastard Sieberling kicked them out like dogs."

"I'm sorry. I really am." Rennie was soothingly calm and obviously not surprised at all.

"You knew?"

"I heard some stories."

Flo stared, defused momentarily. Rennie shook her head warningly. "You're going to give yourself hives carrying on like this."

"You know why they were canned?" Flo cried out. "Because they were my friends, that's the only reason."

"Flo, you could have been home with no fuss or feathers, instead of here. You know how uptight people are over what's been happening, but you come driving into the compound, pick up your friends . . ."

"Ah—I was spotted. Of course." She clamped a hand on Rennie's shoulder for contact. "And the rat told the wolf and the wolf went right after the lambs. What was it his business anyhow?"

"Flo, why don't you just go home? What are you trying to prove? All Michael is hoping is to make the best movie ever on Vietnam."

"Oh, Lord." Flo wanted to shout but restrained herself. "Everything for Michael's movie. Anything for Michael's movie."

162

"I've got to go now."

Rennie walked away stiffly. Flo called after her, "It *was* Gordon who told them, wasn't it?"

She watched the slim figure disappear into the theater and felt bereft, stripped of function and friendship, robbed of purpose and filled only with the thumping anger she had brought with her.

Stella's morning had been spent in contemplation, a peace allowed by the efficacy of the medicine Paul had provided. Later, with the absence of discomfort and the accompanying bout of self-pity, a more hard-headed reality began to assert itself. She had moved by instinct—a motivation not exactly her most productive—into an untenable situation thousands of miles from home. She was an intruder in this complicated nest, and what did she hope to accomplish here? What was she reading into Paul now that she could not, apparently, have him? Was this Rennie really good for him? What did it matter? Head-to-toe muddled, she put the coffee cup down hard and set her mind to linear cerebration. A glimmer of the inevitable shimmered. Direct action was called for.

She marched to the lobby and approached the small catercorner desk of the Tecla Travel Service. The desk was unoccupied, as it almost always was at any time of the day or night. The travel agent, mysterious and slick as one of his posters, kept his office hours to himself. It took a determinedly patient traveler to catch him in the act of working, what with siestas and fiestas, christenings, weddings and deaths; he was a devoted holidaymaker and today was no exception.

When she asked the desk clerk at what hour the agent was expected, she received the bright smile and the eternal "Soon, madame."

She had been sitting for fifteen minutes when she heard a female voice speak Paul's name and saw a young woman writing a note that was to be put into his box. She signed it, sealed it well, handed it to the clerk and turned to go back to the brass-framed doors of the Jaime.

As the woman came on, Stella examined her with interest. Was she before Rennie? Or was she current as well? Why not? De Luca managed to juggle expertly and Paul, in his orbit now, might be trying the same moves. Dispassion vanishing, she felt the small hairs on the back of her neck rise and stared, openly hostile, as

163

the woman came almost abreast of her. At her knee the woman paused, in some seeming confusion, pushed the glasses back on her nose and, bending toward her, said, "Excuse me?"

"Oh, I'm sorry," Stella covered. "I was staring into space, that's all."

"That's okay." The woman started off and Stella, feeling herself in command, said, "I just happened to hear you leaving a note for Paul Gordon."

"Oh?" The woman turned back and was instantly apprehensive.

"I happen to be a friend of his," Stella said, "a friend from New York."

"Oh," the woman repeated, then with surprise, she said, "You're *her*."

"I'm who?" Stella sat up.

"You're Paul's New York lady, ex-lady, all right. I heard about you from someone I know very well. I used to work with Paul. My name's Flo Ankrum."

The words tumbled out eagerly, as though there were other, more important words waiting behind them. Stella was slightly discomfited and nodded formally.

"Hello. I'm Stella . . ."

"I was fired off the picture," Flo rattled on, "for no reason except that De Luca's a fascist. Now, two friends of mine have been fired— and shipped out. Because of Paul, I think." She plunked herself down on the couch. "Can I talk to you? I really would like to talk to you."

Stella took in the energetic hair and the flashing eyes. Not Paul, she decided; this would not be a choice Paul would make. "Talk about what?"

"About Paul. About what happened. It's so important."

Stella hesitated. There was an unsettling quality about this young woman so filled with tension, but there was also an eagerness and deep need that was appealing. She took Flo back to the restaurant, ordered strawberries. Flo wanted only talk.

Hunched over the table setting, she told Stella how she had worked with Paul when he first came to Oacala, how she had felt he was a good man, how, in a matter of weeks, so much about him had altered, altered enough for him to have been the hatchet man who fired her without cause, altered enough for him to have become the instrument through which her friends had been brutally dismissed. She had come here to ask him why he had done this.

Her note asked for a confidential meeting; she had to confront him.

"Hold it," Stella told her. "Are you sure of what you're saying?"

"He's Michael's man," Flo insisted, "and you have to know what kind of contempt Michael really has for people in order to understand how . . . evil this all is."

Stella felt she was hearing about someone she did not know. To begin with, Paul had never been resolute enough about anything to do something even remotely evil. In addition, this woman was talking about a man sensing a career opportunity and grabbing at it with eager hands. Not Paul. A distortion of Paul seen in a funhouse mirror, perhaps, but not Paul.

"You're wrong," Flo persisted bluntly. "He's going to be as dangerous as Michael, as harmful as Sieberling. I just want you to know that."

"Dangerous?" Stella swallowed a berry carefully. "I think you're a little out of balance right now."

"No." Flo jiggled in her chair. "De Luca's hated here. Since I left the company I learned a lot about what's happening to this town."

"What is happening?"

"People have gone to prison, people have been hurt, corrupted."

"What has that got to do with Paul?"

"He's part of it now, don't you see?"

Stella clanked her spoon down to the china. "You're talking about a man you've just about met and I'm talking about a man I know— or used to know," she tacked on.

Flo flopped back, disjointed, limply vulnerable.

"Have a strawberry." Stella inched the dish forward across the table, and surprisingly, Flo took one.

Stella watched her chew for a moment. "Can you tell me," she asked cautiously, "a little about Rennie?"

Flo fingered her glasses. "Rennie's all right. She's messed up but she's all right."

"What do you mean 'messed up'?"

"Michael is her god, the artist wanting perfection. Her mission is to help him any way she can—crap like that." She put another large red berry into her mouth.

"But"—Stella stepped carefully—"he dropped her."

"So what?" Flo said impatiently. "That's not important. She still feels he's . . . oh . . . up there in the clouds. He's just a man, goddamn it. If Rennie would just get that through her head . . .

He's used her. But she doesn't give a damn. That's messed up."

"And Paul?" Her voice was calm but the queasiness had returned to her stomach.

Flo looked at her searchingly. "I guess she's made him . . . part of Michael."

"If you're so disappointed in Paul," she felt the need to ask, "why are you leaving him notes?"

"To get to him." Flo, quiveringly, leaped on that. "To make him understand what he's done, and what else he might do."

"You listen to me." Stella's voice turned tight. "I do not believe that Paul would knowingly do something brutal to anyone."

"Okay." Flo rose up like an avenging angel. "You'll find out." She shoved the chair back and strode rapidly across the dining room, disappearing quickly.

Stella saw then that the travel agent had arrived, but she did not go to him.

Two days passed during which Stella, in sneakers, did her best to be a good tourist. It took much effort. Twice she received messages that De Luca had called. She ignored them.

Somewhat unaccustomed to unreturned calls, De Luca asked if Stella had left Oacala. Paul reported that he didn't think so.

"She's ducking me," Michael said ruefully. "Now that's not nice."

The production drove ahead. De Luca utilized every daylight hour. Night shooting lasted till dawn. As main sequences progressed, Allan Marcus kept pace with his second unit. Plans were speeded up for the flooding of the rice-paddy location. Drawings were completed for the Jericho sequence. Paul was more involved than he had ever been, and De Luca picked out another short but important dramatic scene for him to cut his directorial teeth on.

In this burst of activity it became natural for Paul to transmit De Luca's orders, to check on other departmental progress if Sieberling was unavailable. Faced with squabbles, he found himself able to cut through by announcing icily that "Mike wants it this way," or "We all have to shape up or we'll all be shipped out." The cold approach worked miracles. Even Sal Sieberling was impressed. For Paul it was a game played with hesitation at first. But as he became more familiar with the rules and more comfortable

166

with the role, he hesitated less and understood what Michael meant by "them" against him. Above all, there was the picture, to which Michael was allowing him to contribute on so many levels that every frame would hold some small imprint of his own. There was never a high like it.

When, toward the end of the week, cutting across the Zócalo, he came face to face with Stella, he felt fortified, equipped to be open and honest. Falling into step, guiding her away from a pile of steaming burro dung, he asked how long she intended staying in Oacala. She answered that she might leave on the next day or she might stay on, she didn't know. It was not exactly what he wanted to hear. His arm uncomfortably on Stella's elbow, they stepped carefully to the corner, where they waited for a vintage bus, gasping for air, to move. There, he turned to her.

"Stella, can we be honest with one another?"

"Well, let's try." She bent down to rub her ankles. "Touring is horribly hard work, it really is."

"Right," he agreed. "Let's rest here."

A small, open-air café held the choice corner spot, in perfect position to absorb all the exhaust fumes of the Zócalo. They dropped into chairs and he ordered coffee.

"Stel, listen to me. I'm not sure you came down here just to see Monte Tecla."

"Not just," Stella admitted.

"Not just. Okay. What else did you have in mind?"

"I don't know," she said a little tremulously. "That's the truth. I came on impulse."

He nodded. That was honest. He decided to be even more so. "Stel, I'm not thrilled you're here. It makes me uncomfortable. Maybe it's rotten of me to feel that way, but I do."

The coffee came then and obviated any necessity for an immediate response. Stella sipped, put sugar in, sipped again, put more sugar in, stirred. Finally she asked, "How's the work going?"

"Good, but that's not what I want to talk about."

She put her cup down, searched for a cigarette. "I was speaking to someone who used to work with you. Flo—somebody or other."

"What?" Unbelievable.

"She said some things about you"—Stella shook her head sadly— "about changes you've undergone since you've been working with De Luca . . . not very flattering."

Paul opened his mouth to explode a reply, but a wizened girl of eight or nine came up to the table, waving bark paintings at them. "No," he said angrily. *"No quiero. No."*

"Muy bonito, señor."

"Damn it, no!"

The shout was almost loud enough to be heard over the traffic sounds. Half the café patrons grinned at each other. Embarrassed, Paul gave the girl ten pesos and waved her off. She moved away, slightly spastic and satisfied.

"My God," Stella said, "that child . . ."

"Never mind her," he managed to say fairly quietly. "Let me tell you about Flo Ankrum."

"She said De Luca was a fascist and you—"

"She's crazy!"

"She said—"

"She's a foolish kid," he broke in. "She shouldn't be in Oacala at all. She should have been gone by now."

Stella opened her eyes wide. "Really."

"Michael wanted her out of here, but she wouldn't go. Now she hangs around being bad news. This picture is tough enough without anyone making it tougher." His anger had found a fine displaced target and now it steamed over. "Doesn't she care at all for what we're trying to do with this picture?"

Watching him, Stella concluded that he had found religion, movie-making religion. You didn't argue with religious people, so she kept silent. Paul, however, went on, saying, "Rennie says—" Realizing the gaffe, he stopped in mid-sentence, but it was enough to dissolve Stella's resolution.

"Rennie says what—boil the girl in oil?"

He shook his head in despair.

"Well, what does she say?"

"She doesn't criticize me, look for the faults. I can tell you that."

"Oh." Stella collapsed. "I see."

"I know," Paul said, unhappily, "that there were always things about me that bugged you."

"Oh, I bugged you, too," Stella murmured, "but there were other things, for both of us."

"Yes," he admitted.

She toyed with the coffee cup. "So, that girl is all wrong about you."

168

"Doesn't matter. What matters is the picture."

"That was her point."

"I don't want to talk about her."

"She said Rennie made a tin god of your De Luca . . ."

"Rennie's ways are bad, right?" He kept his voice low. "They have to be bad—because they're not yours."

That stopped her and she took a deep, hurting breath.

He leaned across the table. "I think you ought to leave Oacala, I really do."

"And take Flo with me?" She regretted saying that the moment she let the words out.

He bristled instantly and tossed some coins to the table with such violence that one spun off to roll away on the pavement. "I never could budge you." With that he rose and walked across the Zócalo. Watching him go across the plaza, tears started to pump in Stella's eyes. She pawed at the flow and asked herself, with despairing sternness, what she was doing to them both, but she had no answer.

The answer, part of it, came only when she returned to the hotel, where she snatched drawers open, piled the panty hose, the socks, the blouses, the bikinis and bras on the bed, ready to pack. She wrenched open the closet door, stepped into the cedar vastness and dragged her three dresses from the wire hangers. She hurled the three pairs of shoes and the two pairs of sandals from their repository and was stalking into the bathroom to lay steaming hands upon the scattered cosmetics, soaps, shampoo and Braun International hair drier when the telephone jangled.

De Luca chuckled over the wire. "Ah . . . got you."

"I don't have much time," she said.

"Neither do I. But I want to set our deal."

"What?"

"The job." De Luca laughed outright. "Remember?"

"I don't believe you." She sank to the bed.

"Believe me. I'm always serious. I need you and I want you. But you know that already."

"But I told you . . ." Stella began plaintively, then stopped. Satisfying visions presented themselves. The irrationality boiled over. The urge to strike back, somehow to hurt, grew, swelled within her like a mushroom under rain, excited and finally possessed her. She could hardly, when she spoke, get the words out.

"All right. I agree. Let's do it. Let's make a deal."

"What?" His voice held initial disbelief, then jubilation. "Terrific. Really terrific."

"I mean," she said, wavering momentarily, "let's make some kind of . . . temporary deal . . . so I can explore if I can really be of any professional help here."

"You'll be of great help," De Luca assured her. "When can we get together and finalize things?"

She hesitated. "Tomorrow. We'll get together tomorrow."

"I'll call you."

"Okay."

"It's going to be very good."

"I'll see you tomorrow," Stella replied. She hung up, started off the bed, found her legs were wavering and sat down in the midst of the clothing which would now go back into the drawers.

In the late afternoon, De Luca stopped in to see Paul and, almost as though it were an afterthought, told him that Stella would be working with the company for a time. Paul was so shocked he let a piece of film go through the Moviola gate and flap-flap-flap on the other side, whirling and beating itself until he shut the power off.

"She wants to do that?"

"Uh-huh." Michael picked a strip of film from a barrel and held it up to the light.

Bewildered, Paul said, "Oh."

"She's very special." Michael smiled at Paul and replaced the film. "But you know that."

When Michael left, Paul sat down on the little stool, feeling his pulse throb wildly in his throat. What is she doing? he asked the walls. What is she doing?"

CHAPTER
17

For days after his visit to the Red House, Captain Quesedo pursued his search for the limping Carlos of the *bajo tierra.* He learned little and cursed his informers for being so transparent, so ignorant and so drunken a bunch that a flea would not be taken in by them. Nothing came his way, no one he could exploit, twist a word from. Late one afternoon there had been a whisper that a charcoal seller who limped had been seen in a cantina. Quesedo and five men surrounded the bar. Taken, the limping man proved to be an ancient fisherman, grizzled and senile, talking only of his days with Pancho Villa. At precisely that time, Quesedo later learned, the Aguillar band had mounted an attack upon the hacienda of Oacala's leading factory owner, nailing a manifesto to the door which accused him of exploitation and warned him of the consequences. To underscore the warning, they had killed his matched pair of Russian wolfhounds, separating the animals from their tails and heads, nailing the grisly remains to the door with the manifesto. Quesedo suspected then that the tip he had received was all part of the terrorists' plan; the timing was too coincidental.

That affair had been disturbing enough, but the Aguillar band was recognized by the state police as an ongoing problem. If, however, it was compounded by something truly serious happening to the *yanquis* who had brought so much money to the valley and spent it so valiantly . . . The captain found himself not only unable to shake his fears but with no one with whom to share the problem. He had the unreasonable idea of knocking upon the door of the Ankrum woman and talking to her about it, but it struck him as a ridiculous thing to do. He did, however, come back a number of times to the cinema people.

"Okay . . . okay." De Luca would nod impatiently. "It's all taken care of, it's cool."

"It is my duty to tell you this," Quesedo would say.

Blocked, he took to tossing in his siesta sleep no matter how his wife tried to please him.

At six P.M., making final preparations for filming the beginning of the rice-paddy sequence early the next morning, De Luca was called to the phone by Elvira. She had just discovered a sealed envelope addressed to her lover which had been slipped under the door. He adjourned the meeting and raced to the *casa*.

At Elvira's, as the Indian girl stood by, he ripped open the envelope and held the single sheet of paper under the lamp. The note was laboriously handwritten, smudged but legible.

> My Dear Comrade,
> Now is the time when we must to help Jesus, as we talked. I am so sure of your *simpatía* that the arrangements have already been made. On the other side of this paper you will to see a map which tells your pilot where Jesus waits and then where he is to go for our brave people to meet him. He will to be at the place in the sierra at 7 hours in the morning. He will to make the smoke fire so your pilot will be sure. God will to bless you for this revolutionary act. In the sierra we all salute you.
>
> Your comrade,
> Luis

He turned the paper over. On the reverse side was drawn a crude map of the mountains. A town was circled: XANO. Nearby, a small cross identified Jesus.

"Where is Xano?" He showed Elvira the map to make certain she understood.

"It is high up with one burro trail. Maybe eighty kilometers. Ten, fifteen Mixtec people live there. It is hidden, hard to find."

He examined the map. Another X had been made on a spot near the main highway to Ixtepan. This, he imagined, was where the helicopter must be set down.

Flushed and expectant, he kicked the car up to ninety all the way back and, finding Paul, waved the envelope exultantly.

"The rescue plan. Luis sent it."

Paul was surprised. "He meant it."

172

"Of course. It goes tomorrow morning."

"Tomorrow? We do the rice paddy tomorrow."

"Sure," Michael reassured him, "but we're not using the air corps for that."

"What about Denny? Does he know? He's got to do the flying."

"He'll do it, don't worry."

De Luca rang Sieberling's office and demanded that they locate Burns immediately.

"What if there's trouble?"

Michael jerked his head up sharply at that and Paul equivocated. "I'm not saying there will be, but what if there is? Shouldn't we have a cover story of some kind?"

Michael relaxed and agreed. "Right, a cover story's important. Let's see."

He plunked himself down on a couch, staring intently at the floor. Again, Paul had the feeling he was in a story conference; fiction, not reality, was being discussed.

"Okay." Michael looked up with satisfaction. "If anything goes wrong, we say that Denny was flying in the mountains and had engine trouble. He had to land. When he does, these people come out of the bush with guns and force him to take this wounded man on board. This wounded man holds a gun on Denny and forces him to land where he's to be picked up."

"Not bad."

The phone rang. Denny had been located in the cantina but was reluctant to leave his beer.

"Come on," Michael said, moving rapidly toward the door, "let's get this rescue on the road."

When they entered the cantina, the jukebox was doing its sentimental Mexican best. Denny was in the midst of elaborate recollections of the sexual preferences of Vietnamese women.

"You've got a mission, Denny." De Luca spoke softly, leading Burns into a corner. "And let's keep the voices down."

"A mission?" The flier looked from De Luca to Paul searchingly. Paul nodded. "Just listen."

De Luca bent toward the flier. "Here's the thing. Tomorrow morning, I want you to get into your chopper—alone—go up and fly north about eighty kilometers and be exactly here at seven A.M." He put the map on the table, smoothing the wrinkles.

Burns wrinkled his brow. "What for?"

De Luca coughed.

Burns turned his eyes to the rough map. "What the hell am I taking a chopper up there for?"

"Someone's waiting for you to pick him up," Paul explained. "You set down and do that. He'll have a smoke fire going so you'll know exactly where to land. And the map's marked where to take him."

The flier's eyes narrowed suspiciously. "Who am I picking up and why? Now, come on."

"Okay, Denny." De Luca kept his voice low. "He's a political."

Denny's cat eyes opened wide again. "A political?" He hesitated and his voice dropped to a surprised whisper. "You mean a . . . terrorist guy?"

"Kind of," Paul said, weakly.

"Holy shit."

Burns's hands fell to his sides. De Luca leaned forward swiftly. "He's wounded, Denny. Shot by the police, for nothing. If he doesn't come out, he's going to die. You'll do it, Denny, won't you?"

"What the hell?" The flier grinned. "Why not?" The grin bloomed into a laugh. "What a kicker."

The laugh, after the uncertainty, was infectious. When the flier asked, "Do you think the *terroristas* will give me a medal?" Paul and De Luca joined in.

At six A.M. the following morning, as the first Oacala light stroked the sky, Denny climbed into his Cobra gunship decorated with a winking death's head and the sardonic legend WE KILL FOR PEACE splashed on the side. He slipped a Barbra Streisand cassette into the player, lifted his machine expertly, rising up and swinging away to his left in a graceful arc, watching the earth drop away from him. Glancing at the map on the seat, he adjusted the pitch for more altitude as the sierra began to come in on him and headed for Xano.

He skimmed the mountain-borne ridges and the boulder-strewn hills on hills at two hundred feet, munching a papaya, humming along with Streisand and watching the scrub vegetation come out from under the night shadow into the first golden touches of the sun. A strong thermal came up, veering the copter to the right. "Hey, baby," he muttered, and kicked her straight again. Ahead, the great orange orb was suddenly in the sky, blaze streaming from the edges and looking altogether like an Aztec ornament. In Vietnam he had often flown early-morning missions, swooping down, cannons spitting, just as the sun broke through. It was a familiar and pleasing sight. He had rarely felt fear then, experiencing instead a sense of power and control. No one below had the armaments his Cobra possessed. He had never been hurt, never even came close. And he had never thought of what he had to do as anything but a job. Some men drove trucks; he drove a gunship. The rest was incidental.

A plume of smoke sprouted lazily up from a gully, but he decided it was in the wrong place for his target and chopped on. Pulling up to move over a jutting rock spire, he laughed to the wind. A terrorist. He would be helping some bomb-throwing Mexicano to get away from the cops. He would pluck him from his hideout and drop him into the arms of his buddies so that he could live to bomb another day. He laughed louder. Would the man freak out when he saw the camouflage paint, the dummy guns and the U.S. Army number painted on the Cobra?

He checked his watch. This Xano should be near. Looking down, he could see a depression in the foothills. Going lower, he made out a number of huts. He slowed, slewed left and came over a stand of trees. From the center a thick roll of choking dark gray spumed up. An oil fire. He throttled back, overshot the smoke, circled right and, dropping altitude, angled in at forty-five degrees. Peering down from three hundred feet, he saw the oil drum burning hotly. Two men stood around the fire. As Denny watched, they waved white cloths to him, vigorously.

Throttling back further, he dropped to 250 feet, then to 200, then to 100. The men stopped waving and moved away from the blaze as the downdraft caught the flames and whipped them fiercely, causing the thick greasy smoke to spread. Ten yards from the oil drum and still within the circle of screening trees a strip of earth had been cleared of stumps and boulders. Coming down over it, Denny hovered as the two men huddled and watched; then, gently, he set the skids on the dirt and cut the power to idle the blades, but kept his hands ready, as he peered about, lest this be a trap of some kind, a police come-on. The two men seemed to be the only ones about. They leaped up from their crouch, waved their arms and shouted something he couldn't hear. He leaned out and beckoned. The men started toward the Cobra on the run. One of them, small, powerfully built, with a straw hat and ragged beard, held a rope-tied cardboard suitcase by its half-broken handle and kept waving as he came on. The other, an Indian with a flat fore-head and slight figure, ran with him. They came up to the doorway and Denny asked, "Which one's Jesus?"

"Sí. Jesus, Jesus," the intense, bearded man called excitedly. He started to clamber in. His companion pushed him over the door-way, almost upending him in his eagerness. Grabbing his arm, Denny pulled him upright. He reached for the battered suitcase but the Mexican held on to it, lifting it with both hands and de-positing it, with a grunt, on the floor of the machine. Then he sat, quickly expelling his breath with a wheeze. Outside, to Denny's surprise, the friend charged off quickly, without a word. Denny sat down and strapped himself in. Before he gunned the motor, he took one swift glance at the terrorist. The man seemed to be in his late twenties, eyes clouded with worry as he hunched over. Denny wondered if his wound was in the gut. He had seen men with gut wounds like that. Vibration really shook them up.

"Buckle up." He pulled on the harness. The Mexican nodded. Buckling, he braced his feet on his suitcase. Smiling reassuringly, Denny gave it throttle, released the brakes carefully, and they rose without a bump, like an elevator. From the corner of his eye, Denny saw the Mexican gulp as the Cobra increased speed, banked left, still rising, and arrowed into the sky in seconds, darting forward at almost full speed. Minutes later, they leveled off and headed west to the rendezvous.

Relaxed, Denny lit up and offered the pack to the Mexican, who nodded, took one, accepted a light and blew the smoke out with a deep sigh.

"Speak English?"

"No Eng-lish. No." The Mexican shook his head, puffed nervously and looked over the side at the Cobra's shadow skimming the hill. Jerking his head back to the front, he made the sign of the cross and touched a medallion at his throat.

"Where you hurt?" Denny asked. "*Donde* . . ." and searching for communication, he made a pistol of his fingers. "Boom-boom!"

The man sat straight up then, mouth open in question.

"*Policía* . . . boom-boom. *Donde?*" Denny asked again. The Mexican seemed to understand then. He reached behind him and pointed vaguely to his back.

"Oh," Denny said.

"Sí." The man looked ahead of him again and it was obvious to Denny that he had never flown, never been in the sky, and he was occupied with that. Still, he did not seem to be in great pain. Mike had said the man would die if he didn't come out and that indicated painful wounds. He was being stoic Mexican macho, Denny decided, and half-admired him for it.

It was time to check the map. On that sketch, the X was marked on a road leading north, out of Oacala. He estimated fifteen or twenty minutes to it, but there was no way of knowing. He held his course firm and turned Streisand off. As he did he felt a heavy tap on the shoulder. Turning, annoyed, he saw his passenger staring, apprehension in his eyes, to the right. He had a thick arm raised and pointed at three o'clock. A few hundred yards off their flank and slightly higher, a small plane was closing in. The Mexican, head turned to keep the plane in view, blurted anxiously, "*Policía* . . . maybe *policía!*"

"Be cool, buddy." The small force of Mexican flying police knew the Jericho company ships, standouts in their war decorations, but the terrorist became agitated, scuffing his feet on the suitcase and pounding the seat.

"Go fast. Go more fast."

Denny stared at the man. "Don't tell me how to fly this thing. And how come you're talking English, mister?"

"Little. I speak little," the terrorist muttered.

"That's not what you said before."

"*Policía* airplane no good."

"Let me take care of that."

He throttled back, slowing the Cobra. Its shadow planed gently over the foothills below. The Mexican's face turned grim, eyes hooded and tight. Behind the copter the airplane gained rapidly. When it came within fifty yards, the pilot cut back his engine as well and Denny could see the state police logo and number on the fuselage.

"Is *policía*—sí," the Mexican said, grabbing Denny's arm.

"Stop that!"

Violently, he broke free and kicked his rear control pedals in a tattoo. The Cobra tail wagged like that of a dog making friends. In answer, the police plane waggled its wing, and increasing speed, it veered away to the right. In moments the Cobra was alone in the sky again. The Mexican watched the plane streak off and, when it was gone, slumped back in his seat.

Denny looked at the man. His eyes were closed—in exhaustion, Denny thought. Took a lot of energy to be a terrorist. Man had to

177

be suspicious of everyone and everything or else he'd be a goner. He turned back to the controls and drove his machine for another ten minutes. When he checked again, the Mexican had his eyes wide open and was searching the earth below, anxiously. Denny dropped lower. The map X was on an auxiliary that fed a main road, and it might be hard to find. Still, it was full light now and the sky, serenely blue, held little powder-puff clouds through which they darted, blades beating at the fluff. As they emerged from one the Mexican called, excitedly, "*Aquí*. Down. Down!"

Below, Denny saw the main road, paved two-lane, snaking along the valley floor. Leading off was a single hard-packed dirt trail which wound up into the hills and disappeared into the trees. Just before it vanished, a small truck was parked. The meeting point, X.

"*Aquí*." The terrorist pointed at the truck. Denny nodded, went lower, banked strongly left. As he did so, a man hopped from the truck cab and watched, shading his eyes. At that, the Mexican became excited, almost rising in his seat.

"Easy, man," Denny said. "We'll be right on down there. You'll be off in a flash. Home free."

As though he understood, the terrorist nodded and the beginnings of a relaxed smile crept over his face.

Denny lowered to fifty feet over the road, ten feet from the truck, and then set down easily, keeping the rotors going. Instantly, the Mexican threw off the safety harness and clambered out. Feet thankfully on the ground, he shouted something in Spanish to his friend at the truck. Denny reached down to the suitcase. It was surprisingly heavy and he had to strain to lift it. As he jerked it up, the man at the truck called sharply to the terrorist, who, turning to see Denny, made a lunge for the scarred bag, almost tearing it from Denny's hand and ripping the rest of the handle off. Surprised, Denny let go. The Mexican's stubby fingers dug at the ropes, tugging the suitcase up and pulling it from the cabin. The pressure popped the pressed paper near the rusted hasp and something brown fell to the floor. Denny bent down to retrieve it and the Mexican jerked the case up, powerfully, cradling it in his arms, and ran, legs churning madly, toward the truck. He jumped to the running board and swung himself into the cab, the driver's arm steadying him. The engine cranked to life with a terrible mufflerless roar and with an aching screech of its tires, blowing purple dust and exhaust behind it, the truck careened off, speeding down toward the main road.

Denny didn't see it go. He was looking, with astonishment, at the brown sprig in his hand and sniffing a mild, familiar odor. His fingers felt the thickly resin-coated leaves and he exclaimed in bewilderment to the cabin, "Jesus Christ!"

Dope. The suitcase had held fifty or sixty pounds of dope. That Mex son of a bitch was on a dope run. He stared at the dirt road, dust still playing in the air, the truck nowhere in sight. He looked back at the weed in his fingers, feeling the hairs on the leaves, assuring himself that what had just happened was real. He had taken part in a dope run. There was nothing political about it; it was a scam.

His first reaction was anger. He had been taken for a sucker. But as he whooshed the Cobra aloft, he began to chuckle. Mike had been told the guy was a terrorist hero, a wounded, near-death terrorist hero. Some hero. Not a mark on him, either, not the way he ran with sixty pounds of prime marijuana in his arms. The chuckle slid into outright laughter as he pushed the engine hard to get back as quickly as possible so that he might see Mike's face when he told him. His laughter became a full-throated, joyous roar, merging with the blade chatter as the Cobra spun home over the sierra. Burros heard but paid no attention.

CHAPTER
18

At the location, the parched desert brushland had, magically, become transformed into watery plots of gently waving rice shoots set against a background of Vietnamese straw huts and a guardian grove of vibrant and fresh bamboo trees.

It was a minor triumph of movie-making artifice. Huge hoses, throbbing with pressure, snaked back to four pumps fed by the estuary and spewed out their brackish loads. The thousands of rice plants and the hundreds of trees had been flown in, sprayed with stiffener and cunningly planted in the newly minted mud. Now their delicate buds quivered in the air. Nearby, two cud-chewing water buffalo rested in the shafts of their wooden cultivators, and already tiny local birds were delightedly pecking the vermin from their hides. Fifty locals, outfitted in black pajamas and conical hats, lounged about self-consciously, waiting for orders.

Near a camera tripod stood Ybarra, the rotund land agent, gaping in amazement. He plucked at Paul and declared how *fantástico* this was. Señor De Luca was *muy ingenioso*, a veritable genius. Americans could do anything they wished, even change the face of the entire earth. What he saw before him, he declared, was just like the *televisión* pictures of Vietnam.

Meanwhile, Kodály, having the "blushing morning light" he wanted, was eager to get started. Checking his light meter, he hissed at Paul that the angle De Luca had chosen for the opening shot was going to give plenty of trouble.

"It will be beautiful," Paul reassured him.

"Of course," Kodály sniffed, "but trouble."

The Hungarian was annoyed by many things this morning. Too many extraneous people had come out to see this desert made to bloom, including the director's father, who sat in his son's chair and beamed beneficence at all who passed, but who asked in-

180

numerable questions. De Luca had even let him look through the camera finder. Another critic. Kodály turned Paul in the direction of a large umbrella and rolled his eyes.

It was Elvira. She sat, her small body erect, in a canvas chair, dressed completely in white, hair flowing down her back, gold bangles on her arms and neck. Her face was composed, serene, yet Paul sensed nervous currents beneath her skin. She had come to the location like an Aztec princess, in the Mercedes. On the set, the crew stumbled over themselves in their attempts to move around her chair.

De Luca poked him in the ribs. "See Elvira?"

"How could I miss her?"

"Hasn't Sal done a great job on this place?"

He agreed. Exactly what they had envisioned; muddy water thrusting up the life-giving rice, peasants up to their knees in the rich muck, the plaintive sounds of water buffalo. None of it real, all invented, manufactured by experts, yet all of it would be made to have its own reality by the camera, by what he would do at his editing table. The artifice would make the audience see this rice, feel this rice, smell this rice, smell the sweat, experience the thrust of the animals, know deeply the ancient rituals of fertility by which a people lived thousands of years unchanged and unchanging.

"The light's so beautiful," he murmured.

"Just fantastic," Michael agreed.

Across the watery fields, where the desert began again, a cloud of dust moved forward. Shading his eyes, Paul saw that the cloud was caused by the rapidly moving hooves of half a dozen burros carrying men. Keeping pace, on foot, were a dozen other people. In the distance they were quite small but grew, rapidly, larger and clearer.

"Mike, what's that?"

Michael swung about and shaded his eyes. By now most of the crew were aware of the approaching burros and men. Sieberling, staring at the cloud, turned to Ybarra.

"Who are these people?"

The land agent shrugged. The elder De Luca rose from his son's chair, whispering, "Mikey, be careful."

As everyone watched, the oncoming cloud became less and less dense. Burros and men became clearly visible. The burros were uniformly scraggly animals. The men were all huarached peasants in broad-brimmed straw hats, machetes at their waists. They came on till only a few yards separated them from the movie crew. The land agent called to the three policemen, who had been laughing and sitting on the ground only minutes ago. They came running, machine pistols out and ready, but worry in their eyes.

Two peasants stepped forward. Both were slight-framed, with hard eyes in their leathery faces. The land agent shouted at them, waving his hands. They stared blankly at him and turned away in deliberate affront, looking at De Luca. The taller of the two said quietly, but with strength, *"Queremos hablar."*

Angered at being ignored, the land agent shouted again, but the peasant leaders continued to look away from him and the shorter of the two repeated, *"Queremos hablar."*

By now the land agent was dancing in rage. His feet hopped. His hands sawed the air. When he spoke, his head thrust in all directions.

"These men are troublemakers, señor—*terroristas.* I advise you to say nothing to them. We send back for more *policía.*" He spoke, in loud, exaggerated tones, to the policemen, who stood by, obviously uncertain of what to do.

"What are you telling them?" De Luca wanted to know.

"To push them away from here," said Ybarra. "Here is private property. They have no right to come on here." He plucked at the arm of a youthful policeman, pulling his gun forward.

"Wait a minute. I don't even know what these people want." De Luca looked behind him, calling, "Elvira, I need you." The Indian girl rose quickly and walked to De Luca's side. Seeing her, the peasants exhibited emotion for the first time, their surprise evident. De Luca commanded, "Ask them what they want."

Elvira looked at the peasants calmly. Amazingly calmly, Paul thought. She showed not a flicker of fear or concern. Was it an Indian trait, he wondered, to simply accept whatever came along? She spoke briskly to the two leaders. To her they responded as Ybarra shook his head and stepped back, fuming.

"What do they say?" De Luca asked. "What are they doing here? Why won't they speak to him?"

"They are farmers," Elvira reported, "from this part of the land."

"Okay," De Luca urged. "What else?"

"They say that they will not speak to this man because he is the land agent and he lies and cheats them all the time."

De Luca turned, with surprise, toward Ybarra, who glared at the peasants and spoke again to the policemen. Paul tensed, but the police did not answer; they simply waved their guns about in vaguely threatening movements which the peasants ignored.

"Ask them what they want," De Luca demanded irritably. "The light is going, damn it."

As Elvira addressed the peasants, De Luca looked at Kodály, who stood near his camera and shuffled, his eyes to the heavens. When the Indian girl finished, she listened as both leaders spoke, their voices rising angrily at one point. It was then that Paul saw the first look of surprise that Elvira allowed herself. Turning to De Luca, she translated.

"They say that this land is their land. It is not the land of Don Lopez or of this man. The government gave this land to them many years ago. They have claim to it, but the government looks away from them."

"Never," the land agent shouted, "never. This is not their land. We have the deeds, we have the rights."

"They say Don Lopez has never farmed the land," Elvira continued. "He will not use it but he will not let them use it."

De Luca turned to Paul with a groan. "God, we're in the middle of a land dispute." He looked solemnly at the peasants. "Tell these people that we respect their rights."

"Mike," Sieberling interjected, "you can't do that."

"Tell them," De Luca insisted, "that we will rent this land from them too. Tell them also that we sympathize with their struggle. Go on, tell them." He looked at Paul, who nodded in approval. Meanwhile the entire crew stood by, amazed, listening intently as, once again, Elvira spoke and listened to the peasants' response. As Paul watched carefully, he saw, once more, a flicker of surprise.

"They say," Elvira reported, her voice rock-steady, "that it is no good, no good at all what you will do."

"What?" De Luca looked stunned.

"They say it is already bad what you have done to the land here."

"We watered it!"

"Sí," the Indian girl said quietly, "but the water is from the sea. It is salt and already, maybe, has made this land so bad that it cannot grow anything for a long time. If you put more salt on the earth it must certainly be bad."

Paul was dumbfounded. Elvira continued, "So they say you must to stop now and go away. That is what they wish."

The faces of the peasants were grim. De Luca's was confused.

The elder De Luca burst out angrily, "Who they think they are, these *paesanos?*"

"Mike," Sieberling said, "let's just get the *policía*. These jokers have no legal right to this land. We arranged it all with the Don."

"Sí." Ybarra's face twisted in anger. "Here is my country, señor. And here we do not speak to burros. We beat them with a stick. Go now and call the *comandancia* and we soon see what happens."

"Hold it!" De Luca probed deeply into the eyes of the peasant leaders, desperately trying to make contact. Then he asked Sieberling, "Is it salt water, Sal?"

Sieberling nodded. "So what?"

"I don't know." De Luca looked at Paul, stricken. In desperation he ordered Elvira, "Tell them I'll buy the damn land from them. I'll give them more money than they could ever make farming here."

"They cannot sell this land to you, señor," Ybarra choked out.

"I'll buy it from you *and them*," De Luca shouted. "Tell them, Elvira."

She spoke rapidly, but it was obvious to Paul that she was meeting a stone wall. When she spoke English again she said, "They do not sell the earth. It is their land from the day of their birth to the day they leave the world. It was stolen from them by the Don and they will have it back for their children and their old age. So you must to stop the water and go away from here."

"Go away?" De Luca's body shook with frustrated shock. "How can we go away? Look what we've done here. We're ready to shoot. Elvira, listen, listen to me . . ." He calmed himself down. "Tell them they have to understand. Tell them they have to listen to reason."

"Reason?" Ybarra's tolerance snapped. He loosed a torrent of Spanish at the peasants and excited murmurings rippled from his audience. De Luca grabbed Elvira's arm.

"What's he telling them?"

"He tells them they will all be arrested and sent to the prison."

The murmurs became louder. Two of the mounted men shouted angry responses, pounding upon their machete handles. A third whirled his burro about. Instantly, the other animals bucked and stomped. The peasants on foot moved back, tensely uncertain. From the bank overlooking the feeding creek there came a series of sharp sounds and unintelligible calls. Sieberling started toward the water pumps on the dead run. Half a dozen crew members took off behind him. De Luca and Paul were swept after them. Running, Paul felt, once again, the unreality, the dreamlike quality of "movie" happening before his eyes. It snapped as he reached the bank to be met by a hail of stones sailing from the opposite bank ten yards away.

One of the stones hit De Luca's face, cutting it slightly, and he sank to his knees. Bending low, Paul ran to the creek edge, dodging. When he reached the bank, he saw a dozen young boys standing across the water, hurling the stones and screaming. The crewman who had been working at the pumps was floundering in deep water, clambering toward mud amid heavier rocks that had been aimed at the pumps. As Paul crouched, some of the boys picked up small boulders that had been set in prepared piles and heaved them. A few hit their targets, thunking off the pumps' metal sides and slipping into the swiftly rushing stream. Sieberling, appalled, called, "Where are the cops? Get the bastards. Kick their asses."

The police, who had rushed to the creek with the crew, dropped to their knees, aimed their machine pistols, screeching in Spanish. Horrified, Paul looked for Michael and saw him still on his knees, eyes closed, and waved his arms like a windmill, shouting, "No shoot. No. No." The policemen looked up at him, startled, raised their muzzles above head level and fired off bursts which froze the boys on the bank. The sound galvanized De Luca, who rushed to his side and shouted with him, "No . . . no shooting!"

No more was necessary. The boys fled across the scraggly land, leaving their piles of stones. All except one. Taller than the others, long Indian hair tousled, face contorted with wrath, he rose defiantly to his full height and howled imprecations at them. He reached down to a stone pile and from behind it plucked a Coca-Cola bottle filled with a colorless liquid, its neck stuffed with a rag. He flicked a wooden match head with a dirty thumbnail and touched the flame to the stuffing, which flared up.

"Look out!" Sieberling yelled, diving to the earth. "Get down!" The crew followed him. The policemen flung themselves down as well. Only De Luca and Paul stood upright, in horrified amazement, as the boy threw the Molotov cocktail, turned and ran.

The gasoline-filled bottle, thrown in a high arc, sailed toward the opposite bank, tumbling end over end. It fell short of its target, however, and glided gracefully down, a sputter of pinwheeling yellow where it shattered on a pump housing, exploded into a fierce but brief blaze, which flared for only seconds, producing a choking smoke before sliding into the water and snuffing out. As the last glint of fire disappeared, the *policía* jumped to their feet and ripped off burst after vain burst at the retreating boys.

Everyone rose then. Behind them, the men and burros, wrapped in the swirl they had brought, were moving rapidly away. The *policía* drew together, like chickens in a barnyard, turning their heads nervously, this way and that. Ybarra, brushing the dust from his clothes, stalked over to De Luca.

"You see? You see? You do not give dogs even one bone, señor, not one."

Sickened, De Luca walked away from him, repeating, "Terrible, terrible." Paul followed to where Elvira waited. The three stayed silent, De Luca staring off into the distance, until Paul asked, almost in a whisper, "What are we going to do?" Somehow, after all the noise, small voices seemed necessary.

"I . . . don't know." De Luca turned to the Indian girl as though she had an answer for him. Her hand moved gently over his face and touched the already dried blood.

"*Pobrecito*," she said, "you wish only to do good."

"I want," De Luca corrected with a groan, "only to make my picture."

Looking at the lush synthetic crop, Paul, for the first time, wondered if they would.

At the compound word of the attack had already spread and an electric excitement rippled from building to building. Always the realist, Sal Sieberling pointed out that word of the confrontation on the creek would surely get out; that bitch, Ankrum, was probably on the phone already, and the day of reckoning with the studio could come that much sooner.

"I know that." De Luca pulled at his beard and suddenly shouted, "Get me the Hotel Jaime, room three-thirty-two."

Paul came alert. What did Michael want with Stella in the midst of this? De Luca did not explain, and Sieberling launched into his plan for getting the sequence shot.

"We put a gang of our own guys and Quesedo's *policía* all around the place. Anyone comes within ten yards of the location gets a bullet up his ass. I guarantee nothing happens."

Michael would never do that, Paul thought; doing that would be acknowledging the warfare, placing themselves on the side of

186

the police and the landowners. Sieberling waited. Finally De Luca shook his head as Paul knew he would.

"We can't do that."

"What else are you going to do?" Sieberling demanded. When there was no answer forthcoming, he adjusted his glasses and said, "So, okay."

In the midst of the silence that followed, there was a pounding on the door. When Sieberling yanked it open, Denny Burns came in, still in his flying suit. He had stopped only to swig coffee at the cantina and was bursting with strange good humor. Angry at being interrupted, Sieberling said, "Damn it, Denny . . ." But the flier grinned.

"Got to see the boss, in private."

"Jesus, didn't you hear what happened?"

"Oh, sure—"

Sieberling glared at him. Burns sang out to De Luca. "Mike, will you tell this joker we got business to talk over?"

"Sal—"

Sieberling slammed out. The moment the door closed, Denny locked it elaborately and put his hands on his hips.

"Okay, men, mission accomplished, ready to be debriefed."

"I'm sorry," De Luca said, "that's on my back burner. We've had a few problems."

"Did it go off okay?" Paul asked.

"Piece of cake." Denny crossed his arms, waiting for more questions. None coming, he broke into a deep chuckle. The chuckle changed to a rich laugh and the laugh to a solid roar that poured from his throat in a hypnotizing, mystifying stream until Paul broke the spell.

"What's so funny?"

"What's so funny?" The flier caught his breath and wiped the spittle from his lips with his baseball cap. "Well, what's funny is that this sumbitch I picked up wasn't wounded at all, for one thing."

"What do you mean?" De Luca wrinkled his brow.

"Just that. You tell me the monkey is dyin'. But this Mex is strong as a bull, no wound on him, anywhere."

"I heard Aguillar," Paul interjected. "He said the man had been wounded by the police."

"He *said*. Well. I could say my grandma was a countess in old Killarney, couldn't I?" He winked. "Now, here's the real kicker,

187

fellas. This Jesus character had a suitcase with him. This suitcase was full of—guess what?" He waited. "Come on, take a guess. . . . Never mind, I'll tell you. *Dope.* Great dope." Satisfied at his effect, he finished his saga. "And there was maybe fifty or sixty pounds of it this cat was draggin' out—hell, maybe more. Courtesy of you and me."

He plopped himself down in a chair, stretched his legs straight out, crossed his ankles on a stool and admired his hand-tooled cowboy boots. Paul didn't think he'd heard correctly and was going to ask Denny to say again, but De Luca, stricken, wobbled over to stand directly in front of the flier.

"Denny." His voice was tiny. "Is this true?"

"Mike, I swear."

Paul came over. Denny was wild. Denny was crazy. You never knew what to expect from him. A hundred possibilities sundered themselves against reason and he ended up asking lamely, "Are you sure you picked up the right man?"

"He was at the spot on the map, Paul, for chrissake. He called himself Jesus. There was an old truck waitin' for him when I put down."

"How did you know it was dope he had?" De Luca challenged.

"Take a look." Burns produced the sprig from a pocket and held it up for inspection, daylight glistening from the oil. "This spilled out when he took off. Took off like some big bird too. No thank-you-ma'am. *Whoosh.* Grab that stash and run hell-bent for that truck and they took off like it was derby day in Mexicali. *Wham!* They went. Nothin' left but smoke, the cheap kind."

He broke into laughter again. De Luca, shoulders slumped, walked to the window. Paul looked at Denny with disbelief but the flier nodded mockingly.

"Mike," Paul said with some desperation, "it can't be just like that. There has to be an explanation."

Ashen-faced, De Luca said, "We have to see Luis again, we must."

"Hey," Burns called, "do you guys know something I don't?"

De Luca steadied, taking a succession of deep, chest-filling breaths. His voice became stronger.

"I want you to go to Ismena. Tell him it's a matter that can't wait. We must see Luis."

Paul was startled. "Me?"

"Paul, I need help. I've got to figure out what to do here."

"Now?"

"As soon as possible."

Fleeting objections rose and vanished with resolution. He found himself calm, almost eager.

The car stopped four blocks from Ismena's. Noon was minutes away. The sun was high, the shadows were short and the streets, here, were empty and very quiet. Walking toward the small shop as briskly as he could, short of a run, Paul felt totally exposed, conspicuous, the gringo.

When he reached the shop, he passed, thankfully, through the rope curtain and hesitated. Ismena was behind his counter talking to two slight men. At Paul's entrance their conversation ceased and their heads turned to examine the intruder. The shopkeeper nodded an expressionless greeting and murmured words to the two men. They left instantly, not looking at Paul at all, for which he was grateful. Not until they were gone did Ismena call in his musical voice, *"Buenos días, señor."*

"Buenos días," he responded, coming forward quickly. "We must talk again. It's most important that we talk again."

"Talk then," Ismena said.

"With Aguillar, I mean."

"Why? Why do you wish to talk with him again?"

He searched the man's eyes. They were totally neutral. "Okay. This morning something very bad happened to us. We have to see Señor Aguillar and speak to him about it. We know he'll want to speak to us."

The shopkeeper took time to absorb that. From outside, hands parted the rope curtain, sober faces peered in, then vanished. Paul grew increasingly tense. Finally, Ismena appeared to have made up his mind.

"Is hard."

"I don't care," Paul insisted. "We'll go anyplace. We know he has to protect himself. But it has to be soon."

Ismena came out from behind the counter. "You wait." He walked to the curtain and darted through it out to the street.

When Ismena came padding back in, only five minutes had gone by; Paul could have sworn it was thirty. The Indian man went behind his counter briskly; that was obviously his *querencia* where he felt the safest.

"You can to see the one you wish to see, now," he said.

Paul was taken aback. "You mean right now?"

"Sí, sí. Now. I say you now. You wish to see him then is now. For he is near." The Indian said it impatiently as though he wished this business to be done.

"Okay." He had not expected this at all. It would be alone, without Michael, but there was no alternative. "I'll go now, then. Where is he?"

"You know where is the Calle Libertad?"

"No, but my driver can find it."

"No driver." Ismena's voice took on a worried tinge. "This is not for others but for you. I tell you where to find it from here and you must to go alone. You *comprende*?"

"Okay." He was ready to agree to anything. "Just tell me what to do."

Carefully, Ismena tore a small edge of brown paper from a bag. Taking the pencil stub that hung from a string tied to a post, he proceeded to draw a crude diagram of the way to Calle Libertad, the number of the house he was to go to.

"When the door is open, you must to say that you come from the Deer Dancer. You *comprende*?"

He nodded. "The Deer Dancer."

Ismena handed him the paper. "You go now. For it is no good one *hora* from now. You will not to find him and it will be *mucho* danger for all."

"Okay."

"You will be . . . careful . . . for you, señor, yes?"

Paul was surprised. The eyes had lost some of their neutrality to concern. Suddenly, he liked this man.

"I'll be careful," he told him. "And I want to thank you because this is very important."

Ismena said nothing more and Paul left. Outside, he blinked against the sun and felt the heat, but no one was about and he felt a strange sense of being protected as he walked back the way he had come. He looked at his map. The Calle Libertad was to his left, and he struck out in that direction.

Following the diagram, he traversed a series of small angled streets, losing his way only once. He emerged, finally, onto a fairly wide avenue. Here and there imposing haciendas rose behind protective stone fences often topped with jagged broken glass. A street sign on the side of one such building told him he had found the Calle Libertad. Ismena had written the number six on his paper.

190

This was number twelve. He set off down the calle, passing eleven, ten, nine, eight and seven. That house ended the block. He crossed the street to the limestone mansion on the corner set in the midst of a splendid wrought-iron-gated garden, but the house bore no number. He passed it, went on to the next. That one had an elaborate five carved in wood. Puzzled, he went back to the number-less house, examining it from the street. A short flight of steps led to a graceful landing; set in the center of the landing were two huge red-painted doors.

He went through the unlocked gate into the grounds, inhaling the jasmine and verbena, struck by the airy beauty of the trees which spread huge, delicate canopies over the flower beds. Close up, the hacienda was even larger than it had seemed from the street. It had many windows, each completely covered by wine-colored curtains. He walked up the landing steps and over to the blood-red doors. The knocker was startling, a large, highly polished brass water nymph holding her arms up in a beckoning gesture. Picking up the arms, he rapped with them on the brass plate below.

The door opened almost instantly. A large woman in a purple dressing gown trimmed with lace looked at him and said, obviously well acquainted with English, "Good morning. I think maybe you make a little mistake. We do not open our doors here till much later. You come back tonight, ten o'clock, and then you will have a good time."

She smiled winningly, flounced the skirt of her robe to straighten the hemline, and Paul realized where he was. "Oh" was the best he could do, and Señora Revueltas laughed, with amusement.

"I hope you will come back. *Buenos días.*"

She was about to close the door when, recovering, he asked, "Excuse me, but where would number six be?"

Señora Revueltas's laugh vanished. Her entire manner altered from seductress to suspicious guardian. Her voice went deep into her throat, lowered to a near baritone. "This is number six."

"This?" He stared at her dumbly.

The madam frowned. "I told you we closed now. Do not make trouble, please."

"No." Puzzled, he decided to chance it. "I have to see someone at number six."

"You come back tonight. You see all the girls then."

Once again she was about to close the door when he said, "Wait a minute. I've come from . . . the *Deer Dancer.*"

191

Señora Revueltas stared at him. "You come . . ."

"From the Deer Dancer," he repeated.

"Quick in," she said, pulling the door wide.

He stepped through the portal. She closed the door behind him rapidly, her hand reaching at the same time to the velvet drape covering a floor-to-ceiling window nearby. She pulled the drape back two inches and peered out to the sun-stroked street. Dropping the cloth, returning the entrance hall to its soft, electric-candle gleam, she said, "You come."

He followed her into the great parlor, silent and deserted, past the ornate grand piano and up the thick-piled carpet of the curving staircase. He followed her past a corridor of doors, each of them closed, each of them with a symbol painted on it. One was a vine of lush grapes, another a dragon breathing orange fire, another, he saw, was a pink woman's garter. Here, as below, the light came from electric candles. Señora Revueltas stopped in front of a door bearing a rendition of a single black, spike-heeled shoe. She gestured for Paul to stop behind her, knocked on the door and whispered something in Spanish. She waited, her ear to the door, then she nodded. "All right. Go in."

She turned and started back. Paul put his hand on the knob but the door jerked open. In front of him stood Luis Aguillar, bare-chested and grave-faced.

"Ah—you found me."

He pulled Paul into the room. It was painted black. Even the brass bed held a rumpled black coverlet. A small table, dark ironwood, was spread with notepaper. Aguillar pulled forward a chair.

"Sit. *Por favor.*" He lit a cigarette and sat on the bed. "You are surprised to find me here, eh?" He inhaled deeply. "Señora Revueltas is *muy simpática* for what we try to do. Sometimes, when it is important that I stay for a few hours in the city, I come here."

"I see." By now the surprise of finding the terrorist at the bordello was wearing off and Paul felt driven to get to the point. "Señor Aguillar—"

"Luis, you call me Luis."

He nodded. "Luis. You know what happened this morning, but . . ."

The terrorist's brow wrinkled. "This morning? What happens this morning?"

"You don't know? You haven't heard?"

"What happens? Tell me."

192

By the time Paul came to the gasoline bomb, the terrorist was pacing, his face wrathful. When Paul finished, he smashed a clenched fist down onto the table, scattering papers everywhere.

"The fools!" He glared at Paul as though he were the enemy. "I go to these people and they say they understand what I tell them, that you are friends. They tell me okay, Luis, then they do this?" He whirled in a towering rage. "They don't understand *política* and they must learn. *Política* cannot have *tontos* like that . . . fools."

"Luis, we have to make our picture, and to do that we have to shoot those scenes without trouble."

"*I* understand that," Aguillar said. "It is the ignorant ones. Those ones I will take and—" He broke off, blowing a wreath of smoke around his head, collecting himself. He reached for his shirt and his pistol on the bureau.

"All right, my friend. I will take care of this." He shook his head grimly. "They must understand that they are dangers to the movement and to themselves. No discipline."

"We even told them," Paul said, "that we'd buy the land, give them cash; they said no."

"Ah . . ." Aguillar buttoned the shirt. "Sí . . . like burned children they have no trust."

There was a soft, insistent knocking on the door and a voice hissed from the corridor. The terrorist called, "Sí," quietly, then extended his hand.

"Now, I must go."

"What's going to happen? Will they stop?"

"Or someone pays," Aguillar said, "pays hard."

"Luis," Paul said hesitantly, "that Jesus, the man our flier took out . . ."

"Sí. Jesus. He is safe now."

"He didn't seem to be hurt, our flier said."

"What?" His eyes opened wide with question. "Of course he was hurt."

"He had a suitcase with him."

"So?"

"Our flier says"—Paul felt ridiculous—"that it had dope, marijuana, a lot of it. He showed us a leaf that was dropped."

Aguillar smiled. "No. He makes some mistake, your flier."

"We just didn't understand it," Paul said uncertainly.

"Jesus?" Aguillar scowled. "*Sin semilla?* I don't believe that. He is a good fighter. Much courage. I will see about this."

193

Fingers scratched at the door. Aguillar put his pistol in his belt under the loose shirt. He touched Paul lightly on the shoulder and was gone.

Paul waited a full minute before opening the door. Seeing the corridor empty, he walked quickly to the head of the stairway. Eyes alert, he saw the door with the garter emblem an inch ajar. As he stared, concerned, the door closed and he heard two high, giddy voices. He descended after that, as fast as he could, racing through the grand parlor and out to the entrance hall.

Señora Revueltas was there. She opened the front door, and with jarring abruptness, her voice tinkled.

"Oh, señor, we adore the Americans. But, you see, no one is ready for business. You must come back tonight and enjoy."

She pulled him to her, giggling, put a finger to her lips, removed it, then pressed it firmly against his mouth. In a moment, the red door closed behind him and the sweet taste of raspberries shocked him.

With distaste, he realized it was her lipstick.

CHAPTER
19

Manuel Quesedo's gold-braided uniform cap perched on his head at an unaccustomed square angle; no tilt, no tilt at all. He had jammed it there, rushing from his office after the terrible calls had come, first from Sieberling and then from that slime of slimes, that *cojone*-less piece of putrid flesh, Zocado, the mayor's assistant.

Sieberling's anger he could take; after all, they understood one another; but Zocado was out for him, he knew that. And he had that other piece of burro turd, that strutting, cuckolded-six-times-over mayor, under his thumb. The trouble was, Quesedo reflected, that venal men, wicked men, were in power while decent people like himself were mere organs of the state. The trouble also was that the naive gringos like De Luca made nothing but trouble with their illusions. It had to stop, he vowed; he would not be the sacrificial goat.

"With respect," he told De Luca when he arrived, "these farmers must to be put in their place. You are a gentle-hearted man but t'ings now go too far. My men tell me of a fire bomb. That is serious. If these *bandidos* will do that you must to have the protection, no? I give you plenty of my mens but you must to let them act if some t'ing happens. That is what they have guns for."

De Luca walked to his desk, moved from there to the window, walked back. Quesedo sighed; the *jefe* was considering all sides.

"Is there any other place we can find for the rice-paddy stuff?" De Luca asked, startling Sieberling.

"You're not serious?"

"Absolutely."

"Mike, we've got it all here," the production manager protested. "To try to find another place now . . ."

"I'm trying to deal with the problem," De Luca said, biting off his words.

"Let those bastards see a gang of police with guns and the problem'll take care of itself."

De Luca was in another place. "If we could bring fresh water in by trucks, the damn land wouldn't be hurt. What do you think it would cost to—"

"There's no way, Mike. Not even with money. That place is a sponge."

Quesedo watched the byplay with feigned interest. Nothing would come of this, nothing.

"I know," De Luca said, thoughtfully, "that what we're doing doesn't really have long-term consequences—probably. I can get experts to tell me that, anyway. And even if it did, we could bring agricultural people in here with fertilizer and stuff. If we could convince them of that . . ."

He didn't need the skepticism in Sieberling's eyes to know it was a delusion—he could never convince them, he was a gringo.

"Mike," Sieberling asked, "are we shooting the rice paddy tomorrow? I've got to know."

"I want to talk to Paul," De Luca said. "He's out doing something very important; then we'll see."

He sat down at his desk and stared blankly at the wall.

Quesedo left the Jericho compound as he had come—with no plans resolved. And yet, something had to be reported to the hated Zocado; there was no escape.

His mind created one. Daydreams of the round American girl slithered into his visions and flooded into erotic possibilities. Painfully, he shook himself into the present and decided to stop at Señora Revueltas's establishment. A good policeman who achieved results kept up unflagging pressure, relentless pressure; pressure was his specialty.

Maria was ironing a long satin dress when he walked in on her. She was in a torn kimono, her hair was in curlers and, seeing him, her response was a frightened giggle.

Quesedo was direct. "Well, what about that charcoal seller?"

"My mother has not seen him again."

"Haven't you asked about him?" he insisted.

"No . . . I . . ." Iron in hand, the girl started trembling, and her left breast, emerging through a jagged rip in her wrapper, began to shake.

"Stop that," Quesedo ordered. "Just cooperate and you have nothing to fear."

"Forgive me," she stuttered, pulling the hole closed.

"So?"

Desperate to assuage him with something, anything, she blurted out, "An American came here today."

"Today?" It did not sound correct. "You mean in the daytime?"

"Yes," she said quickly. "I peeked out the door when I was in Rosa's room and we saw him when he was going back to the stairs."

"Who did he see?"

"I do not know. I saw him go, only. But the señora must have let him in."

Quesedo stepped closer to her.

"How do you know he was an American?"

"One knows."

"Yes," he agreed. "Describe him."

Maria tried to remember the man, his tan trousers, his blue shirt, his height, his hair, the way he held his head. As she spoke, Quesedo realized with a flash of absolute certainty that she was describing the Judío, Gordon.

When Maria saw the surprise light his face, Quesedo was recalling what De Luca had said, that Gordon was out doing something very important. What was important to them? It came to him with no hesitation. They were trying to make contact with those who were wrecking them, of course—what else? Exactly what they would do, those idiots. But here? Whoever came here came with the full knowledge of Señora Revueltas.

He nodded approval to the girl. "Good, good. Now you must help me even more."

Her tongue flicked out to moisten her lips.

"You must watch," Quesedo continued, "for someone, not a gringo, who comes when this place is closed. That someone will be important to me, you understand?"

The girl nodded.

"When you see who comes here, you call and tell me, all right?"

He wrote the telephone number down on a scrap of paper. When she reached out to take it, he smiled and playfully poked at her nipple.

"Be careful with that fancy dress," he said, and left her in peace.

* * *

197

Stella was in the bath when De Luca's phone call reached her. Hearing his voice was a shock. Agreeing to work for him had been an act of defiance toward Paul with no thought of any consequences. Now, here was the master saying he needed her expert advice and that a car was already on its way. Worse—before she could utter an objection, have a second thought, he was gone and the line was dead. She blamed Paul for getting her into all this.

De Luca welcomed her, but soberly. The hug she could not evade was perfunctory; his fingers around her flesh were cold. He was, clearly, elsewhere, which confused her.

He quickly and vividly described what had happened on the creek. She was stunned but still had no inkling of why he had summoned her.

"Look," he explained, "I'm worried that I can't keep this from getting out. But I've got to try. The studio is looking for any excuse to come down here and get rid of me; this could make it for them. You're a pro, I know you are. What do you think? What would you do?"

Professional advice! De Luca had commanded her presence to ask professional advice, as contracted. She was so relieved that she smiled and said the first thing that came into her head.

"There is no way to keep this from getting to them. And the exaggerations will make it even worse."

"Damn straight," De Luca agreed.

Stella thought a moment and then said, "Turn the tables."

"Huh?"

"Turn the tables." She leaned forward, selling hard. "Call them. Insist that they come down here as soon as possible and see things for themselves. That indicates to them, first off, that they've been hearing some tall tales. It takes them off the case a little. Then, when they do come, it's not with quite so much of a bite. By that time, of course, you have to have things in order and be ready to charm the pants off them, but the basic notion right now is to defang them, you see."

"Defang them." De Luca stared at her, astonished. "It's brilliant." He whirled on one foot, gracefully. "You're marvelous. I knew you would be. It's great. And you're right, of course. Here we've been trying to keep them away and all it's done is make Lufkin suspicious as hell. It's gorgeous." Instantly, he called Sieberling.

From the moment the production manager entered the room, Stella perceived his taut body as a tank and his dark glasses as the menacing guns. It was, however, a belligerence composed of his coolly ignoring her. Even De Luca's introduction of her as "one of us" elicited nothing more than a skeptical acknowledgment. And the explanation of her strategy drew a single searching look.

The suggestion De Luca loved had come from Stella spontaneously; zombie-thought, end product of a hundred such meetings in her life. As she sat by the window, barely listening to the men debate the possibilities, watching a trail of donkey urine on the paving stones, she felt very alien. To the country, to this room, even to herself. She was on automatic pilot and it depressed her. Yet, within the depression was a kernel of dimly apprehended need, and it propelled her forward.

Though almost unaware of what the men were saying, she was very aware that, from time to time, the tank would turn its dark-glass turret in her direction for a quick check, testing—measuring the range. She was enemy terrain and she knew it. She heard clearly, however, when Sieberling asked about the next day's shooting possibilities and De Luca answered that he was waiting for Paul. Minutes after that, Sieberling left. When she rose to her feet and said, lying, that she had some errands, De Luca insisted they could wait; he wanted her with him for a while, a million things were spinning through his brain, she might help sort them out.

Aching to leave, she found herself accompanying De Luca to the cutting rooms, where Murray, the new editor, ran some helicopter footage that Allan Marcus had shot.

"Good stuff," De Luca commented. "Allan can still do bits and pieces. I love that guy."

A scraping noise and an intake of breath turned her toward the door to see Rennie there, film can in hand, eyes blinking with surprise. De Luca took it in stride.

"Hi. We were just looking at Allan's Cobra stuff. Stella's helping us out for a while with some P.R. advice."

"Oh." Rennie nodded, gave the film to Murray. In the process Stella could see the constriction in her shoulders, and the tightening of her jaw muscles made her face appear almost square. De Luca appeared to be uninterested. He took Stella by the arm. "Let's go."

As she left, Stella passed within inches of Rennie and saw the trembling of her bare arms, the tiny hairs alerted and rising at the hormonal signals.

Walking back to the production office, feeling swamp muck rising to waist level, she told De Luca she had to go, absolutely had to go. Instead of answering, the director, looking beyond her, called, "Paul!"

By the time she focused down the street, he had moved away rapidly and was almost on the run toward Paul, who was approaching from the Zócalo side. She waited, breath in her throat, observing, irrationally, that Paul's khakis looked good on him, that the blue shirt set off his tanned skin and firm shoulders. She also knew, with hurt, that his reaction at her being there would be less than loving. The look he launched across the distance between them was an arrow of inquiry. By then De Luca had reached him, was talking rapidly, pulling her toward them.

"Surprise," she got out.

"Oh, yes," Paul said.

"Let's get inside." De Luca pushed them both. "This is too crucial."

"I have to go," she insisted.

"I want you to know what's happening." De Luca was firm. "That's the only way you can help me."

Paul looked at her with disbelief. Her deepest instinct was to flee, to avoid the look of pain in his eyes.

"Michael! Michael!" Laszlo Kodály, driving by, had his head out the window. "We must speak, Michael."

"Two minutes," De Luca muttered, going toward Kodály's braking car.

Paul looked at Stella and shook his head. "This is crazy."

"I'm just doing him a favor."

"Do me a favor and don't."

"It's a temporary thing, a little thing," she excused. "It might even help you in the end."

"Why, just bloody why, Stel?"

It was the hurt and anger she had expected, and helplessly she said, "Oh, I'm here anyway."

Having soothed Kodály's jangled nerves, De Luca returned. When he took Stella's arm, possessively, she moved his hand away and said, "No, I'll be in touch later, but I have to go now." She walked away rapidly before either of them could see that she was shaken.

In her hotel room she removed the kerchief and was struggling with her hair when there was a knock at the door. She went to it, a tangled web of conflicting notions about what to say to Paul, but when she pulled the door open, there was no Paul. Flo Ankrum stood there anxiously.

"All right." Stella sighed. "What now?"

Flo stepped in, shuffling her feet. "I'm sorry I became angry with you. Running away wasn't very mature."

"Okay."

"You have really good instincts, you're a really good person, I can tell that."

It was almost an accusation. Stella nodded patiently.

Flo looked at her, uncomfortable intensity gathering in her face; then she burst out, "Why did you go to Michael's after what happened this morning?"

Astounded, Stella asked, "Wait a minute, are you keeping tabs on me?"

"No, someone I know saw you and phoned me."

That was even worse. "Why would they do that?"

Flo pushed her glasses back. "They thought I'd like to know."

Stella shook her head. "I don't like this."

"I told you," Flo erupted again, "Michael's trying to wreck these people. They're fighting back. Someone could have gotten killed on the creek this morning. They came to talk to him peacefully, but the police were there with machine guns. I know Sal's behind that, but Michael will do anything to get his way with a picture."

"I don't understand a damn thing you are saying."

"I am saying"—Flo's eyes opened to moons behind her glasses and the leather bag strung across her shoulder whipped up with every twist of her body—"that Michael and Gordon are already responsible for putting innocent people in prison and getting some of them shot, that they're already responsible for making landowners and businessmen rich at the expense of the workers and peasants, that they're polluting and poisoning the atmosphere, and while you said to me that you'd never believe that about your friend, look what happened this morning! Now, you go to see Michael—and he only wants things from people, I know that. So why did you go? What did he want?"

"Exactly what business is it of yours—any of this? Or what I do? Or anything else?" This girl was impossible.

"Because I'm a female member of the human race, and I care about these people," Flo declared. "They're not going to stand still for being raped and I never thought that someone like you would collaborate with—"

"Collaborate? What are you talking about?" She found herself a breath away from a shout. "Who's collaborating? And with what? And why? You come running up here screaming at me—"

"When things are so important, you scream." Flo stood her ground.

"Do you? Well, I could scream over a lot then."

"I'm not talking about personal things. I'm talking about people living or dying," Flo said in a suddenly quiet and reasonable tone that defused Stella's anger.

"Listen," she said, "right now I can't reason too well, you understand? My glands are acting up, my brainpower's failing. I can't see too clearly what's ahead of me. Don't involve me in this business."

Flo plucked at her skirt and said, "I thought maybe you were something else, you and Gordon. That's all." She was gone before Stella could answer.

In his office De Luca stared at Paul in surprise. Aguillar in a whorehouse wasn't the point, but an Aguillar who had not even heard of the conflict on the creek was something else.

"How could he not know? How is that possible? He knows everything that happens in ten minutes."

"He didn't know," Paul said, a vague feeling of failure attacking him.

De Luca's muscles trembled angrily beneath his beard. "How do we know he'll ever be able to convince those crazies, Paul?"

"We don't," Paul murmured.

"Maybe," De Luca said, "he will, but meanwhile . . ." He thought a moment, then said resolutely, "This picture is too important to be wrecked by a bunch of people who don't understand a goddamn thing about social problems. Shit, if we weren't gringos, would they be doing this?"

"They don't love us for being *yanquis*," Paul said, "that's for sure."

"Okay, then, I believe we have to move and move like the wind. I want to wrap in six or seven weeks." To Paul's startled look he responded, "We can do it if we hump." He plucked a script. "It's all here now; it's all ready."

Paul knew it was. It hadn't been when he came here but it was ready now. De Luca started to pace.

"You and I may not like Quesedo and what he stands for, but damn it, we've got to use him." His voice shook with determination. "We'll get the whole Oacala goddamn police force for security if we have to, from now on." He touched Paul on the shoulder beseechingly. "What do you think? I want to know what you think."

"I think you're right," Paul agreed. "These people don't understand where we're at. Maybe later they will, when Luis hammers at them enough."

De Luca clutched the edge of his shoulder. "Right. The point is you and I know, even if *they* don't, what we're doing it all for."

Paul nodded.

"So, tomorrow morning, we're going right back to the creek. Sal will arrange what we need and from then on, we move."

It had to be that way, Paul thought—what option did they have? "Oh," he remembered, "I asked Luis about that Jesus and the dope business."

"And what did he say?"

"He didn't believe me at first, then he said he'd find out about it pretty quick."

"Huh," De Luca said, and turned away.

By the time siesta was over and life returned to Oacala, Sieberling and Quesedo had completed plans for a ring of police guards to be on hand for the rice-paddy filming. Sieberling was grimly pleased that he had prevailed. Quesedo complimented the production manager for bringing a sense of reality to the *jefe* who was, after all, a creative man, a dreamer. Sometimes these men had to be protected against themselves by more practical people such as Sieberling and himself.

"In spades," Sieberling agreed.

By the end of the work day, announcements had been made to the company that police protection was being provided. Laszlo Kodály muttered that he had not signed on to be a war photographer. The head gaffer vowed that if any son of a bitch harmed one lamp, he'd shoot him himself. The transport captain, stung by the immobilization of his trucks, conspired with the special-effects men for smoke bombs with which to scare the hell out of any greaser coming at him with a machete.

As the evening hours wore on and Señora Uribe served endless *cervezas* and *hamburguesas*, the talk turned to deep indignation. Denny Burns pronounced the Oacalans to be two-faced bastards.

203

The local gasoline dealer serving his planes was raking it in on fuel bills. The guys who worked for him were getting plenty *mordida*. The supplies man reported astronomical payments to local food merchants. The lumber dealer was making a million. Everyone had a story of Mexican profit on the company's back and only bad behavior in return. To have some damn group actually sabotaging, dangerously so, was the last straw. These people were assholes and always would be. To blame the gringos for "corrupting" the women or checking out local smoke was a laugh. Every corruption had been available long before they had arrived. These people were eager for the dollar, very eager, always were and always would be. For some jokers to make a big deal of it had to be some kind of politics, nothing more.

Rennie thought that Michael was simply protecting his artistic vision. She was confident that Paul had helped him come to that decision, and serving coffee, that night, in her motel patio, she deplored those who simply did not understand what Michael and Paul were all about. Paul, exhausted by the day's events, hardly heard her.

"I'm going to go and get some sleep." He yawned. "We're due to be out there about five o'clock."

"Sleep here," Rennie urged.

"No, I'll just go back." He had no idea why he did not wish to sleep in her bed that night, but he did not.

"That friend of yours has wormed herself into a job with Michael," Rennie said. "Did you know that?"

He nodded.

"She shouldn't be here. She has no business here."

"That's a fact." He yawned again.

"She wants to hurt you, I can tell that."

"No," he said, "she doesn't. I think . . ." He hesitated. "I think she doesn't know what she wants to do, that's all."

He stumbled into a taxi, and only when he was undressing for bed did he remember that Stella was above him and wondered if she were in . . . or out with De Luca; then sleep sandbagged him.

An hour later he came awake with a cry. He had seen, again, the rage-filled face of the Mexican boy as he rose up to hurl the flaming bomb. Only this time the bomb had arched over the creek and exploded on Michael, setting him alight, and his body hopped and jerked with the burns, pushing screams from his chest. It was those screams that woke Paul. He heard them still and smelled the smoke,

204

awake though he was. Ninety minutes later, he was still fighting both wakefulness and sleep, needing rest but fearful of what lay in wait in the darkness. When he did give in, though, he did not go back to the creek.

CHAPTER
20

All night, as Oacala slept, preparations for filming the rice-paddy sequences went on. The repaired pumps sucked up creek water in greedy gulps and gushed it out on the checkerboarded plots. The production designer, masterful perfectionist, son of a Scottish carpenter, demanded more water and still more water. In spots the earth had already dried out, leaving a thin white residue here and there that required further inundation to obliterate.

Floodlights, illuminating every leaf and pebble, blazed in the night like so many silent furnaces; Sieberling wanted no darkness in which mischief could be worked. On both banks of the creek, harshly lit, Quesedo's *policía* took up positions. Another contingent stretched in a wide arc, straddling the road across the property.

As the night began to dissolve, Quesedo himself drove up to inspect his troops. Pronouncing everything satisfactory, he proceeded to wolf down a company breakfast of ham and eggs. Pronouncing that satisfactory as well, he sat back, contentedly puffing his second cigarette, reflecting upon the riches of the *yanquis* and the slim backsides of the girls moving about doing their jobs.

Most always the owners of these trim, firm backsides sought, he knew, yogurt. Since no one in Oacala even knew what yogurt was, the *jefe* had arranged for the plane from Mexico City to bring the stuff in. That's what they liked to eat—yogurt. It gave them their slim asses. They avoided flesh like the plague, these young women who were always dieting. He smiled to himself. All over the valley and up into the hills were stalk-thin women who also dieted constantly. Only they were forced to diet; they had little food, were always hungry and, if faced with this yogurt, would think some terrible joke was being played upon them. And these slim-assed young women had big jobs here, menlike jobs, not cooks or office girls. In the cities of Mexico men dreamed of jobs, ran to the new oil fields; here the girls held them. And what of the men of America? They were always busy with shiny toys—little tractors they rode on to cut their beautiful grass, garage doors that opened and closed when you pressed a button, electric shavers that spoke to them; he had seen it all on the *televisión*. It must be a funny life for a man in the cities of the North.

He rose to check the creek banks again. How far would this *bajo tierra* go? Would they be stupid enough to try something with armed men about, ready and waiting? His countrymen could be very stubborn. Still, he hoped that nothing happened on this creek. If it did, his men would have to respond boldly or else that fountain of evil, the deputy mayor, would hold him responsible. He had to find the leaders of this insane movement and cut them away. He had to push harder. Perhaps it would be wise to watch the Judío and catch him in his next move, for surely he had been to the Red House to meet one of them. Could it possibly be Señora Revueltas herself? The thought shook him. She was too practical a woman. Also, she had many influential friends, and if he were wrong, she had the capacity to make much trouble for him. Through his cap he scratched his head, which hurt from so much thinking so early in the morning.

Paul arrived with a head full of cobwebs. He had coffee and found that people not involved in the day's work were there. Allan Marcus, sitting with Denny Burns and his fliers, deadpanned that he had come to see if the Mexican police could shoot straight. Only when they were high, Denny responded. His fliers thought that hysterical. Allan, looking down his nose at them, offered the possibility that prolonged flying in noisy helicopters gave one irreversible brain damage. The fliers laughed at that too.

At the creek Paul noted the *policía* guards, two by two, stretching for fifty yards in either direction, some in jeeps with machine guns uncovered, some patrolling slowly, rifles ready, and he grimaced. As the sun broke out, De Luca's Mercedes zoomed up. He came alone, having persuaded his father, with difficulty, to stay at home. Quickly, he emerged, wearing a green khaki jump suit and baseball cap, his location shooting uniform. Paul greeted him with a somber good morning. De Luca nodded, squinting at the opposite bank. Sieberling came over and said, with satisfaction, "Quesedo's on the ball this time."

Understatement, Paul thought. The whole Oacala police force was here. Who was left in town? De Luca said, briskly, "I don't like it, but we don't have any choice." He turned his back to the creek and looked at the morning sun burnishing the gently waving fields. He pulled at his beard and narrowed his eyes. The police no longer concerned him. His course of action had been decided. What concerned him now was a hut too near the water which would have to be moved, a pile of bamboo logs he wanted made higher.

"What do you think of cutting from them to the bodies of the dead Cong in the bombing sequence?"

A little too pat, Paul thought, and said so. But they could try it and see how it looked. He too had already forgotten the police. Kodály approached, exploding with impatience—the light, the light, the endless question of the light. De Luca set up the first shot: rice stalks. Beyond, one of the actors playing a Vietnamese would walk behind the primitive plow pulled by the water buffalo. The schedule had been changed and no extras would be needed today, only the principals, including the Chinese actress who was, just now, descending from the costume trailer, her eyes hidden behind dark glasses. She was extremely nervous at the sight of the police. She didn't like guns, she explained.

"Don't concern yourself with them," De Luca advised. "Just get into the character and the moment. This is all peace and tranquillity here in the village. This is ancient life and ancient ways and you're one with the flow."

"Yes," she said, "but I still don't like guns."

She went off to the makeup trailer, and he ground out, "I'm getting to dislike her. Elvira would have been wonderful."

"Will they shoot?" Paul asked. "I mean if those kids come back."

De Luca didn't answer. Instead, he shouted for his assistant. Paul wandered back toward the flooded field and caught sight of Ybarra, the land agent, holding a steaming mug of coffee. The Mexican saw him and waved a jovial greeting. Paul nodded curtly and hastened by, passing Quesedo near the camera. The policeman smiled broadly and wished him good morning. The communications truck called for Paul. It was Rennie, wanting to know how things were going. He told her nothing had happened yet. She just wanted to make contact with him, she said.

As the first shot was lined up, foreboding filled the air like a poison cloud. Conversation ceased. Silence hung over the paddies, broken only by the sound of equipment being pulled and hauled into place. Here and there a muttered curse broke out into the open. On the banks the *policía* caught the fever and kept silent as well. Sieberling, perched high on a camera platform, swiveled his head around the horizon. Finally, the hoses were withdrawn. The Chinese actress was in place in the mud. The water buffalo were ready to plod forward.

"Let's make it," De Luca shouted.

Paul never saw the shot. For the three minutes of the lengthy take he watched the fields, half-expecting the peasants to rise from the earth itself, screaming and waving machetes, but when De Luca finally called "Cut it," the fields were still tranquil.

All morning they filmed. At noon, with the sun blazing overhead, Sieberling called lunch. No farmers had appeared, no interruptions. It had all been intense work, and Kodály swore it would look magnificent.

Paul began to feel his shoulders unknot. Ybarra, fanning himself with his hat, said, "You see, señor, it is all a puff of air. You show them iron and you are never troubled." The man was a little tub of lard, Paul thought, with a mustache on top.

At five-thirty he decided to return to his cutting rooms. A helicopter was coming in and he could return to town in it, sparing himself two hours of back-breaking auto ride. In minutes the whirling-bladed bug came shooting in over the mountain and sank, gently, to the landing pad.

He went to it, and when the cabin door opened to discharge a passenger he automatically moved aside to make way, but his head came up with a swiveling jerk when he recognized the familiar blue slacks and the kerchief and the wisps of blond hair. What was *she* doing here?

"Michael asked me to come," Stella told him.

"Oh." He examined her closely. She seemed very tan and very assured.

"Nothing bad happened today, they tell me."

"Under control."

He swung aboard and Stella waved a little good-bye. She did not smile, but her face was set in gentle lines, her eyes deep and moist in a way he could not recall seeing before. As the blade speed increased and the helicopter lifted, he peered down to watch her walk away.

At seven De Luca called a halt. There would be a break until the sun went down and night sequences could be shot. The *policía*

209

would be fed in staggered groups so that they might continue guard duty, needed or not. Jubilant over the day's outcome, De Luca gathered Stella and Sieberling into his blue bus and placed a call to the studio. As Stella watched, De Luca produced an impressive performance. Speaking to an obviously guarded executive, he became, by turns, demanding, conciliatory and finally totally open. The Jericho company had nothing to hide, not their books, not their actions, no matter what garbage was being retailed back home. He requested—no, he insisted—that someone come down and see for himself. It was a twenty-eight-minute bravura turn. Stella had seen some performances but this was star quality. Hanging up, De Luca shook his head.

"You feel so slimy doing a number like this, but you have to outwit those bastards in order to achieve anything."

"What did he say?" Sieberling asked.

"They have the world of confidence in us, but if we really would like to talk things over with someone, face to face, well, it can be arranged."

"What bullshit!"

De Luca laughed. "We can handle it. We're rolling and we'll keep rolling. God, it was good work today. I can feel it in my bones."

Stella listened as they talked. De Luca was almost euphoric. He turned to her, gleefully. "How would you like to get into some black pajamas and be a Vietnamese woman's back tonight?"

"No thanks."

A discreet knock on the door introduced an apologetic wardrobe assistant. The Chinese actress was having a tantrum. She hated her costume and was screaming in Cantonese.

"She wants to wear a slit-skirted *ao dai* in the rice paddies to show off her legs, the stupid bitch. I'll be right back."

When De Luca left, Sieberling promptly turned to the telephone and talked in low tones, his back to Stella, who stood, awkwardly, near the shaded window. She could have refused the summons, but she had been curious. Now, she felt totally misplaced here, trying not to look at Sieberling's profile hunched over the telephone. She thought about Paul. His eyes had looked very tired. Seeing him step into the helicopter as she stepped away had produced a dull ache which settled into her chest and was still there.

Sieberling hung up the phone, turned back to her, but said nothing. He straightened his glasses, stretched his neck, coughed.

Outside, the water pumps commenced their monotonous chant. Unable to bear the silence, she said brightly, "All that water will make this place an oasis. Giant trees are liable to spring up."

Sieberling's dark glasses faced her unwaveringly. "That's salt water," he said. "Nothing grows with salt water. That was the whole hassle."

She did not understand. "What do you mean?"

"Forget it."

Why forget it, she thought, if it was the "whole hassle"?

De Luca returned, complaining about the Chinese actress.

"She's crying because she thinks she doesn't look good. Can you imagine? That's an actress. She only wants to look good. I told her she looked so good I was falling in love with her." He gave Sieberling instructions for Kodály and the production manager left.

"Okay, now, a little time for us, a little time to unwind." De Luca bounded to the refrigerator for a bottle of white wine, turned to grin at Stella. "A great day—a breakthrough day." He ripped the cork from the bottle joyously. "Did you hear me on the phone? Did you hear me feed it to them?" He threw back his shaggy head and roared. "It was your great idea. Just marvelous." He filled two glasses to overflowing and handed her one.

"What's the salt water thing?"

"What?" He cocked his head in surprise.

"The salt water thing that made the whole hassle."

His energy stopped for a moment.

"Not important anymore, not relevant."

"But what is it?" She persisted, half-wanting to know, half-wanting conversation.

He frowned. "There is such a thing as priorities. Later, after they bring the supper in."

"I'm not sure I feel like having supper here," she said.

His frown deepened. "Why not?"

"I just don't."

"I see. You just don't." He drained his wine, refilled, started to sip, then suddenly removed his glasses and flung them clear across a table, where they skidded to the carpet. The move was sudden and violent.

She tried to keep a quaver from her voice. "Why did you ask me to come? All I've done is sit around and watch."

De Luca gulped half the wine. "Some people would think that's a privilege."

211

"I like seeing movies. Seeing them made bores me."

He glared at her. "How would you see them if I didn't make them?"

"I'd go see Mickey Mouse, then."

He slammed his hand down on the table. "Damn it, brains don't give you the right to be cruel." She said nothing. He gestured toward her glass. "Why don't you drink the goddamned wine?"

She was so startled that she lifted the glass to her lips. He laughed, drank, refilled his glass. "That's better. Unbend. Take your shoes off." With a sudden move, he reached to her feet and pulled her sandals off. She froze, then slowly reached down, retrieved them, slipped them back on. He scowled. "It's hard to figure you out."

"It shouldn't be," she said. "It doesn't thrill me to service either someone or his talent or both."

"Service?" He was angered. "I relate. I relate on an enormous number of levels!"

"If you say so."

He glared at her. "How much am I paying you?"

"I don't remember."

"You took a job with me. I'd like to know why."

Well, she thought, he would not be satisfied with leasing her; it might as well come out.

"You *offered* me a job. I'd like to know why, really why?"

He hesitated a moment, then said, "You've already earned your money."

"That's good." She bent down to adjust a sandal strap. "We've both gained then."

He watched her, brushing his beard, then he rose and walked to the opposite end of the trailer. She felt, during the six seconds of that walk, the air change.

Suddenly, he asked, almost innocently, "What do you think of Paul these days?"

She looked up in surprise and he went on. "You don't think he's any different? You think he's the same man he was when he was with you?"

"Not . . . exactly," she said.

"Not exactly. Not exactly." He mocked her tones. "Oh, no, not exactly. He's very different is what he is. His talent is emerging. He is beginning to understand what he never understood before."

She wondered what he was getting at.

"He couldn't have done that—before," De Luca jabbed. "Before, he was all locked up, choked."

"Before—oh."

"With you, yes."

"What's Paul got to do with this?" She asked it quietly.

"Conversation." De Luca smiled. "We're making conversation." She took a deep breath. "I'd rather go back to town."

Instantly, he stepped to the door and opened it. "There will be a car leaving."

"I loved the helicopter ride," she said.

"Did you?" The smile was still on his face. "I'm afraid it's busy. Speak to you later." She walked through and the door closed decisively, almost hitting her back.

Walking toward the parked cars, she retied her kerchief. The sun had not yet vanished; its last rays were spreading molten gold over the artificial trees. She could not help turning back to look at the blue bus, and despite the warmth she felt chilled.

The first night sequence went like a dream. The moonlight on the rice stalks, the breeze (manufactured by the giant fans) soughing through the bamboo, the dim, ponderous shapes of the water buffalo limned against the shimmer of the paddies were magical somehow, and everyone felt it. De Luca was all manic energy, filming angle after angle, altering, urging, shaping. When he called "Cut!" and returned to the blue van, he was coiled tight as a camera drive.

The scene with Stella seeped back into his mind. She had not wished to understand him in the slightest. She had, in fact, deceived him. Her interest in Paul was paramount. She had been too clever by half. He had not expected a second rebuff. When a knocking at the door disturbed his anger, he shouted through it, "Don't disturb me, damn it."

But the knocking continued. When he opened the door, ready to shout again, he was greeted by the Chinese actress. Her eyes were downcast and her delicate features were drawn into a supplicating mold. In her arms she held the black pajama costume. The costume, he fumed, the goddamn costume again.

"I know you very busy," she said, "but must have one little minute for me."

"Okay," he said brusquely. "Come on in."

213

She entered swiftly and was about to speak, but he spoke first. "All right, now this is what the Vietnamese peasants wear. If you wear something else—"

"No, no," she said quickly, "I have them make this one not so big as before. I wish you to see."

"You can't stand out, don't you understand?" No, she did not understand.

"But it is the same, only better. I try for you, please."

He felt the knot in his stomach tighten and pull. Why did she not understand? He felt like slapping her. "All right, put it on, put the thing on," he barked, and went to find the wine. When he turned around, she had shed her brocaded robe. Under it, she was almost without hips and the bikini panties were caught by her bones while her white brassiere superfluously covered what were obviously barely raised nipples. She smiled unself-consciously.

"You will see."

He put his wineglass down and moved toward the girl reflexively. Saying nothing, he reached for her. She was genuinely surprised. "Oh," she said, "but . . ." When he put his hands upon her, she giggled and wiggled her small frame. When her underclothes came off, he lifted her bodily, like a toy, pushing and pulling, handling her with no regard for her sounds or the distortions of her legs and spine. When his surges ceased, she was still in his hands, limp, her head against his chest. He put her down on a couch and turned away drained, eyes closed, rocking on his feet. The girl sat up.

"You bad." But she giggled again.

"I'm sorry," he mumbled, "I just . . ." He turned to the wine, not wanting to look at her. She stood up, retrieved her underclothes, covered herself with the robe, hesitated, picked up the costume and held it out.

"But you like this, no?"

"Yes," he said. "It's fine. You wear it."

"Thank you," the Chinese girl said, a small shade of victory in her black eyes. She closed the brocaded robe and left without another word.

The night sequences went well. Sieberling was wary until the final "Cut!" was called, much after midnight, but all was peaceful. The crew's tension had long since disappeared and a mild case of euphoria set in, abetted by Ybarra's "leetle present" of half a dozen bottles of tequila, not to mention a cache of hand-rolleds.

214

Paul had flown back in at ten with Rennie. The last hours, though he had not spoken of it to Michael, were worrisome. There was always the possibility that the peasants were waiting to make another move. When it proved otherwise, he knocked back his ration of tequila, like the others, and felt the weight lift from his back.

"Luis . . . maybe Luis finally reached whoever gives the orders."

"Who's Luis?" Rennie quizzed from her place on the floor, back against a chair.

"A friend, a very important friend." Paul smiled. "*Salud*, Luis." He raised his glass.

"Luis, you crazy bastard," De Luca toasted. They drank and broke into laughter.

"You guys have some deep dark secret," Rennie complained.

"You betcha." De Luca thought a moment. "Tomorrow, there's that action sequence with the two Cong and our girl. The way the schedule looks now, I'll have to be in two places at once to shoot it, unless I get some help." He hesitated. "I had thought of letting Allan handle it, but I don't know, I feel now that you could give it more than he can. Want to take a shot?"

Paul's buzz vanished instantly. The sequence contained action, but there was emotion there as well, relating, not just second-unit. Still, he felt he must question. "Mike, are you sure?"

Rennie rose then with a serene smile of purest satisfaction. "Of course he's sure." She moved, regally, to the bathroom, leaving her shoes behind.

De Luca laughed. "We'd get a real jump on the schedule that way, so when we get the extras in on the day after, we'll be able to close out the location. What do you think?"

"God, yes."

"I'll be able to shoot the indoor stuff then." He did not say that he had little desire to work with the Chinese actress again, though he knew he must and would. "I had a talk, today, with your friend Stella."

From the way he said it, Paul knew something had happened.

"We didn't exactly agree on the way things ought to be handled."

He could understand that.

"I'm not sure I can work with her."

He could understand that, too.

"I'm not judging her, Paul, and it's not really personal, but I'm not sure I find sympathetic vibes there . . . for either of us."

She had not gone to bed with him then, Paul reasoned with an improbable sense of relief. But Michael was right, all the same; she had no sympathetic eye for this movie or for his own opportunities.

"She's funny," he said, slowly. "She's . . . rigid." He laughed. "You know, that's what she used to accuse me of being."

Rennie returned then and De Luca lazed himself up. He had decided to be flown back to his hacienda for the rest of the night, and the three left the blue van together. Outside, the powerful work lights were on and Sieberling was assigning watch duty to his crew as the hoses worked again to replenish the rice-paddy water levels. A new squad of *policia* had arrived, dispatched by Quesedo, to replace their comrades on the outer perimeter.

As De Luca flew off, Paul walked the location, with Rennie, searching for the perfect spot to film the scene Michael was entrusting him with. As they paced, in the glare of the floods, Rennie reached up to kiss him.

"Michael knows how good you're going to be," she murmured, "and so do I."

"Well, I don't," he said.

She kissed him again, but he did not even feel her lips. He was looking out, beyond the lights, to the hypnotic darkness of the silent desert. His ears could not detect the noises made by the tiny creatures that lived by sundown, who slithered and slid, who crab-walked and rustled, tunneling through sand castles in search of even more minuscule prey to devour so that they might survive. But they were there, creatures that darted, played dead and changed color so that they might avoid being devoured, resist receding into tiny bowels, from which, eventually, they would touch the desert once again as a new, replenishing source of life.

CHAPTER
21

Asleep, pressed tightly against his wife's nightgowned back, De Luca awakened suddenly, uncertain of why, totally alert in an instant. Wide-eyed, he became aware of whispers and scrambling noises. He thought, at first, they were in the room but realized they must be outside. Beside him Catherine slept, beautiful in her suspended state, hair in place, face unblemished. He left the bed, padded to the window and pushed the shutters open to peer down upon a horrifying moonscape. In the harsh glare of the night lights, the gardens, shrubs and trees were no more. In their place were twisted limbs and tortured earth. Every shred of vegetation had been ripped out, slashed down. Trees, half-chopped, half-sawn through, were bleeding on the ground. The riotously colored acacia lay in heaps, already withering. Huge holes were everywhere. Roots jutted into the air like awkward severed veins. It was a nightmare of carnage. A horde of rampaging elephants might do this, might leave nothing of decades of loving care, might rip and butt so that it would not be beautiful here, perhaps ever again.

"My God—Jesus," he groaned.

Catherine came awake and called, "Michael . . . what?"

"They wrecked everything," he shouted back at her, grabbing at his robe and charging out of the room. On the stairs he was met by his ashen-faced father.

"Mikey . . . you all right?"

"Look what they did!" He threw open the front door as the housekeeper came struggling from around the rear. Her face frozen in horror, she crossed herself.

"*Madre de Dios. Ai . . . ai . . .*"

Catherine ran downstairs to her husband and saw, fully, what had been done. Her mouth opened wide in surprise.

"Michael, who did this?"

"Where are the guards, goddamn it, and the gardener? What happened to those bastards?" He raced across to the small gardener's cottage.

"Mikey, be careful," his father shouted.

He reached the cottage, bare and sterile now where before it had been overgrown and dense. He pulled at the door and it gave at his touch. He lurched inside. There were no lights on, but he was able to see enough to make him stop. Three bound figures lay, like effigies, on the floor, one alongside the other. They were so still he thought they were corpses. When he went to them, cautiously, he saw that was not the case and breathed easier. The two guards were bleeding from blows to the head but were otherwise unharmed. The gardener, an old man, had simply been bound and gagged. De Luca released them, and they rose to their feet, unsteadily. The gardener trembled so that he could not speak, could hardly stand and had to sit. The two guards, blood matting their hair and smearing their temples, blinked and looked at the *patrón* worriedly. Their story came out in fits and starts. At some hour, they were not even sure when, a band of totally silent men had appeared and made them captive. They had come with a wagon pulled by hand which contained tools, spades, machetes, saws, special things. They seemed to know exactly what they were doing, how to proceed. The guards observed them for only minutes before they were blindfolded and gagged, but in those minutes they saw how expertly the men were destroying everything on the property.

Dazed, De Luca went back outside. Catherine was shivering. "It's horrible, horrible. How could they?"

Within twenty minutes, Paul and Sieberling arrived, responding to De Luca's alarm. Quesedo took longer.

"They suckered us," Sieberling analyzed. "We had fire power and they cooled it, so they came in here and did this."

"How they do it and nobody hear, nobody?" the elder De Luca demanded.

Quesedo glanced from one horrifying scar to another. "They be farmers; they know what to do to be quiet."

Paul looked away from the wreckage, feeling it like a body blow. Secretly, he had been convinced, as the rice-paddy shooting progressed, that Aguillar had finally turned the trick, and it had given him a pride of accomplishment. Illusion. He looked back to the moonscape, frustrated and angry.

"If they could do this to me"—De Luca's voice faltered—"if they

218

could come into my home and attack me, personally, there's no hope, none at all."

"I tell you so before," Quesedo said feebly.

"Those bastards aren't going to stop." Sieberling glared at Quesedo. "And what the hell are you going to do about it? If I get the federal police in here, it's your ass."

"We will to find the leaders of this," Quesedo choked out. "It is you who have believed, till now, that all would be well."

"I accept it won't be." De Luca's voice rose. "They're blind. Misled, maybe. People get some kind of power and that's the end of the purity."

Quesedo looked at Paul. That one had been in contact with one of the leaders; why did he not say so now, halt the games?

"They don't understand," De Luca muttered. "I'm not going to be driven away. I'm going to finish what I have to do here, and we're going to protect ourselves any way we can."

After Sieberling and Quesedo left, Paul stayed on. It was a vigil of mourning, silent and somber. As the daylight began slanting in, shining the floors, he and De Luca sipped coffee, looking away from each other. At six-thirty De Luca curtly said, "Let's go." Rising, neither of them looked out the windows and went out the back.

By the time they arrived at the location, word had reached the set. Quesedo's *policía* were all about again. Denny and Gimper took to the skies to monitor the miles around but had to be waved off whenever the noise of their motors impinged upon the sound man's ears. This was so often that the maneuver was useless, and Sieberling called them down.

De Luca, filming his sequences, took over the right side of the location. Paul, with his short scene, set up at the spot he had chosen the night before. Curiously, despite what had happened, despite the tension all about him, he felt calm, even confident. The Chinese actress evinced disappointment and a little bewilderment when informed that De Luca would not be behind the camera, but she entered into the scene with relish. It all went well, Paul thought, and was over in three hours. When he relaxed his concentration, he saw that Rennie was standing outside the ring of lights, a wide smile on her face, applauding with silent palms. He was about to go to her when there was a shout from the camera truck. Instantly, crew members converged upon it. Three *policías* nearby ran with guns in the air. Sieberling shouted into his walkie-talkie for De Luca, legs pumping as he called.

Inside the truck, Kodály was choking paroxysmally. His trembling second assistant, a wiry thirty-year-old, was holding a film magazine that De Luca had shot. The side had been ripped open as if it were a sardine can. The black metal jutted up, bent and jagged; the darkness-needing film lay exposed to the destructive light, its coils thick and silent.

Paul stared in horror. Michael's moments had gone into that reel, prayed-for, sweated-for moments, gone now—only blinded frames remaining.

"Jesus Christ," Sieberling shouted. "Goddamn it, what happened?"

"I—I—" The assistant tried to speak but his voice failed. Kodály managed to wheeze, "He puts this magazine down, just thirty minutes ago. And when he comes back to take out the film, it was like this."

At the door De Luca, coming in, heard. The blood drained from his face, leaving his cheekbones dead white. He reached for the mangled metal. There was silence, broken only by Kodály's wheezing. Paul thought Michael might have a heart attack. His hands shook, knuckles blanched. He turned the magazine over and over again, staring at it, pleading with it as though his eyes could heal.

Sieberling's voice cracked the silence, raging at Quesedo. "Your men aren't worth shit. And maybe it's even one of them who did it!"

Quesedo flushed. Kodály, who had been scanning the logbook to see exactly what the reel contained, shook his head in despair.

"The reel has many takes you say to print, Michael. Good stuff. What do we do?"

"Reshoot," De Luca said, and Paul heard a flatness enter his voice, a steel edge that would be there from now on. "And reshoot again, if we have to."

He dismissed people with an exhausted wave, but Paul stayed and finally, after long minutes, De Luca whispered, "After what happened last night, I guess they didn't think I'd shoot today."

He fingered the curled metal sides of the film magazine with loving, grieving fingers. As though he's lost a child, Paul thought, or seen one lose an arm.

Signals had been crossed somewhere, had to be; Luis was a force.

220

Yet, he had indicated there were serious conflicts between the *bajo* peasants and the politicals of his movement, the primitives and the revolutionaries; it could be that the production was caught in the crossfire.

"Luis," he said, but Michael waved the name away in a new concern.

"I demanded that someone from the studio come down here. If they do, they'll walk right into this mess. I can't call now and say, 'Stay away.'"

"If we could only meet these people, talk to them," Paul said gently, but Michael was not listening again. Paul continued thinking of a face-to-face meeting between Michael and his tormentors. The idea gripped and grew, but he did not mention it again.

In pursuit of any clue to the film saboteur, Sieberling backed Manuel Quesedo to the wall. How would any Mexican working around the production know anything about cameras or film loading —when it was done, where the reels were put?

Quesedo was mystified by the query, but Sieberling soon enlightened him. Someone had to tip them off about how important a film magazine was, someone who worked around movies, who worked around this one.

"I'm talking about Ankrum, damn it. She'd know all about that stuff. If they asked her how to sabotage, she'd be able to tell them."

"Oh, now," Quesedo protested feebly, "she not be like that. She don' do such a bad t'ing."

"Wouldn't she?" Sieberling planted himself directly in front of the policeman. "She's bad news. Get her out of here."

"I go to see her. I look at her papers again."

"Don't look—tear them up."

Driving back, Quesedo wished the steering wheel was the *puerco*, Sieberling, and he could push him this way and that. He left a man no pride. With affairs slipping out of control all he could think about was revenge upon a girl.

He found her in the marketplace. She was bargaining for a black pottery bowl, and when he saw her almost familiar extending bush of hair, he felt an affectionate glow and cursed Sieberling again.

"Let me make you a present of this; is nice."

He paid for the bowl over her protests and took her to an open-air cantina for chiles rellenos. He plucked two Dos Equis from the

221

counter and opened them with a flourish. He could see her waiting for something to happen and said, his voice gently soothing, "Florenza, I t'ink it be good we talk."

"About what?"

"Ah—this *bajo tierra* does bad t'ings and I know you have a soft heart."

He tapped her chest boldly, feeling the roundness for a second. She said nothing.

"Myself, I don' believe you do bad, but others like to see you far away."

She still said nothing, but the set of her head and her vulnerable eyes brought the girl from Chicago back with such force that he shook his head in wonder. A feeling swept over him that if he sent her away, some magical chance would be missed.

"What are you going to do?" she finally asked.

He considered. Sometimes things worked out without action. It might be possible to keep Sieberling at bay until matters were under control again.

"What I do?" He spread his arms, theatrically. "I take chance on you is all."

He put his hand on her shoulder, close to the pulse in her neck, smiling with reassurance. "And you must to take chance on me, okay?"

His palm cradled her collarbone. He felt her moist skin and the vein through which her quick blood moved, and a sweet series of future meetings bloomed in his mind. He rolled her body under him like a living log.

Flo moved away, appraising him. He was not forcing her to leave, and his liquid eyes swam with only the slightest film of deceit. There seemed, in fact, to be some pool of decency struggling to surface. Paradoxically, he was gentle toward her—what he was toward others she had inklings of—but she was as weak as anyone, as helpless. Thus, when he reached out, touched her hair and said, "No girl in Mexico has hair like you, no person," she did not flinch but only replied, "Lucky for them, maybe."

By the time he left her, Quesedo's depression had given way to excited contemplation of a sensuous future which was possible only if, as he was doing, one grasped the present firmly.

Flo watched him go, knowing something must have happened to send him here. It could only be the *bajo*, fighting back. She started toward her motel, half-running, to find Señora Coyopan.

Just before nightfall De Luca returned home. The gardener had enlisted five men in an attempt to clear the grounds, but the earth resisted pacification. Raw holes were everywhere. The hacienda, graceful though it was, stood revealed, naked on a barren plain, crying for cover. Catherine was miraculously calm. She had already been in touch with a landscape architect from Mexico City who was arriving within twenty-four hours to supervise new plantings. Nothing could replace the old, leisurely growths, but, the architect assured her, if money was no object, much could be done very swiftly.

The elder De Luca was not so accepting. His Mikey had brought artistic light to these miseries. His Mikey had brought refrigeration to the cantina. His Mikey, just by being there, would bring importance to this town. And he was repaid this way?

De Luca soothed his father. More guards were coming. He hated to get so involved with the police but, for now, it was the only way to protect them all. Later, at Elvira's, he pressed his face into her cheek and confessed his fear that the *bajo tierra* were escalating their actions, that various elements among them had obviously gotten the upper hand. He stroked her long plume of hair and said they were uninterested in the risks he was taking to make this picture. He drew his hand across the small curve of her belly and concluded, bitterly, that they had their own motives—prejudice possibly, but he would not stop making his picture.

Elvira said nothing. She listened and turned to kiss his chest. Her hands, like a healer's, touched his face and he slept. When he did she looked at him for a long time before closing her own eyes.

CHAPTER

22

In the bed Paul shivered awake and beside him, attuned, Rennie woke also. She moved closer, calling his name. He sat up, rubbing his lids, and whispered for her to go back to sleep. She opened her eyes and reached for him. He muttered that he was all right and, leaving the bed, went to stand near the window. Through the shutter cracks he saw the black vault outside, brilliantly stippled with southern stars. The sliver of moon, a teal arc, blessed all with mystery.

A soft roundness pressed against his back, and Rennie's arms went around his middle. She murmured for him not to worry; he and Michael together could fight the world, their art was powerful and they were doing a beautiful thing and she loved him for it and for what he would become.

From the window he could see the Zócalo and the cathedral bell tower rising up near it like a square finger admonishing the Hotel Jaime. Below that finger Stella slept.

At five o'clock he dressed and went into the all-but-deserted streets. The cantina, however, was bustling. The aroma of burned Mexican coffee was pungent, and the counter held mounds of sweet rolls under protective plastic. Paul found a chair next to Allan Marcus, who, red-eyed, a deformed denim hat covering his head, ran a finger over his gums and proclaimed that his teeth were rotting as a result of the local diet.

Kruger, transport captain for the day, checked in with his list of the extras being trucked in for delivery to the set. They were scheduled to be on their way by now and would arrive at the location and be ready for costumes, some 150 buggers, at six-thirty. Fifteen minutes later, Paul left with Allan to be flown to the rice paddies by Denny himself. Marcus insisted they be given no treats, no stunts, no jokes; just transport. Denny suggested he walk.

At the location the water pumps were gushing again, and some of the wilted rice plants were being replaced with more richly lacquered ones, the better to glisten. Kodály was directing his light arrays. De Luca, in his safari shooting outfit, was already discussing the scene to be shot with the Chinese actress and an American playing a Vietnamese village chief with the aid of extensive makeup. As Paul approached, De Luca gestured, unhappily, at the ring of Quesedo's *policías* which sealed off the entire area.

Minutes later, the first setup, a high crane shot of the peasants working, had been decided upon and the crew started to rig the camera. Paul talked to De Luca about how the entire sequence might be cut together.

"Are you reading my mind?"

"Trying to." Paul laughed.

By now it was almost six-thirty and De Luca was eager to get started, but nothing could be done until the extras arrived and were outfitted as Vietnamese. At six-forty-five the water pumps were shut off and the hoses pulled from camera range. Kodály and his camera operator rode the crane platform impatiently. The costume racks were all out of the van and waiting. The Chinese actress sat close to her American colleague, and together they concocted bits of business that would reveal their true characters but that no camera could ever catch. Paul sipped coffee from a plastic cup and waited, admiring how Michael had organized the sequence, with his infallible visual sense, using every element of landscape.

At seven o'clock the sun came up full and hot over the valley. His eyes glued to the horizon, Paul saw no sign of approaching trucks.

"Where the hell are they?" De Luca uncoiled from his chair. "We've got a hell of a lot to shoot today." Kodály shouted, though the day had just started, "The light is going!"

At that point the communications man waved frantically from his jeep. Sieberling stepped over quickly to engage in animated conversation. Abruptly he snatched up the radiotelephone and barked into it. The squawked response made him drop the instrument and come running back. His voice, slightly muted by shock, called, "The trucks are rolling empty. They just found out. No one's in them."

The moment the words came from Sieberling's mouth, Paul knew. He looked grimly at De Luca, but the director was already shouting, "What do you mean no one's in them? Where are the extras? What happened to them?"

"I don't know," Sieberling said in confusion. "Something went wrong."

Beyond the production manager, beyond the police, a cloud of dust was raised by a jeep racing along the valley floor. It bounced on its tires, and the driver fought rocks and hard brush, jamming the pedal down, hacking at the gearshift. Hypnotized, the silent company watched the four-wheeler tear over the mesquite and jerk to a halt at the paddy's edge. The driver, young and hard-muscled, jumped from his seat and ran to De Luca. As he came within an arm's length, Sieberling grabbed him by the shoulder and demanded, "What happened? What's going on?"

The young driver, his face wound up with worry, said, "Nobody was there, not one Mex. The extras were supposed to be at the collection points, you know. Then we'd load them up. But nobody came, nobody was there, there was nobody to load. It all got crazy, nobody knew what to do."

De Luca froze. Paul, taken aback by his own lack of surprise, asked calmly, "Who hires these extras?"

"A contractor," Sieberling replied. "Runs a butcher store. He always gets them for us."

"Maybe he made a mistake. Maybe he didn't give them the right time and place."

De Luca sat slowly. "It's more than that."

"I'm going to damn well find out." Sieberling cupped his hands and shouted. "I'm flying back. Get me back right now."

De Luca whispered hoarsely, "It has something to do with *them*, I know it."

"Let's wait and see." Paul tried to be reassuring, but he knew that Michael was right.

The butcher shop was the usual fly-ridden stall with its chunks of jagged meat and dripping guts hanging from hooks. The butcher, as loaded with lard as the pork behind him, beady-eyed, with a paper hat on his head, pleaded innocence as two fat tears rolled slowly down his cheeks like misplaced cooking oil.

Yes, he had arranged for the extras days ago. He had done a proper job, but then yesterday—

"What happens yesterday?" Quesedo screeched at him.

Yesterday, the butcher reported hesitantly, some people had spread the word not to work for the gringos or else there would be

226

consequences. It was a situation beyond his control, he pleaded.

The *bajo tierra*, Quesedo translated for Sieberling, had frightened the people away from working, and what could be done about that?

"Why didn't he tell us yesterday?" Sieberling demanded.

The butcher's fear was its own answer.

As it became appallingly clear that the day's schedule would have to be scrapped, De Luca hastily arranged for Allan Marcus to shoot cover material; then he and Paul flew back to the Jericho compound to confront the realities. The picture was impossible to shoot without hundreds of extras. The final sequence alone would require four to five days of intensive work with the Viet Cong streaming in, the entire peasant village running away, the air strafing. They had planned to have almost a thousand extras clogging the roads, becoming panic-stricken and rushing like terrified buffalo, mindless, doomed and guiltless, to their destruction.

Pacing, gesticulating, his voice bitter and anguished by turns, De Luca railed. "Selfish, ego-tripping, macho kooks. Maybe Luis had something. They know nothing about real politics, about real political struggle. I could have helped them with that. I could make a picture here that would tear the lid off and tell their story so the whole world would listen. Instead, they do this to me."

"I still think Luis is the key," Paul insisted.

De Luca shook his head. The key was extras. What were the alternatives? Army troops? He had made a film in Yugoslavia and the government had been delighted to sell them the army as extras. Sieberling, when he joined them, had already explored that possibility. He had been on the horn with someone high up in the administration. He had not received a good reading. Federal soldiers would have to be flown into Oacala and billeted there. That presented difficulties apart from the resentment it would cause. This was a comparatively new government and it had to step very carefully over possible mine fields. To be accused of using government facilities to help a U.S. project—well, it took some thinking about.

De Luca wrapped himself in gloom. Paul grappled with any shred of possibility but nothing real occurred to him. A lump of anger rose in his throat. Hundreds of peasants out there spending their time staring vacantly at the ocher earth, and their bodies were not available. No one wanted their hearts and minds—simply their shells, their physical envelopes. They would be, truly, "atmosphere," as the extras were habitually called on the set, designed to provide that simulacrum of reality, but it was not to be. This "atmosphere" had evaporated.

"Listen." Sieberling said in a low key, "I happen to know a guy from New York who lives in Mexico City, right now. He knows all the scenes. He has lots of contacts all over the country."

What would he do? Paul wondered.

"I've already gotten to him and explained our problem. He has a friend here in Oacala, he told me—guy named Machado. This Machado can get us what we want."

"Extras?" De Luca shook himself alert. "He can get us extras from the local area?"

"My guy says Machado can get them easy, yeah."

"Easy?" Paul sat up. "How does he do it? You saw what happened this morning."

"He has his ways; he gives them protection and stuff," Sieberling said. He saw the look of apprehension well up in Paul's eyes and appealed to De Luca. "We pay him and he pays them and makes the arrangements. We give him a percentage on top, we supply the trucks and he gets them."

"Who is this Machado?" Paul asked.

"A Mexican."

"No." Paul found himself unaccountably raising his voice. "I mean *who is he?*"

"Wait a minute." De Luca hunched his head down and his eyes glinted. "Let's keep cool here." He turned to Sieberling. "You're telling us this Machado can deliver?"

"Definitely. My guy says it takes one phone call to him."

"Call him," De Luca ordered. "Ask him how long he needs to get people. You take care of the details, Sal."

When Sieberling left, De Luca heaved a deep sigh, flung himself down on a couch and squinted over at Paul, who shook his head and asked, "Who's that man he called in Mexico City?"

De Luca looked away. "I don't know and I don't want to know."

As Paul worked with Rennie for the rest of the morning, he decided that Michael was right. You had to see beyond the moment to the goal. Rennie asked him what was going to happen, and he assured her there was a plan in the works; extras would be found. She looked at him with eager eyes. Despite the problems, despite the travail, she told him fiercely, the picture would be made and would be a triumph, she knew that. Nobody could stop what he and Michael had it in them to do. She clutched at him with an intensity he had not seen in her before, and he realized how inextricably she was bound up with the production, almost as though its future was hers, its success her vindication.

Later, he went alone to the cantina for a quick lunch, and when Señor Uribe approached with a beer, he asked him if he had ever heard of someone named Machado.

"Machado?" Uribe's eyes shifted with a hint of discomfort
"Machado, yes."

Uribe shrugged. "Is couple Machados here."

Paul put his beer down. "This one is important, would have to be."

Uribe hesitated, then leaned over. His right hand went out, became a pistol; his index finger changed from barrel to trigger, pulled sharply, Paul could almost hear the explosion.

"What does that mean?"

Uribe leaned over further and whispered hoarsely into his ear. "*Bandolero*. Gangster." He winked and left for another table.

Paul sat back uneasily. It was no great surprise. Sieberling's man in Mexico City was probably Mafia, in temporary seclusion. They did business everywhere. This Machado was a local he did some of that business with. But what could be in it for him to undertake contracting extras? The money was peanuts. But then, these people did favors all the time and held the markers. Where would Machado get extras, however—how would he get them? The more he thought about the prospect, the more uneasy he became.

And yet what else was there to do? There was Luis. There was that slim possibility of a face-to-face meeting with the *bajos*. If that could be made to happen, Michael would win them over, there was no question of that. Finishing his beer, his anxiety mounting, he reasoned that Machado had to be a last resort. Though Michael might not agree, a try at finding Luis and explaining the bind had to be made, absolutely had to be. He rose and strode from the cantina into the baking street. He made his way to Calle Juarez and Ismena's shop unerringly, only to find it closed, the iron shutters locked.

He pounded on the hot metal, hoping someone, beyond, might hear him, but it proved futile. Frustrated, he stepped back. The post-noontime heat settled about his head, and it was difficult to think rationally.

He walked to the avenida. There he found a taxi, clambered in, and when he asked to be taken to Calle Libertad, number six, the driver's lips split in a salacious grin and he rolled his eyes.

The driver knew the city. His cab cut through back streets and donkey paths to arrive at the Red House in minutes. Beyond the iron gate, as before, thick curtains covered every window and the veranda light was out.

As Paul left the cab, the driver called, *"Mucho calor, eh?"* Then he drove off, beeping his horn.

Going up the path, Paul heard no sound but remembered that he had heard nothing the other time as well. He took the steps rapidly, picked up the brass knocker and rapped heavily. He waited, anxiously, for only ten seconds, then knocked again and again. Finally, he heard latches being thrown from inside. As soon as the door opened a crack, he burst out, "Señora!" But he saw that it wasn't the madam. It was a tall, thin girl who held the door open a bit to look at him with obvious fright. She clutched a faded green wrapper at her throat and winced seeing him.

"The madam," Paul said quietly. *"Por favor."*

The girl stared at him blankly. He reached out a reassuring hand but she jumped back, calling in a choked little voice, *"Temprano. Cerrado. Cerrado."*

She started to close the door, but he pushed against it in desperation. *"Momento . . .* please."

At this the door swung fully open. The madam, behind the girl, had simply reached over and pushed her out of the way to confront Paul herself. Her hair was down. A lavender belted gown hung open over a lacy negligee, and even in this state of undress a string of pearls flashed from her throat. She was nastily belligerent.

"What you want here? You go. Go away!"

"I have to speak to you, please. It's about . . ." He hesitated, then finished, ". . . the man I saw before."

The madam gritted out a few angry words to the girl, who scurried away and up the stairs. Turning, she glared at him and said, "Is impossible. You understand? Cannot to be. Don' know nothing. You go now."

"Let me in," he pleaded, "just let me in."

The madam pursed her lips, jerked herself away from the door, and he stepped inside quickly. She slammed the door behind him and burst out, "Why you do this? Is much danger. You cannot to come here anymore. No more. Is finished."

"I have to see Aguillar." He spoke rapidly. "It's very important. Ismena wasn't there. I don't know where else to go to find him."

The madam implored the heavens. "I wish I never see him or you. *Policía* could be waiting out there, you understand that, mister?"

"Yes," he acknowledged, "but that's how important it is."

She glared at him and finally ordered brusquely, "You wait. Sit." Her mules slithering on the polished floor, she disappeared behind a door. Obediently, Paul sat on one of the red plush chairs.

In the musty thickness, the heaviness of the choking velvet hallway, he felt his head begin to throb. There was no air in this place; nothing came in, nothing went out. The million exhalations here floated, stagnated, were breathed in again. Windows were never opened, never. He felt the sweat collect under his arms and in the cavity below his neck. The throbbing became more pronounced, and he pressed at his temples for relief as Stella used to do for him.

Her mules slapping again, the madam returned. "You know where is the Oacala club of tennis?"

"What?" He did not think he heard her correctly.

She smacked her palms together impatiently. "The club of tennis. Tennis."

How would he know where that was?

"You ask the taxi man, then. He takes you. Is near Inigue." Inigue, he knew, was a wealthy suburb, and he wondered if they were communicating at all.

"You don't understand me," he said. It enraged her.

"You go there, to the tennis," she said angrily.

"To the tennis club?"

"Sí, sí . . . the club of tennis."

"But what do I do if they stop me?"

"They don' stop you. You are a gringo. Is no *problema* to walk in. All right?"

He nodded, believing finally.

"You go to small building near the road, in back. Wooden building, little house. Stays there the man who takes care, you understand?"

"The caretaker?" Things started to clarify themselves.

"Sí, he takes care." She nodded vigorously. "You go there and you find . . . who you must see. You go now. He waits." She stopped speaking, gripped his arm hard. "You don' come here no more. Don' care how important you say, don' come here, okay?"

"Yes," he said, apologetically, "I'm sorry I had to come now." She removed her claw. A sudden wry smile attacked her. "But if you want good time, you can come at night. Understand? Then you

231

have the best time in all Mexico. Mine is the best house of all. Everyone knows this." Opening the door before he could respond, her fingers waved him out.

On the veranda he filled his lungs with the warm, scent-laden air and felt the throbbing begin to subside. He had pulled it off. Aguillar was at the tennis club and knew he was coming, had to be aware of what was developing—and must have some way of dealing with it. Jubilantly, he took the steps two at a time and rushed down the avenida, determined to find another cab even at this siesta time. Running, he found himself laughing. The tennis club. *The tennis club.* It was perfect.

CHAPTER
23

Inigue, with its jacaranda-treed winding road bordered by great intertwined clumps of vibrant sunflowers, with its private parks hidden behind concrete walls and wrought-iron gates, was Beverly Hills, Paul decided, only vastly more affluent. One such gate was open, allowing a look at a hacienda far more impressive than De Luca's. In the courtyard a young woman worked a snorting, steaming Arabian; whoever lived in the dolce grandeur of Inigue owned a goodly piece of Mexico.

Passing estate after estate, the T-shirted driver kept repeating, "*Mucho dinero aquí . . . mucho dinero.*" After twenty minutes, leisurely rounding a bend, he pointed and announced "Tennis."

A stone portal lay ahead and a small building pleasantly drenched with ivy and hydrangea. As they came under the stonework, a tall, green-uniformed guard held up an imperious hand. The driver braked so hard that Paul fell back in his seat. Through an open door he saw another guard at a table, newspaper in hand and a holstered pistol close by.

He found a phony, expectant smile somewhere. "Hi, is this the tennis club?"

The guard peered in at him.

"*Buenos días, señor.* You meet someone?"

With startling speed and conviction, his lawyer's name popped out. "Yes . . . Señor Becker."

"Beck-er?" The guard's brow wrinkled with nonrecognition.

"Yes," Paul said. "He has all my things too."

"Ah . . ." The guard waved them on.

The madam was right. *Yanqui* opened all doors.

He left the cab and walked toward a terraced clubhouse in the distance. There, waiters in mess jackets served umbrella-protected tables. Alongside was the car park—an assemblage of Bentleys, Mercedes, Alfas and BMWs, leavened here and there by Lincoln

Continentals and Cadillacs. They all rested in careless formation, creating a mosaic of superbly painted machines, German gunmetal setting off Italian blood red and austere English black, a rare collection.

He passed the car park on a footpath bordered by graceful fruit trees, dripping willows, beautifully clipped box hedges and lavish rose beds. Where, in all this splendor, would the caretaker's place be?

Where, for that matter, were the tennis courts?

It took him a few minutes to realize they were below ground level, some ten feet down, lined with concrete and floored by red clay. When he looked down at one, the sight was bizarre: two men slashing away at a yellow ball in a pit—where the valley winds could not get to them.

A girl in a blue-and-green tennis dress, her shoulders all deep beige cream, passed him on her way to the sunken court. Her look was quizzical, and he felt conspicuously out of place in his denim shirt and khakis.

He saw a small pebbled path cutting across the greensward and headed for it, anxious to get away. He kept to it until the courts were almost out of sight and a narrow car path appeared, bordering open field.

A service road, he thought—then he froze. Not a dozen feet from him a green-uniformed man chuffed intently along behind a heavy-bodied alert guard dog. The animal had its head to the ground and its great muscles rippled.

Paul stopped, then forced himself forward again, and as he made the move, the dog cut directly across his path and halted, a soft growl rising in its throat. At this the guard looked quickly over at Paul, but the look was simply one of embarrassment.

"*Vamos.*" He slapped the dog hard on its flanks, urging it forward, and moved after his animal. Paul swallowed phlegm and stepped up his pace.

Fifty yards later, the pebble road curved sharply. Around the bend a small wooden cottage came into view. The windows were curtained; the roof was in need of repair. One step of the four leading up to the door was crumbling. Containing his excitement, he scanned the vicinity, saw no one and went quickly toward the building, where he mounted the creaky steps with a fake air of assurance. Hesitating again to scout from there, he saw a car and a truck parked on the service road, but they were devoid of occupants.

He put his hand on the knob, took it away and knocked instead. Nervously looking behind him to make certain that he was still unobserved, he knocked again. Suddenly, the door swung open, loosing a shaft of light into the darkened interior, and an arm reached out and pulled him inside.

It was a small, rough room, primitively furnished. The arm was Aguillar's. He stood close by, wearing white peasant clothing and a straw hat.

"Pablo," he said solicitously, "are you all right?"

"I'm fine," Paul said. He shook his head admiringly. "The tennis club."

Aguillar allowed himself a little smile. "I understand, but this is a safe place; we have good friends here. How is Miguel? I think of his trouble in all this."

"He's in a bind. We're all in a bind." He hesitated. "You must know what's happening."

"Sí." Aguillar's lips tightened. "I do know, and believe me, I have tried to stop them. They always say someone does something on his own, but I don't believe them. My patience is at end. Where there is no political education, there is only *anarquía*."

"Michael is being forced to do things we don't really want to do, Luis." He thought it best to come right out with it. "There's this man we're about to use, Machado."

Aguillar looked incredulous. "Machado? The criminal?"

"He can get the extras," Paul said uncomfortably. "We pay him and—"

"I know what he does."

"Luis, you're the only hope we have. Because Michael's going to make this picture no matter what, and we have to have those extras."

Aguillar frowned. Paul pushed on doggedly.

"If we could meet the leaders face to face, if we could get together, you and them and us, if they'd just listen to Michael only once, they'd understand, they'd see he's together with them, I'm sure of it."

Aguillar concentrated, turned the idea over in his mind. Paul watched for signs. Aguillar nodded slowly, acceptingly.

"Face to face. Men to men." He gathered enthusiasm. "We all sit together and talk together and listen to Miguel. Yes, yes, that is the way it must happen. I make it happen. Oh, yes—I take them by the neck and I pull them to such a meeting." He punched the air with a powerful fist.

Paul felt vindicated. It *was* the way. Michael's sincerity would sweep them all.

"As soon as possible," he pleaded.

"Sí," Aguillar agreed, but disturbingly, the fire left his eyes to be replaced by a morose gray film.

Paul waited. It was apparent that the Mexican was struggling with something unpleasant. Finally, he braced his shoulders and said, "I must tell you something sad now."

Paul stiffened, expectantly.

"I must say to you that I was wrong about Jesus and you were right."

"Jesus. Oh," Paul said softly.

"Sí. He does bad business, like you say, very bad for a revolutionary man." His voice took on stern depths. "He is gone now. He was once a good man but he is gone now."

What did that mean, Paul wondered—gone? Was it a euphemism for being shot? He did not ask. In the ensuing silence the muffled roar of a small tractor became audible.

Aguillar stepped to the window and, lifting the curtain an inch, glued his eye to the opening. In a moment he turned back, jamming his hat closer down over his face.

"That is the signal for me. If something is not good, then Francisco comes on his tractor. That is him."

"You mean dangerous?"

"Something not right, not good. I don't know what. But I must go."

"The meeting?" Paul pleaded.

"Sí . . . sí . . . you will have a message from me." The terrorist gripped his hand in a quick good-bye. "I will force this. I will say to them they must to listen to you or I will be against them, and if I am against them it will be no good. And this they know." He took two steps to the door but swung about again.

"Oh, Pablo, is it possible that the *jefe* has an extra camera he gives us, a little one?"

"Little one?"

"To show the cinema."

"A projector, you mean?"

"Pro-jector, sí. We have a revolutionary cinema from Cuba. We would like to show this to the farmers."

"We can get you one, I guess."

"We must always make the propaganda," Aguillar said. "The

236

cinema is very strong for this." He gripped Paul's shoulder hard once more. "Tell Miguel we will overcome everything."

There was a flash of the door and he was gone. The tractor drone faded. A bird tweeted sweetly somewhere, in tune with Paul's new hope.

Captain Quesedo watched the caretaker's cottage from the old Ford behind the truck.

When the whore had telephoned him, it had been difficult to understand her. The man, she had repeated over and over again, the man who was here. Finally, he had understood that she meant the Judío, Gordon.

When she told him what she had overheard—the caretaker, the tennis club—he had sworn her to silence, borrowed the nondescript car and raced to the spot. From this vantage point, crouching uncomfortably in the rear, he had seen Gordon enter the cottage. The whore had been right. Whoever he was about to meet was already there then, and the meeting was, at that instant, taking place.

Minutes passed. Quesedo breathed in the soft afternoon air, gluing his eyes to the cottage. A golden bee flew near and probed the open window. It started into the car and Quesedo jerked away, slapping at it. Unimpressed, the bee lazed back outside and Quesedo returned his attention to the cottage. With dismay, he stared across the open field to where a white-clothed figure was moving rapidly away.

Quesedo ground his teeth. This man had to have emerged in the past five seconds and now, after all this, was disappearing. He pounded at the wheel in frustration then gaped, instantly alert, for his quarry had turned back for a last look at the cottage. Catching a glimpse of the man's face, Quesedo moved his nose to the windshield, his palms going clammy. As the man adjusted his straw hat and trudged on, the captain fell back, astonished. Slumping, he saw Gordon leave the cottage, but that no longer interested him. The face he had seen was *Luis Aguilar's*. Unmistakably. Why was Gordon meeting *him*? The *bajos* were the troublemakers.

Mind whirling, from sheer instinct he detected, within the puzzle, the kernel of opportunity. A feel of fuzz on his left wrist distracted him. The golden bee, returning, sat there quivering slightly. Without hesitation Quesedo smashed his right palm down and felt the satisfying crack.

CHAPTER
24

In her morning shower, Stella weighed everything and found a clear result—time to go.

She phoned the airline office, got through to them with shocking speed and arranged for a seat on the late plane since the one P.M. was booked.

She composed a good-bye note to Paul, tore it up, wrote three other versions and destroyed them all, deciding, finally, that notes were nonsensically melodramatic; a phone call would do. Having decided that, she looked into the center of the Zócalo where the band shell rose on its gilded legs and she became, momentarily, ludicrously nostalgic.

On this morning Flo Ankrum held a cup of black coffee and felt the pressure mount in her chest.

Ten minutes ago, Señora Coyopan had come by. There had been a quiet bond between them ever since the woman's husband had been taken, and she told Flo what everyone in the market already knew—the extras had not shown themselves. The cinema people were furious and now there was fear. A *maleante* was coming in, she'd said, a *bandido*, and would force them to go. Who knew what would happen after that?

"How could this man force people?" Flo had asked, astounded.

Because of the fear, Señora Coyopan had responded. No one would go against him or his house would be burned, he might be beaten—or worse. This was not the first time with Machado.

Was it possible, Flo wondered, that Michael would go this far? Sieberling would, of course.

Her room confined her. Sitting on the patio watching the flowers was even worse. She jumped into the VW, thinking she would visit a new Mixtec dig, but when she came to the road going there, she veered off on sudden impulse. She drove, instead, foot down on the gas pedal, losing her way twice, until she reached the crushed stone link to the pink stone *casa*.

Braking, she saw the small, long-skirted figure seated on the steps, a bowl in her hand, and knew who she was.

"Excuse me," she called. *"Buenos días.* I'm sorry to come like this, but it's very important."

The Indian girl rose quickly, her face clouding with suspicion.

"Michael is dealing with that Machado," Flo called urgently, "and he mustn't. There's big fear. You're Indian, you understand . . ."

"You are who?" The girl stopped her.

"I used to work . . . with them," Flo said, "but they—"

In one quick movement, the girl went through the open front door and closed it behind her, leaving Flo to stare at the hand-rubbed cypress wood helplessly.

She drove back to the town, deflated. It isn't her fault, she thought somberly; Michael has her brainwashed; he does that to all his women. When she entered the Zócalo and came abreast of the Jaime, the need to talk, to share, was so overpowering that she ran into the hotel and found Stella in her room.

Stella looked at the breathless girl, once again, in her doorway, and said, "Whatever it is, I can't help you. I'm leaving this afternoon."

Flo sagged. Her knees bent, her shoulders slumped and even the flare of her hair seemed to lose its thrust. All the bumpy defiance changed into a soft despair that impelled Stella to relent and say, "Oh, all right. Come in."

Flo stopped just inside. "I heard something that's so terrible . . ." She poured out what Señora Coyopan had told her. When she had finished, vocal cords tense, Stella said firmly, "I'm sorry—whatever it is, it's not my affair."

"No," Flo agreed humbly, "I just thought maybe Gordon could see what this is going to lead to. It could really come down."

"He's just the editor," Stella objected. "What makes you think he even knows about this—if you've got it right?"

Flo flashed for a moment. "I have got it right." When she saw Stella tighten, she said, "I'm sorry."

"All right," Stella said, "so now you've told me."

"Are you going to see him before you go?"

"No, I'm phoning him, that's all. Now could I be left alone, please?"

"Yes," Flo said, but she didn't go to the door. Instead she added, "When you speak to him, just ask him . . ."

The woman never gives up, Stella thought. "That's it," she said, and reached for the knob. "Good-bye and good luck."

"Right." Flo moved then, but turned back and asked almost plaintively, "Would you like me to drive you to the airport? I could come back and—"

"Thank you, no."

"Right." She delayed a moment more, then, defeated, said good-bye.

When Flo left, Stella went to the phone and called Paul. She was connected to his cutting room and told him, straightforwardly, that she had just called to say good-bye; she was leaving on the afternoon plane.

"Oh," he said, and she detected a note of relief in the single word. He asked about her *turista*; she said she was fine. He said that was good, and then there seemed nothing else to say.

In the uneasy silence, more to fill the gap than anything else, she said, "I hear there are some problems with the extras."

"Oh," he said, and she could tell that he was stepping carefully, "there have been some problems, but they'll work out. Who told you about this?"

"Someone," she said.

"Who someone?"

"Ah—around."

"It's not *around*."

"Maybe the waiter," she said airily.

"I don't believe you," he said with irritation. "It's very complicated; some of the people who want to work for us have been scared away."

She paused for a moment; Flo was somewhere near the mark, anyway. "How are you going to get extras then?"

"We will, that's all. We're just—arranging for someone else to handle it."

She did not respond, thinking again of Flo, and he said, defensively she thought, "Or have you heard about that, too?"

"I heard—something," she admitted reluctantly. She had not envisioned this kind of good-bye and regretted the whole thing..

"Anyway," he said, "things will probably return to normal because there's someone important working on it."

"Okay," she retreated. "You've got some political Mr. Big; that always helps."

That eased the mood, and he told her he was sorry she hadn't had a better vacation. She assured him that it matched Club Med—and she would have better stories to tell.

She hung up, feeling she should have stayed with a note after all.

After talking to Stella, Paul went back to the Moviola and unreeled the first rice-paddy sequence. The camera, fluid as the paddy itself, moved with the stalks, strained with the buffalo, searching deep into the mud. His own screen, however, was too alive with kinetics of other times and other places. He switched off the motor and went to see De Luca, who was conferring with Denny about the planning and shooting of the Operation Jericho sequence. His thought that De Luca had thrown him a searching look upon entrance was substantiated the moment the flier departed.

"What did she want?"

He took a moment—too long for De Luca, who snapped again, "Your friend, what did she want? She called you, I know. The switchboard girl told me." It was the tone Michael reserved for enemies.

"She called to say good-bye," Paul said. "She's leaving."

"Fine."

"But she . . . heard something; that's what I wanted to tell you. Someone told her we were planning to use Machado."

"What?"

De Luca picked a crystal paperweight from his desk and flung it to the carpet. It rolled, harmlessly, to a corner. Paul understood his anger.

"Who told her," De Luca ranted, "who's the *someone*? Who knows what we're doing?"

"I don't know."

"What has she got to do with this? All she can do is make trouble for us."

"No," he said quickly, "she'd never do that."

"What *does* she want to do then, help you?" De Luca marched his bulk toward Paul. "She doesn't want to help you, believe me."

"She doesn't want to hurt us," he said stubbornly.

"It's important to know who told her, Paul."

"I asked; she didn't say."

241

"That's how much she's trying to help us," De Luca roared. "Who would tell her such a thing? No Mexican is going to walk up to her in the street and tell her that. What else does she know? And why is she poking her nose into this?"

Helplessly, he said, "We should give Luis some working time, Mike; a day at least."

"That's another delay. We can't afford more delays."

"Mike," he pleaded, "it saves us getting involved with that guy."

"Yes," De Luca said, grim-lipped, "but I am trying to see where I stand. My house gets ripped up and Aguillar does nothing. My whole schedule gets shot to hell and he still does nothing. There's this . . . dope thing. Now he wants a projector, for God's sake. How long can we wait?"

"I know," Paul mumbled, "but I've heard these things about Machado."

De Luca dropped to the couch next to him. "Paul, what you did, finding Luis and confronting him, was . . . heroic, actually, yes it was. I don't know who else would have done that for me. I was amazed when you told me and I'm still amazed, but Paul, we have to be prepared for the possibility that he can't get these . . . people . . . to listen to him."

"It's . . . possible," he acceded, grudgingly.

"Let's do this." De Luca jerked himself up again. "Let's wait till midnight to see if we get some kind of word from him. If we don't, we shoot in the morning, no matter what. Is that fair? Is that reasonable?"

"Midnight?" That was only ten hours from now.

"Paul, we've got to move; we've got to get it in the can, now." De Luca retrieved the crystal ball. "Believe me—I know. There's a time when you think and you plan and you junk it all and start again, junk that too. But there's the time when you *go*. The energy's there—it happens. You'll see. You'll find out when you do it." He stood directly over Paul. "We've got to shoot tomorrow, got to."

"I guess."

"And what," De Luca asked suddenly, "did you finally say to . . . your friend?"

"Stella?" For a moment he was disoriented. "I told her Machado was just a . . . kind of casting service."

"What did she say to that?"

"Mike, it was a good-bye call, really—that's all. She said good-bye." He felt it advisable to try to lighten things up. "She's just a

242

little . . . kooky, that's all. She said she was taking the plane out and would have some stories to tell back home and that was it."

Before the words were completely out, De Luca asked sharply, "What did she mean, stories?"

"Mike"—he rose impatiently—"just about her trip here. It was good-bye."

De Luca frowned and said, instead, "Let's forget about her."

"Okay." He started for the door, but before he could leave, De Luca caught him by the arm.

"Paul, I respect what you feel and I know you respect my feelings—because we're both trying to do just one thing: make our movie our way, right?"

There was a soft, beseeching light in De Luca's eyes that pleaded for intimacy and understanding. Finally, Paul thought, that was what it was all about—making their movie. *Their movie.* He nodded and De Luca, satisfied, allowed him to leave.

Barely moments after Paul had gone, De Luca called Sieberling into his office, told him that Paul's friend was booked on a flight and that he was concerned about her.

"But if she's leaving . . ."

"I have this gut feeling," De Luca insisted. "She said she would have some stories to tell. And she will. She knows a lot of people, important people. It makes me queasy. I'm not sure she should be going and doing that right now."

"Oh." Sieberling came alert. "I understand. Yeah. Absolutely."

"She has no right to come on down here, hang around and go back to retail gossip that might just build pressure. Don't you think we have a right to protect ourselves?"

The phone rang then and the conversation ended abruptly. Sieberling had disliked that woman from the moment he laid eyes on her: a smart-assed broad with too much cool. He looked at his watch to check how much time he had to work.

Stella left the hotel for the airport half expecting to see Flo Ankrum lurking somewhere in her VW. She was not, of course, and settling into the taxi, Stella sighed with relief. The drive with her would have been a ten-mile political exercise. Certainly, Flo Ankrum had no reservoir of small talk. She had wells of large important talk, however, and walking to the frescoed terminal, Stella caught herself smiling at the girl's powerful earnestness, her life-and-death pronouncements. For Flo Ankrum

243

everything led to politics; sex, food, eye shadow, all were way stations on the Marxist theoretical road, and all were approached with equal intensity. Still, Stella thought, there was something engaging about her.

The terminal was without its usual crush of tourists and bewildered peasants. The buses and taxis had just hauled a load of new arrivals to their destinations. The customs men smoked and discussed the finer points of passing women. A smiling, jet-haired, round-faced porter approached. Chattering amiably, he relieved Stella of her suitcase, walking with her toward the ticket agent, who, morosely, punched buttons and observed his computer screen, not looking up. She presented her ticket, saying, "I'm on the plane to Mexico City." Head still down, the ticket agent reached for her envelope, opened it with a distracted sigh, extracted the ticket, was about to insert it into a time punch when, frowningly alert, he looked up.

"You are this lady?"

"Every inch, yes."

"Moment. Moment, please." The agent thumbed through a batch of papers. Stella looked at the porter, who smiled reassuringly. The agent looked up. "Is little something here. Your reservation was taken by mistake. That flight is all booked up. I am sorry." He handed Stella her ticket and looked down again.

"Wait a minute," she said, mystified. "What am I supposed to do now?"

The man looked up, his face grave. "Clerk makes mistake on the telephone, madame. There is no place for you." He shrugged. "What can we do?"

Stella stared at him with disbelief. He turned his eyes downward again but she leaned in and said forcefully, "I have to leave. I must."

The agent looked to heaven for help and flapped papers at her.

"All right," Stella calmed herself, "I'll take the late plane, then."

The agent grimaced. "That is full-booked too, madame."

"Now, listen," Stella said grimly, "I've checked out of the hotel; I've arranged to be in Mexico City. You have a responsibility to me."

"We find hotel for you, madame." He picked up a phone but she shook her head.

"I don't want a hotel, I want a place on that plane."

"Is no place."

The agent spoke sharply to the porter, whose smile had faded and whose eyes had turned cautious.

244

"He finds you taxicab."

"I don't want a taxicab, I want to see your supervisor, your boss. I want to see the chief agent, you understand?" Overbooking. Here in this sleepy southern city, the airline traveler's curse had overtaken her.

The chief agent turned out to be a red-faced bull of a man with the horn rims of his glasses so thick they almost obscured the lenses. He was harsh and uncompromising. Mistakes could be made and were made all over the world, even in the United States, he was sure.

"What about standby?" Stella asked in desperation.

The chief agent shrugged. "Go tomorrow. Is good tomorrow."

"I'll wait now," Stella insisted.

Thirty minutes later, she heard the loudspeaker declare that loading was open for the Mexico City flight. She watched as a line of tourists, souvenir-laden and chattering, formed. She tried to count heads but lost track. Stationing herself at the picture window, near the gateway to the aircraft, she observed the passengers drifting past, walking up the ladder-gangway to the plane's yawning opening. She waited there for twenty minutes watching, then heard the loudspeaker call for final boarding. In surprised gratification, she realized that less than half the plane must be full; the passenger line boarding was a thin, straggling one. She peered at the row of windows where faces could be seen and saw many empty spaces. There had to be seats.

As the loudspeaker spewed multilingual instructions, she ran to the desk, where one final couple was being checked in, waited and, when they left, thrust her ticket forward.

"There's lots of space. Get me on it."

The ticket agent looked at her as though she had never before passed before his eyes. The blank look made her frantic.

"Please," she said, "look at your list. There are seats there, I know there are. Get me on."

"The flight is complete, señorita," he said, but this time his voice was soft, almost hesitant.

"No," she cried, "it's not."

Through the window she could see the last couple hurrying up the top step and into the airplane. Two ground crewmen put their hands on the boarding steps and wheeled it away rapidly. The curved door slammed into place. Confused, Stella turned to the ticket agent, but he had moved away from her, down his counter, and was studying a clipboard. As the plane commenced to move, earthbound and ponderous, away from the boarding area, Stella's suitcase dropped from her clammy hand. No porter came to pick it up. They all had their backs turned as she angrily watched the airplane grow smaller in the distance.

CHAPTER
25

Sieberling's phone call produced a meeting at a café on the Zócalo. The swarthy Mexican who turned up had a wrestler-thick body that spread sweat stains through the armholes of his white silk jacket. He had a cratered face and a gift for shooting tequila between his thin lips in one quick movement. He denied being Machado, however, saying, in an English learned in the inner cities of America, that the "gee" didn't come to town much, but he was "connected" everywhere and there was "no problem" in getting these "characters" to work. The details were easily arranged. Machado's twenty thousand American dollars was fair. Payment to each extra of the equivalent of ten dollars a day was on the generous side. Trucks to be provided by the company. After arranging for delivery of the cash payment, the bulky man produced a knobby handshake which almost damaged Sieberling's middle finger. After squirting a last tequila down his throat, he told the production manager, "Don' worry 'bout nothin'. All taken care of." When he ambled off, Sieberling could see that the seat of his suit held a burgeoning dark ring.

As the afternoon waned, Paul worked with Rennie, saying little to her. His concern, deepening with the passing hours, increased even further as he reflected that there had been no arrangements for Aguillar's signal this time. How would it come to them? Where? Who would make it?

Night fast approaching, Rennie kneaded his spine gently, soothingly, pronounced him incredibly tense. She kissed the back of his neck and insisted that he come to her bed that night. Despite himself, he told her of Machado.

"What are you getting so worked up about?" she asked. In the end, these extras would be getting paid more than they could earn anyplace else in Oacala for a day's work. Why was it so bad? Why

247

was he so gloomy? Paul found that he couldn't explain and decided to remember only that whatever the picture needed, it had to get. A movie had a life of its own that had nothing to do with the logic of the outside world. It was a closed universe. And this universe required extras. If Luis couldn't arrange it, then Machado could. And that should be enough. But it wasn't, quite. Later, De Luca called and asked Paul home with him for dinner and to await the deadline hour. Approaching the hacienda in the Mercedes, De Luca looked away from the attempts to erase the landscape devastation, while the sight of the collected brush and newly exposed earth increased Paul's apprehension.

Catherine De Luca was calm, however. She held to an unshakable conviction that all turmoil was temporary. In the end, things would be taken care of. Michael was born under a special star that would keep rising. The silver and china laid out on the great table attested to that conviction. Turbulence might exist outside. In her house, however, serenity and *solidity* were the watchwords. She created some other encapsulated world which served, somehow, a need for domestic order in her husband, created a refuge from those other urges which rioted through him.

After dessert, the elder De Luca took Paul aside. His Mikey was depressed by what was happening, he knew. That was terrible. Those *brutos* did not understand the artistic spirit. His Mikey, he confided, had always been too soft-hearted, too easy. Perhaps, he reasoned, that kind of sensitivity was an inheritance from him, the father, but the real world was different; it required a strong hand. Mussolini, he recalled, as terrible a man as he had been, understood Italians very well. They required discipline, order. He had not gone far enough, that was the problem . . . not with the Jews, he hastened to add, not that, but with his own people. As a result, Italians had come out of the war with a reputation as buffoons, Commedia dell' Arte people.

Paul wondered why the old man was going through all this. Moments later, he had the answer.

"Pauli, you are so close to Mikey . . . I know how he thinks about you. When things like this happen, we must all do whatever we can to . . . make it easier for him, to help him, eh?" Voice husky with emotion, he reached over to pat Paul's cheek with avuncular affection. "I know you want to do this. I just say it to you because I feel it in my heart, that you are close, and we all wish for Mikey what is good and best, eh?"

248

He looked at the old man, astonished, disguising the sudden surprising current of envy that raced through him.

At eleven o'clock, they were alone, sitting at opposite ends of the oversized couch watching the television screen glow with the primary colors of "Fiesta Mexicana." A long-haired blond singer gyrated her way sinuously through a ballad of lost love. A chorus line of extremely short girls in halters and sailor hats did a nautical routine.

At eleven-thirty, as a male dancer stamped and posed his way through a flamenco, De Luca rose and began a window-to-door pacing with the flashing feet as counterpoint.

At midnight the station went off the air, and it was now absolutely out of his hands, Paul thought.

De Luca reached for the telephone.

"How about . . . the other house?" Paul asked in a final delaying tactic.

"She would have rung me." But he called Elvira's number nonetheless. When she answered, he asked if there had been any messages for him. There hadn't been.

Paul expected him to hang up then but he did not. Instead, he listened, becoming more and more agitated. He hung up, finally, and whirled to Paul and said, "That bitch, Ankrum—she barged in on Elvira!"

"Ankrum?" It seemed crazy.

"She wanted Elvira to stop us with Machado. Jesus."

Paul stood up. "Flo went to her?"

"Flo, Flo. And I'll bet she went to your friend. But who told her in the first place?" He talked into the telephone then. "Sal? Get moving. We'll need three hundred for tomorrow. And that Ankrum is involved somewhere. She knows our moves. That's our business, Sal, not hers; you understand me?" He hung up and spun about. "Incredible. You try to be good and they cut your balls off. It's not your fault, Paul."

"I just don't understand it." He didn't. What possible connection could Stella have with Flo Ankrum?

"You stay here tonight, Paul. We'll be going out to the location early." Suddenly Michael grinned. What the hell was there to grin about? Paul wondered, but an exultation had entered Michael's voice.

"Listen, we'll kick all the ass we have to to get our picture done, okay?"

It was a celebration of battle. Nothing ever would be easy, but it would come out . . . *good*. It would be something they made that no one else could.

"Right, Paul?"

As he stared, Michael raised his arms above his head, hands curled into defiant fists and chanted, "*Movie power.*"

Satisfied, he called, "Sleep well," and bounded from the room. Later, Paul called Rennie to tell her he was staying over at De Luca's. She said that if they were sleeping in the same bed she'd love to join them. When, finally, under the covers in the guest room, Paul found it difficult to sleep. Double visions, transpositions, blurs . . . collided behind his eyes. He twisted, groaned at his incongruous erection and wished Rennie were at hand. Finally he slept, tossing and mumbling.

In her bed, the paperback copy of *They Shoot Horses, Don't They?* beside her, Flo heard the jeep arrive and its engine cut. She lay still for a moment after the sound stopped, knowing that it concerned her. Before the knock could vibrate her door, she slipped from the rumpled sheets and put her robe on. Then she called out, "Who is it?"

Quesedo's voice, hardly muffled by the door, came at her.

"Manuel Quesedo. Please, is very important, very *serio*. Open."

Not entirely surprised, Flo considered refusing him entrance. She temporized, calling out, "What do you want?"

"You must to open" came back at her.

She pinned the neck of her robe together and unlatched the door. Without invitation the policeman stepped across the threshold. She tightened her lips.

"It's after one o'clock. What do you want? Make it quick."

"Señorita"—Quesedo closed the door—"this be all bad business. No sleep for no one." He glanced around. "You have coffee?"

"Not now, no." She looked at him with cool defiance.

"Tequila?" Before she could answer he laughed. "I don' t'ink you have. Is joost a joke."

"I don't feel like laughing."

"Señorita Ankroom, you must to listen to me." Quesedo removed his cap and delicately scratched his balding spot. Flo regarded him warily, wondering what the best course was if he tried going at her. Would a piercing scream bring anyone? Could she risk hurting him physically, or would he lose control and crack her skull? Would it be best simply to submit, lie there indifferently, stonily staring at him all the while, and thus avoid real physical damage? She heard the horned owl hoot in the forked tree and the crickets chirp. They only increased her sense of isolation.

"You make bad trouble." He shook a finger at her.

"What?"

"You go to some woman, American woman, talk to her of the *bajo tierra*. She goes to *jefe* De Luca and I—"

"She went to Michael?"

The words exploded from Flo with such force that Quesedo took a step backward.

"No," she went on, refusing to believe this. "She left Oacala, I know she did."

"She does not leave," Quesedo said, recovering, "no. Is *problemas* from this and I am called now to arrest you, okay? So late at night I am waked up, and I must to do this. I don' like to do this, but I must."

"Arrest me?" All her fears of rape vanished in an indignant cry. "The king gave the orders, didn't he—and everyone jumps, even her. Oh, God." She turned away from the policeman, quivering with impotent rage, then, hating to appear weak, turned back, defiantly, pulled her glasses from her head and flung them down on the bed.

"Señorita Ankroom, you listen to Manuel now, eh?" Quesedo's voice turned soft. His eyes gleamed with something that, unaccountably, calmed her fears. "I don' want to take you to the . . . prison. Is no good there for a woman. I don' like to t'ink of you there, okay?"

She lowered her eyes for a moment. "I appreciate that."

He clapped himself on the head with his cap. "I t'ink and I t'ink what we can do. I have idea." She looked up at him and he nodded. "Now, this time, you put everything in suitcase. We go in jeep to little place I know. Is rooms there. No one says not'ing to nobody because Manuel Quesedo is friend to them. I say to Señor Sieberling I don' find you, I cannot to arrest you. He must to believe. You stay till we talk again, see what to do." He drew a deep breath and watched her.

"Rooms?" She fingered the neck of her robe in new fear.

"You stay here what can I say to them?" Quesedo asked. "Señor Sieberling be angry man."

Yes, of course, that bastard wanted to punish her. A jail sentence would be just right, in his eyes. She had heard about Mexican jails with the rats and infested meat and the toilet holes and the brutal guards. Still, the prospect of leaving here was very frightening. She allowed her distress to show, and Quesedo reached out a hand. She backed away, deciding.

"Okay, I'll go."

"Is good. Is very good. I help you."

"No." She did not want him handling her clothing. "I can do it. I'll be a minute." She swept her underwear from its chair, grabbed her jeans from the stool, reached into the bureau to fish out a blouse and disappeared into the bathroom.

Waiting, Quesedo lit up a cigarette and felt his tiredness leaving him. When, once again, Sieberling had roused him from sleep, he had felt such rage he had shaken the bed with his quivering, but his wife had slept through it all.

Flo stepped back into the room buttoning the top button of her blue blouse. It seemed such an intimate gesture that Quesedo exhaled a sigh of pure enjoyment. She started packing and, not looking at the policeman, asked, "Could you tell me why you're doing this?"

Quesedo shuffled, almost in embarrassment, she thought.

"I don' . . . like you to be in the prison," he said, cautiously. "I t'ink is better if we be . . . friends."

"Friends?" How friendly did he mean for her to be? She reasoned, however, that if he had come for sex, he would have blackmailed her then and there; either she submitted or she went to prison. But he had not.

"Friends, sí."

She tried to read his face and, finding something in his smile she took as genuine, said, "Thank you. I appreciate what you're doing."

"Sí, would be bad for you in prison now. They work with Machado tomorrow and be very nervous."

Flo looked up; she had almost forgotten the immediate cause of all this. "The Mafia man?"

"Businessman," Quesedo corrected, "but sometimes he does very hard business."

She hurled her sandals into the suitcase with such force that the lid closed.

Outside, there seemed to be no moon in the lampblack sky, but here and there a hint of its cool power glinted through rifts and slatted the road as the jeep droned along.

"My car," Flo erupted suddenly, "my car's back at the motel."

"Ah! . . ." Quesedo grimaced. Then he said, "I arrange it goes to the *garaje* of an *amigo*. Give me the key."

He held out a hand. She hesitated. He said, "You must to trust me or is no good. You t'ink I do bad for you? I save you from bad, okay? You want to go to the prison I take you now."

"No," she said quietly, "I don't want to go to prison," and found the keys in her bag. Taking them, Quesedo smiled reassuringly, but she felt chilled and drew the shawl tighter around her shoulders. Avoiding the avenidas, Quesedo maneuvered the jeep through the back streets, past the marketplace, through to the other side of the town. There, a miscellany of tiny adobe buildings, cardboard shacks and rude wooden huts arranged themselves in and around the trees like vacation homes, each well separated, each with a small garden plot. The stench of the open sewer in the center, where a lazy fecal flow stagnated, signified permanence, however, not holiday. As Flo wrinkled her nose, Quesedo murmured apologetically.

"*Malo* here . . . Much bad. *Pobres*. Poors but no one comes here for you, eh?"

He swung the suitcase from the backseat and led her toward a darkened adobe building. The door proved unlocked, and he kicked it open with a foot, urging her inside. He set the suitcase down in a corner and lit a small kerosene lamp perched atop a wooden box. When the light flared, Flo saw that the room was unoccupied. A straw-mattressed bed poked up, bumpily, at one end. A roughly made chest of drawers, a table and two straight-backed chairs with incongruous velvet cushions, torn and mended, completed the furnishings.

"Where are the people?"

Quesedo looked at her blankly.

"The ones who live here?"

"Oh. They go." He waved his hand vaguely. "You be here by yourself. The woman comes to see you, cooks for you, does anyt'ing you say."

"I don't want anyone to do for me."

"Okay. Okay."

"How long do I stay here?"

"We see." Quesedo frowned. "Is not like motel but is better than prison, believe me. We see what Señor Sieberling do. They too hot now. When is more calm, they be not so *loco,* then maybe I say I find you; but for now is better for you this way. Maybe few days is all."

She stared at the wisp of oily smoke spiraling up from the lamp. A few days would be possible. Thinking that, she chided herself; if she were a committed activist, places like this would be the norm, hovels her natural habitat, hardship her sign of identification with those who, unlike her, had no way to escape. Still, it was frightening.

"Will I see you?" she asked.

When she said that, Quesedo smiled happily. "Sí . . . but you wish me, you telephone, is *bodega* not far from here which has one. You do not have to give a name if I am not there. You can joost to say it is a friend, and I will know. I will come here like the wind." He put a hand on his chest, in courtly gesture. "I would like to take you to my *casa.* There, it would be most comfortable for you. But . . ." He sighed. "This life is not always what we wish, eh?"

Flo blinked back her surprise. He would like to take her to his house? If it wasn't sex, what was this man getting at? She lifted her glasses and rubbed her eyes.

"Ah . . ." Quesedo said quickly. "You must to sleep. Of course. I go now."

"The motel people . . ." She started, thinking not really of them but of Señora Coyopan, who would find her missing this day and be concerned, but perhaps she might find some method of getting a message to her.

"I take care," Quesedo assured her once again. "I fix. They don' say no t'ing to Señor Sieberling."

He adjusted his cap. "So." He extended his hand and gently rested it on her shoulder. She steeled herself to the touch, but it was so light, so gentle, she found it surprisingly comforting. "*Bellos sueños,* Florenza." He tossed a book of matches on the bed and quickly left the hut.

Examining the door, she quickly discovered it had no lock at all and set one of the chairs up against the knob. Then she tried the bed. It was harsh and soft at the same time. Sitting there, in the dimness, a sudden wave of fear and despair claimed her. She lay down upon the bed and huddled into herself.

On the way back to his *comandancia* Quesedo was attacked by

254

qualms. He had taken a bold step. If there was even a suspicion of his action, he was finished, he knew; everything would be taken from him. Yet the urge had been overpowering. Had he arrested her, jailed her, any chance of being what he wished to be to her would have been destroyed. There grew a dream, in his mind, of her staying in Mexico, at least for a time. He would find a small house for her. There, he would share her bed, caress her body, feel her hair with his tongue and his teeth and afterward, while talking, discussing, she would come to see that he was *worthy*.

The reality of the headquarters intruded. He waved away the idiot sergeant and proceeded to his office. Resolutely, he telephoned Sieberling, knowing he was waiting, even though it was only hours from daylight. The phone rang only once and he plunged in recklessly.

"Señor, it is Capitán Quesedo. Listen, I go to this Ankroom to arrest her, like you say me to, and she not be there."

"So why didn't you wait for her?"

"She goes someplace, señor. Nobody knows where she goes. She stays no more there in the motel."

He braced himself for the explosion. It came, with Sieberling's voice rattling the earpiece furiously.

"How can that be? What are you talking about?"

"Don't know, señor. They say . . ." He thought of a likely lie. "They say she goes away with a man."

"A man?"

"Sí."

"What about her car?"

"She takes it, señor."

"You think she's taken off for Mexico City?"

Quesedo considered. "Maybe she goes south—with this lover."

"Son of a bitch. She's up to something, Quesedo. Notify the police down below. They can spot her. She's an American."

"Sí—of course I do that." Changing the subject quickly, he asked, "You bring in people for the cinema tomorrow?"

"It's in the works; they'll be loading soon."

"I send my men for the protection."

"Don't bother. But you be there; we've got to talk about this."

"Of course I be there."

He heard the click-off next, hung up the phone and swore at the underground that had caused all this. He would find the leaders and break their bones. Remembering suddenly that Gordon had met with Aguillar, he debated informing Sieberling of that fact, deciding, finally, to hold the puzzling card for the time being. He poured himself a tequila and brooded about Machado. The man knew how to get these peasants to work. What might come afterward was another story. He finished the tequila and, deciding not to go home, he removed his uniform and lay down on the cot in the corner of his office. In the darkness he saw the girl from Chicago, saw her plainly and clearly.

CHAPTER
26

⌖▬⌖▬⌖▬⌖▬⌖▬⌖▬ **26** ▬⌖▬⌖▬⌖▬⌖▬⌖▬⌖

The trucks, jammed cab to tailgate with Mexicans, started to arrive at six o'clock. In the still-hanging mist, they looked like vertically stacked human cordwood. Body to body, the pressure swaying them in one mass, they were warily silent rolling into the rice-paddy location. The helicopter had dropped Paul only ten minutes earlier, and coffee mug in hand, he surveyed the scene with a still-befogged mind. Near the camera platform De Luca was already deep in discussion with Kodály. Light blaze cut through the swirl as the crew began to set up. Hoses poured water onto the fields, jerking spasmodically as the pumps pushed. An assistant directed the extras' emergence from the trucks to a makeup and costume shed. There, wispy beards would be attached to the men, eye outlines altered. The women would have their hair rebraided. All would be furnished with straw hats, Vietnamese pajamas, rubber sandals. They would be transformed from *campesinos* to "atmosphere."

Allan Marcus, rubbing his eyes blearily, loomed up.

"Well, we got 'em."

Paul nodded. Nothing seemed very wrong. The Mexicans were quiet and wary, but this must be so foreign to them, so beyond their experience, that it would make them slightly fearful. By now there were almost two hundred men and women and even a group of children. They stood patiently in a triple line, serapes and rebozos muffling them against the dawn chill, waiting to be made Oriental. Marcus drifted away as De Luca came over, gesturing, with satisfaction.

"I was afraid for a while, you know—but it's working out."

Paul agreed.

"You know what we ought to do?" De Luca mused. "Schedule the Jericho sequence at Ixtepan within a couple of days. Use this same bunch and get rid of the whole extra problem quickly, once and for all."

There was value in the plan, but could all this construction be finished in time?

"It damn well better be."

The Chinese actress came near, adjusting her conical hat. De Luca turned away, frozen-faced. "She really rubs me the wrong way. It's incredible. She's a woman and Elvira's a woman. Yet look at them, worlds apart. She's ego-ridden, disgusting, pandering. Elvira is . . . female, gentle, spiritual—"

Paul wondered where Catherine placed in this line, or Rennie.

"And you know what?" De Luca's face lit up with delight. "We can build platforms right on Monte Tecla and have high stationary shots down below. We can really control the shooting then, so we don't have to rely on helicopter shots."

"Will they let you shoot from up there?"

"*Mordida* to the right parties. Sal can make the connections. Anyway, we're not going to alter a thing." He wiped a coffee drip from his beard. "I'm getting antsy, Paul. I always do when I see a clear way. I want to get it all in the can and go home." Suddenly he asked, "Have you read that screenplay yet?"

Paul was at a loss. "What screenplay?"

"Mine. The one I think you ought to direct."

"You're serious about that?"

De Luca glared. "Damn straight I am. Paul, it's going to happen. We're going to come out of this smelling like roses. I know we are."

"You never gave me that screenplay," Paul said. "You put it back in your desk."

"Oh." De Luca was sheepish. "Did I?"

Steve Kruger, at the wheel of a truck still disgorging silent and apprehensive people, waved a greeting. Waving in reply, Paul caught sight of four late-model American cars parking one beside the other. The doors swung open, loosing five men from each vehicle. What was striking about them was their similarity; each was well fed and strong-looking and wore shoes. In addition, they all wore felt hats and double-knit, pastel-colored slacks with bell bottoms. Machado's envoys; as they walked arrogantly toward the canteen table, shouldering their way through the crowd, there was no doubt.

As they reached the coffee urn, taking possession, a thick-browed young man glared at them. Instantly, one of the intruders raised

258

two warning fingers, formed them into a V and moved them slowly and steadily toward the boy's eyes. The boy stood his ground until the dirty nails had almost made contact with his eyeballs, then he flinched away from his tormentor, who put his hands on his hips and, having made his mastery clear, swaggered on.

Minutes later, when De Luca came by, Paul said angrily, "These are hoods, Michael."

Looking up from the tattered script, De Luca said, "Really . . . who?"

"The double-knits."

De Luca chuckled. "Looks like there was a fire sale."

"They're pushing the extras around."

"I don't have time for that," De Luca said impatiently. "The extras are getting well paid. Someone has to organize them."

When he did not reply, De Luca said, "Paul, it's a couple of days' work and then we're through with them. Okay?"

The shooting proceeded on schedule. The transformed Mexicans tended the plants, walked behind the water buffalo, looked wise and ancient. None of them could handle chopsticks, however. Most of them had never even seen such things and were incredulous when told they were actually used to pick up food. Given a demonstration by the Chinese actress, they oohed and ahed at her ability to shovel rice into her mouth from the bowl, but remained unable to maneuver the delicate pieces of wood. De Luca solved the problem by altering the shots so that the peasants were never seen actually eating, only holding the chopsticks and staring into the rice bowls contemplatively. On film later, as photographed by Kodály, these shots would turn out to be incredibly moving, evoking a feeling of timeless sadness.

The chopstick sequence served also to reduce, momentarily, the level of tension that had been evident from the moment Machado's men had arrived. Moving from one spot to another, making his notes, Paul saw the furtive darting of eyes, the whispered comments, the jerks of the head toward the well-fed polyesters, who, though they were few in number, seemed to be everywhere. He wondered if there were others, unseen, out beyond the location, where Quesedo's police patrolled. When the lunch break came, Sieberling, grimly pleased by the morning, was dispatched to Ixtepan to speed up the construction work. After that, De Luca invited Paul to share lunch.

Before he entered the blue bus, Paul saw that the hundreds of

259

Mexicans were sitting at tables eating out of their boxes in absolute and stunning silence; even the children were quiet. Seated together, separated from the extras, Machado's men ate with loud chatter and intimidating gusto. Troubled, Paul made a vague reference to the tables, but De Luca hurried him into the bus and launched into a discussion of the work to be done.

Before nine in the morning, after a restless night at the Jaime, bypassing the telephone, Stella appeared at the air terminal to book on the early plane to Mexico City.

The aggressively blond ticket agent at the counter reached for the credit card and a computer page simultaneously. Then her hand stopped and an actual expression crossed her face, a puzzled frown. She checked schedules, lists, still frowning, then finally looked up. "Señorita, I am sorry—we are all booked on that flight."

She pushed the plastic back across the counter. Stella pushed it forward again.

"Listen," she said firmly, "I was here, yesterday, and was told there was no space, that there would be plenty of space today. Now book me on that plane."

The clerk swept her long, tinted blond hair aside again. "I am sorry, but there is no space on that plane." She shoved the card toward Stella once again.

"What is going on?" Stella demanded. "Just what is going on here?"

The girl said nothing. Stella debated calling the supervisor again. This was madness, complete and total madness—or was it? A chill suddenly ran through her. Half-formed fright coagulated in her stomach. She decided to ignore it.

"Surely," she said, keeping her voice under control, "there is a seat on the next plane. There must be."

The clerk ran a blood-red thumbnail down a clipboard. "Hm . . ." she said. "We are very tight. We are holding twenty seats on standby for a party of tourists who may be going or may not so," she shrugged, "I cannot book you on that plane."

"But if they don't take that plane?" Stella asked, desperation edging her voice up.

The clerk shrugged. "We must see then." She turned her attention to the telephone, leaving Stella flushed. Was there a train? Could she hire a car and drive out—through the mountains to Mexico City? It was too dangerous for that; there were too many unknowns. She had heard too many horror stories of women traveling alone in cars in deserted areas. Whom could she call? Paul came, naturally, to her mind, but an instinctual reservation held her back, even as an instinctual suspicion grew. She decided to wait till the one o'clock plane.

The terminal had no facilities for any kind of long wait. As the facade was revolutionary, so the interior was functionally spartan. Stella returned to the Jaime. There, she alternated between the lobby and the dining room, reading the *Mexico City News*, munching fruit, drinking coffee and trying to find a reasonable course among the possibilities infiltrating her mind. She was ignored by the desk clerk, but when she spotted the elusive travel agent she approached and, as innocently as she could, requested a seat on the next flight out.

There seemed to be no problem whatsoever as the agent, his professional smile working at its best, rapidly did the paperwork, called the airport, bantered with whoever was at the other end of the line, started to write up a ticket, checked her credit card, spelled her name and then—the smile vanished. Hanging up the phone, he looked at Stella apologetically and reported the slight mistake—no more space.

She rose without a word. Outside, rage-enshrouded, she tried to calm herself. Could they do it? Was it possible? Given need and power, anything was possible, of course, in this day of computers. All it took was the right word to the right connection to put the right name into the network and there it was; there would be no escape. The name, and whatever code followed, would be everywhere—with a simple tap-tap-tap of the keys.

She found a cab and directed the driver toward the Jericho complex. The guard outside the main building sensed danger in her walk, but she was a *yanqui* lady and he did not question her. She swept past him, walking by company members, until she halted at De Luca's door. At that point a strong-faced girl volunteered that the director was out on location. Nodding thanks, Stella about-faced, marched back through the hall and out again. The guard blinked as she strode by him, continuing, rapidly, toward the camera and editing buildings.

Inside editorial, she went directly to Paul's domain and, without knocking, opened the door to step across the threshold. Setting her bag down, she saw Rennie's surprised face. The editor was holding a film reel and, at the door slam, almost dropped it, the film spring-

261

ing free and uncoiling to the floor. Stella looked directly at her.

"I have to see Paul."

"He's not here."

"Are you sure? Are you damned sure?"

"I am very damned sure. He's at the location, working."

"Umm." Stella swiveled her eyes to the closed door of the private cubicle.

"You want to see for yourself, go ahead."

"I'll take your word for it." She tried to think straight, keep her anger under control, make it work for her, but underneath the anger was a pain she also had to keep under control.

"If you want to leave a message—"

"Yes, *I do want to leave a message*." The words burst from her. "I want to leave a message for *both* of them." She took a deep breath. "You can tell them, and it better be soon, that the airline's not letting me out of Oacala and I know, *absolutely know*, that somehow and for some reason I can't fathom, except for his weirdness, that Michael is behind it, okay? Will you tell them that? And will you tell them further that I'm going back to the hotel now and I'm going to wait there? And if I can't get a guaranteed reservation on the morning plane, I am going to call every wire service in the States and discuss a few of the activities here." Rennie's face turned ashen at that, she noted with satisfaction. "Do you have all that? Is it clear?"

"I don't know what you're talking about," Rennie managed to say, "but I'll tell them, yes."

"Good." Stella picked up her bag.

"Just tell me this," Rennie asked. "Why do you have to destroy what they're doing?"

Stella turned back, startled, as Rennie continued, "Is it because you're unable to be part of the changes Paul is going through, his growth?"

"Yes, that's it," Stella murmured, "that's the whole thing. You've got it cold." She opened the door and darted through. Forcing her legs to operate, she moved herself to the gate where she hailed a cab. As she clambered in, she noticed a man in a policeman's uniform staring at her, speculatively. She slammed the door, sank back into the torn velour seat, pawed at her eyes and managed to control her trembling.

Seconds after Stella closed the door, Rennie dashed to the production office looking for Sieberling. He had just returned from

Ixtepan and was in conference with the explosives specialists when she broke in upon them. Informed of Stella's visit and threat, Sieberling sat back in his chair, pulled his dark glasses from his eyes and muttered obscenities.

"She's hateful," Rennie said. "She just wants to wreck everything."

Sieberling told her he would fly out to the location within minutes to inform De Luca.

"And tell Paul," Rennie urged. "I want him to know what she's really like."

As Sieberling walked toward the helicopter pad, Manuel Quesedo came up to him, beaming, and said, "Everyt'ing goes fine, this morning, eh?"

"So far," Sieberling continued, walking fast. Quesedo kept up with him.

"The *campesinos* all come with no trouble. That Machado—" He shook his head in admiration.

"I'm going out there. You want to come?"

The captain had no intention of going. "Oh, would be very good for me to go there today, but is much other t'ings to do, señor . . . There is much responsibility on me."

"Oh, sure." Sieberling tried to keep the derision from his voice. He was annoyed at the lockstepping; he wanted to be alone. Twenty yards from the helicopter, Quesedo put a restraining hand on his ›arm.

"Señor Sieberling, I t'ink I tell you somet'ing." He had decided it would be in his best interests to share what he knew. Accordingly, he informed the production manager that Gordon was playing a dangerous game, that he, Quesedo, had certain knowledge that there had been personal contact, not with someone from the underground but with the *terroristas*, with Aguillar himself. To his surprise, the news did not faze Sieberling at all. He merely grunted.

"I say with Luis Aguillar," Quesedo repeated. He had hoped for a coup.

"I heard you," Sieberling responded.

"I tell you this because we must to trust each other," Quesedo covered up. "Like I tell you, the *artistas* must to be protected against themselves, eh, because they do not know the real world."

Sieberling nodded, ran to the aircraft, ducked under the rotor and hopped aboard. Belted in, watching the earth fall away, he thought about Quesedo's words. Probably true. Like his other

263

director friends, movie-making whiz kids, millionaires before they were thirty, rebels against the system, any system, Michael had strong feelings about wars, poverty—even frozen orange juice for that matter. It damn well could be that he was fooling around with this Aguillar. Sieberling fiddled with his glasses in despair; this wasn't Beverly Hills with built-in political protection. He decided, for the moment, to keep his own counsel.

When the copter set down, it was already late afternoon. De Luca was lining up a shot and Sieberling waited till it was made, then walked over quickly and said they had to talk. De Luca called Paul and the three men stood in the shadow of a tall camera crane as the production manager reported Rennie's experience, to which Paul listened, open-mouthed. When Sieberling finished, De Luca, clenching his teeth, said, "If she actually calls the wire services, I'll throttle her, so help me." He glared at Paul. "That's all we need right now, more stories back home so those bastards can cut our legs off."

"This plane thing," Paul questioned. "I don't understand it."

"She's out of her head," Sieberling said flatly. "If she can't get a plane, is it our fault?"

"She'll get a plane." De Luca smacked his hand against the crane's aluminum base. "We'll pull every string to get her on a damn plane out. But if she goes back and starts spreading stories anyway . . ."

"She's a bitch," Sieberling murmured.

"She doesn't know," Paul said quickly. "She just doesn't understand what's going on, that's all."

"Maybe," De Luca said, "I'll give her the benefit of the doubt, so it's up to you, Paul. You go to her and tell her that if she has any feelings of friendship for you, she has to promise not to talk about our problems in the States."

"Absolutely," Sieberling concurred.

Paul shifted balance, uneasily. It was right for him to do, yet—

"Paul." Michael put his eyes an inch away. "What's important to me is important to you; make her understand that."

"That's a fact," Sieberling chorused.

"I can try," Paul finally agreed.

He went, immediately, to the helicopter and De Luca, watching him go, said, "I misjudged her. I shouldn't have done that. Bad mistake."

"She'll be out tomorrow," Sieberling soothed.

"But, she's got to keep quiet," De Luca said. "You know that, Sal."

What was he supposed to do, Sieberling thought bitterly, get her legs broken? Or have acid thrown in her face? Sometimes De Luca was bitten by his own movies.

When the phone rang, sometime after five o'clock, in her new room at the Jaime, Stella was surprised. Hearing Flo Ankrum's breathless voice at the other end compounded the shock.

"How did you know I was still here?"

"I was told. I'm not at the motel. I'm in hiding."

Stella thought she had misheard. "Did you say *hiding?*"

"Yes, they want to put me in jail."

"Who told you I was here? What is this all about?"

"A policeman."

"A policeman?"

"Don't hang up. Please," Flo said desperately. "I don't know who else to call. Allan won't do anything, I know that."

"Do anything about what?"

"What's going on, what they're doing . . . forcing those peasants to work for them. They're terrified of that Machado. And he takes half of what they get paid, too. Tell somebody what's happening here. Please. I have a phone number to give you, someone who can get the story to the papers."

"I don't want it. I'm going now. Don't call me again."

She banged the phone down and stood over it, breathing hard. When the knock on her door came, she almost jumped.

"Who's there?"

"It's Paul, Stella. Could I see you a minute?"

She unlocked the door. He appeared very tense, and she was torn between being angry with him and wanting to hold him. He shuffled inside and quickly said, "Stel, I'm not going to get into what you're thinking, but you'll be leaving tomorrow and—"

"Oh," she said, "Michael got the message."

He passed his hand over his forehead, tiredly. "Listen, it's been a very long day, very tense-making."

Instantly she was sorry and her anger fled. As he rubbed his eyes she asked, "You want to sit?"

"Believe me," he said, "it's nobody's fault, the airline here is . . . you know." He shrugged.

265

"Paul," she said quietly, "paranoia doesn't run in the family. For some reason Michael worked his magic."

"I'm not going to quarrel with you," he replied. "I want to ask you a favor, that's all."

She waited.

"Stel, this picture is important to me. Personally. Michael's giving me a chance to do things that—" He broke off, not wishing to stray from the point. "The studio's out to get him, they really are. They'll use any ammunition they can. What's happening to us here is not our fault. All I want is . . . your word to not, well . . . tell stories, I guess, because they might get back to the wrong people."

She sat down on the bed, dismayed. The room was silent for almost a minute and the drip from the bathroom faucet sounded as loud as a kettledrum. Finally, she said, "I just want to get this straight. Michael sent you here, didn't he?"

"It's because of *me* you're here," Paul defended. "That's a fact."

"And you and he are going on to greater glories, right?"

"What's the point of saying that?"

"Because," she said, "I think he's got hold of you, he really has."

"Stella." He made an effort to keep his voice down. "I'm asking you to do something that is not unethical or immoral or going to hurt somebody."

"Let me see." Her tones were deceptively silken. "You want me to promise not to tell anyone back home that a bunch of people here think that you're hurting them badly, that you're riding rough-shod over what they want, that I was prevented from leaving, that a Mafia type was brought in to force people to work for you, that he's even ripping off half their pay, and that a woman is hiding out because Michael wants to put her in jail for absolutely nothing. Do I have it right?"

As she spoke, his body grew tauter and tauter. By the time she finished, he was almost quivering and shot out, "That's your version."

"What's yours?"

"Stel, no one's putting people in jail."

"Why would she tell me that?"

"People just say things about Michael, they do."

"Are you going to tell me this Mafia man is a pussycat?"

"Stick to the point."

"Paul, Paul . . ." She stood up, fighting to keep her arms from stretching out to him. "You're in over your head, it's not you."

"Damn it," he shouted, "you don't *know* what's me. You think of me as some—I don't know—some furry mouse, maybe, but furry mice don't make pictures." He quieted abruptly. "All I'm asking is a favor."

Stella shook her head slowly. "I won't give him that satisfaction, Paul. There's a lot about this trip I'd like to forget, but I won't promise him anything, *anything.*"

"Okay, Stel." He stumbled toward the door and she watched him, unyielding. When he left, she sat down on the bed again, numb.

CHAPTER

27

Slightly dazed as he crossed the Zócalo, Paul almost walked into a burro which kicked, viciously, at him. The Indian nearby beat the animal hard with a stick, and Paul hurried away. Around the square the cafés were filling up. Recalling his first delighted look at this lively scene, he searched the dark faces now and all he could see was how the eyes were hooded, the manner guarded, the secrets preserved. Any of these could be in the *bajo*, hating, probably, even the color of his skin.

A delicate man in a white *camisa* on the south side of the square caught his eye. The high-cheekboned face and the small frame seemed familiar. He turned full face and stopped in his tracks. At that moment it came to Paul clearly—it was Ismena. Quickly he moved toward him, but Ismena—if it was he—turned abruptly and disappeared into a side street. By the time Paul reached the opening, the white-shirted figure was nowhere to be seen. Only a yellow dog was there, whimpering in front of a butcher stall, and the butcher came out to kick it in the ribs.

Though eager to fly back to the location, Paul thought it best to stop at his office. There he found Rennie, unnerved at Stella's interference but more concerned over the effect upon him.

"Did she upset you? Don't let her do that? She's not worth it, Paul. She's the past. She's back there someplace."

She put her arms about him comfortingly and kissed him. He tried to respond but found his glands affected by the thoughts of Machado, Ismena, Luis and Stella's stubbornness. He assured Rennie that he was all right, but there were a million things to do and he had to get back to the location; he would see her later that night. At the door she ran her fingers through his hair and said, "The thing is that when you feel something for somebody you're loyal to them;

you don't hurt them. The past is a covenant, too. Even if it's over, there are echoes that go on forever."

The helicopter on the return trip was piloted by Gimper. Paul was the only passenger and had to endure the story of the pilot's affair with a woman who was kinky for men with any deformity. That put Gimper close to the aphrodisiac department. "She was a nut case for crazy positions," Gimper explained, "and legs and arms got in the way. I couldn't take too much of her." The fact that Paul was obviously not interested did not deter him.

On the ground, daylight had almost disappeared, but Kodály provided his own illumination which made the rice paddies appear silken.

The Chinese actress, in the center of a group of contemplative peasants, was moving in a small dance. In moments a Viet Cong would appear, parting the palm fronds, his helmet covered with camouflage, his clothing blending with the jungle. De Luca pronounced the scene "beautiful" and called for another setup. Emerging from the helicopter, Paul saw that Machado's double-knitted men had spread themselves about the shooting area. He asked Allan Marcus if there had been any trouble.

"Not a peep. . . . Things are going great." Marcus waved a hand, expansively. "We got a good defensive line here. They're not going to score." He puffed a perfect smoke ring with assurance.

Watching the circle, it came to Paul with absolute certainty who had been in contact with Stella.

"Have you heard from Flo?"

"Uh-uh." Marcus drew in tar and nicotine. "I called her a couple of times to see if she was all right—she's a little whacko, you know—but I could never get her in." He gestured in front of him. "Going to look real good, this stuff. Production people did a hell of a job making this a rice paddy. Christ." He bent down, picked up the dusty soil and let it slip through his fingers. "Some fertile farmland."

"You heard anything about Machado taking half of what these people get for a day?" Paul nodded toward the extras.

Marcus looked at him, quizzically. "I don't speak the language."

Shortly after nightfall the extras were dismissed to be trucked back. The Machado retainers, in their cars, led the way. In the blue bus, De Luca produced his usual white wine, curled up on the couch and asked if Stella had been seen. Grimacing, Paul reported that no promise was forthcoming.

"Sal is right—she is a bitch," De Luca muttered. "We'll just have to see how to handle that."

"Mike," Paul said tentatively, "she really believes you pulled some strings to cancel her space."

"She can think what she likes," De Luca snapped. He rose from the couch and roamed the room. "So many people want us to fail. Sometimes it's like we're fighting the world."

"You're right," Paul said softly. He felt like a traitor even speaking of this now, but a degree of guilt had been set into him and he needed to assuage it.

"Mike, is it true that Machado rips these people off of half their wages?"

De Luca said, wearily, "I don't bother myself with how they get paid, that's Sal's job." He saw that did not satisfy Paul. "Look, if he really rips them off, I'll make it up to them later. Somehow. I'll tell Sal. But right now we have to have those bodies—and we have to have them in time for the Jericho sequence or we're in the toilet. At this moment, this man is a necessary evil."

Damn fact, Paul thought—damned hard, stinking fact of life.

For the second time in twenty-four hours, Manuel Quesedo drove to see Flo Ankrum. The morning visit had been cursory, just to see how she had spent the night, how and where she had eaten, how the others had taken her presence. Tonight, with soft darkness lying over the valley, was to be more personal, he hoped.

Together, in the small room, lamp and candles lit and the bottle of Cuervo Gold he was bringing on the table, it would be intimate; she would get to see the man beneath the uniform. He hummed a few bars of "Flores Negras," a song of deep emotion he had heard first as an adolescent. It had been sung then by the reigning favorite, Elvira Rios, a voluptuous, jet-haired woman who sang in a smoky contralto that stirred the loins and plucked sad notes from the soul.

Turning into the neighborhood, his headlights first attracted attention at the outdoor cooking fires, but as soon as his jeep was recognized, the heads turned away abruptly. He stopped in front of the block house, took the paper-bagged Cuervo and knocked on the door. She opened it, wearing an ankle-length skirt, a sweater and a rebozo wrapped about her head and shoulders, country-style. He stared with admiration.

"Florenza, *buenas noches.* You look Mexicana."

Flo stood in the doorway uncertainly. "Hello. Is something wrong?"

"No . . . I just come to see you. See how everyt'ing is." He flashed a grin. "Better I come in, eh?"

She nodded and stood aside. He came in, whipped the Cuervo from the paper and held it aloft, triumphantly. "Is good for you, makes the blood move."

She eyed him narrowly. "Okay." She fetched two plastic cups as Quesedo put the bottle down on the table, removed his cap and unbuttoned his uniform jacket. She removed the shawl from her head and her hair crackled out, full. Watching her, Quesedo was struck by the roundness of her movements; there was the grace of rippling flesh there.

"Goes okay today?"

"I called her, after you were here. I called Gordon's friend, the one you saw. She wasn't interested in what I had to say."

He unscrewed the cap and poured the amber liquid into the cups. "You don't tell her where you be or anyt'ing?"

Flo shook her head. "An hour ago I saw a truck come by here and drop some people off. They were working with De Luca. Some ugly mug in a car was shouting at them. Somebody said something to him and he hit her. She was an elderly woman and he just smacked her in the face. I wanted to run over there and scream at him or hit him with a rock or something, but I knew I couldn't so I just watched, like the others."

"Drink," Quesedo said softly.

She raised her cup, but her face remained cloudy and the lips stubborn.

"Drink," he commanded again. Lifting his cup, he saluted her. "Salud . . . to you and to me too." He drained almost half of what there was. Flo sipped.

"Hateful!"

"Forget this . . . for the moment." Quesedo was a shade annoyed at her obsession. "We have beautiful night. You are not in the jail. We can to get to know each other." He reached his hand out to her cheek. When Flo tensed, he touched her glasses.

"You wear these always? Maybe not for now. Is not necessary to see so good, now." With a daring gesture he lifted the frames from her bridge. When she jerked her head away, he dropped the frames back apologetically. "Please . . . I joost wish to see how you look without them."

271

Wordlessly, she took her glasses off and regarded him.

"Beautiful," he breathed, "you are much beautiful."

"I am much blind," she said, and put the frames back on. He laughed and drank again.

She sipped a bit more of the Cuervo. It burned her throat slightly and she coughed.

Quesedo grinned. "Best way is to drink quick . . . down. . . . Makes you to feel warm in the belly."

"Captain—" she started.

"No, no," he protested. "You must to call me by my name. Manuel. You say it now. Manuel."

"Manuel," she repeated reluctantly.

"Good," he approved. "Always now it be Manuel—and Florenza." He leaned over, thumped cups and drank again. She hoped he would slow down; a drunken policeman would be more than she could handle. And yet he had come this far for her, kept her from jail, found this place, seemed basically gentle.

"I can't stay here forever," she said. "What's going to happen?"

"You leave this to Manuel."

"Damn his eyes!" she burst out.

"The *jefe*?"

She nodded and sipped again.

"Florenza, I know you have big idea of joostice. But the life is not joostice and you must to learn to accept."

"It's all around us," she cried out.

"Sí. I know, I know." He bent toward her gently and touched her hair.

"It's so sad." She sipped the last of the tequila, held the cup to her lips, broodingly.

"Is much sad 'bout everyt'ing," Quesedo intoned, bending lower and putting his other hand on her thigh. Feeling its firmness and her lack of objection, he began kneading it slightly.

"Yes," Flo said, "oh, yes." She leaned forward then in a blaze of indignation. "But why does it have to be that way? Why can't we change it all?"

"Dunno," Quesedo said, wishing she would stop all of this and respond to the feeling in his blood.

"But how long can it go on without total war?"

"It go on," he said impatiently, "it go on so long as be men and be women."

"Yes." Flo sat back limply in her chair. Frustrated, Quesedo rose

272

from his uncomfortable crouch. If it were some other woman he would reach out and pull her to her feet, slap her, bite her, force her into submission, not to him, but to the true dictates of her blood, into the passion he knew roamed beneath the surface, leashed but ready to have its fetters removed and explode into a frenzy of lovemaking. But with this one—

"Florenza," he tried once more, moving nimbly to her side and thrusting himself against her. She shook her head sadly.

"It's bigger than Marx, more complicated. It's confused—we're all confused today, isn't that it?"

Quesedo muttered, "Sí—sí."

Flo sat up again, ignoring his pulsating trunk. "I'm not sure why you're helping me this way," she said, slurring her words slightly, "but I'm grateful. *Muchas gracias.*"

He nodded, thoroughly disgusted, the words coming as ice water to his groin. "I try to help is all," he managed to say. Rising and retreating, he smoothed out his trousers.

"Can real socialism change things?" she persisted.

"I go now." Quesedo reached for his cap. He thought about taking the tequila with him but decided there would be other times here.

Flo rose from the chair with a certain majestic sway. "Good night."

"Sí, good night, good night." He hurried from the house. Before she closed the door behind him, he saw her stumble. The tequila was having its effect, and he thought for a moment of going back and trying again but decided not to. He buttoned two buttons on his jacket and got behind the wheel of the jeep. Why must she be that way? He liked intelligence, but there were limits. The Judía from Chicago had been intelligent but had made love with him from the beginning. Her passion had been overwhelming, ever-present, and he had assumed that this one was like that. He vowed to break through her armor. Once that was done, her natural womanly liquids would do the rest. But that did not help release him tonight, and he turned the jeep toward the Red House, anticipating the possibilities.

It was barely ten-thirty when he arrived at the Calle Libertad, too early for any crowd. The girls had just finished their meal, eating in half-slips and teddies and elaborately flowered robes. Some ate in their occupational dress, covered carefully at the top with pinned towels to prevent sauce stains. Maria, he noted, was miss-

273

ing. When he inquired about her, Señora Revueltas, annoyed, told him she had been gone since five o'clock and if she took off this night she was finished in the house. A large party from the coast was expected, oil men who had flown into Oacala, and she could use more girls tonight. She had even considered borrowing a few from the rat hole near the Zócalo, but those girls were second-raters, some as old as twenty-five and twenty-six, and these clients would never go upstairs with such ancient merchandise.

Quesedo wondered what her game was. To have sheltered Aguillar was audacious. This was not a local matter, the federal police wanted the man, and anyone who helped him was in trouble. She had powerful protectors, but even they might shy away when it came to *terroristas*.

"So, *capitán*." Señora Revueltas moved to the personal. "A little champagne, eh?"

Quesedo smiled. "You send it up. Maybe I go see your new little blonde, eh?"

"Some eye . . . you have the expert eye. You wait a few minutes? I'll tell her you're coming upstairs."

She called to a thick-bodied maid in a white cape who said, "Sí, señora," and ran to the staircase.

"She is in the room with the blue moon on the door," Señora Revueltas said. "She comes from the north and is fifteen and this is her first year." She barked an order to another maid.

Quesedo lit a cigarette. What a fortune she made here, that woman. Every time a prominent lawyer or doctor or businessman had an erection, she made a percentage.

He was about to start up the grand staircase when he heard steps behind him. Turning, he saw it was Maria. She was obviously surprised to see him, and frightened, for her eyes grew wide and her tongue flicked in and out of her mouth nervously.

"*Capitán*," she hissed. "I call you. For hours I call you. I am gone all day; she will kill me, the señora."

"Why? What happens?" He saw her begin to tremble and clutched her arm. "Control yourself, woman."

"Carlos." She whispered the name. "The man who limps, the charcoal seller, he comes back."

"Where is he?" Quesedo found himself whispering also.

"In my mother's *barrio*, there is a widow, Conchita. Her man dies of a bad stomach; she has little children."

"To hell with her children," Quesedo barked. "Is this man there, with her?"

"Yes, with her."

"When did he go there?"

"In the afternoon."

"He will stay the night with her?"

"Yes." The girl hung her head. "She has not had a man since her husband died. She is young . . ."

"Her name is Conchita?"

"Yes."

Quesedo laughed. The girl stared at him, open-mouthed, and he said, "That is how we get them—when the devil is between their legs."

"Please," the girl pleaded, "you don't say that I tell you this."

"Never. You're a good girl, you're all right." Quesedo reached out to tweak her nipple good-naturedly then, stimulated, cupped her flesh.

"I must go upstairs," she faltered.

Quesedo released his hold, patted her face. "Don't worry about the señora. I will tell her you are my favorite here. You tell her I had to go. I will come back later and I will go upstairs with you, I promise."

He walked rapidly to the door. She looked after him, her eyes still wide with fright.

Outside, a soft night wind flitted through the leaves. Inside the house, Elvira held De Luca tightly, spooning her belly to his back as he murmured, "They will do something, I know they will."

She said nothing, only pressed harder. He reached back with a hand to feel the reassuring outlines of her face. From outside the house, a muted cough floated back to them.

"Sal says I had to have this man with me when I come here."

"Yes. You sleep now, *mi corazón*. Does not matter."

It did matter. On the seat next to him in the car, Machado's man had a compact machine pistol, a French weapon. Driving to Elvira's, he had proudly displayed it. But he had laughed; they would do nothing, these *idiotas*, with him around, the *jefe* could be assured of that. De Luca had not laughed.

He turned himself about to face Elvira. "I've decided to shoot the big sequences as soon as possible. I want that in the can. And

275

I'm going to shoot right from the top of Tecla. Sal got the permission. We'll have a sweep of everything that way."

She could not know what he was talking about but it didn't matter, he had to talk.

"*Bueno*," she said softly, responding to the rush of his words.

"What will they do?" he asked into her breast. "And why won't they try to understand?"

At seven A.M Allan Marcus, having spent one of his better sleepless nights, appeared at the Cantina Uribe. Outside, he found Steve Kruger checking a tire on the small pickup and cursing. According to him, no Mexican understood tires; they all assumed air pressure was eternal. He hitched a ride with the driver, and they headed off for the main highway.

A mile down, they detoured a stretch of closed road. The Mexicans were always loath to detour and Kruger growled, "Can you imagine what it's like if they closed it?"

He made his left to a dirt track and swerved quickly to avoid hitting a moped that suddenly turned into him.

"Jerk," he muttered, recovering smoothly, but the moped driver came on his left side and, leaning low over the handlebars, gave his one-lunger all the gas it could eat.

"Look at that putz," Marcus called.

Kruger footed the accelerator, but before the engine could respond, the reckless moped driver had sped six feet past the pickup's bumper and now, insanely, was turning right to cut directly in front of the truck.

"Goddamn nut!" Kruger shouted, jamming his brakes. The pickup wheels locked, skidding forward on the hard-packed dirt. The moped nimbly leaped to the left, skidding as well. Marcus grabbed for the door handle, bracing himself.

In seconds the skid was over, the pickup coming to rest across the road, but as Kruger, enraged, flung open his door to get at the moped driver, a tan-shirted boy in heavy goggles, three men broke from behind a crumbling wall and advanced, shouting in Spanish. Looking up as they came toward him, Kruger saw that two of them held very large revolvers while the other waved a machete.

"Marcus," Kruger bellowed, "in the compartment!"

Inside the cab, Marcus had not seen the three. When Kruger's voice came at him, he had no idea that inside the glove compartment was Kruger's forty-five. He leaned to the left, in shock to see the three Mexicans rush at the riveted driver, waving guns. His first thought was disbelief. Real violence had never happened to him before. He had manufactured violence for the screen, but it did not look this way. This way was jerky, fear-filled on all sides. The clumsy men with the guns poked and shouted as Kruger eyed them like a dog at bay, not knowing what to do and fearful that some move might actually get him shot.

Marcus clung to the door, dumbfounded. The man wielding the machete ran to the cab and wrenched open the passenger door. He made no attempt to enter, simply held his blade threateningly and stared at Marcus, who stared back.

One of the revolver-armed men looked from Kruger to Marcus in the cab and back again. He spoke in low tones to his companion. They swung their heads between Marcus and Kruger in obvious uncertainty. Finally, the shorter of the two shoved the muzzle of his weapon hard against Kruger's stomach, forcing a shout from the driver of "No—wait!"

In the cab, seeing Kruger, gun against his belly, being backed off behind the crumbling wall, Marcus froze. His guard, hard-eyed, turned the machete over and over in the air, making the honed edge gleam in the morning light.

This is unbelievable, Marcus thought; they're going to kill Kruger. And then what?

Watching, he saw the driver back away, stiff with fear, hands in the air, saying things he could not hear. In a moment he disappeared behind the wall, one attacker going with him. As Marcus braced himself for a shot, the Mexican at the door leaped up, grabbed him and shoved him from the seat to the floor between the seats. Spotting a paper bag behind him, he swooped his hand down, picked it up and, depositing the bag on Marcus's head, pulled it down over his face. As the bag cut the light off, Marcus felt a rough palm shoving him, pushing him, folding him almost double into the small space. Then he heard the sound of running feet, felt a body lurch into the driver's place, slam the door, and in another ten seconds he felt the engine burst into shuddering life and the wild jerk as the Mexican accelerated from a standing start with the gas pedal jammed to the floor.

I am being taken, Marcus told himself, incredulously. Kidnapped. The bag came below his nose and he strained to breathe. The bumping threw him forward, but a hand dragged him back by the shirt. He slumped in place, closing his eyes. He would try to be calm, wait and see what happened, but his throat was parched and his hands shook.

CHAPTER
28

By nine o'clock, sloughing off night fears, Paul was at his Moviola. At the rice paddy three scenes were already in the can. The trucks had wheeled in with no delays, their cargo of extras upright and silent. The polyestered guardians had also returned, relieving others who had spent the night playing cards and drinking pulque.

Everything seemed well in hand until the door shot open and Steve Kruger burst in, his shirt torn, an angry red lump thrusting out from his cut forehead and his face covered with grimy sweat.

"They've got Marcus," he announced in a hoarse voice, kicking the door shut. "They kidnapped him!"

In his shock, Paul rode the gain up and the sound track screamed until he slammed the power off.

"Three Mex guys took him. They stopped us on the road and banged me on the head. They told us we had to quit, go home. They took him away in the pickup. I came back on a wood seller's cart." He touched the lump on his head and winced. "Those mothers."

Rennie came forward, wide-eyed. "You mean they . . . took him . . . took him away? Deliberately?"

"They had these old-fashioned pistols . . . big long things." Kruger seemed to need to relive the scene. "One of them pushed his piece right into my gut. It had cartridges. I could see the barrel. Jesus. My gun was in the car. I yelled to Marcus but he didn't hear me, I guess." He fell silent, closing his eyes. Quickly Paul went to the telephone, waiting anxiously as the communications man called for Sieberling. Rennie asked the driver if he wanted a doctor, but he simply slumped into a chair, pressing his fingers against the swelling.

"They've got my forty-five," he muttered. "Sons of bitches will find it."

After what seemed an interminable time, Sieberling came on the line. Tersely, Paul informed him of what had happened.

"Jesus Christ. Let me get to Mike. Hang on."

Paul heard the receiver thump down. Rennie came over, whispering, "What are we going to do?"

Kruger groaned and opened his eyes. He rose unsteadily from the chair, but sank back again. "I should have had the gun in my belt," he muttered, "and shot their asses off."

The second assistant popped his head out of his cubicle and went pale at the sight.

"Murray, keep working," Paul said. "It's some kind of accident." Murray removed himself quickly. Paul heard Michael's intense voice in his ear asking what the hell was going on. Once again he repeated the story, adding, "They said we had to go home."

"My God." De Luca's voice shook. "Those bastards."

"I think you ought to speak to Kruger yourself. You want us to come out to the location?"

"Let me . . . let me finish the morning. Let's keep it low-key. I'll come back as soon as I can." His voice was guarded. "I have to think this out."

"I want a beer," Kruger said plaintively. "Could someone get me a Bohemia?"

"I'll get it," Rennie offered, and left, her face blotched with worry.

Kruger shook his head gingerly. "That poor bastard. I hope they don't hurt him."

But what if they do? Paul thought. What if they do more than hurt him?

It was after twelve when De Luca and Sieberling marched into the Jericho compound. A sanitized Steve Kruger, gauze on his wound, repeated his story. Listening, De Luca sat, shoulders hunched. When the recital ended, Paul volunteered that the crazy *bajos* had obviously mistaken Marcus as someone key to the production. Sieberling, outwardly calm, considered.

"Okay, it's a snatch. The question is, what'll they take for him?"

"They said 'go,' " Paul reminded him.

"They *said*. But if you find the right party and make the right offer . . ."

"Not them."

"Anyone."

"Who do we find? Where do we find them?" De Luca injected.

"Mike," Paul asked, "shouldn't we notify the police?"

280

De Luca glanced over to Sieberling, who grimaced and shook his head. Startled, Paul said, "But we have to do something to get Allan back."

"Forget the police; we ought to speak to Machado," Sieberling countered, "lay it out. Make him an offer. Let him do it any way he thinks to get Marcus back."

The phone rang. De Luca snatched it up and snapped, "I don't want to be bothered." But his eyes came to attention and his body sagged. "My God."

Paul went to him. "What?"

"Lufkin," De Luca hissed. "That bastard Lufkin is at the goddamned airport." Then into the phone, "Put him on."

"Lufkin?" Sieberling's face went white. It took Paul seconds to recall that Lufkin was the studio man, the hatchet man. It seemed inconceivable that he would do this—arrive without warning. But of course he would do that.

De Luca cleared his throat; his face took on an expression of boundless enthusiasm; his voice exploded with welcome. "Ben, you sure do love to surprise people." He produced a deep chuckle. "We'll send a car for you right away. Can't wait to see you and rap and show you the great stuff we have."

He was attentive to the earpiece, then, "Great. Terrific. And call as soon as you get into the hotel." He replaced the phone and metamorphosed back. "That bastard, that son of a bitch, he came here behind our backs, trying to catch us off guard. That bastard, that goddamn—"

"Mike," Sieberling interrupted, "what the hell are we going to do? He'll find out about Marcus."

De Luca froze. He will find out, Paul thought. How could it be kept from him? Allan Marcus was an American citizen kidnapped by Mexicans.

"If he gets one whiff of what's been happening," Sieberling continued, "he'll go back and kill the picture, sure as hell."

"Yes." De Luca winced. "It's bad—very bad."

He walked the length of the room in what seemed to Paul almost physical pain, his hands opening and closing, his shoulders twitching. Finally he said, "He must not find out. Never."

Paul waited for more, but there was none. De Luca stared into space, Sieberling into himself.

"But what . . . are we going to do about Allan?" Paul asked cautiously.

"I don't know," De Luca said, his desperation evident. "All I know is that Lufkin has to be kept from knowing. Sal, if we told Quesedo, would he keep quiet?"

"It's possible."

How was Quesedo to do anything, keeping quiet? Paul wondered. With something like this he had to mount a real search, call for state police.

"Listen." De Luca thought his way into a plan of action, "First of all, Lufkin has to be shown a good time and hustled out of here before someone puts a bug in his ear. One or two days at the most." He saw the question in Paul's eyes and came close to him. "We have to play this by ear and not throw the baby out with the bath water. You think I'm not concerned about Allan?"

Paul wanted to say that if they kept shooting it would be a clear rebuff, defiance; what might they do to Marcus then? Instead, he nodded, but muttered, "Allan—"

"I know, I know!" De Luca groaned. "But we have to play for time; it's disaster if Lufkin hears a word." He groped the air. "I think . . . I think Allan will be all right. They're using him for a pressure point. If they let anything happen to him, they know all hell will break loose. They don't want that, do they?"

No, they would not want that, Paul agreed, but the *bajos* had been proven to be less than rational. Some action had to be taken, shut down for a few days, perhaps.

"Now—shut down now?" De Luca agonized. "With Lufkin here?"

"You give them an inch," Sieberling said, "and you can kiss it good-bye. They tried to stop the extras on us, didn't they? But Machado knows the moves. Turn him loose."

De Luca turned to the driver. "Steve, how you feeling?"

"Okay."

"Good. Now listen. No one but us knows what happened, right?"

Kruger nodded. De Luca patted his shoulder.

"Keep it that way. Anybody asks you about your head, you got into an accident. The pickup's being repaired." He turned to Paul. "Who else knows?"

"Rennie."

De Luca waved that away. "Now, I'm going to arrange to give Lufkin the tour. You'll show him some stuff and sure, he and I will come to some nitty-gritty about costs, but I'll handle that. This other thing is just not to come anywhere near him."

Clarity had returned to him; the shock was wearing off. Not for Paul, however.

"Suppose some locals find out about it. You know how it happens."

"I know Lufkin," Sieberling answered. "He speaks dollars and cents, not Spanish."

"What you have to do, Sal," De Luca urged, "is just spread the word to keep our troubles to ourselves, so when Lufkin tries to tap anybody, he gets nothing, even if he pays for it."

"That can be handled." Sieberling's face clouded over. "But there could be other problems—the Ankrum girl, for instance. No one knows where the hell she is, and if she knew Lufkin was here, she'd be the first to shoot her mouth off to him."

De Luca sagged. Sieberling turned to Paul. "And are we sure that your friend's taken off?"

"Stella?"

"If *she* knew Lufkin was here, maybe she'd put a bug in his ear."

"Never. No."

Sieberling was unimpressed by his indignation. "How do we know? And she speaks English."

"Paul." De Luca went behind his desk. "Sal is right. Follow up on that. Just make sure she's gone. All I want is one more day at the rice paddies with nothing happening," he continued prayerfully. "Then we can shoot the big stuff at Ixtepan."

"What happens," Paul asked, "if we don't hear anything more from the *bajos* and they just don't send Marcus back?"

De Luca hesitated. "Let's cross our bridges," he finally said, "when we come to them."

When the plane arrived from Mexico City, Stella was already at the airport. When she advanced, belligerently, to the counter, the clerk disarmed her with his sunny smile, his memory of her name and the presentation of her ticket and boarding pass.

"Beautiful day to go to the capital, señorita. I wish I were going with you."

She had been, Stella mused, absolutely correct. Roadblocks before and now—smiles. Oh, yes, that slimy aide-de-camp had pipelines everywhere. Her watch told her she had almost an hour to kill before boarding. Settling herself in the muraled coffee shop, she watched the flow of the new arrivals, a mix of Mexicans and

American tourists. The time passed slowly and she searched for interesting details, finding little to engage her attention, which sent her mind to Paul; she speculated that if he had seemed, to her, indecisive all the time they had been together, uncertain and searching, he had found some other pattern to cut his cloth to. Could one call De Luca an inspiration?

Interrupting, the loudspeaker crackled out Spanish and she prepared to stir. Then, in English, a female voice: "All passengers departing on flight number sixty-two to Mexico City are advised that there will be a forty-minute delay in departure."

She groaned with everyone else and peered out the picture window. Three mechanics in blue overalls were attacking the inboard engine. She sank back in her chair. An airline-announced forty minutes compounded by a Mexican forty minutes added up to who knew how many hours. For a flashing moment she felt conspiracy at work again, then became more rational. She wasn't the only one delayed. But it was hateful, nonetheless. In her mind she was already not only in Mexico City, but in New York, at her apartment, in her bedroom with the cool light and Sony and stacks of books, with her baby picture in its ivory frame. Her body, however, was here at the airport coffee shop and promised to be for quite some time. She told herself to be calm and patient.

The next announcement came at two o'clock. To the groans of all those departing, the ubiquitous loudspeaker pronounced departure of the one o'clock to Mexico City canceled. Passengers were advised to stand by for further announcements. Outside on the field, the mechanics were clambering down from the plane with an air of jovial finality.

There was an immediate rush of bodies to the ticket counter, where the clerk waved his hands in an ineffective attempt to stem the rebellion. Caught between a large red-haired woman and a blustering Latin man, Stella fought for space and heard the clerk say, despairing of even being heard, "Please . . . please . . . this plane cannot depart. You will all be on the seven o'clock plane that comes from Mexico City and goes back."

"How can we all get on that?" a beefy man shouted. "What about the people who have reservations?"

"It will be arranged."

"I hate this country," a young woman in a denim suit announced in a fury as her equally denim-clad husband looked on, misery etched on his round face. "I just hate it."

Fighting her way out of the crowd, Stella found open space and was pulling her blouse down when she was startled by the loudspeaker calling her name with a request for her to pick up the white telephone. Having found it in a corner, she discovered it was Paul at the other end. He had wanted, he said, to say good-bye, but there seemed to be some kind of trouble. What was going on?

"What is going on," Stella said, "is a malfunction. I am malfunctioning and the airplane is malfunctioning. We are both canceled."

"There's no flight?" His voice held a tone that was either pleasure or anxiety. She could not decide which.

"They say we'll be on the night flight. The one that leaves at seven. That's hours from now."

"Stel, I'm coming to get you."

"Why?"

He hesitated a fraction of a second. "Because I want to. We'll have some coffee away from there."

"I just had coffee," she wailed, suddenly overwhelmed.

"Wait there. Just wait."

He hung up before she had a chance to protest. It would have been perfunctory anyway.

He arrived barely twenty minutes later by cab. He lifted her suitcase and they were back inside the taxi returning to the town, to the Jaime, which was, at least, familiar territory. Seated in the garden, coffee and sweet rolls on the table, she said, "Well—still here."

"I'm sorry," he told her, "I know you really want to go home."

He seemed distraught, unhappy, and yet, in the midst of whatever was going on, he had called the airport to speak to her. That was touching.

"How are things going?" she asked. "Did anything—bad—happen—as that woman said it would?"

"No, no, nothing." The words tumbled out. "Everything's moving right along. We're going to wrap here in a few weeks."

"Are you going back to L.A. with him to edit there?"

"I guess." He rose suddenly. "Listen, excuse me for a minute, I've got to make a phone call."

At the telephone booth, Paul rationalized his discomfort. He was *not* betraying her in any fashion. There was no evil intended. There was simply a situation to be taken care of. How could she be injured by his actions?

"Listen, Michael," he whispered into the mouthpiece, "I'm with Stella now. Her plane's been canceled. Mechanical trouble."

"Oh, shit."

"It's not important," he soothed. "She's leaving on the night plane now."

"I want her gone. And I want you to watch her go, Paul."

"I will, I will."

"Lufkin's coming over in ten minutes, though. Get back here and arrange to show him some stuff."

"Okay."

"And I want you to have dinner with us, tonight, at my house."

"I'll be there."

Mind racing, he returned to Stella, trying a reassuring smile but could not manage its frozen falsity. As he fumbled with his coffee cup, she observed him tolerantly and his guilt level grew. She smiled, patted his hand, and he wished she would snarl something that would take him off his private hook.

"It was a mistake coming here," she said, instead. "Confession time."

The more she talked, the more miserable he became. She was quiet, thoughtful, nonjudgmental, and he ached to lean over and whisper what was really happening. Instead, he looked at his watch and pretended surprise.

"I have some things to do for the next hour or so, but I want to come back here and drive you to the airport."

"You don't have to," she demurred, but he smothered that quickly, insisting upon his rights as an old friend.

"I'll meet you here," he told her, "without question. So don't go off without me."

Leaving with a vague feeling of regret, turning back to look at her, he was troubled by what he saw, the outline of her face against the trees, a certain brooding grace in her eyes and the blond bangs slightly dampened by the moisture of her skin.

At the Jericho compound, Rennie was waiting excitedly. "He's come," she announced. "Michael's in with him." She clutched anxiously. "He can't stop the picture, can he? This is the most important picture of Michael's life."

On the way to De Luca's, someone shouted his name from the doorway of a building and he saw Denny Burns coming at him. The flier waved a shooting schedule in the air and shouted, "Hey—

where the hell is Marcus? He's supposed to come up and shoot some hand-held with me and the sumbitch ain't nowhere. What am I supposed to do?"

"There's been a change," Paul improvised. "Didn't you get notified?"

"No."

"Sal's working it out. Just hang loose."

"Goddamn it," Burns said irritably. "We been lookin' for the mother all morning. He shacking up with some new piece of tail?"

"Probably." This, he knew, would be an explanation Burns would accept.

"He's still gotta take care of business," the flier muttered. "I'm going to the cantina; it's too goddamn hot out here. Shit, Nam wasn't even so hot, sometimes."

Getting a little out of hand, he thought, watching Burns stride off; it's getting a little out of hand. He continued on, shakily. What might they be doing to Marcus? Bound, gagged, blindfolded, someplace in the hills, they could be doing anything, anything at all. And nothing was being done about it.

He did not, at first, notice the two men standing idly near the green Pontiac. Only when their sudden swift movements caught his peripheral vision did he recognize the polyester slacks. As he watched, they plucked up one of the three Mexican helpers who were putting down coils of wire. They lifted him off the ground by his neck, despite his struggles, and, with casual practiced ease, pulled him into the car, folding his flailing arms neatly. In seconds the door closed and the man was gone. Paul looked at the two remaining men with questioning surprise, but they averted their eyes and walked away.

What had happened out there? Disturbed, he took a minute to collect himself before approaching De Luca's door, where he knocked and entered upon command.

Great false joviality. Michael, wineglass in hand, waved at him expansively. Sieberling, holding a wineglass as well, was perched, uncharacteristically, upon the arm of a chair, a grudging smile attacking his face. The visitor, whom Paul judged to be in his early fifties, was a straight pin of a man with the slightest of paunches. Wearing a white sharkskin suit with a blue tennis shirt open at the throat, he had just told a joke. Under his graying razor-cut hair, his features held a deceptive blandness; nothing stood out.

287

All one could tell of that deeply tanned face was that it had been well taken care of; massaged well, oiled well, anointed well. That face was its owner's pet.

He shook Lufkin's well-manicured hand and saw his eyes suddenly become computer chips making an immediate calculation. De Luca took over quickly.

"First thing I want you to do is show Ben some of our stuff, then later we'll get him out to the location." He turned to the visitor. "I'll have the figures for you sometime today and we can have a chat about them."

"Great. Perfect." His enthusiasm seemed absolutely genuine and Paul wondered how he did it.

"I'm still surprised I didn't get your wire," De Luca said smoothly.

"Me too." Lufkin shook his head, his smile sunny. "But I guess these things happen when you leave the States."

In the hallway, with De Luca and Lufkin ten feet ahead, Sieberling warned Paul, "We should have someone with him every minute, never let him alone. I know that son of a bitch. He laughs at everything and then puts the knife in."

"Sal," Paul said anxiously, "just now, outside, I saw two of Machado's men grab one of the Mexican laborers. They dragged him into a car."

"Maybe they were going for a beer."

"No, Sal—" He felt a strong pressure in his chest. To expel it, he planted himself in front of Sieberling and said, "The man was trying to get away."

"Was he?" Sieberling's face tightened. "Then maybe he knows something about who took Marcus." He sidestepped quickly, but Paul reached out a hand to stop him.

"Does Mike know what's going on?"

Sieberling twisted away from him. "Damn it, you want Marcus back on the QT? Or do you want to make a federal case out of this? Lufkin hears one word and he blows the whistle, which he wants to do anyway. How the hell are you going to get Marcus back without *somebody* doing something?"

"Yes, but—" He cut off, feeling the words churn in his throat. Luis, Luis was the way, but Sieberling was no part of that.

Lufkin was enthusiastic about everything he saw. Every shot was a "knockout," every sequence a "killer—Oscar material."

"He lies," Sieberling warned tersely, "about everything. Don't believe a word he says." De Luca had gone back to the rice-paddy location, having warned Paul not to leave the visitor unescorted, even for ten seconds. Sieberling had whispered the same injunction to Rennie. After the forty-minute screening, when Lufkin asked to be taken back to his hotel to get some material, Paul felt apprehensive, but Rennie, cheery and bright, stepped in, offering to drive him and even take him to lunch.

"Love it," Lufkin agreed, "but no Taco-Rico stuff."

"Promise." Rennie laughed, snapping her fingers in the air. "Spanish music and everything."

He watched them go, depression enfolding him. Screening the footage with Lufkin, he had become morosely aware of how little time he had been spending in actual work on the film, how much there was to be done. He sat down at the Moviola for the lovingly familiar rituals, and only when there was a knocking on the door and he opened it, dazed and somewhat sullen, was he aware that over two hours had passed.

"Great lunch," Lufkin enthused. "This girl really knows the town."

"I think Michael might be waiting for us at the rice paddy," Rennie announced. "Shall we go?"

De Luca had called "Cut!" minutes before they arrived, and the black-pajamaed "atmosphere" were relaxed into Mexican postures, awaiting orders. In the shade of a makeshift tent, Paul glimpsed a few polyesters, and he felt an automatic stab of anger colored with some fear. On a keg of nails, near one of the water hoses, Steve Kruger sat, a modest dressing on his head. He walked swiftly over to Paul looking uneasy and, from the side of his mouth, asked, "Anything happening? I don't want to ask the boss."

"I don't know a thing," Paul told him, "but it's being worked on. How are things here?"

"Sieberling's put out that Marcus went up to Mexico City to get some stuff for a day or so."

Something had to be said, Paul knew. Turning away from the driver, he saw that Lufkin was deep in a private conversation with Kodály. Rennie, greeting a friend from the costume department, seemed not to have noticed, and who knew what the wild Hungarian might be saying? Strolling by, he discovered that they were old acquaintances and made a note to report that to Sieberling.

De Luca, it turned out, was in his blue van, awaiting them. When Paul delivered Lufkin, eager to be relieved, he discovered it was not to be; Michael wished him to stay. Lufkin appeared to

289

be uncomfortable with another presence but De Luca insisted; Paul was working with him on production and there were no secrets between them. De Luca exuded absolute confidence, padding about with his usual wineglass, posture erect, eyes dancing. Lufkin, a small, elegant leather case in hand, sat quietly, in contrast, the open face present but, Paul noted, altered, creased by shadowed furrows, which transformed that tanned visage into something feral.

"So," De Luca began, "what do you think of the footage?"

"Mike, we always love what you shoot." Lufkin snapped open the case. "But it's been over a year here." He held up a rainbow of accounting paper. "The money's flying away. Over twenty-two million already."

De Luca was unaffected. "Ben, do you want a budget up there on the screen, or do you want a great picture?"

Lufkin sighed. "A great picture. Of course—all the guys want a great picture. But the guys keep asking, and I have to tell you this, whenever we take a meeting the question comes up—are we going to come out of this place with a picture at all?"

"Ben, I'm not down here for my health."

"Mike, people keep coming back with stories . . ."

"You listen to that garbage?"

"Mike, we had to pay off big names you gave deals to then flew in and out without one foot of film coming from them. There's God knows how much for sets you built in Mexico City and flew down here, then junked."

"Ben, Ben, listen to me. I change my mind. That's how I make pictures. And I've made a lot of money for you people that way, right or wrong?"

Paul watched Lufkin's face settle into agreement.

"Absolutely. But Mike, this time is the longest shoot in company history. Every day costs a fortune." He shifted uneasily in his seat. "And we can't get a handle on what's causing the delays. We hear things that are giving my people a lot of problems."

"More garbage. You know how people love to talk garbage."

"I know. But we get stories about crew fights, arrests, trouble with the authorities. All that eats up time and money."

"The authorities? They love us." De Luca smiled, sipped his wine, unconcerned.

"Mike, we heard someone tried to blow you up with a bomb. You had to shut down."

290

De Luca laughed. "Ben, whoever's doing your spying is sniffing too much coke. There was a dumb little problem, a misunderstanding, that's all settled. Am I shooting? Am I shooting like hell now—right outside?"

Lufkin nodded. "Looks like that."

De Luca played his trump card. "Ben, did I call you and insist you come down to see for yourself?"

"Absolutely."

"If I had something to hide, would I have done that?"

Lufkin considered. "Probably not."

"Then look around. Ask anybody anything you want. Everyone has orders to cooperate. But Ben, I think this is all about something else . . . about the kind of picture I'm making." He was shifting the ground, Paul saw, and marveled. And he had hit a nerve, for Lufkin looked up, momentarily startled.

"Well, the guys want to be sure, Mike, that people will want to go see this picture . . ."

"Ah," De Luca said.

"You have this whole Vietnam thing, but the country's changed. Iran, all that stuff. People don't feel the way you think they feel about Vietnam anymore."

"I can't help that."

Lufkin put his papers down. "Mike, some of the heavy hitters on the board are saying this should be finished back home."

De Luca's eyes actually twinkled. "I tell you, Ben, let's do it this way—let's make a country-and-western out of it . . . with Dolly Parton, maybe."

Lufkin smiled wryly. "We could do worse."

De Luca moved to refill his glass. Lufkin changed his position on the couch. It was an intermission, Paul perceived.

"See much of the town?" De Luca inquired.

"Town? Who looks at towns? I see airports and hotels and offices and locations. But the lunch was good. She's all right, that girl."

"Rennie? Oh, sure, she's terrific." De Luca sat down next to Lufkin; his voice became warmly intimate. "Ben, I'm really glad you're here. You're not one of these baby geniuses running the studio. They'd be just as happy making plastic toys or toilet paper, if the percentages were right. But you've been around movies for a long time. People say you're tough, but you have a feeling for movies those nerds could never have."

"They're smart . . . some of them."

"Ex-agents, ex-lawyers. None of them knows how to take a lens cap off a camera."

"Mike, a couple of them are talking about a cutoff, a hiatus."

"Are they crazy?"

"Look at the financing contract." Lufkin smiled reassuringly. "But that's not for now. Still, so many months here and so many delays." His brow wrinkled contemplatively. "What's really holding things up?"

"Me, I'm holding things up, Ben. Because I want to get this picture just right." De Luca hovered over Lufkin like an oak over a scrub pine. Another fine performance, Paul thought. "But you happened to come at a time when I know exactly where we're going and how to get there. The problems are all behind us." He bent toward the visitor. "I'm telling you we can wrap very soon now—a matter of weeks."

"Weeks?"

"I'm telling you that for a fact." Confident energy flowed from him. "Now, why don't you take a ride to Monte Tecla? That's a real spectacular. We start shooting there tomorrow. I'll get Rennie to take you over."

Lufkin was agreeable. He replaced his papers, saying, casually, they would talk some more. De Luca called for Rennie and she came in, smiling. As the visitor had a final word, Rennie managed to tell Paul she would see him later.

After shutting the trailer door, De Luca dropped his jovial manner like a discarded shirt. "That son of a bitch. You know what he was threatening? Did you get it?"

Paul did not.

"He was telling me, with that business about calling a hiatus, that they'd start up again, with another director. On *my* picture. My guts out there all over the place and they'd cut me out without a wink, change everything. Over my dead body." He drained the wine. "How do you think I did? Did he buy my story or is that bastard just making believe?"

"I think he bought it," Paul said, cautiously. "You made out a great case. And we're shooting. But if someone says a word about Marcus . . ."

"No one in the company knows."

"You think so?"

De Luca pulled at his beard. "I'm praying hard. And Rennie's

292

got to keep him busy." He looked at his watch. "Still some daylight left. I want to finish here."

They left the trailer. Kodály was waiting impatiently. The sky was an incredible blue, so deep it appeared endless. The Mexican extras were sitting together, one waiting organism. The hoses throbbed with water and the rice paddy took on a fresh sheen. Denny Burns, primed to go aloft for aerial shots, drank from a can of Bohemia. As Paul walked at Michael's side, his attention was drawn to the polyesters. A new man had joined the group, and with a sharp intake of breath, he recognized him as one of the pair who had attacked the laborer.

"Mike . . ." he started to say, but stopped the complaint; the *bajos* were the ones creating the violence. When Michael turned an inquiring look upon him, he shook his head. "Not important."

They reached De Luca's giraffe-legged director's chair where the dog-eared script flopped in its usual place on the high canvas seat. Beside it, now, was a small, paper-wrapped foreign object. Occupying space, it sat there centered, shadowed, waiting to be moved. The deliberation of its placement was unmistakable; it floated on the beige sea like a white beacon.

Paul looked at it apprehensively. "What's that?"

De Luca bent down and poked. The paper sprang crisply open and something shone. He picked it up, looking closely at what appeared to be a silver circlet with an engraved *M*. Then he let out a stifled cry, "It's Allan's!"

Paul, whose mind had already seen the finger or the ear, a film of blood at its cut edge, said, "There's something written on the paper."

Apprehensively, De Luca smoothed the creases. Thick crayoned lines revealed themselves, became formed into numbers and letters: 24 HORAS.

"Twenty-four hours," De Luca whispered.

"The *bajos*." Paul spoke tensely.

De Luca rose up. "Those crazy bastards." He squeezed the paper into a ball angrily and whirled to scan the mess tables.

"Could be anybody," Paul muttered. "What are we going to do, Mike?"

Grimly, De Luca shoved the ring deep into a pocket of his bush jacket. "We're going to finish the day; then we'll see." He moved forward purposefully, shouting for Kodály. Paul felt his toes touching the edge of a precipice. They meant what they said. They were

293

fanatics, and fanatics would go to the end of the line. Quesedo had pegged it—when money was involved, people were reasonable, deals were struck; when it was something else, there was no bargaining. Fanatics made their own rules and so they meant "24 *horas*."

He looked at the polyesters. That way wouldn't work. They could beat everyone in sight, it wouldn't intimidate those who were truly *bajos*. Luis was the way; Luis was the best hope. Almost trembling, he looked over to the helicopter landing circle where he saw only Denny's death's-head craft. He made his way to the flier and took him to one side.

"I know you've got to shoot aerial," he said, urgent concern drying his throat, "but I have to get back to town, quickly. It's really important. Could you take me?"

Burns examined his face shrewdly, then nodded, with no hesitation. "Let's go, cap." As they walked, he suddenly asked, "Have anything to do with Marcus?"

Paul tripped and gaped. Burns said quietly, "He didn't go to Mexico City on the cargo flight. I asked."

"Oh?" Paul executed an elaborate shrug.

Burns said no more, but in the air, as he banked left to swoop over the rice paddies below, he grinned. "Another dope run?"

"That's right," Paul said. "Another dope run."

CHAPTER
29
⌖═⌖═⌖═⌖═⌖═⌖═ **29** ═⌖═⌖═⌖═⌖═⌖

Captain Quesedo held his throbbing head. No sooner did you discover one pinhole in this pig's bladder and stem the outpourings than another was discovered, and another.

He had sent a man to follow up on the whore's information about Carlos, the charcoal seller. Espido, who had the usefully innocent look of a man starving but not resenting it, had reported back that the charcoal seller indeed was there in the hut with the widow Conchita, had been there for forty-eight hours servicing her, in fact. Espido had caught a glimpse of him as he came outside, for a few minutes, to relieve himself. He was ugly and he limped, but God knows he must have something for this widow.

Quesedo had decided not to arrest him but to have Espido trail him when he left, and perhaps he would lead them to someone important.

All this had put him in a fine mood until the summons from Sieberling. At that point his headache had started. He had feared something like this. They would have to, now, call for the state police to search the hills, mount a sweep of the lower sierra, and even then it was doubtful that they could find the man who had been taken; the peasants of the *bajo* knew hiding places no one else did.

When Sieberling ordered that the state police absolutely *not* be notified, Quesedo had felt a wave of nausea. If an American died in his district, that would be the end of his career. He would be broken, finished.

"The *jefe* is *loco,*" he had cried. "You are all playing with fire."

Sieberling had insisted that it still had to be kept quiet; those were De Luca's orders. They were taking measures, however, to locate the missing man.

"Ah, Machado," he had said then, unhappily. "And who is this man from California?"

All Sieberling would say was that he was important and no word of the abduction was to reach him, and since they did not know where Flo Ankrum was, there existed an immediate threat.

"You have got to find out where she is. Got to, you understand me?" Sieberling had said. "This is the crunch and you've got to show what you can do."

Quesedo took his hands from his temples, tried to overcome his dejection and knocked at the door of the hut. When Flo opened it, her hair was bound up in a kerchief and her face was scrubbed clean. He would have preferred lipstick and eye shadow, but the intensity of her features, the changing play of expression, pleased him and his spirits began to rise.

"*Buenas tardes.* You look much nice."

She shrugged and tried to read his face. Though by now there was a grudging trust of him, the reasons for his kindness were so mysterious she had spent half the night working on them. Still, she was grateful for his gentleness and concern; it was a damn sight more than she had come to expect from Allan Marcus.

"What's happening?" she asked. "At the water spigot today, someone told me the Mafia mob is going after people. Why?"

Quesedo frowned. "Why you talk with them? That no good."

"I was getting some water and it happened. They don't know who I am."

"I don' t'ink this place be good for you anymore."

"Why?"

"Is here no . . . no protection." He struck the chord again. "Can to come in here any *borracho* and make the attack on you. I cannot to let that happen." Persuading himself by his argument, he let his fantasy roam. Despite her strength, she was fragile and in the face of a drunk would be helpless, would be pawed, clothing ripped, forced to endure some wild-eyed animal pounding at her. It was intolerable. "Somet'ing bad happen to you, I feel so much to be my fault I don't know what I do."

His declaration of guilt astounded her. In a soft voice she said, "No . . . I'll be all right, honestly. I can take care of myself."

"Señorita," he pleaded. "You don't know how bad men can be when they drink too much. They don' care for not'ing. Is no good to stay here; I change my mind."

"Where will I go?"

"You must to listen to me, Florenza. You must to have the *confianza* in me, eh?"

She nodded, and he moved close enough to see the slight dew on her upper lip and to breathe in what emanated from her, that odor of earth and breath and body. He inhaled deeply, intoxicating himself. She waited intently for what he would say next.

"I t'ink 'bout all this. I t'ink what really be best for you and it comes to me that you be okay near where I be, eh?"

"What do you mean where you are?"

He heard the suspicion in her voice and said, hastily, "In the station. I see you get good place. You eat good. I don't let no one bother you."

"You mean in jail?" she gasped.

"For a few days," he said quickly, "and when you say what you want to do, where you want to go, you go. Is all to protect you."

Her eyes burned. "Did they put you up to this again?"

"No," he lied. "Why I do this now for them if I don' do it before?"

She did not know. "Suppose I . . . just want to leave Oacala later today, or tomorrow. Why can't I? Instead of going . . . to jail?"

He tightened his lips. Why must she do this? He had invented a wonderful reason for her not staying here, a marvelous reason for everything to work out, but she insisted upon fighting him.

"Is much complication," he finally said. "You go away from the place you say you stay in your visa, you see. That be 'gainst the law. Take time to make all this okay again. Just few days. And I give you big room. We bring in good bed. Make every t'ing private for you. You go to my toilet. Not be hard."

"You're going to tell them, aren't you?" she said bitterly. "De Luca and Sieberling and Gordon, you're going to tell them I'm in jail."

"I must to do this, but they do not'ing to you, I don' let them do no bad t'ing to you. Believe me."

He quivered with the passion of his resolve, and Flo asked herself what option she had. She should have just given up and left at the beginning. They had the power. They did what they wished in the end. Oh, Allan, Allan, she cried to herself, come back with me, get out of it, you have things inside you you don't even know are there. You hide everything tender and graceful, you cover up your talents, you give your gifts to him and he sucks you dry the way he does everyone, pulls the breath from them, leaves them limp

297

and fleshless . . . and when you learn I am in jail, what will you do?

Aloud, she said, "Do we go now?"

Paul crossed the shadowed Avenida Juarez, avoiding the heaps of dung, and walked quickly toward Ismena's shop.

All during the chopper flight he'd felt anxious wings beating at his chest. Burns noticed and just before touchdown told Paul that he had all the earmarks of a pig crossing a road near the bacon factory.

"Listen," Paul had said, "Allan's on a kind of . . . secret job. It would be good if you didn't talk about it, okay?"

"You got it, cap," Burns had responded with a disbelieving wink. Then he had boosted his machine back into the air for the return trip.

As Paul came up to the shop, he stopped and stared in surprise. The corrugated metal shutters were drawn down. It was well past siesta but the place was closed. Why? Why today, particularly?

He tapped the gray armor futilely and it rattled like small thunder. He tried to find a single open niche to peer through but could find none.

He turned to the deserted street, eyeing the frame buildings, wondering if Ismena lived in one of them, but they stared back at him, totally silent. Casting a final, frustrated look at the shop, he retreated slowly. A moped engine buzzed angrily behind him and he whirled in time to see a rear wheel disappear down an alley. He clenched his fist in angry frustration; if they wanted Machado's tactics they could damn well have them, but neither Michael nor he was to be held responsible. Michael would have made that rice-paddy location ten times as fertile as it could ever be, but no—they simply wanted *yanquis* out of their valley, that was the bottom line, and to accomplish that they had put a man's life in danger and would not meet, would not talk, wanted everything their way.

A small girl in a dirty dress, face blotched with impetigo, came out of a doorway to observe him. As he passed, the child raised her hand, silently, open palm up. His first reaction was rage. They wanted Jericho out and yet they let their children starve and beg and die of disease. Guilt overtook that and he gave the girl ten pesos, at which she vanished abruptly, her eyes as flat as they had been before.

He trudged on through the streets, obsessed. It had to end and

298

Luis had to end it. He had promised. Did he know about Allan? Surely he must, absolutely, and yet—he thought he heard footsteps behind him, but it was only a cat, pouncing. He stopped again as the only other possibility flashed into his consciousness, then started rapidly toward the Zócalo, trying hard to recall the directions Ismena had given him, those directions which had led him to Calle Libertad and the Red House.

He wove his way through the maze of alleys and dead ends, finding the turns with an ease he simply accepted. Cross, right, left, diagonal, the short street to the longer, to the shorter and then out to the broad avenida, he moved through it all precisely, emerging finally at the iron fence with the parklike garden beyond, and beyond that the house rising aristocratically, its red velour drapes marking it inviolate.

He passed through the gates onto the malachite walk and half-ran up to the house, where he slammed the brass knocker down three times. Even after two long minutes there was no answer, no rustle of life, and he beat the knocker onto its plate again. When nothing happened, he pounded on the oak with his fist, but there was only silence from within the house.

"*Oiga*—what you do here?" The deep male voice spun him about. It belonged to a squat policeman who had come up the walk soundlessly and now stood at the foot of the stairs, examining him with suspicion.

Composing his face into a lopsided grin, Paul tapped his watch. "Too early, I'm too early."

The policeman relaxed in amused response. "Sí, *amor* at night."

"*Adiós*," Paul called. He walked rapidly down the steps past the uniform. Once outside the gates he slowed and looked back. When he did, he thought he saw a curtain part in the upper story, and he was two steps back before he looked again and saw that the red velour had not moved after all.

He continued on to the street then, finding it hard to lift his legs.

CHAPTER
30

When half-past five showed on the ornate lobby clock, Stella unwound from the deep, comfortable couch and wondered whether Paul would come to take her to the airport. As the afternoon had passed, with the two margaritas numbing her brain and the two espressos sending their charges in to awaken her, she had gone from newspaper to paperback to thinking. Were the changes she perceived in Paul products of Oacala defocus or organic? And where was he? She decided to give him another fifteen minutes.

She stretched, languidly, and the desk clerk, by now almost an acquaintance, smiled at her. She smiled back. Probably, she reflected, if Paul had greeted her with open arms and said what a mistake it was for them to have broken up, she would have recoiled and taken the next plane back home. Maybe. No matter. She had come down and gotten into this thing, run through the changes and was on her way out. Watching the trim-figured travel agent unlock his desk reminded her that she had no reservation home from Mexico City and, pushing her way out of the reluctant cushions' pleasant grasp, went to the travel desk. The agent looked up at her, his standard smile arriving, but he appeared distracted.

"*Buenas tardes.* You excuse me, señorita, I am much busy."

"I just want the schedule from Mexico City to New York, direct."

He has woman trouble, Stella thought, or wife trouble, or mother trouble, or all three.

"Is here, madame." He plucked a folder from the rack and gave it to her, busying himself again.

"Is the seven o'clock going to leave on time?"

"Sí . . . leaves on time."

It was a quarter till six. She looked out the glass doors to the street, wondering if she should wait even ten minutes longer. It was getting a bit ridiculous. What difference if he came or not, if he took her or not? But there was a difference.

"You wish a taxi, madame?"

"I . . . don't know," she said. "Maybe I'll give it another five minutes. A friend is supposed to pick me up here."

"Ah . . ." She saw unaccustomed curiosity come into his eyes. "An American?"

"Yes," she answered, surprised.

"Ah," he said again, and went quickly back to his papers.

Uncomfortable, she asked, "Why did you ask that . . . about his being American?"

"No reason." But he was, clearly, nervous.

Stella leaned in. "What's going on?"

The travel agent slithered his body forward to meet hers. "Madame, you go to the airport or you miss the flight. Maybe your friend is late, or he don't come."

Something in the arch of his body, in his reptilian eyes, sent an alert through her. "What do you mean?"

"Señorita, is better you go to the airport."

She calculated, then opened her leather bag, probed inside and plucked out the first bill her fingers touched. It was a crumpled hundred-peso note, which she slid along the desk. The travel agent's hand covered it almost immediately, scooping it toward him as his voice went low.

"Something happens—something bad. Some American is taken away, madame, from the company that makes the cinema."

She felt her head buzz with blood. "What do you mean taken away?"

"Take away . . . by . . . *bandidos* . . ."

She snapped back in her chair, horrified. "Kidnapped."

"Sí, like you say . . . kid-napped. I don't know maybe he is one you wait for."

"When did this happen?" She gripped his hand tightly. "What's his name?"

He pulled his hand away. "Don' know more. Is talk just. But it happens. *Bandidos* take somebody."

The buzz changed to a pounding in her head. She jumped up, ran out of the lobby to the front of the hotel. An Opel taxi stood five paces away, the driver refreshing himself with a Coca-Cola. She pulled open the door, calling, "Cinema company . . . *por favor*. Please. Cinema company. Over there." She waved wildly in the direction of the Jericho compound.

"We go," the driver said. "We go quick."

He kept his word. The cab bounced off the stones, caromed off the curbs, brushed flanks and carts and, in minutes, was there. The two police on duty, hearing Stella's voice, waved her through.

She hurried to the editing office and burst through without knocking to be confronted by a startled Murray, who told her he had no idea where Paul was. Her fears compounded, she strode to the administration building.

Inside, someone at a desk asked what she wanted, but when she answered, voice reeking with confidence, that she worked for Michael, the woman directed her to the special-effects people at the end of the corridor where a meeting was taking place. She marched down to a door marked DEATH SQUAD—KEEP OUT! De Luca's voice came from inside the room and she grew uneasy at the sound. Automatically pushing her hair from her eyes, she knocked. De Luca's voice came roaring back

"Stay out!"

She opened the door. De Luca was surrounded by four sun-creased, strong-bodied men. A blackboard at one end of the room was labeled BATTLE PLAN, and on it was drawn Monte Tecla and the valley below with notations and crosses and hatchmarks. The special-effects men stared at her in surprise. De Luca froze.

"I'm sorry to break in on you," she said, "but I was waiting for—"

"I thought you were gone," De Luca interrupted.

"That's just the point," she swept on. "I heard that someone—"

His hands reached out as though to stop her mouth. "In my office," he said quickly. To the men he barked. "I want the first part of the action to be in place for tomorrow, all the wires laid, all the trips ready, all the smoke. Got it?"

She stood by, uncomfortably, as the men assured him there would be no problem. Watching their relaxed responses, she became uncertain of her ground. If Paul had been abducted, would there be business as usual, this way?

"Come on," De Luca said brusquely, edging her from the room. In the hallway he turned angrily. "What the hell is this all about? Why are you doing this to me? What kind of a person are you?"

"Where's Paul?"

"What is it your business?" His face clouded with wrath. "You don't have any claim on him."

"He said he'd come and take me to the airport. He didn't. That's not like him to begin with. And then I heard . . ."

"Heard what?"

302

"I heard that some . . . bandits . . . he said they were bandits, kidnapped Paul sometime today."

"Paul?" De Luca stared at her, astounded.

"Yes."

"That's a joke," De Luca said. "That's some kind of a sick joke."

"It's not true?"

"No, it's not true. Now will you leave, please?"

"I want to see him," she said stubbornly. "I just want to know that he's all right."

"He's all right." De Luca set his face so close to hers she could see the patches of gray in his beard. "It's none of your business, but he's all right. Nobody's . . . kidnapped him. Somebody's putting you on."

She heard voices down the hallway and turned to see Rennie approaching, laughing, a man holding her arm. De Luca became agitated. His voice was low but hard.

"You go back. I'll tell him you were here."

"Why can't I wait for him?"

He glanced quickly at the oncoming couple. "Because I say so. Now if you don't leave, you're going to find yourself in a mess of trouble."

Down the hall, Rennie saw them and pulled her companion to a halt.

De Luca waved. "Be right with you."

With sudden conviction Stella said, "It's true, isn't it? And it's not bandits, it's because of the trouble you're having."

"It is not true." De Luca spat the words out through his teeth. "Go back to the hotel. Paul will call you later. I swear he will. I swear on my children that he'll call you."

She hesitated.

"You have my word," De Luca said, "that Paul has not been . . . kidnapped and that he will call you."

She looked into his eyes and saw fear, but what was the fear about? Down the hall she saw Rennie, obviously tense, the man with her puzzled. Something, she told herself, yes . . . something, but what?

"I'll wait for his call." She started down the hallway, increased her pace and, when she passed Rennie, looked straight ahead.

Outside, she stopped to take some air into her lungs and looked at her watch. Six-thirty; too late for the seven o'clock anyway. She would go back to the hotel and check in for the night. She decided to walk a bit but found her legs leaden. A blanket vendor planted himself directly in her path and she pushed through him blindly. A spindly-legged girl approached with flowers, holding out the misty blue and yellow bouquet, fresh and beautiful. She wore a ragged little skirt, and a scabrous insect bite festered in her delicate brown shoulder. Stella knelt down and, clutching the child to her, began to cry. The child, with no change of expression, continued to call, softly, *"Flores . . . flores."*

The moment Stella left his sight, De Luca changed gears, shooed Rennie and Lufkin into his office, went back to special effects, called Sieberling, replayed what had just occurred and announced, grimly, that mistaken though Stella was, word was spreading; the woman had to be watched every minute till she left, and Lufkin was certainly to be isolated from anyone who could tell him anything, and where the hell was Paul, anyhow?

Sieberling didn't know, but he wanted to assure De Luca that Machado's people were active in their own way.

"I don't want to hear about any of that," De Luca called into the phone. "That's *your* business, not mine." He rushed to his office, where Rennie had already poured wine for Lufkin and herself. They had had a fine time at the sacred mountain, she reported. Lufkin agreed; Tecla was impressive. And he had been thinking about the picture; if you made a Vietnam story that people wanted to see . . .

"Not that again," De Luca groaned.

"I've been telling him"—Rennie laughed—"that what you really have here is a love story, with shooting, that's all."

"She's almost convinced me, too." Lufkin appeared to be much more relaxed, but De Luca judged that to be, possibly, deceptive. Wording it casually, he asked if Lufkin had seen any evidence of the so-called problems.

"Lot of police, with guns," Lufkin responded.

"We get equipment stealing," he explained. "That's a fact I won't hide from you. So, we have to protect the stuff. It's all for show."

Lufkin's response to that was agreeably understanding, but he and Mike still had much to talk over, he insisted. Right now, however, he needed a shower and was heading back to his hotel; Rennie would be giving him a lift if it was all right with the boss.

It was Sieberling who later brought Lufkin's attitude into focus.

He had managed five minutes alone with Rennie after her return from Tecla. Lufkin, it appeared, had spoken to a couple of crew members who had closed ranks and told him funny Mexican stories. He had attempted nothing else. Rennie was steering him well, and, most important, he was accepting her guidance.

"That's good," De Luca said. "That's useful."

"Can be," Sieberling agreed. "But we have to face the fact that we're under the gun. What if . . ." he hesitated, searching for words, ". . . if there's a . . . a development with Marcus . . . if they . . ."

"It's a bluff," De Luca asserted. "I don't think they'd dare hurt him. If they did that, no one could prevent federal police from coming in and all hell would break loose around here." He calmed himself. "So we just do what we're doing, get rid of Lufkin fast, and when they see I'm not running, they'll come to their senses." He looked at his watch. "Where the hell is Paul? That woman is unnerving me."

Within fifteen minutes, as the cathedral clock chimed seven, Paul dashed into the office. Only as he crossed the threshold did he remember his promise to Stella, and a pang of remorse struck him. It vanished at the sight of the hot-eyed, waiting De Luca, who described Stella's visit in scathing terms and accused, "You were supposed to see that she was on that damn plane out of here. Now she's got wind of something. Sure, she has it wrong, but it means there is word out."

That was a shock. "She didn't go?"

"And you damn well have to telephone her right away and show her you're okay," De Luca ordered. "We're walking a tightrope here and you disappear."

Immediately Paul called, attempting to erase all tension from his voice. He apologized for missing the airport date, but he had been doing something important and had simply forgotten; he was sorry.

"Believe me," he said, "nobody's interested in me for kidnapping purposes, and I'm sorry you're stuck here for another night." As he spoke it struck him that she had been deeply concerned about him, and his voice softened.

"I hope," she said, "that whatever troubles you're having go away and that all goes well."

"It will straighten out, but who told you that story, anyway?"

305

The moment he said it he regretted the saying. He was fishing; she had been anxious about him and he was using her.

"Somebody in the hotel. They didn't say it was you, but I just had this fantasy that it was—since you weren't here. I just reacted."

"All these misunderstandings. You'll be back home soon. More misunderstandings could hurt the picture."

He heard only her breathing then for seconds. Finally, as though having made up her mind, she said, "Nothing's going to come from me, Paul. When people ask me how my trip was, I'll be enigmatic."

Feeling manipulative and unhappy, he said, "Tomorrow, I'll absolutely take you to the airport."

"Okay."

"And I'll call you in the morning."

"Do that."

He hung up, wincing.

Flo had been in jail before for only one night of her life, after an antiwar demo. That had had an aspect of communion; bodies, hearts and minds together, and the civil liberties lawyers working to get the bail bonds ready. This dank place was redolent of sweat and despair, despite the efforts of four convicts who swept and scrubbed to restore some semblance of passable cleanliness to the six-by-eight-foot cell with the bare bulb and the hole in the floor. They had brought in a fresh mattress and hung cloth ticking over the bars, giving some privacy and less ventilation. They brought in a ceramic bowl and pitchers of water. They brought in a rude chair, a tiny round table and, finally, a bowl of papayas and mangoes as welcoming gifts.

Ushered in, she had ignored the improvements, feeling only the chill of fear. Quesedo assured her she would spend little time in the cell; his office was her home. If she wished to sleep on the couch, even that was possible. What was important was simply that she be someplace there, so that he could report the fact. He had given strict orders to allow her anything she wished. She would not, of course, eat the jailhouse slop; her meals would be brought in. It was country food, true, but from an excellent, *muy típico* restaurant that he himself frequented. Quesedo's aspect was not that of a jailer but a gracious and caring host; his was a poor, unworthy hotel he was striving to make acceptable to his North American guest. Flo left her unpacked bag in the cell, stood, a mixture of defiance and compliance, in Quesedo's office and demanded to know how long she was going to be there. It would be only till things straightened themselves out, Quesedo assured her, a few days, certainly no more.

She sank into a chair, brushed her hair back, pushed her glasses up on her nose and decided she would go along, for the moment.

Quesedo started to leave and she called, "The telephone?"

"Use," he said reassuringly, "for sure."

Outside, voices were raised. A cell door clanged. Approaching the *comandancia*, she had been filled with apprehensions. Mexican jails. Entering, with the uniformed guard and the convict trustee both touching fingers to their heads in salute, she had been hurried away from a dimly lit passageway beyond which was a cell block whose fetid odors reached out to invade her nostrils. In comparison, the isolated cell prepared for her was, in fact, the Ritz of Mexican jail cells, and Quesedo's office seemed insulated from even that. She felt a wave of gratitude; he was trying to be decent.

She picked up the phone, a vintage instrument that had, on some caprice, been painted purple. After clicks and bleeps, she managed to get Allan's number. To her surprise, with no trouble at all, the ringing began. She let it ring half a dozen times before concluding that he was not there. Nine o'clock. Drinking someplace, dreaming of his corned-beef sandwiches. She hung up, disappointed. She had wanted, very much, to hear his voice, to tell him she was in Oacala jail, to challenge him. Did he allow a thought of her to enter that thick skull of his?

The door opened and the captain returned. He looked at her warmly and announced that their dinner would be sent in. He waved his bottle of Cuervo and produced two water glasses.

"Come, Señorita Ankroom," he invited.

As she wavered, he clicked on the battered transistor radio that was sitting on a file cabinet. It buzzed angrily. Beneath the loud hum, two men sang of passion and revenge.

"I make you *ambiente*, so you forget is here a *comandancia*." He poured the tequila and offered her a tumbler. She capitulated with a shrug.

"I t'ink"—he raised his glass in a toast—"that you be very beautiful."

Embarrassed, but not resentful, she sipped and felt the fire in her throat. The telephone rang harshly. Quesedo glared at it. It rang again. "Excuse," he muttered, relieved the instrument of its

307

pain and barked his name. The voice on the other end whispered, in sepulchral tones, "This is Espido."

Instantly, he became alert. "Where are you? What's going on?"

"The rooster left her bed."

"And?"

"I followed him."

"To where?"

"He went to Calle Juarez . . . to a shop."

"To a shop?"

"Closed, *capitán*, the shop is closed."

"Ah . . ." Quesedo jammed the receiver against his ear. "But he goes in? Someone lets him in?"

"Just so. And soon two other men come and they go in, too. I come right away to call you."

"Tell me the shop on Juarez." He snatched excitedly at a scrap of paper and pulled a ball-point from his pocket. He looked back at Flo, smiling reassuringly—"Business"—then turned back as Espido spoke again, and scribbled the information.

"You go back. Keep watch. I decide what to do." He hung up, his pulse beating strongly. There was something here; he felt it in his bones. The charcoal seller had two interests, women and politics. He would leave the one only for the other.

Miraculously, the speaker's buzzing eased, allowing the guitar sounds to float tinnily but unhampered through the room. He took it as a sign and reached happily for his glass.

"Everyt'ing going to be good, soon, Florenza."

Paul tried to lose himself in checking footage. He dreaded the approaching evening with Lufkin, phony talk, false joviality. He slumped in front of his Moviola, confused and unhappy. The prospect of the lanky, silver-haired Marcus tortured or worse, and no effort made on his behalf, was bone-chilling, but he had to believe that Michael was right, the *bajos* were bluffing; they would not bring destruction down upon themselves.

At nine, knowing he would be late and half-grateful, he locked up and went out into the new night. As he walked to the compound gate, he thought of Stella in her room. His original flood of anger had ebbed away to leave a stretch of melancholy beach, the sign of finis, like postcoital blues. He was so absorbed that he failed to hear the soft voice calling. "Señor Gorrdon . . ."

The second time his name was called, however, he turned and,

308

with great surprise, saw Elvira. She wore an intricately sewn blouse, embroidered with gold thread. Her waist was cinched with a narrow belt of twisted golden strands. In the gathering darkness, she appeared like an errant ray of amber light. He took a step toward her, saying, "Oh . . ." She reached out, her fingers gripping his sleeve, her voice calm, but he felt the urgency beneath.

"I come to see Miguel, but he is not here."

"He's over at Ixtepan—or was—making preparations."

"Ah, I cannot leave a message for him, this man says."

Instantly alert, he asked, "What man?"

"This man who speaks to me the other time speaks to me again. He says I must take Miguel tonight, to the *brujo*."

"The *brujo*?"

"Man who makes medicine. Magic man. In the hills."

"Are you sure about this?"

"Yes. And he says I must not tell this by telephone, so I come."

"Why? Why would Michael go to the medicine man?"

"There will be the Deer Dance," she said, and with a rush of excitement he recognized the words with which they made entrée to Ismena.

"It will be done tonight at the *brujo*'s cave. You come to me and I lead you there. It is done at midnight, between one day and the other."

Elation sparking him, he burst out, "Luis!"

"He does not say this."

"But it has to be Luis, has to be."

It was the only possibility. Luis had come through. And tonight they would finally be face to face with the *bajos*.

"I'll tell Michael. How long will it take to get up into the hills?"

"Not long. We go by auto, to the foot, and then we climb for a little. The *brujo* is there."

"Right. Okay. We'll pick you up."

She nodded, took her hand from his arm and moved away silently. In seconds she was out of sight, and he walked quickly, heartbeat very erratic, toward the Zócalo.

CHAPTER

31

When he reached the De Luca hacienda, the lights were burning brightly and the sounds of laughter teased the night. He saw that most of the landscape carnage had either been concealed with canvas, as though new plantings were in progress, or filled in ingeniously so that Lufkin would not question, even casually.

Inside, Catherine De Luca, hair in a smooth bun and gowned in blue silk, exuded a madonna-like calm. She pecked Paul's cheek and chided him for being late. At the piano, the elder De Luca had Lufkin on one side and Rennie on the other, a captive audience, and was illustrating bel canto. Rennie called a luminous hello and leaned down to answer a question that Lufkin had murmured as Sal Sieberling sipped his Campari near the terrace doors.

Utter unreality.

He stared at the parody of domestic tranquillity, bursting with his news. Michael was upstairs on the telephone and Paul quickly volunteered to get him, but Catherine insisted they go in; dinner was ready to be served. Reluctance in every cell, he found himself marching into the dining room with the others. Only when he was already seated did Michael come racing in. He had been making final arrangements for the start of the Operation Jericho sequence, in the morning.

"Going to give you a bang-up finish, Ben." He laughed, sat, poured wine expansively. Paul waited until the bottle hovered over his glass, then tried to signal with his eyes, but the director was unaware.

"We've got hundreds of extras coming in," he continued talking to Lufkin, "terrific effects planned, all kinds of goodies. And, very important, we have official permission to shoot right from the top of the pyramid itself . . . gives us some viewpoint. Three hundred

310

and sixty degrees in all directions. That's cooperation."

"Sounds good"—Lufkin twirled his glass—"sounds real good."

"Mike," Paul said, with desperation, "I had word from Kodály, he wants us to call him."

De Luca looked at him, surprised. "Kodály? I just spoke to him."

"No . . . that was something else," he said hurriedly. "We'd better call back." He rose up. Catherine shook her head in disapproval, tinkled her bell. The two maids collected plates but he moved away, quickly, De Luca following him, obviously puzzled. Three steps up the staircase, Paul told him of Elvira's appearance. De Luca listened, wide-eyed.

"God, if we could settle this once and for all . . ."

"Maybe they'll have Marcus with them, and we'll come back with him."

Their huddled whispering built into feverish speculation, interrupted by the appearance of the elder De Luca, sent by Catherine. He looked at them, eyebrows raised, and asked if they had a woman hidden away. They returned to the table.

The four courses congealed in Paul's stomach, the wine not so much lubricating the mass but bloating it and fluttering his abdomen even more.

Not Michael. He ate with gusto, drank with ease, and his eyes betrayed no hint of quease. He kept up a rapid-fire conversation, and had not Paul known that, at midnight, they would be facing a crucial test, it would be impossible to deduce from the performance that he was anything but the confident host. When they left the table to have coffee in the parlor, Rennie slipped past, managing to say, breathily, in Paul's ear, that Lufkin was under control. She then went to sit next to him on the couch, where Catherine stood over them, balancing her espresso cup and telling the studio emissary she knew of a very special place for his wife to shop in Beverly Hills.

Looking at his watch, Paul saw that it was after ten. Brandy must come now and more aimless chatter—another hour of torture. He cradled the goblet and concentrated on Luis and the *bajos* and the impossibility of failure. He went from that to thinking about the picture itself, about the screenplay lying tantalizingly in De Luca's desk drawer, about the future. He observed Rennie's assured, quick movements, Michael's mesmerizing Lufkin with what he would be seeing in the morning at Ixtepan, Catherine's telling a glazed Sieberling, in detail, of a lacemaker she had found in the town. It all went with agonizing slowness. Finally, he saw Lufkin yawn, rise and move toward imminent departure. De Luca suggested that Rennie might drop the visitor off, since Paul and Sieberling would be staying to discuss a few things. That arranged, it took only minutes for the actual departure, with Rennie murmuring to him about speaking later and Lufkin exclaiming over the splendid evening.

As De Luca closed the door, his mask of affability dropped away. "I can't make him out. He's just lying back."

Catherine disappeared without a word. The elder De Luca waved and went to his bed. Sieberling asked, "You need me anymore?"

"Yes," De Luca said. "Paul and I are going to meet someone. I want you to stay here till we get back."

Sieberling came alert. "Now?"

"Could be awhile," Paul added.

"Got it," the production manager said. "I'll be here."

They left him thumbing through an *Esquire* magazine. In the floodlit glare De Luca led the way to the parked cars and chose the Mercedes.

As they drove in silence, Paul sat tautly, his eyes wandering from the circles of light in front to the darkness behind in the rearview mirror. Unnecessary. They were going to the important confrontation and it would be illogical to follow them. Still, he could not keep his eyes from the mirror.

There was a single light on at the small house when they reached it and Paul saw Elvira's face framed in the window before she let the curtain drop. He moved to the backseat, grateful for its shadows. De Luca's fingers drummed nervously on the wheel as Elvira emerged and came toward them. Seeing her, tenderness glided over his features. He opened the door and she slid inside, pulling her long skirt in and closing the door.

"It would be better to wear the blue jeans," she apologized, "but the *brujo* does not like women in them." She was composed, and De Luca, reaching over, kissed her on the forehead and stroked her hair. She smiled and touched his face, in response. Watching, Paul felt a bridge of gentleness between them and was surprised at Michael's ability to sustain that.

"Where do we go?"

"Go to the big road," she answered, "and when I see the small road, I tell you."

De Luca turned the Mercedes back to the blacktop and gunned it along. Ten minutes later Elvira called out, "There . . . the little road is there . . ."

She motioned left and Paul, peering, saw a narrow opening between the trees. De Luca slowed, swung the car left, and they passed through by inches, onto a jouncing dirt lane.

"How long do we go on this?"

"Till it stops."

The rutted, pocked and pitted dirt strained even the Mercedes's capacity to keep level. Paul felt one yawing bounce after another. The lights rose up and violently dipped, rose and dipped.

"Soon," Elvira said.

Abruptly, so abruptly that they were within two feet of crashing into the side of a rock-strewn hill, the road ended. De Luca turned the engine off. When he did, the headlights cut as well, and overwhelming blackness plunged in upon them.

"Wow . . ." Paul reached out to feel for the door handle. Managing it, he stumbled out.

"Damn it. We should have taken a flashlight." He heard Michael's voice but could not make him out.

"In a minute you see," Elvira said, calmly.

It took more than that. It took fully five minutes of standing rooted to the spot, but finally Paul managed to see De Luca reasonably well, and Elvira, who stood near him. He looked up and saw only a slim piece of the sky cut by a dark shape looming up.

"Montaña de Pobres. Is a trail here. Come."

She walked confidently forward. De Luca followed and Paul fell in behind. He could see a bit better now, and what she called a trail was a narrow line of trodden brush ascending and curving. Silently, they worked their way up, Elvira, sure-footed and swift, moving with confidence, stopping every now and then to wait for the men, who lagged. At times the trail was almost flat, then suddenly it would angle up forty-five degrees so that the suddenness of the change alone caused the breath to come hard. After twenty minutes Paul felt the pull in his muscles and the shallowness of his lungs.

"Let's hold it for a minute," De Luca whispered, gulping hard.

They leaned against a huge outcropping of rock, recovering. Elvira waited patiently, almost unexerted.

"This medicine man sure lives way the hell up," De Luca complained.

"He does not live here," Elvira explained. "No one knows where the *brujo* lives. It is bad medicine to know, for bad spirits might attack him. Tonight he makes medicine in the cave of the Pobres; another time someplace else."

313

"Why is Luis putting us through this? Why can't we just see him and have the meeting?"

"Some kind of security thing?" Paul suggested. "What is the Deer Dance, anyway?"

"Very old dance. With much meanings. Much magic. It tells of the deer in the sierra. It tells of the hunter coming and the finding the deer and shooting it with his arrow. The deer dies."

"*Afternoon of a Faun*," De Luca muttered. "Life and beauty and death. They do it too. Damn."

They struggled up again, going higher and higher until they saw first traces of sky, stars vibrating clearly; and finally the whole arc-like sweep was revealed as the jagged top of the mountain came into view. Scrambling, pushing against gravity into the thin upper reaches, Paul followed Michael and the woman to a wide, plateau-like ledge. At the back, the mountain pushed up again, but here was surcease from the climb.

"Come," Elvira whispered, and led them forward. A sudden elevation sprung at them from the right, and a gaping hole in the rock revealed itself. Beyond, flickering tongues of light wavered. She stopped abruptly before the cave and raised a hand. From the darkness a small, blanket-wrapped form moved toward them. When it was steps away, Paul saw that it was an Indian of great age, cheeks crisscrossed with deep channels, not an inch untouched by the clefts. His eyes were rheumy, and his legs, kindling on his frame, jutted awkwardly from the rough wool over them. He stared at them expressionless and turned back to the cave.

"We go," Elvira urged.

As they moved forward slowly, the flickering resolved itself into smoky oil lamps placed in niches in the rock. On the earth a fire burned fitfully.

"Was that the *brujo*?" De Luca whispered.

"No." Elvira shook her head. "Just an old man."

The neck of the cave widened, and in the opening Paul saw a semicircle of twelve blanketed Indians seated on the earth. Wrapped in wool, the majority old, faces scored by time, hair in braids, it was almost impossible to tell gender as they stared, with lowered heads, into the fire. On the opposite side of the flames a man hunkered down, drawing lines and circles in the earth with a pointed stick. He was younger than the others. Dressed in a long leather singlet, he wore a headdress of feathers and yellow metal, and before him was a carved wooden bowl. As the three intruders entered his field of

314

vision, he raised his arms as though in welcome, then lowered them and continued his scratching.

"The *brujo*. Sit." Elvira lowered herself, in one flowing motion, to the cave floor and they followed her example. From the *brujo's* mouth came a low-keyed muttering which rose to a singsong and then to a mournful keening, an intense, controlled ululation. The congregation seated before him responded with vowels of their own. The ritual was repeated, repeated again and yet again, echoing from the cave walls hollowly and hypnotically so that Paul, watching the fire and the *brujo's* fingers, felt his anxiety dissolving into peace.

Quite suddenly, the *brujo* reached behind him for a deerskin bag. He pulled from it several small, round objects and, with the practiced fingers of one hand, as his other hand made incantatory movements, pulled them into bits, depositing the fleshlike shreds into the wooden bowl. He stood up, after that, raised the bowl in both hands and with a voice unlike his other, a voice originating from some ancient time and some other species, a voice in his throat, gasping, strangling, suffering, he groaned a prayer to some deity, dropped to his knees and, moving along the semicircle, offered the bowl. Each of the Indians, in turn, dipped, took a morsel and slowly pushed it between their teeth and chewed slowly, deliberately, eyes closed.

De Luca looked over to Elvira, questioningly. Her lips formed a silent response.

"Peyote."

The bowl came to Paul. He looked down at the brown flecks of earth still clinging to the skin and froze with indecision. Elvira murmured something and, to his great relief, the bowl went away. It passed Michael and Elvira and came to rest upon the ground again. The *brujo* reached behind him once more and a small drum appeared in his hands. He picked up his stick and, settling back on his heels, beat a slow rhythm. As he did this, Paul became aware of a dim rattling sound from the darkness beyond. The rattling was accompanied by a soft shuffling, a snakelike, sidewinding sibilance, and Paul felt gooseflesh rise on his arms. As the drum rhythm quickened, the rattles kept pace, the shuffling becoming louder and louder. Paul leaned away from the sound and prepared to jump. Without warning, a figure hurtled over the heads of the group, over the fire and into the open space. It was a young boy, naked except for a strip of deerskin tied about his loins. Around his neck gleamed a necklace of deer's teeth. His right hand held a feathered tin rattle

315

tightly, and from his brow, fastened by thongs, projected the horns of a buck. He stood in the firelight, his strong oiled body shining, his head raised alertly, his nostrils moving, scenting, and he quivered in place, the shiver of intermingled fear and anger, the movement shaking the rattle into a sustained, drawn-out, ominous hiss.

The drum tempo quickened and the boy began to move, to stamp delicately, paw the earth, his antlers low. In that confined space he ran, doubled back, leaped high in the air, lay belly to loam; he saw the hunter, evaded him, raced off as though loosed from a bow, only to be trapped again, and, crouching, forced aching breaths as his flanks heaved. Then, with a mighty jump, he hurtled to the attack, fought, was wounded. Running no more, he made a stand, attacked yet again. And again, an arrow struck him, and another. The drumming became rapid now, throbbing, a heartbeat racing against the inevitable. The rattling became continuous, defiant. Another arrow struck and pierced. The boy, caught in a full leap, arched, twisted. The rattle moaned. He came down limping, still thrashing, but his head was lower, his body weakened, the breath coming faster and faster. The drumming became frenzied, the rattle screamed. The boy, sweat covering his bronze skin, dodged away now, twisting, contorting, and finally another percussive arrow struck, staggering him. A final mighty surge into the air and he was down, in a heap, eyes trembling, dimming, head straining, neck pulling, pulling and then collapsing. In the dust the body heaved for the last time. The drum stopped, and in the loud silence the body twitched, inducing one long, slow, fading rattle. Then, in the firelight, the body was still.

For seconds there was no sound and no movement in the cave. Inexplicably, Paul found himself on the edge of tears. The dancer *was* the deer; the two were intertwined. For a moment he feared the boy would not rise again. But he did. He rose easily to his feet and silently walked behind the *brujo* to disappear in the shadows. Paul felt a hand on his shoulder and turned in alarm, but it was Michael, awed.

"Magic," he whispered, "absolute magic."

"Miguel." Elvira's voice snapped the mood. She looked toward the cave entrance. A stocky, bareheaded man stood there staring at them. He beckoned, turned and left the cave.

After the smoky semidarkness, the night seemed almost bright. Rapidly, not looking back, the man who had summoned them

316

walked toward the mountain wall. De Luca followed intently. Paul was slower, still caught by what he had seen. The man reached up and pulled aside what seemed to be a piece of the wall but which revealed itself to be a black curtain masking another cave entrance. Straining, Paul could see moving men inside. Laughter floated out into the night and the pungent odor of garlic sausages sizzling in oil.

From the wall, their guide tossed back *"Alto!"* at them. They halted instantly, five paces from the cave. Before he disappeared inside, the Mexican shouted something, holding the curtain wide. In that moment, staring, Paul caught a flash of a tall figure with graying hair, in a corner.

"Marcus," he muttered excitedly. "Mike, he's in there. I just saw him."

De Luca gripped his arm with equal excitement. "They have to understand. I'll buy them all the land they want. I'll get their pictures published all over the world. But they have to understand."

Before he could say anything more, the cave flap opened again and Luis Aguillar was coming toward them, a warm, welcoming smile on his face, clearly visible in the light of the small oil lamp he carried.

"He's here," Paul said jubilantly.

The terrorist, setting the lamp down, called out, *"Buenas."*

"Buenas—am I glad to see you," De Luca said fervently. "It's crazy, Luis; they've gone crazy."

"Be all right," Aguillar soothed. "You see the *brujo*, eh? I am sorry to send you there, but we don't know maybe somebody follow you so we do it this way, to make sure first."

"Is Marcus all right?" Paul asked. "They haven't hurt him, have they?"

The shadow of a frown moved across Aguillar's face and Paul's heart jumped.

"Don't think he is hurt," Aguillar mumbled uncomfortably.

"Think?" Paul reacted. "But he's in there, in the cave."

Aguillar sighed. "No."

"Paul saw him," De Luca insisted.

"No, you make a mistake."

Paul looked at Aguillar in astonishment. The smile had left his face. A brooding look had replaced it, and in the dim lamplight, points of defiance glittered in his dark eyes. From the cave a thin man holding a Kalishnikov rifle emerged, but Aguillar waved him back.

317

"He's not in there?" Paul demanded.

Aguillar shook his head.

"Where is he?" De Luca asked.

"Someplace. They don't tell me."

"But is he all right?" Paul insisted.

Aguillar's tone was guarded. "They say he is all right."

He said no more. De Luca took a deep breath. "Okay. We'll get to that. Let's go in and have the meeting."

"Is a problem." Aguillar grunted.

Paul felt his throat start to dry out.

"What do you mean?" De Luca asked.

"Like I say!" It was a small, angry explosion that caused De Luca to step back a pace. The Mexican lowered his voice and repeated, "Sí—is a problem."

Dreading the answer, Paul asked, "Luis, aren't they inside the cave?"

"They don't come," Aguillar said shortly.

"Luis—" he stuttered, "Luis . . ."

De Luca's eyes opened wide in disbelief. "You said—"

Aguillar turned to him with bitter accusation "You bring Machado in. You don't know he is a gangster, *fascista*? He cuts the ears from peasants when the landlords tell him to. When he rapes a woman, no one dares to say nothing. He is hated here."

"Are you blaming me for that?" De Luca retorted. "I hired him to get me extras, that's all. Extras whom I pay damn well, people who would be glad to work for me if the *bajos* would leave them alone."

"They say to me, they don't speak to you while Machado beats them and steals from them. They say you send him away and then they see."

"Stop shooting?" De Luca was incredulous.

"Luis," Paul faltered. "We can't do that. Someone is here, someone—" He broke off, knowing it would be impossible to explain. He felt drained. After all this there would be no face-to-face meeting; no *bajo* was in the cave beyond, only men cooking sausages. He looked toward Michael helplessly.

"Listen," Aguillar said in a more conciliatory tone, "by now everybody is too hot. The *bajo* people say—"

"What about what I say?" De Luca cried. "Me!"

Aguillar shrugged and reached for a cigarette. A sudden blaze of yellow light appeared behind him as someone pulled the cave

318

curtain aside to peer at the visitors. Paul could hardly make out his features, and in the next second, voices from within the cave cursed the man loudly and fluently, forcing him to drop darkness back over the mountaintop as he retreated.

But amid the curses Paul had heard something that turned his spine rigid and shot his eyebrows up. Michael saw his distress, and Aguillar, startled, turned behind him to see what had caused it.

"That man," Paul said, "they called him Jesus. I heard it distinctly."

"Jesus?" Aguillar looked puzzled. "I don't understand."

"Jesus," Paul said softly, "was the dope smuggler we flew out, the man you said you 'took care' of."

A look of surprise settled over Aguillar. "No, no," he said swiftly. "That is another Jesus. Jesus is an ordinary name. We have two Jesus."

"I don't believe you," Michael said.

Paul sucked in his breath. The terrorist scowled, weighed a response and then said, "You believe or not, makes no difference."

"I don't." Michael stared at him intently.

"Maybe it is another man," Paul said uneasily, but he saw that Michael had wound himself up and was discharging energy now, his voice reeking with scorn.

"That's supposed to be a revolutionary act? Putting dope on the streets of America so ghetto kids can get zonked?"

Paul winced, stepping back as Aguillar discharged a stream of smoke through his nostrils. But when he spoke, it was with no malice but almost pedantically.

"I don't say this man is Jesus, no, I don't say that. But you must learn about a revolution, Mr. Jefe. Takes much money. We do not make bank robberies too good so far but maybe we learn. We must buy food, buy guns, buy bullets, pay the *mordida*. We get money where we can. If the *yanquis* will pay for the *sin semilla*, we will sell it to them. Let the ones who use it burn their brains out; what do we care? That money can make here the revolution, you understand." He turned to Paul. "You must understand what Lenin says, what Mao says. It is wrong to think like a bourgeois, have morality like them. That blinds you to real struggle."

"You want proof of *my way* to struggle?" Michael demanded. "Have I told the authorities about Marcus being taken?"

Aguillar shrugged.

"If I had, there would be planes and state police swarming all

319

over these mountains, you know that." He threw a quick veiled glance at Paul. "But we've kept quiet, for one single reason—because we hoped that these people would be reasonable."

"Luis," Paul interjected, "their note said twenty-four hours. If they hurt Marcus, God knows what will happen."

Aguillar considered. Finally he spoke.

"I tell you this; you make for me much problems with Machado. Fifty kilometers from here is a big landowner—best land. Only the land is not his, no matter what the government says. Just like where you make the rice grow. Belongs to farmers. Landowner says no. He buys Machado to keep them from coming. So here again is Machado. And all around the countryside people say where is Aguillar? Where are the revolutionary fighters when Machado's *fascistas* do what they like? Is a good question, eh?

"What can I tell them? I must think about that we come down from here and show them something, take some ears from the *fascistas*. Is a political strategy, eh?" He nodded reflectively. "You are political men, you understand that."

"My pictures are my politics," Michael said stiffly.

"Maybe. But this is not a cinema for us. Here, we live all the time, here we die. A few pigs, some rows of corn, roof over the head, these are the questions."

"I want to talk to these people about those questions," De Luca said, "but they don't want to talk to me."

"Marcus," Paul whispered.

"Maybe we can do this," Aguillar said. "I tell them you do not know what a *fascista* Machado is, but I tell you. You understand and will finish with him, now."

"Will you guarantee extras so that I don't have to stop shooting?" De Luca interrupted passionately. "Because I can't. I absolutely can't."

"Guarantee? I just tell you is bad if people say I am a friend to men who buy *fascista pistoleros*."

"It's not that way," De Luca declared.

Aguillar frowned. "You see like you see. But a man can only do what he can do." He snatched the lamp up. "I must go now. My people, inside, do not like me to be so much alone, out here."

Paul felt everything slipping away and called, "Luis, tell them to give us more time; we'll think of some way out of this."

"I must tell them the truth." Aguillar's reply was solemn. In the next moment he was gone, back to the cave.

They descended in silence; nothing was said to Elvira and nothing needed to be said; De Luca's grimness was evident and Paul's disappointment was mirrored in his face. Only at the bottom of the mountain did De Luca lose control. When the door of the Mercedes stuck, he yanked it open with a lunging pull.

They drove as they had come—in silence. When they arrived at Elvira's *casa*, still nothing was said. She opened the door, whispered, *"Buenas noches"* and left. In seconds De Luca was back on the main road, shooting the car along the moon-drenched asphalt. Glancing at the digital clock, he said, in flat tones, "Almost one-thirty. We start early at Tecla."

"What about Marcus?"

"They won't harm him," De Luca replied savagely. "I'm telling you it's a bluff." He swung hard toward the town. "Let's get the Jericho sequence finished and Lufkin out and then we'll see." The car met the cobblestones and they were into night-quiet Oacala, the *paseo* over. He jockeyed the Mercedes across the square, jerking the car to a halt at the hotel. As the seat rocked, he looked at Paul, eyes bristling with anger.

"That money ended up in his pocket, you know."

Paul squinted at him quizzically.

De Luca shook his head with vigor. "I'm telling you. It's in his pocket, someplace. And that dope run was his, never mind what he says. Those crazies don't even want anything to do with him. He's as corrupt as any banana republic general."

"I don't know," Paul said warily.

"I know." De Luca's voice was filled with contempt. "He's just been conning us all along, bleeding us."

Paul looked at the sharp outline of the bell tower. It was not impossible. He hadn't delivered, and speeches were, after all, easy to make. "Maybe," he breathed.

"And maybe even," De Luca went on, "he's told those *bajos* to keep up the pressure and God knows what they can get out of us. They hate us, for openers. Never mind that I'm putting myself on the line, never mind that I've been involved in *their* cause all my life. All they know is to hate us because our skins are white and we come from north of the border. Screw my picture, screw what I'm trying to do." He slammed his hand down on the leather-covered steering wheel.

"It could be," Paul responded, not entirely certain.

De Luca calmed himself. "Okay . . . come over at seven and we'll fly out to Tecla—and get some sleep."

Paul clambered out. The Mercedes shot off, and he went through the Jaime's bronze doors. On the second floor he reminded himself that Stella was still on the third. He would have to return from location to get her to the airport but he could manage that if nothing interfered.

In his room he tried to force a yawn but couldn't. Shirt off, he stood before the open-shuttered window and stared out at the rim of the sierra in the distance. The night was cloudless and the mountains were blue. A dog yapped. Another mistaken rooster strained its throat. He leaned forward, finding himself so powerfully awake that his stomach clenched with tension and the muscles of his eyes strained open. He sat down on the bed, picked up the phone and called Rennie. He would not tell her what had happened, but it would be good to talk. She would relax him, ease him. He listened to the ring for half a dozen times, but she didn't answer. Surprised, knowing she was attuned to emergencies, he let it ring another six times. She still did not answer. Disappointed, he hung up, turned the radio on. A rock group attacked. He spun the dial, found only that, snapped the radio off, lay down on the bed and looked up at the ceiling. The fantasy came to him of calling Stella, awakening her just to talk. The idea amused him and relaxed him somewhat, but he still could not sleep.

When De Luca came in, Sieberling was in the exact same place on the couch he had been earlier. He looked up from the magazine, and De Luca wondered if he had ever moved. Probably not. He was the one solidly dependable element. He corrected himself. Paul was solid also. He was wildly lucky to have found him. To have managed this, with Aguillar, despite the outcome—

"Have a nice ride, Mike?" Sieberling tossed the magazine down. A nice climb, De Luca thought bitterly, a nice, useless climb, and worse. He hesitated, but decided he was right, absolutely right.

"I was up in the sierra," he began cautiously. "I saw Luis Aguillar."

"Jesus," Sieberling muttered.

"Listen to me," De Luca flared. "The man's a dope dealer and a conniver. He pretends to be this revolutionary figure, but he takes his from the top."

"Why should he be any different?" Sieberling shrugged.

"Because people are suffering around here, damn it!"

How could he expect Sieberling to understand? The man suspected all people, all motives; he was never disillusioned, disappointed.

"What has he got to do with us?"

"We hoped he could help. We hoped . . ." He groped for words. "Marcus."

He started to sit but found himself too agitated for that. "The son of a bitch led us on, led us to *think* he was a force. He's a zero." Rage began to boil in him as he recalled Aguillar's calm manner; he had *patronized* them. "And Sal, I have this feeling he's going to make some kind of trouble for us."

"What do you mean?" Sieberling was instantly alert.

"It's a gut feeling, that's all . . . some things he said about my stopping shooting."

"With Lufkin here?"

"Exactly." There would be enough trouble with Lufkin, anyway. The quiet creep was waiting. "I wish," he burst out, "I hadn't started with Aguillar, that he was out of my hair." He stalked to the sideboard and poured himself a glass of Barolo to calm his nerves. He should have stayed with Elvira tonight of all nights. He should press close to her slimness and feel her silken hair on his face. He should look into the incredible depths of her eyes, feeling the calm there as though it were a physical embrace.

"The guy hides out," Sieberling called to him. "How'd you find him?"

"Paul made a contact." He stared at the wine bottle and the color gave him an idea. The entire Jericho sequence might have a faint red cast . . . from the sun at dawn to the fiery blasts later, the entire sequence might be suffused, delicately, with the color of blood. He would speak to Kodály; they would work it out. But it had to be delicate—a metaphorical shading, nothing more.

"Who took you there, Mike?"

There was no point in mentioning Elvira. "What difference does it make?"

"I mean," Sieberling asked, "where was the guy?"

He swung around and saw that Sieberling had risen. He had removed the sunglasses and his eyes were red-rimmed and blinking as though having difficulty focusing.

"He was in this . . . place," he said offhandedly, "where some

323

medicine man did his thing. Montaña de Pobres, they call it. I'm going up to get some sleep," he added quickly. "You can stay here or go home."

"I'll go," Sieberling said quietly.

He left, and for long minutes after he was gone, De Luca stood in the center of the huge room, glass in hand, motionless. He was almost unaware when his fingers opened and the glass slipped, falling to the thick Indian rug, spilling the Barolo and creating a purple stain.

CHAPTER

32

The clang of iron doors and the buzz of excited voices, reaching her even at the other end of the jail corridor, awakened Flo, and, fully dressed, she twisted on the cot to listen. Boots rasped over the concrete floors; sudden loud laughter erupted. She rose, went to the bars and tried to look past the dim fluorescent toward where vague uniformed shapes milled about. As she peered, two men in soiled white smocks lurched into her field of vision carrying a stretcher upon which rode a blanketed heap. Two excited *policías* strode after them, and they were all soon gone from sight. Seconds later she heard an engine boom into life and tires crunch.

She looked at her watch. Minutes after five. Her body ached in every joint. Her glasses were clouded and her head itched. No lice, she prayed—please, no lice. As she tried to clear her lenses, two more policemen materialized, advance guard of a party approaching. Seeing her, they halted, uncertain of what their attitude should be toward the captain's guest. One, vaguely, waved her deeper into the cell; the other, a beer bottle in hand, winked.

"Mucho excitación."

The rest of the party appeared then. First two more police. Between them, hands bound behind his back, Flo saw a delicate-framed, dark-skinned man in a torn white shirt. His resigned eyes found hers for a fleeting moment of communion, then turned away. One of the police opened the office door and shoved him inside.

"Florenza." The captain stood in front of her animatedly, a stubble of beard sprouting.

"My God," she said, "is it always this way at five o'clock in the morning?"

He laughed. "No, no . . . but today is big day." He shouted in Spanish to one of the men, who produced keys and opened her cell door.

"Come."

Taking her arm, he propelled her forward and into his office. The captive stood in a corner.

"Sit down," Quesedo urged. "We have coffee." He rippled an order, and one of the jailers ran off.

"You don' sleep too much, I am sorry."

"It doesn't matter." She collected her hair. Her head still itched. Against the opposite wall, the sad-eyed man looked away from her. "Who's that?"

Quesedo smiled, a certain smugness plain. "You see that man? Is big leader of the *bajo tierra*."

She swiveled toward the thin figure. Quesedo hitched his trousers up, proudly. "Oh, sí . . . tonight we catch them. I have man who finds them and I make big raid. Catch him, catch five more, is all over, this *bajo tierra*, and I do it. His name is Ismena, has little place on Juarez."

Not even the mention of his name changed the flat look on Ismena's face. His eyes were glass, his chiseled face stone. Flo stared at him, shocked, hoping to send a message of solidarity with her vibrating being.

"The cinema be all right now," Quesedo interrupted her process. "No more bad t'ings."

She turned back to the captain with sorrow and said, "I saw somebody go by, on a stretcher."

"Ah . . ." The captain nodded. "Tonight I pull in everyt'ing." His arms embraced the world. "They hear 'bout me in the capital. Was Luis Aguillar, goes to the hospital. He takes two bullets, maybe three."

The words hit her like the bullets themselves. She felt them strike her ear, then her brain, then her heart, felt them explode inside her, fragment, turn her limbs cold. Quesedo saw the blood leave her.

"Florenza," he quickly said, "'he knows what is the game, what happens maybe. That is chance he takes. You be for revolution and you don' die in your bed. He do his job and I do mine, Florenza." He looked at her, asking for understanding. "I don' feel he is bad man. Is not personal t'ing, you must to believe."

Aguillar. The grief welled up in her. Who now would help these helpless? Suddenly terrified that, in some mysterious and unknown way, she had been an instrument in his capture, she asked, "How did you find him?"

Quesedo glanced at his prisoner and shrugged. "I do . . . tonight I get everybody. I show them all."

"But how?" She shifted in the chair, and her voice was so desperate, so needful, that it aroused his compassion.

"Florenza," he said. "For you I have much respect."

"I know that," she said, her brain whirling with guile, "and I know you have only tried to help me. I appreciate that. I know we have . . . much to say to each other."

"Sí," he murmured. "Sí."

"But we have to be open and honest with each other."

"Of course," he lied, longing to put his hands on her hips.

"So if I ask you this—"

He could not deny her. "I learn where he is this night. Someone tells me. In a cave near the Hill of the Poor. We go up, quiet like goats. He is so surprised he cannot to make a good fight, but he tries. His people run, but I don' care 'bout them, only him." He chuckled with some private whimsy. "I tell you this, I don' t'ink Señor De Luca be so happy with *terroristas* like he says."

Her eyes went wide at that, and he grinned at having made his point.

"What—" she started to say, but he stopped her.

"Joost like I say—sometimes a man says one t'ing and does another. Is funny t'ing." Quesedo interlocked his fingers. "*Bajo tierra* and Luis, they work like this together, 'gainst De Luca."

The policeman returned with two cups of steaming instant coffee, and the sight made her sick to her stomach.

"Captain," she whispered, "can I leave? I'm no damn danger to anyone. I want to leave. I want to take a shower. I'm filled with lice. I'm crawly." Her voice became stronger. "You've got *him*. Aguillar's in the hospital. What else do they want? Let me out!"

Quesedo took only a moment. "I do. Sí. I take you home, myself." He buttoned his jacket with resolve. "Is my responsibility, because everyt'ing fixed." He shook his head with amusement. "*Bajos* be fools. We find this man they take, in little hut. They say they will do much bad to him, but when we find him, he only has bad stomach from tacos."

"Someone they took?" She had not known anything of this.

"Sí . . . take tall man, name Marcus, you know him?"

Her hands started to tremble, and she clenched them together in her lap. Controlling her voice with great effort, she asked, "Is he all right?"

"If he don' eat tacos." The captain put an arm about her shoulders familiarly. "Come."

Leaving, she saw Ismena's eyes follow her, and she choked back tears.

At this hour of the morning, the fireflies convened. Driving, Quesedo, in buoyant spirits, remarked they were like living fireworks. Flo tried to respond but could think only of what the captain had told her at the *comandancia*. *Michael was not so fond of Aguillar as he pretended to be.* And the revolutionary was in the hospital now.

"So now"—Quesedo changed the subject—"you go away from here?"

"Yes," she said, "I'll go."

"Sí, of course." He smiled as he let his little secret out. "And I go too, on little trip to your country soon, to Los Angeles."

When she looked surprised, the smile became a confident laugh. "Oh, when a man travels, sees other t'ings in the world, that makes him more wise. You believe?"

"I suppose."

She looked down at the road, slightly confused.

"Now, would be much good you tell me where you live in Los Angeles, eh? I write you when I come and then I see you. We can to know each other more better there. In Los Angeles is more free for people, is new country." His eyes warmed as the vision took hold. "With money is possible anyt'ing, no? I bring plenty money. We talk about what I can do. We be good friends. I have for you much respect, much *emoción*."

Flo heard his declaration with dismay. "I was thinking of not going back to L.A.," she said carefully. "I'd like to go south. I hear the women run things in Tehuantepec; I'd like to see that. Or maybe Guatemala, I don't know."

"Guatemala?" The word burst from him. "Is men on the streets with machine guns in Guatemala. *Fascistas, comunistas.* They shoot, shoot, shoot. Anyone in the way, die. You be kill for nothing. No, I don' like you do that."

"Well, then maybe I will go back to L.A.," she said quickly, pacifying him.

"Sí. Is better there in Los Angeles." Quesedo calmed again. He reached a hand over to stroke her cheek.

"You will to see how good it can be."

She did not even feel his hand, thought only of what Michael had done to Aguillar, and it burned in her chest like a live coal.

The first light had invaded the night sky when they came in through the kitchen door and over to Elvira's bedroom. There were two of them. She recognized neither; one was young with murderously glowing eyes, the other older, colder, with a hawk nose and thick lips. They stood over her bed pulling at her, lifting her. She thought at first they were thieves and said she had money, would give them money. The younger one became angry at that.

"They took him," he said. "They came tonight and took Ismena and others. Everything is in confusion. How is it you didn't warn us?"

Elvira was shocked. "I knew nothing of it."

The older man leaned down. "It was your job to know. You sleep with the man; did he not say anything?"

"He did not."

"Are you sure?" The younger one sat heavily on the bed.

"He said nothing." She had to appear calm, she knew—any flash of emotion might be mistaken for guilt. When the old man had approached her to do this and agreed to let her keep everything De Luca gave her, it had seemed not to hold any danger. To report back his plans, his movements, was simple; it had only grown more complicated later.

"Get him here." The older one pointed to the telephone. "We should have taken him first."

"He won't come," she said. "He goes to Monte Tecla this morning. Light is precious to them. He won't come here."

"Tecla." The younger one pounded a fist into the bed. "And the government lets them. Tecla is *our* place."

"Call him." The older one picked up the phone and handed it to her. "Tell him you are sick. You are dying. You are bearing his baby; men are raping you. Tell him anything, but get him here."

She took the phone as the men waited, riveted upon her. At the hacienda, the phone rang three times before it was answered and a woman's voice said, "Hello?"

It could only be his wife. "Excuse," she said, "I must talk to Señor De Luca."

The woman did not answer.

"I must speak to Señor De Luca," she repeated.

A click. The connection was broken. She held the phone out to the men. "They hang up, you can hear for yourself."

"Call again." The younger one jammed his hand down on the receiver cradle. The older one wiped spittle from his lips.

"It will be no good," she whispered.

"No?" The younger one whispered back, his eyes burning. "It will be no good because you have told him, eh?"

"He knows nothing." She felt fear begin to grow. These were ignorant, brutal men and they were capable of anything, like most men.

"He buys you," the younger one spat at her. "A whore to begin with to do this, so he buys you."

"No," she said softly.

"I think so," the older one said, a certain sorrow in his voice.

Enraged, the younger one flashed a hand out, grabbed her long hair and jerked her head up. Involuntarily, a cry of pain escaped from her lips. His other hand pulled a hunting knife from his belt, and in one swift stroke he slashed just above her forehead, dropping the thick thatch of severed hair onto the coverlet before her startled eyes.

Impassioned by his first move, he dove at her, slashing again, whipping her hair off in a scythelike motion. He did this over and over as she sat stalk-straight, rigid with shock, not daring to thwart him, holding back breath as his razor edge sliced away until only a jagged inch of brush was left, until her scalp shone through, until the effort was too great and the fear in her eyes satisfied him. He stood up then, and, his own breath coming fast, the orgasmic flailing completed, he replaced the knife in his belt, looking at his companion with challenge. The older man shrugged.

"Now, everyone will know," the younger man said. "Everyone will know who loves *gringo puercos*."

When they left, Elvira did not move. For minutes she sat stiffly amid the long black shards of herself. Finally she reached up to explore her head. Feeling the coarse stubble was painful, and she quickly removed her hand. She lay back on the pillow and thought of Michael who had never hurt her, Michael who had invested her with grace. They would be waiting for him, someplace, she knew. If she warned him, they would, somehow, know that too. She had no weight with them; she was a feather.

She sat up, slowly. He would be at Ixtepan and his people could reach him with their radios. She plucked up the telephone but

330

heard no sound. Nothing she did produced the usual hum; there was only ominous silence. Cautiously, she left her bed and followed the telephone wire along the wall, through the wall and out to the parlor. Halfway across the parlor wall she found it; the wires had been ripped from the retaining tacks and cut; copper edges reached futilely for the other ends which had been ripped as well and twisted into an angry ball.

The fear returning, she crept to the still-shuttered window and, staying well to one side, moved the opening apart imperceptibly. She looked out to the walk. A red-backed bird pecked at seeds and squawked, then flew off over a bush, and following its flight, she saw a dark shadow on the ground where there should have been only early dawn light. She focused her eyes on the spot, and when, unmistakably, the shadow moved, she knew they were there and jerked herself away from the window.

Seated on the floor, she put her head in her hands and felt powerless again.

At near seven, as planned, Paul arrived at De Luca's and found bedlam. Captain Quesedo was reliving the raids for the benefit of De Luca's father and one of Denny's air force. Catherine De Luca, in an ice-green dressing gown, already had the sideboard loaded with bacon, toast, rolls, oranges and steaming pots of coffee. An assistant director was busy on one phone with instructions to Monte Tecla, where the elaborate preparations were coming to fruition. Sieberling was on another phone to the transport captain getting reports. Seeing Paul come in, he went to him quickly and, in machine-gun bursts, sketched what had happened during the night. He himself had only been called less than an hour ago by Quesedo. Marcus was back and unhurt; everything was on track.

Paul listened with amazement.

"Pauli," the elder De Luca shouted to him, gleefully, "we got the animals." Quesedo, smiling broadly, waved a good morning.

Michael was in the den with Marcus, and when Paul hurried there, he was pulled inside.

"I told you he'd be all right."

Allan Marcus was seated on the daybed, drinking coffee and munching a sweet roll. He had a four-day growth of beard; his hair was matted and his bare feet were coated with dirt, but he appeared unharmed. "If you want to know," he said, gravel-voiced, "I can tell you how it feels to sit in a hut with a couple of unwashed

Mexicans for four days while they go over the pictures in *Playboy* magazine again and again."

De Luca laughed delightedly. Stunned, Paul went closer.

"They never tried any rough stuff?"

"Tacos." Marcus rolled his eyes theatrically. "Tacos were rough. And hardly any sleep."

Paul sat.

"Actually, I was dozing off when the police jokers came crashing in. They scared me more than the other guys. They started shooting up the place even while the guys jumped up and put their hands in the air. It's a miracle no one got killed."

"I knew we just had to be cool and lie back," De Luca said, "I knew it."

"You know what I want to do?" Marcus announced. "Take a shower, take a shave, sit down on a regular toilet seat and then I'll be ready to go to work."

"Give yourself a day," De Luca said, but Marcus was adamant. He had been scheduled to shoot hand-held camera in a helicopter for Kodály and he was going to do it. He rose from the daybed and mused, "When they put the paper bag over my head, I was scared to death, but after a while I knew they were as scared as I was; funny."

After Marcus left, Paul felt disoriented. All this had happened as he lay on his bed staring at the ceiling, dazed. De Luca was jubilant. The past trials seemed to have dropped from him like a molting skin. "It's all a dead issue now—and we're on firmer ground with Lufkin." He paused in his tracks. "Did he tell you that the Indian in the pots-and-pans store was one of them?"

"Ismena? No." Paul jerked erect in his chair.

"He should have told us. He should have talked to us. If he had, none of this would have happened."

"Ismena?" He tried to understand it. "What happened to him?"

"Quesedo picked him up."

That, Sieberling had not told him. It was all so interwoven. The somber Indian captured. And Luis—

"Sal told me they went up to the caves and shot Luis."

"Yes. He's in the hospital, poor bastard, poor, ineffectual bastard."

"How did they find him? And last night, just after we saw him?"

"Seems like Quesedo's been after him for weeks. He had no idea we were up there—still doesn't; what's the point? He told me he infiltrated one of his men and last night they closed in. He's smarter than he seems."

Paul sat back in his chair. He had envisioned the *bajos* as obdurate, steely-eyed fanatics. This one, at least, was simply—an Indian.

"Paul," De Luca said, "this was the fire. There's always some kind of fire. Now, let's make our picture. Let's break their balls."

Catherine came in with a mug of coffee and a plate of food, and De Luca left for another round of instructions to special effects. Paul sipped the coffee only once before he reminded himself.

"I'd better call Rennie and tell her what happened and where I'll be." He had already picked up the telephone when he heard Catherine say something he did not understand and asked, "I'm sorry, what did you say?"

Her arms were crossed and her eyes were very bright. "I thought," she repeated, "that you might not find her at her place."

"What do you mean?"

"Well, go ahead and try."

He looked at her, trying to pierce the green eyes and the steady face. "But what makes you think that?"

"Because." She flicked a stray hair back. "Paul, if you really need her, call Mr. Lufkin's hotel." When she saw his jaw drop, she added, "And don't make such a big deal about it."

"Jesus Christ," he said, hanging up the phone.

"He likes her." Catherine smiled. "So—"

"He likes her?"

"It's not important," she said. "But I thought if you were looking for her . . ."

"Wait a minute . . ." He could not believe she would be saying this.

"Paul," she said patiently but with a deep satisfaction that Paul did not miss, a certain settling of scores, "he is important here, and he . . . likes . . . her." Her hands lifted the silk gown a bit and she walked out. Instantly, he tried Rennie's motel. As it had the night before, the phone rang but no one answered. He hung up slightly dazed, but he was roused by De Luca's voice calling energetically, "Paul . . . let's go. They're waiting at Tecla."

Flo looked in the mirror, and red-rimmed eyes stared back at her. Automatically, she pulled the brush through the coiled springs of her hair. Her chest heaved, moving the cotton robe like a sea, and suddenly, she found herself bent over the dressing table, smash-

333

ing the brush down on the wooden face in frustration. Michael always won—always.

She pushed herself back up, rubbed her red eyes vigorously with a coarse tissue. The burning in her lungs had started with the sight of Aguillar and continued even now, unlessened. To smash Michael. Once, to tell him face to face what she knew about him, to tell the world! To reveal him for a fake, a fink, a rat, a liar. Impulsively, she reached for the telephone.

"Allan? It's Flo."

"Hey." His voice was welcoming. "How are you? I just got back from four days in a hut."

"You're all right though?"

"Okay. Sure. What's going on with you?"

"Allan, I have to see you. It's overwhelmingly important."

"Yeah . . . well, I'm shooting all day at Ixtepan. Maybe tonight?"

"It can't wait. You don't know what Michael's done this time, Allan. If you knew—"

"Flo, don't start with that stuff again."

"He put me in prison. Don't you have any feelings for me?" she shouted. "Any feelings at all?"

"We had this out, I thought. Jesus . . . I've had a hell-time myself. My stomach—"

"Allan, I'm going to leave, maybe tomorrow. Come with me."

"I've got to go to work now," he said, "I really do."

The connection was broken. She sat silently for a moment, staring at the dead phone, then reached for her glasses. Some reckoning had to be made. She pushed the frames onto her nose resolutely, quickly put on her clothes and walked out.

Before eight, Stella rose, opened the shutters, looked out over the sierra in the distance and the sunlit square below, took deep drafts of the gentle air, heard the hummingbird outside the window near the vine and felt at luxurious peace.

She started the bath thinking about Paul. That was settled. Some other plane had been reached, some new level of rapport between them. Changes had taken place in him, she understood that; but the essential man, the *thing* inside, the combination of sensitivity and intelligence she had been drawn to, initially, was unaltered. They would be friends in the future and so be it.

334

She thought the soft knocking on her door was the maid, wanted to say "Go away" in Spanish but had no Spanish to say it in, so she opened it instead, with a ready shake of her head, and saw not the slim maid's body but the robust wild-haired girl in a soiled red blouse peering at her intensely. After surprise, anger came up in her throat.

"Go away!"

She started to close the door but Flo pleaded, "Please don't; Michael put me in jail last night. I just got out."

Stella measured her. "You were in jail?"

"Yes. Michael thinks he can get away with anything." There was anguished sincerity in her voice, and her lips were twisted in humiliation and bitterness. Stella moved aside as the peace of the morning fled. Flo came in and, as though Stella knew what she was talking about, said, "I was there when the police captain brought them all in."

"Brought who in?"

"Aguillar," Flo said, near tears, "the revolutionary. He was turned in, informed on—by Michael."

"Sit down," Stella said. "You look a little rocky."

"It's true. He's in the hospital, shot and critical. They did it to him."

Her eyes were wide as saucers and Stella thought she must be careful with her.

"Look, I'm taking a bath right now. Why don't you rest here while I—"

"The underground people, they've got them too. Maybe because of Michael also."

"How do you know about this . . . informing?" Stella asked.

"The police captain likes me. He thinks I'll let him make love to me. He told me."

"And you believe him?"

"Yes!" It was a shout from her vitals. "Because that's Michael. He put me in that jail cell—" She broke off, trembling, then, holding herself together, begged, "Help me."

"To do what?" Stella asked, startled.

"I am going there to tell them all what I think of them. I want to confront Michael face to face."

"That's insane," Stella said.

"Come with me." Flo's voice wavered. "I'm a little . . . afraid

335

to go there alone, and if you're along there's a better chance of my getting up there." Her whole body shook. "Come. Come with me, please . . . please."

Like a smooth mirror cracking, her once-staunch facade broke and she sank into a chair, face in her hands, shoulders quivering. Instinctively, Stella reached out and cradled the girl's head against her stomach, stroking the wiry skein of hair and saying what she did not believe herself, "It's okay . . . honestly, it's okay, it's okay."

CHAPTER
33

For many days and hours, the crew had labored, without stop, to set the final preparations in place. Atop Monte Tecla the two camera cranes rose like the necks of stainless-steel mastodons. Wooden superstructures, mounted on four of the higher stone abutments, also served as camera mounts so that the entire 360-degree sweep could be filmed. Two generators on their trucks hummed diligently, excreting the network of cables feeding vital juice to the huge bulbs angled to the valley below. In the plateau's center, to the sides of the eight-pillared temple, another battery of lamps looked skyward, ready to illuminate the low-swooping helicopter gunships as they would pass on the strafing mission.

Electricians, camera crews and construction men moved from structure to structure checking, adjusting, correcting. The communications van rasped with four channels of talk as the bottom of the mountain communicated with the top. Two assistants with bullhorns shouted their needs and injunctions to hurry.

Down below Tecla, the tourist buses to the sacred mountain had been stopped, by a town order, until the filming would end. Starting at the south face, where the road to Ixtepan had been transformed, by the addition of a Buddhist shrine, the new Vietnamese village stood in place with all the fidelity that the talents of the Scottish art director and unlimited money could provide. The thatched huts, the fields, the pigs and buffalo, the bamboo forest, the burial ground, a more imposing government house of stone and wood, all sat perfectly proportioned.

The extras, still squired by Machado's men, were almost all made up and costumed. An assistant director, through an interpreter, explained what the first scene would demand of them—a simple coming and going along the pathways.

Peopled, the village looked calm and pacific. Hidden in the huts,

337

snaking along the ground, tunneled into hollows were the means of their destruction; hundreds of charges, of all percussive possibilities, from the simulation of a single bullet exploding into the earth to a ripping tattoo of machine-gun slugs, from hand-grenade blasts to huge rocket explosions that would slam into a hut and send it kicking up into the air in a whoosh of flame. Those places to become fire had been carefully prepared with the proper gasoline gel, which resembled napalm and would be set off with an electrical spark controlled by the special-effects team. That team crouched behind a large hut, dozens of switches set on relay boards before them. At a touch, or on a set program, the bullets blew up, the bombs burst, the rockets destroyed. Here and there, small, concealed trampolines stood ready. In the heat of battle, stunt men, dressed as Vietnamese, would jump onto them from a height. The moment they would hit, a timing device would ignite a blast of powder and smoke. The men would recoil into the air, arms akimbo, faces distorted in the fury of a red haze, convincingly blown sky-high. Other men readied themselves in trees. When presumably hit, they would fall fifty feet to the ground, where, hidden by fronds, air mattresses awaited to break their fall.

Huge lights bloomed from stands here too, and giant reflectors ready to fill the shadows, to make shadows, to diminish, to reinforce. Here, Kodály called orders frantically and his men clambered to obey. Beyond the created village, in the desert scruff of Ixtepan, Denny's air force waited. The Cobra gunships sat in military rows of two. The F-105 two-seater fighter-bombers, with exact plastic duplicates of their eight-thousand-pound bombs, squatted behind them. Soon they would be off for establishing shots.

Rising from the controlled chaos was a palpable sense of anticipation and mounting excitement. For almost all of the army De Luca had assembled, this was the true meaning of film; not words but action, movement, violence, effects; all the crafts brought into play, all the tension, all the complex techniques coordinating perfectly to freeze the moment of blast, the moment of chase, the moment of catastrophe. These days were the rewards for endless boring hours of dialogue, close-ups, two shots—hated still lifes.

"The sense I'm working for here," De Luca explained, "is normalcy. Lyric normalcy. An extension of what we've done at the rice paddies."

At his elbow, making editing notes, Paul found it difficult to concentrate. The night, the Deer Dance, the news of Luis's capture, moved with him, stayed with him as the reality, not this Vietnamese plain in the morning sun.

"You look a little blah," De Luca remarked. "You feeling all right?"

"Do you think any of these people know what happened last night?"

"Forget it," De Luca said sharply. "Put it out of your mind. When you get to the location, when you're in control, blot out everything else. Don't let it exist."

Denny Burns approached with Allan Marcus for last-minute instructions. Marcus was clean-shaven and wore freshly laundered clothing. He declared that he had taken a twenty-minute nap and was fresh as a daisy, ready to go aloft with Burns and do his job. Burns allowed as how Marcus was a tough son of a bitch, even if he was a Hollywood character.

Drifting away from them, Paul came upon Quesedo at the commissary table. The policeman's cap was set at a cocky angle and his smile was superior. He had brought a token force of four, who slumped at their posts like wilted brown plants. He winked and, saluting with a doughnut, was about to launch into conversation, but Paul fled to the camera truck. The policeman, too, looked unreal this morning, in his jackboots, his eyes confident with success, his teeth bared and gleaming.

"Paul."

He turned rapidly, hearing Rennie's warm call. She was striding toward him happily, almost dancing, her voice bubbling.

"Good morning. I heard all about last night. It's a mind blower!"

"Yes." From a corner of his eye he saw Lufkin, immaculate in beige slacks and suede loafers, approaching Michael. Rennie reached out to hug him.

"And look at this place. It's going to be fabulous." She laughed. "And we'll make it even better in the cutting room."

He thought of what Catherine had said. "I tried calling you last night but there wasn't any answer."

"Ohh . . ." She waved that away. "And they didn't touch Allan. Isn't that fantastic?"

"Yes. I called you again this morning," he said, "but there was still no answer."

Her ebullience faded into surprise, then sulkiness. "You didn't have to do that," she said.

He knew then that Catherine had called it and tried to locate the strongest feeling he had but found it impossible to untangle one.

"Paul," she said, "don't misinterpret."

"I don't. He likes you."

"He likes me," she agreed, and then, rushing her words together, "and wanted me not to go home, and I know how important it is that he doesn't make trouble for Michael, so I stayed." Her voice, holding no apologies or evasions, unsettled him.

"It's not all that important or earthshaking," she added. "It was more . . ."

"Like a job," he finished.

"No," she said passionately, moving so close to him he felt her breath and drew in her perfume. "I just felt they were meaningless acts, and if I could help you and help Michael that way then I should."

"I see." Hurt, he looked for a flaw in her logic but could find none, if emotions were excluded, violations, prior states.

"My feelings for you," she said tremulously, "have nothing to do with last night."

"And what," he asked carefully, "if he likes you again, tonight? He's still here—or tomorrow?"

"It's different now, the trouble's over."

"But what if it were still going on?" he persisted.

"Why do you have to do this?"

"I'm just trying to get the straight of it."

"I don't know, I haven't thought about it."

"Well, think about it," he said, his anger evident.

She drew away from him, flushing. "You won't understand, will you?"

How, he wondered, did Catherine know that she had pleased Lufkin? Had Michael told her?

"I do understand," he said. "It's totally logical. Did you fake orgasm?"

"I can't talk to you now," Rennie said quietly. "You have your priorities confused. You need a little space to understand this." She walked into the camera van, and as he watched her slim figure pass through the doorway, the lithe spring of her buttocks vanishing, a deep wave of regret enveloped him.

He wandered aimlessly back to the commissary table, saw Quesedo strutting and went the other way. He leaned against a prop

340

tree and watched De Luca and Lufkin—heads together, in animated conversation. Two Vietnamese peasants conversed in loud Spanish. A water buffalo bellowed morosely. A special-effects man with a reel of wire came up and displaced him; the tree would blow up in the air attack. The assistant director's bullhorn developed laryngitis and nothing came through but a grating rasp.

He realized he was seeing and hearing through a curtain of haze and determined to stop being affected by irrelevancies. He started, with determination, toward Kodály, to check on the large camera magazines, but De Luca left his director's chair and came toward him.

"Get this," he hissed. "That son of a bitch was never fooled. He knew all about Allan, knew about a lot of things, but was playing dumb."

Paul shot a dumbfounded glance at Lufkin, ten paces away.

"You're kidding."

"No, he was just waiting, as I thought, to really turn the screws. But we beat him." De Luca's voice was charged with triumph. "We beat him."

"What's going to happen?"

"You always make some deal. Learn that." De Luca looked back toward Lufkin, waving amiably. "I convinced him we were out of the woods. I'd sign a pledge to be out of here in eight weeks and . . . I'd produce a small-budget picture for them that I'd write . . . maybe the one in my desk drawer. We'll talk about it later."

Sieberling approached. Everything was ready up above for the shot. De Luca jumped into a jeep, which instantly took off for Tecla's peak. Caught up in the flush of preparations, Sieberling's mouth twisted into an uncharacteristic smile. "Going to be a goddamn good one," he said before he hurried away.

All right, Paul told himself. Get with it now. Drop everything personal; it was movie time. He had work plans to discuss with Rennie and private matters had to be blotted out, as Michael said.

He gave the commissary table a wide berth and came up behind a group of extras being herded toward a clump of bamboo. Stepping aside to let them pass, he was at the edge of the road when the Volkswagen stopped. He paid it no attention until a door flew open and he saw Flo jump out, a kerchief flying from her head, her face twisted anxiously.

He was startled into immobility, allowing her to see him, and she swooped, instantly, like an avenging angel.

"Gordon," she shouted, "I didn't think you could do such a thing, never. How can you live with yourself?"

He saw two electricians staring at her.

"Flo," he said, in desperation, "calm down and sit down some place out of the way. Michael's going to do a take in a minute."

She did not seem to hear. "I called the hospital," she said. "He's critical. One bullet is in his lung."

He thought of turning his back and charging away. But she was crazed and might follow him. If Sieberling saw her, who knew what he would do? He turned back, trapped, and said, angrily, "Why me? What do you want with me?"

It was then that he saw Stella approaching and peered at her in shocked disbelief. A bullhorn voice advised the cast to take their places for a rehearsal; everyone not in the scene was to take a place in the area marked "Safety."

Coming abreast of them, Stella murmured to Flo, "Take it easy, please," and looked at Paul uncertainly. "This is kind of crazy, but she came to my hotel all upset."

"They put me in jail," Flo said loudly, "and I saw Luis come in, wounded."

"I didn't know you were in jail," he said. "I'm sorry."

"I saw the old man too, the *bajo* one." She looked as though she might cry.

"What am I supposed to do about all this?" he asked helplessly, glancing about. The electricians had left.

"Paul." Stella was almost apologetic. "She says De Luca turned Aguillar in. He arranged to have him caught."

"What? Come on," he exploded, "that's wild, and rotten and a lie."

"Yes," Flo flared back at him, "he did. I know he did. That's how they knew where he was. The police captain told me."

He looked at her, speechless.

Stella spoke softly. "She thinks you knew about it, too. I told her you would not do that."

"I . . . had nothing to do with it," he said, recovering. "Michael didn't, and I didn't, and whatever you were told is . . . wrong."

"I told you!" Flo shouted at Stella, as Paul cringed. "He always has it his way!" She turned away from them, looked up toward the top of Tecla and shook her fist.

"Stel," he muttered, "she's going off."

"He's hurt her." Stella pushed the bangs from her eyes. The bull-horn rasped once more.

"We're in camera range," he pleaded. "Let's move. Please."

"He's a fake." Flo turned back to them. "He's an armchair radical. He's into the *idea* of people but not people. He's into the *idea* of struggle, but all he wants to do is make his movies, that's all. There's nothing else to him. Nothing. He turned Aguillar in."

"Move that VW," the bullhorn roared. "You people get that car out of there and move away!"

"Stella, get her out of here," Paul pleaded.

"Hey . . ." He heard a rush of steps and turned to see Sieberling charging down upon them, followed by a startled Quesedo at his heels. "You," the production manager shouted at Flo, "what are you doing here?"

Flo stared at him icily. "This is Mexico, not Beverly Hills."

"Right now, this is private property." He looked from her to Stella, trying to make the connection.

"They're going," Paul said. "They came to speak to me."

"This is Mexico; I'm going noplace," Flo said stubbornly, glancing at Quesedo, whose face visibly twitched.

Sieberling pushed her in the chest, shouting, "Get out of here!"

"Don't do that," Stella said. "Keep your hands to yourself."

Paul said, "Sal, take it easy." But by now the production manager was ablaze.

"How come you let her go?" he demanded of Quesedo. The captain made a feeble response with his hands and shoulders.

"She's trespassing," Sieberling ordered. "Lock her up."

"Señor," Quesedo stuttered, "is much *nerviosidad* here. No good, this." He looked at Flo, and his eyes begged her to leave.

"I said to lock her up," Sieberling insisted.

A pig, Quesedo thought in panic, a true pig to expose him so. And after what he had pulled off. Without his coup there would be no cameras here today, no anything. He spoke very softly so as not to provoke.

"Cannot to do that, she does not'ing against the law."

Caught by surprise, Sieberling almost dropped his clipboard. "I'm making charges against her. Okay? I'm making charges of sabotage and destruction of Jericho property. And I'm demanding that you *lock her up*."

"You are an incredible bastard," Stella said to Sieberling as the sweat beads broke out on Quesedo's forehead and Paul looked on, helplessly. Meanwhile, Flo clenched her lips and fastened her eyes on the policeman, who, exerting a great effort, managed to look away from her taut face.

"Señor," he whispered, "I take her away. I talk to her. Is better that way."

"How come you let her go?" Sieberling demanded.

"Sal, drop it," Paul said, but Sieberling was implacable.

"She's trespassing and I'm ordering you to lock her up."

Quesedo jerked himself ramrod-straight as a revulsion rose up against this man whose voice dripped contempt, who was one of those he had always smiled to and bowed to, even as he knew they looked upon him as less than themselves.

"No," he said strongly, "you do not order. *I* decide this business. Not you and so it is."

"*You* decide?" Sieberling's astonished voice rose. "We'll damn well see about that."

"Okay, we see." Quesedo looked over to Flo.

An assistant in a jeep zoomed close to them, calling, "Sal, Mike's burning us. Gotta get started."

"If you don't get out of here," Sieberling snapped, "my guys will make you wish you had." He strode away from them.

"He means it," Paul pleaded. "Stel . . . please just go back down the road out of the way."

Stella nodded. "Yes, let the wunderkind perform his wonders." She put a hand lightly on Flo's shouder. "Let's just sit and watch." She noted how gray the police captain's complexion had turned, as though the pressure in his veins had suddenly dropped.

"I . . . go with you little way," he said in a choked voice. He had defied Sieberling and the cost was yet to come, he knew.

Flo appeared to be struggling with words. "That . . ." she said, and her face was so tender, so dear, that he longed to put his own alongside it. "Thank . . . you," she managed to say.

Before getting back into the VW, Stella turned to look at Paul, and when he half-waved, she felt a stab of sorrow which she concealed with a "See you."

Atop Tecla, De Luca stood in the bucket of the crane to the side of the Panavision camera whose zoom lens surveyed the fake Vietnamese village below. At his feet was a bullhorn for general instructions. Strapped to his chest was a microphone for communication with his first assistant. Around his neck was the viewfinder with which he framed shots. Its leather-covered barrel was scarred and pitted, but he would not give it up. His father had given it to him for his first feature and it remained precious.

As always, when orchestrating some complicated piece of action and setting himself apart from it, high above, overviewing, he felt euphoric, blissful, faculties sharpened to a high no drug could duplicate. He waved to his father down below who was just arriving for the show and going over to sit with Lufkin. He saw Paul leaving a jeep and called to him to come up. The crane operator lowered the basket in a gentle hydraulic swoop, and in seconds, Paul had clambered in and they were lofted again.

Watching them rise, Allan Marcus saluted. He would be going up with Denny on the second run but had direct communication with him for this one, in preparation.

"Ground One to Numero Uno," he sang out. "The big honcho and the little honcho have just gone up to glory. You've got three minutes. Over."

Denny's voice came singing back to his ear. "Marcus, how many cute little Vietnam protest girls did you get to screw?"

Looking down, Paul felt conspicuous. Editors did not ride cranes; they stayed earthbound. But up here directors saw the parts of the scheme come together, up here was the command post, and he opened himself to the experience.

"On the start," De Luca explained, "everyone comes out of the huts to begin the day. The cameras down below will stay on small vignettes I've set up. From that house, a man and a woman coming out, after the night, still quarreling. In that house, they come out later than the others because they've been making love. We get just a glimpse of that which I'll shoot later . . . or maybe you will." He slapped Paul on the back merrily. "People straggle out to go to the well, to start fires, all that and all individualized—that's the point. These are *people*, not a peasant village."

He turned Paul to the west. "From there, the first chopper comes . . . high . . . lazy . . . The people look up. An observer plane, they think; they've seen them before. They go about their business. Then the chopper starts to swoop in lower, and the other planes appear in the sky like flying horrors. That's the first section. Oh, shit," he concluded, "look at that." He pointed to the southern quadrant and a speck of helicopter shone against the sky. "That's

Denny, up already. For these shots he'll be lead man and Allan's shooting hand-held to get overhead shots as they come in, but he's previous."

He spoke into his microphone. "Get Denny away, damn it, I'm seeing him and I don't want to yet at all. Get him off."

He peered skyward to see how effective his communication would be and smiled with satisfaction as the speck wheeled and disappeared.

"Crazy bastard," he said affectionately.

Twisting in the bucket, Paul saw the small crowd of Mexicans and tourists at the foot of Tecla behind wooden barriers, yards from the last Vietnamese hut. Already, food vendors, quick to sense opportunity, had set up and were dispensing tortillas and soft drinks. Shading his eyes, he searched for Flo's Volkswagen but couldn't find it. The loudspeaker crackled. "Ready when you are."

"Everybody knows what's supposed to happen, right?" De Luca questioned.

"Supposed to."

De Luca picked up the bullhorn, ready to make adjustments. He turned to the operator seated behind the camera. "Rehearsal. Your first move is left, remember, when I give you the signal."

The operator nodded, settled himself, and put his eye to the rubber-cushioned eyepiece. "Here we go," De Luca said happily, and called into his microphone, "Okay . . . let's try it."

Paul watched the village intently as Kodály's battery of lights switched on, filling the shadows, teasing the darkness from the lanes, providing a golden morning glow tinged with a soft pink that the sun unaided could not provide. Few directors worked their lights during rehearsals but Michael believed it was important to do so here.

"Now," De Luca breathed into his microphone.

In magical response, a water buffalo wandered up a dirt track, a small boy leading it. The boy yawned sleepily and stopped to relieve himself. De Luca grinned. "Going to be just fine." From a hut a man and a woman emerged, shouting and gesticulating.

"Too much there . . . they have to be cooled down."

From the other huts the occupants emerged into the blazing glare. Some of them froze, hypnotized.

"Keep it going!"

A naked baby crawled out into the dust. A mother swooped it up, laughing. A stocky man in a breech cloth came to the door of his

346

hut, vacantly scratching his crotch. De Luca was delighted. "That's his own invention. . . . The man's an actor. Now all the time we're moving in imperceptibly; now we begin to turn into another part of the village. . . ." He signaled to the operator, who cranked the camera so that it moved gently, left. "That's where the single V.C. is . . . sleeping with his wife."

Paul heard the *thuck-thuck-thuck* of a distant helicopter rotor. From the south Denny's machine had come into view again. De Luca craned his neck and groaned. "The son of a bitch is early again. Never mind, let him come." He settled back to watch the advance across the sky.

From the open door of the Cobra, nestled between the quick-firing cannon and the fifty-seven-millimeter machine gun, Denny, flying alone, could see the sweep of the entire valley and Tecla rising, its monuments scaffolded by cameras and lights, the camera cranes reaching toward him like extended steel claws. Clustered at the foot of the hill, the peaked cones of the Vietnamese huts looked like pencil points.

"Hey, Sex Maniac, this is Ground One." Marcus's voice grated in his earphone. "Have you checked your aperture? Over."

He checked the remote-control cable on the camera fixed into the nose and called back. "It's beautiful. Over."

Marcus laughed derisively. "When it was a cannon you had and you zoomed down popping away, must have been like target practice, right?"

"Yeah." Denny banked in a lazy arc. "Ever hear of antiaircraft guns? Sometimes those mothers had them camouflaged so well you didn't know where the hell they were till they started to give you a little rock-'n'-roll. Now, am I supposed to stay level or glide down? We got thirty seconds before I come in lower, I think. Over."

"Stay level, birdman. Over and out."

Denny held level and raised the binoculars to his eyes to scan the scene below. He pulled Kodály into the twelve-by-forty's and grinned at his usual frantic look. He saw Marcus munching what appeared to be a doughnut and wished he had one aboard. Sweeping the edges of the crowd, he caught a glimpse of a female figure shading her eyes against the light. She was there for a split moment and then she was out of his field. He grinned maliciously and called, "This is Sex Maniac to Ground One. I just spotted your girl friend in the ground groupies, Marcus. Where'd she come from? Over."

Startled, Marcus said, "Flo? You're kidding." What would she be doing here? She was so—crazy. Probably she held it against him that he didn't help her. He couldn't. But she'd never understand that.

The radio sputtered with speech Marcus could not decipher, airman's jargon compounded by the crackling and fuzz of the equipment.

"The guys are coming on," Denny announced. He spoke into his air channel. "Remember, keep the choppers in attack formation when you come over the rise, make two passes each and tight right. The fixed wings come in for the rocket runs and give them plenty of room. No accidents today. Now, remember, this is a rehearsal, but let's make it look good . . . look smart." He suppressed an ironic laugh. "This is Wing Commander Burns, over and out."

From experience he knew exactly how it would be. The villagers would look up and the small bodies would hold still, staring up into the sun as they judged whether this machine would be harming them or not. They would be deceived, plod on with their lives. Behind him he could hear the other choppers whirring in. They would catch the village by surprise, start swooping low, guns blazing and rattling. The fighter-bombers would come next to slam their rockets into anything likely, including seemingly open ground —for the waiting V.C. would be in bunkers. He would ride above after the first pass so that the camera could keep rolling. On Tecla, and in the valley, Kodály would catch the panic, the fear and the destruction.

He banked the chopper right, cut the pitch and moved lower in a graceful descending line. The exhilaration of the moment lifted his spirits and he burst out in his tenor—

"Memories—light the corners of my mind—la la la la la la la la . . . of the way we were . . ."

On the ground Marcus said, "Sing it, baby . . ."

Denny's voice grew louder. *"Memories—la la la la la la la—"*

He was only a hundred feet above Tecla and could see De Luca and Gordon below staring intently as the scenario continued to work itself out.

"Going out over the hill now," he called out, and shouted into his air channel, "Let's go. Move in. Make it look good."

He whumped away from the Monte and over the village, feathering till the helicopter almost floated. He leaned back in his seat and sang explosively now, *"The way we werrre."*

Behind him, the other helicopters, like a detachment of enraged bees, were buzzing in, holding formation, chop-chopping the air, the death's-head emblems on the noses fiercely visible, the cannons and machine guns bristling from the doors with men at the sights.

From below and to the right, sudden spasmodic flashes of light broke from the density of the deep bush. Almost instantly, Gimper's voice came through on the air channel.

"What the hell's that?"

Denny peered downward as the flashes increased in frequency. He was about to raise his glasses but decided not to bother.

"Numero Uno to the squad," he called, instead. "Those are muzzle flashes. Mike's got something set up there and the dummies are wasting their blanks in the rehearsal." Into his ground channel he said, "Chopper One to Ground. Some of your atmosphere are shootin' their load. Tell them no one's lookin'. Chopper One, over. Dumb bastards," he concluded. "Let's cool them out."

He opened throttle, headed out over the bush and worked lower, peering at the flashes which continued, and was astonished when, suddenly, men rose up, rifles at their shoulders. He heard the crack of their fire over his rotor chop and felt a jarring double impact forward of him.

"They're shooting live. It's live," he shouted, kicking the craft away. "Jesus Christ!"

As the helicopter jerked and shuddered, he battled the pedals. Down below he saw a man leap up from the tall reeds cradling a machine gun, sighting upward at him.

Vibrating madly, the slim gun barrel loosed a stream of bullets, and he ducked in automatic response. Just forward of him there was a blinding flash, a sound of shattering metal, and the rotor noise lessened.

"Son of a bitch, they've hit something," he shouted into both channels. "Somebody's shooting at us with live ammo."

Fighting for control, he advanced the throttle to full, tried to pull up, but the machine would not rise. Slamming at the knobs, kicking, he saw a helicopter speed by him on the right. A white-faced Gimper waved at him and his voice came over the radio, screeching, "Get out of here, Denny. Get out!"

He saw Gimper pull his thirty-eight and start firing futilely down at the men now rising fully from the brush, hats off, brown faces contorted with excitement. The machine gunner, sweat pouring from him, turned his weapon on Gimper's chopper and threw a lead arc at him but missed.

Disregarding Gimper's puerile fire, the attackers continued to blaze away, screaming, forcing Gimper to spin up and out of their trajectories.

Abruptly, Denny felt his rotor catching hold again and the cabin stabilized. Working the pedals like an organ, he thought he had regained some measure of control when, with a convulsive shudder, his machine started heaving and plunging, every atom of metal struggling to retain its form.

"I'm losing it," he said almost calmly into the air channel. "I'm just going to try to blow it out of here." He leaned over and shouted to the attackers below, *"You motherfuckers!"*

Working throttle and pedals, he contrived to jerk the machine up ten feet, yawing and wobbling, and saw that he had succeeded in leaving the valley and was coming over Tecla.

In the crane basket, stunned by the sight of the battered helicopter limping back toward him, jerking spastically, De Luca shouted, "Get me down!"

Paul had been the one to hear the first shots and point to the Mexicans rising from their cover, blazing away.

"Who are they?" De Luca had shouted into the radio. "Stop them!" But everything had happened too quickly.

The crane basket drove to earth like a hammered nail and Paul clutched the camera for balance. At ground level, Marcus, face in panic, stared skyward, calling tensely into his microphone, "Denny . . . hang in, man, hang in. Denny, hang in."

His was the only voice. Apart from that there was total silence as the crew, the helpers, everyone, fixed their eyes on the wobbling flight. As though the attackers, too, were waiting, the firing stopped. Higher overhead, the other helicopters circled, their rotor chuffs intersecting as they hovered over Denny.

Paul watched the tortured aircraft, riveted to its progress. At his side, De Luca's hands clutched each other, and his face, under its baseball cap, was frozen.

Slowly, a bird in pain, the helicopter managed to rise another twenty feet. As it struggled to maintain that altitude, the rotor turned with an aching twist and the tail shuddered with every revolution. Still, it floated over Tecla and Paul was able to see Denny, working feverishly. Then awkwardly, the machine started to settle.

"He's coming down," De Luca muttered. "Denny'll do it. He can do it. He's coming down!" he shouted. "Give him room."

From the helicopter, Denny could see the knots of people down below scatter, leaving a large open space. He gripped the seat and held his breath, feeling every yaw in his guts.

"Easy, baby—easy," he whispered to his machine, but as he said this, the power went completely. There was a micromoment of sudden, free-floating slackness, then the fall began.

From the ground, at Tecla, they saw a blade tear off from the rotor mast and slice across the silver skin, plummeting the helicopter to the earth. It dove like a projectile, spinning down and around, breaking apart as it fell, but the main cabin was still in one piece when it neared the earth, and with a crackling roar, it caught the top of Tecla's octagonal temple, was impaled by the stone, smashed the stone in turn and was opened by it at the same time, like a gigantic sardine can, and collapsed into the hollow center, exploding what glass remained and throwing up a ton of metal debris, as the watching crowd let out a roar of horrified dismay.

De Luca ran toward the wreck, his booted legs jiggling at a crazy angle. Paul and Marcus ran behind him and the spell broke. A dozen men dashed forward, leaping toward the aircraft, disregarding the heat and the smoke, pulling and hauling to get into the cabin. From every quarter of the plateau came despairing groans. The script girl, who had raced forward with them, shrieked in a high, terrifying soprano, and De Luca pulled up, his hands going to his face in horror.

CHAPTER
34

Kruger, the driver, was the first to hurl himself into the wreck. In minutes he appeared with something in his arms that resembled a torso. Wavering, he sat down on a ledge of rock and openly sobbed. Others came to him, instantly, with drop cloths to cover his burden. De Luca was transfixed, and though Paul watched, he felt disembodied; it was almost impossible to make the link between the twisted metal wedged in the well of the temple and the silver machine it had once been. He half-expected that Denny would suddenly appear to make jokes about his stunt double; surely that small mound underneath the drop cloth could not be connected to him.

He felt a hand clutch his arm and turned to find Rennie in tears. Her other hand stretched out to De Luca, and she pulled both men close to her. Nearby, Allan Marcus, the earphones ripped away from his head and still dangling, like a severed umbilical cord, slumped in shock. Manuel Quesedo, who had come running over with the others, was covered with sweat. His unbelieving voice came up from his dusty boots.

"*Loco*—they be *loco* to do this."

No one listened. Men came out of the split bird with other lumpy drop cloths and deposited them gently on the earth near the temple, like offerings. De Luca half-started forward but Sieberling motioned him back; there was nothing he could do. A breathless *policía* ran up to Quesedo and reported that the gunmen had all vanished into the brush.

"Don' matter," the captain vowed, "we get them all, *jefe*. Others give names."

Someone drove a small panel truck up to the rubble. A grip opened the rear doors and then hesitated as though any act after that was too final to contemplate.

352

Quesedo mopped his forehead with his sleeve. "Federal *policía* come now. When *terroristas* do this . . ."

"Luis's people?" Paul looked at him, greatly surprised.

"Sí—not be *bajos* with machine guns. *Terroristas* know Aguillar be taken last night and they t'ink . . ." He stopped, suddenly uneasy. "Who can to tell what they t'ink?"

"They think we had something to do with it," Paul said. "That's why they did this—it's a reprisal."

"It's so useless," De Luca groaned. "So useless."

Ben Lufkin came toward them, ashen-faced. "Mike, what a . . . terrible thing. Never, never in my life have I . . ." He shook his head. "I'll get with you later. Right now I want to put in a call."

"Ben," De Luca said quickly, "do me one single favor. Don't make that call until we've talked."

Jarred, Lufkin coughed, said, "Okay" and walked, hastily, to the car that had brought him. In seconds he disappeared down the hill.

Where only minutes before there had been panic on the Monte, now a stillness descended. The deformed remains hung, contoured to the temple. The sacrifice was removed to the truck whose driver sat morosely, waiting for his order to depart. There was nothing more to be done; the crew and the Mexican helpers whispered in their separate groups. An assistant informed De Luca that special equipment would be needed to cut the wreckage out. Another came to ask, hesitantly, if the extras, down below, could be released for the rest of the day.

A fresh chill assailed Paul, and he looked for Quesedo but could not find him. How could he have told Flo that Michael was responsible? Why would he?

With no warning, De Luca's father was at his shoulder, controlling his tears.

"Pauli, Pauli," he groaned. "What they do to him, those animals? What they do to Mikey? They try to destroy him."

Denny's the one who died, he thought. The panel truck took him away.

"Of course," he said, and the old man shuffled off.

Rennie came to him, breathlessly. In ten minutes Michael wanted a meeting, before he saw Lufkin; a plan of action had to be worked out.

Paul heard her in a fog.

"I can't get my head together, I'm sorry."

"I know," she said, "but we have to . . . stick together and help him, Paul . . . we have to help him get through this."

Her face had taken on a resolve, yet a certain beatitude was there as well. He fell silent and became aware of a large group of peasants who had come up the hill and were now advancing slowly, riveted by what they saw. They halted a dozen feet from the rubble of the temple and whispered to each other. Seeing them, Sieberling shouted, "Get them out of here. Get them away."

Appearing from nowhere, Quesedo called to them authoritatively, but they stood their ground.

"What do they want?" Sieberling demanded.

"Not important," the policeman replied. He motioned to three of his men, who moved quickly to the peasants, herding them back. Retreating, the peasants shouted in anger. A Mexican helper standing close to Paul said in quick, nervous tones, "They be angry because temple is broken. Much important to them, Tecla's house. Say you break it and brings much bad luck now, to everyone."

At the edge of the hill, the crowd refused to move back farther and one of the *policías* struck a man on the side of the face. As though it was a signal, and with a common roar of anger, the peasants leaped upon the three hapless policemen, engulfing them like an army of ants. Breaking away from the melee, four of the mob rushed to a nearby camera and, with one single heave, broke it from its mountings to send it crashing over the lip. De Luca went white.

"No," he screamed. "Sal!"

"Get them," Sieberling exploded, charging forward. Ten men rushed forward with him, two with pistols already out, but they were swallowed as a new horde of peasants surged up from below to envelop them.

Paul stood, helplessly transfixed, as a splinter group ran to the camera truck. Having reached it, they struck out wildly, with whatever came to hand, at the innocent lenses and shutters and motors, spraying glass and metal for yards around. De Luca moaned as another camera was flung down the hill, the case cracking, exploding its parts like shrapnel. Four gigantic lamps and stands followed that, the hurtling sight goading the mob to rip and shatter whatever it could in a paroxysm of revenge. Quesedo and his *policías* held their guns out, but there was no possibility of shooting without wounding an American. Two of Machado's men were crawling, unsteadily, on all fours, blood dripping from their faces.

And then, abruptly, the mob receded and were gone from the Monte, leaving broken light stands and bulb shards and yet another camera swaying on a loosened tripod, its lens broken off.

At the head of his men, Sieberling looked after the retreating peasants and shouted obscenities at them. He was about to castigate Quesedo when he saw the innermost hut of the Vietnamese village take fire to blaze furiously as the draft swept up.

"Fire," he shouted, "there's a fire!"

Paul ran, with whoever was left, to the rim of the Monte. By the time he reached it, another hut had caught fire and then another.

"Safety men!" De Luca yelled. He plunged down the hill, and Paul raced after him.

When the first shots had come, Flo, peering skyward from behind the barriers with the onlookers, had known they were live rounds. Her ears, attuned to movie blanks, found the difference, but Stella had been skeptical.

She was twenty feet up the mountain when the first fire broke out. The whoosh of the flames and the cries of the crowd spun her about in time to see the next hut catch and flame upward with a frightening intensity. The crowd below screamed and broke up, running. The Vietnamese-dressed extras, hundreds of them, raced to escape from the narrow lanes in which they were trapped. Pushing and thrusting, they ran over each other in panic as the film crew, bullhorns blaring, snatched up precious equipment and stumbled back, retreating to the road.

Bodies bolted by Stella, and when she realized they were coming down from the Monte, she reversed and ran back with them. Reaching the valley, she heard an explosion, felt a blast of heat, and the ground came up at her. Knocked prone, she saw that a wooden hut that had been near a clump of trees was no more, nor were the trees. Instead, there was a huge hole in the earth and four people were in it, dazed.

Rising unsteadily, she heard a barrage of firearms and ducked down in fright but saw, quickly, that the spitting fire was coming from another hut which had obviously stored powder and ammunition that were now exploding, blowing out bits of wood and metal in vicious trajectories. A Vietnamese-dressed woman, hat off, long hair flying, ran in confused and frightened circles, blood leaking from her scalp. A man snatched up a crying child who had been hurt by a flying board and managed to rush away from the now totally fire-engulfed village.

The entire area was filled with sulfurous and concealing smoke. More explosions rocked the earth as other storage huts were touched off. Running blindly toward where she remembered the barriers to be, Stella reached clearer air, her chest throbbing, her shoes torn from her feet. With surprise, she saw Flo. The girl's glasses had disappeared; her hair had been singed and a part of it was still smoking. She had an elderly woman by one arm and a young one by the other and was moving them to safety. Seeing Stella, she screamed, "Are they satisfied? Go up and ask them if they're satisfied." Leaving her charges, she plunged back into the smoke.

By now the fire had spread beyond the invented village and half a dozen small houses nearby were alight, the pigs outside snorting in terror, running against their confining wires, screaming as they did when they smelled the abattoir.

The safety squad, heat shields on, pumped chemicals, smothering what flames they could, but the real enemy was the stored explosives which blew in their casings with a shock wave of compression, hurling earth, sowing confusion and terror, trapping the extras and the tourists alike.

Rushing through the bedlam, Paul spotted Stella leaning, dazedly, against a still-standing tree. He ran toward her, shouting her name. Her face was sooted and she shook as he grabbed her arms.

"Oh . . ." was all she could say. "Oh, God . . ."

He pulled her to where the miasma and heat were less, to an open space between two scorched vehicles. She heaved, spasmodically, and he held her, looking back, meanwhile, to the center of the inferno where De Luca's khaki-suited figure weaved, it seemed, between the smoke. She clung to him silently and he clung to her, rocking gently until her heaving stopped, until she pulled her head away.

"Easy," he murmured.

She nodded, looking at him with an intense, searching look that reached deep down, startling him, jarring him as though the probe were physical.

From out of the haze a black mat of hair appeared and a frenzied pair of red-rimmed eyes. Flo's face was dirt-caked, her blue jeans soaked in mud. Her blouse, slashed and rock-ripped, showed bursts of startling white where her breasts had torn through. Her body was an electric wire. She rose above the flames behind her as though on a tower, on a crane. Her eyes were brighter than any of Kodály's lights.

"Did you think they wouldn't do *something?*"

Wisps of smoke clung to her hair. The skin of her face was reddened and rough. She gave off an acrid odor. Shaking her head in despair, she looked across a burned patch of ground past a concrete storage hut where two water buffalo were on their knees, lowing in pain, their hides smoldering.

With an intake of breath, she ran toward them, moving speedily. A small explosion echoed from the storage hut. She gave it a quick look, skirting it to get to the animals. As she turned the corner, there was an angry hiss as though a snake were locked in the concrete. The hissing grew louder, became a snapping, cracking sound, and in one choreographed movement, the walls blew outward, the roof upward; the hut opened like a concrete petal, the blast of TNT hurling slabs for twenty feet in all directions and rocking the earth.

Flo fell where she was, spun about first by a two-foot chunk of concrete, then she was covered with debris. Stella screamed. Paul shouted and ran toward the pile of dust and rubble. Two safety men reached it with him. He pawed till he felt an arm, then pulled. The safety men went around to the other side and pulled with him. Flo's body jerked loose, staggering all three back. Her head hung down like a rag doll's, and Paul could see a huge gash behind her hair. He turned his face away and the three set her down awkwardly. Not knowing what else to do, one of the safety men stripped off his jacket and placed it over her head. The other murmured tensely into his walkie-talkie and Paul, near to retching, walked back to where Stella had been, but she was no longer there.

Behind him, the fires were dying and the explosions had ceased. The extras and the onlookers were collecting in clumps, subdued and still frightened. A few of the hurt lay on the ground, friends and relatives kneeling worriedly beside them. The earth was pocked and scorched. The Monte's stones were fire-blackened and broken. The hogs still raced about, squalling in terror.

Within minutes, a grim-faced De Luca, an angry Sieberling and a shocked, unbelieving Allan Marcus were at Paul's side, staring at the now drop-cloth-draped body.

"It's her own fault," Sieberling muttered. "She had no right being here."

"Why don't you go over and kick her," Paul said bitterly.

"It's horrible, horrible." De Luca's beard cradled bits of cinder and his eyes were bloodshot behind the smudged lenses. "They set the fire, you know, the *bajos*. It wasn't an accident. Look what they've done to their own."

"The ambulances from Oacala are on the way." Sieberling was more subdued. "I'll radio them about this."

"I'll stay here until they come," Marcus said. He seemed to be half his height and a twitch had attacked his right eye, winking it convulsively.

From out of the still-lingering smoke, Manuel Quesedo appeared like a demon, running at them full tilt. His cap was gone, his jacket was ripped in half a dozen places and his face worked madly. He shot past Paul, tripped, recovered and plunged forward, stopping only when he reached the drop cloth. Hesitating, he kneeled down and lifted a corner of the shroud. Paul saw the back of his head grow rigid and his hand come up to cross himself. He rose, stricken, and stood there, staring into space.

She was gone and it was all gone with her. He would never see her white skin or the roundness of her breast or feel the life in her hair, and they would never talk again.

De Luca called, "Captain!" But Quesedo did not answer.

"Quesedo," Sieberling echoed.

At that the policeman turned, and Paul saw the grief in his face. He walked slowly to Sieberling, stopped before him and spat deliberately, at his feet. Sieberling stepped away, astonished, and Quesedo slowly, contemptuously, turned his back and walked slowly up the Monte.

For half a minute no one said anything. Then Allan Marcus broke the silence.

"But he put her in jail."

Two hours later, after the cleanup had begun, after Sieberling had persuaded De Luca he could do nothing more and they were driving back in the Mercedes, the devastation receding behind them, Paul watched the mesquite and the cactus pass. He watched the dung and the dust and tried to shake off the cold feel of Flo's arm.

"I believe," he finally said, "that if we hadn't gone to the cave, this whole thing would not have happened."

"Maybe," De Luca answered. "But you can't redo the past. The thing we have to do now is see what we can salvage."

"Salvage?" It was a startling idea.

"Yes—do it. Make it, despite everything. Show them. I'll go to Lufkin with an offer to compromise some more. The studio's not going to let those millions piss away; they'll have to go along, somehow."

His eyes were growing steadily less clouded; his voice took on the timbre of confidence. He was, once again, in his natural element, inventing, imagining. It was almost as though what lay behind them, at the Monte, was a scenario, an exciting story conference, bringing with it its own intoxication.

"To stop now, after all we've been through, would be . . . a kind of treason to Denny."

He means it, Paul thought, unbelieving.

"Michael, listen to me. Elvira knew about the cave. You knew and I knew."

"Luis's whole goddamn gang knew. You think that dope runner's to be trusted? Look what he did to us. In the end they were simply trying to milk us dry."

"No," he pressed, "it's all one piece—we went up there and they got him."

The slightest of clouds returned. De Luca struggled with some devil inside him, then said, "I don't think it means anything, but I told Sal where we were." He watched for the incredulous look and added, "I want to be totally honest with you, Paul."

"Sal," Paul said. "Sal turned him in to Quesedo."

"Am I being honest with you?" De Luca demanded. "Would I tell you this if I believed it was our fault, even for a minute?"

"Michael." He heard his voice rise in despair. "They're dead; they won't come back in the next reel!"

"We have to go on." De Luca's voice shook for the first time. "You and I have to go on."

They were in the small street that led out to the Zócalo. As they made the turn, and were still in shadow, from out of a doorway a small female figure in a dirty gray skirt and green top emerged to wave them down. De Luca jammed on the brakes to avoid hitting her. Paul grabbed at the steadying bar as they skidded a bit and saw, with shock, that it was Elvira.

The Mercedes pulled to a stop inches from her. She reached back and picked up a large woven straw bag. Paul threw the door open and she quickly jumped in. De Luca reached over to grasp at her hand anxiously.

"What's wrong? What are you doing here?"

"Do not go to the *casa*," she said in a quiet voice. "They wait for you there."

"*Bajos?*" Paul could readily believe it.

"My God, they've hurt you." De Luca fingered a pale green bruise on her cheek.

"Is nothing. When I see they do not watch too good, I take a few things and go out by the bedroom window."

She was very controlled, Paul thought, but something had happened to her, there was no question of that.

"You're sure you're not hurt?"

She hesitated a moment, then said, "This, they do." She pulled the kerchief from her head, allowing both men to see the spikes.

De Luca gasped. She still looks beautiful, Paul thought, not deformed at all.

"It comes back," she said quickly. "I am young. It comes back. They think I be ashamed this way, but I have no shame for this."

"Damn them!" Michael's shaking voice held a depth of feeling Paul had never heard before. "You'll come home with me and stay there for a couple of days. We'll call the police."

"No, I go to where I work before, the Señora's house. I sleep there this night."

"Elvira, come with me. Please."

"No, I go where I say."

De Luca sat back in sulking silence. Breaking it finally, he said, "I'll take you there."

"I can go alone. Is better. From the Zócolo, I can to walk there in little time."

"Then what?"

"Then we see."

De Luca started the car angrily and drove across the square where, as always, the German tourists snapped endless pictures of dung heaps. Here, Elvira briskly opened the door.

"I go out now."

Paul raised a hand to help her with the bulky straw bag, but she shook her head and did it alone.

"Call me, please," De Luca implored, "later. We'll get another house. I won't let you go back there."

"Be careful, Miguel." She stepped to the street. "And you." She turned the full power of her eyes on Paul and walked away briskly. Two men having coffee stared at her in shock and she thought of what must happen now, how she must leave here before they came to maim her further.

As Paul watched Elvira move down the street, he heard Michael say, "I've got to see Lufkin right away," and was skewered by surprise. Lufkin? Lufkin had been driven from his head. But Michael said intensely, "Lufkin, yes. We can't let everything fall apart."

Drained, he watched Michael drive off. Not even the brass blare of "La Cumparsita" from the bandstand as the rehearsal commenced shook him into a connection with the life around him. He walked slowly to the Jaime and went directly to the third floor. Stella was in the tub, the soapy water above her shoulders. He sat in a rattan chair and looked at the beamed ceiling, where he saw the lumpy drop cloths and the burning village and only roused himself from the vision with a strong effort.

Flo had been right, he called out with contrition—that son of a bitch Sieberling had turned Aguillar in and provoked the attack, though not on Michael's orders, on his own. Stella called back that Sieberling rarely did anything that his boss did not wish done; his sixth sense told him what to do and what not to do.

"Not this," Paul insisted. "No—this is pure Sieberling."

When she came out, his eyes were closed and his face slumped tiredly. She stood over him, wanting to open the towel that swathed her and enfold him. When he opened his eyes and saw her, he asked, "Are you going back tonight?"

"Yes. What's going to happen here now? What are you going to do?"

"I don't know. Michael said . . ." He saw her lips compress and added compulsively, "It's complicated."

"Yes," she said, "I'm sure."

"I owe it to Michael to . . ."

"If that's the way you feel . . ."

He waited for her to say something more, but she did not. Unable to bring himself to say anything else, he rose to go, and she said nothing to stop him.

CHAPTER
35

After showering and changing his clothes, Paul retreated to his cutting room. On the way there, he saw an ambulance, bell clanging, crossing the square, and he knew, without being told, that it came from Monte Tecla. Fighting depression, he sat at the Moviola and stared at the blank screen. Rennie and Sieberling, returning from Ixtepan, reported that it was swarming with state and federal police. Angrily, Rennie declared that the terrorists and the stupid underground had brought it all upon themselves.

"And Michael's trying to keep the pieces together," she said, fighting back tears. "God, how he's trying to do that."

That was for sure, Paul thought, oh, yes. He looked straight at Sieberling.

"Why did you tell Quesedo where Aguillar was?"

"Get off my back," Sieberling grated.

Rennie, uninterested, marched away, a slim, erect, martyred figure. Paul watched her go with surprising numbness. Sieberling was about to leave as well, but he would not let him.

"How do you explain that Quesedo told Flo—"

"Them?" Their names raised rage in his eyes. "Don't tell me about them. She was putting out for him. They had some kind of deal going, don't you understand that?"

"That's another lie," Paul shouted.

"You want me to tell you something?" Sieberling shook the sunglasses in his face. "I'll tell you not to be a jerk, that's what I'll tell you. And wise up—just wise up."

At one-thirty, as he watched close-ups of Denny, intensely conscious that he was viewing a corpse, word came through that two Mexicans, a woman and a child caught in one of the explosions at the foot of the Monte, were seriously, possibly critically, injured. He shut the machine off, unable to watch anymore. As he sat in silence, the telephone rang; Michael was back.

Still in the grip of the news from the hospital, he walked, zombie-like, to De Luca's office, where he found him concentrating intensely. He had just been on the phone to his crew at Ixtepan.

"We've had a lot of damage, but it's being cleaned up very quickly, even with the damn police all over the place." Michael pulled at his beard and prowled with restless energy. "Now, let me tell you what I've worked out with Ben Lufkin. We stop everything here as of now, to take stock, to assess . . . then we go back to the States and reproduce interiors on a sound stage and shoot what we have to there. Meanwhile, I'm having people scout for some other location—maybe in Hawaii—and we go there to finish. It was going back to California that won Lufkin over. I let him understand that once we're there we'll rearrange the deal. I'll take fewer points. He listened hard to that."

"Michael," Paul said, "Jesus Christ, Michael . . . it all happened only this morning."

De Luca whirled about. "Yes, but could I let him go back to L.A. without talking to him?"

"Two people are critical in the hospital."

De Luca's eyes clouded with hurt. "I heard. Yes. I hope the ones responsible really suffer. I hope they hang on the cross." He shook off the tragedy. "Now, these next days are going to be very important for us. Kodály wants out, for one thing. And those pilots want to go on a rampage." He hesitated. "Poor Denny. That poor bastard doesn't even have a widow to give insurance money to."

"And what about Flo?" Paul asked savagely. "What has she got?"

"I feel as terrible as you do, but *it's not my fault and it's not your fault.*"

"We shouldn't have flooded those fields. We shouldn't have brought Machado in."

"What was the alternative—quit?"

"I don't know."

"Well, *I* know."

That was it, Paul understood—that was his secret, *he knew.* "Those people hate us. We came in here and ripped everything up."

"Wrong! Wrong!" The words blew from De Luca's lips in a denying roar. "What did we do? We poured money in. We saved people from starving. And there are worse men than Machado around here. How many times did I try to meet with those murderous

363

bajos? You can ask Elvira; she'll tell you how the people really feel about us."

He felt like screaming, *Michael, do you really believe that?* No deceptions, no quick footwork, no cone of light *only where you want it,* but belief?

For there would be no deliberate cruelty in that, no lies—only flaws. And everyone was flawed, goddamn it, and Michael had done much for him. There was the future to be thought of, and in the vise of circumstance, anyone could do anything.

Silently, he pleaded with Michael for the truth. Openly he said, "I saw Sal. He won't admit informing on Luis."

That was dismissed. "Sal—Sal has his own ways."

"But he did turn him in."

"We're not sure."

"I'm sure."

"Yes, but we're all very wound up here."

"No." He watched Michael keenly. "You have to call him on it and get rid of him. He's vicious."

"We'll talk about it."

"Let's get him in here now."

"That's hardly our first priority."

"His informing started everything."

"I said we'll talk about it, but now's not the time."

"Now *is* the time," he said grimly. "Let's clear the air."

De Luca exploded. "Don't pressure me. This is no time for more pressure. Sal's a side issue. Let's get on with what has to be done." He looked away, clearly uncomfortable.

Paul waited a moment, then said, "Sal told me not to be a jerk."

"Whatever that means." De Luca shrugged impatiently.

"What that means," Paul said carefully, "is that I *am* a jerk. I should have known that you wanted him to do what he did."

De Luca appeared stupefied. "You think that's possible? You think that's even possible?"

"He told me to wise up. When he said that—"

"My God." De Luca's voice faltered. "I came here with hopes and dreams; if anyone knows that, you do. I stayed here, prepared to fight the reactionaries. Luis, despite what he did to us, is someone I could only have the deepest respect and admiration for. Paul . . . if you can believe I wanted something to happen to him—" He broke off, emotionally. "The more important thing is that events are beyond anyone's control now. What we have to do, you and I, is finish this picture. What we have to do is make it so good and so important that the world will listen to us."

He had slipped the question, Paul saw with despair. Why could he not understand that if he answered, if he shared the truth, that was all? But he had not.

"You don't need me to finish it," he said dully.

"Paul . . ." Michael approached him tenderly, his voice low, "we've been like . . . brothers on this. My father said it and it's true. I don't trust too many people, you know that. But it's been really good. Don't break it up now."

Shocked, Paul examined the sensitive face. *He* needed, had always needed, had always felt the piece missing, had searched and yearned for the father, the brother, the friend, for the collaborator, for the being upon whom to depend; *his* was the need, but Michael—? And the plea was genuine; Michael's eyes gave affirmation, his body tensed, his hands were motionless; Michael needed *him*.

"Besides, I'm thinking of you. You have talent, but that's not enough. This miserable world is set up so that it's a permanent battle. The only way to do anything you believe in is to fight your way through everything."

"I guess," he said quietly, "my problem is I don't believe enough."

"You do. You can. You have to."

"No," he said, "I don't."

"Then you'll never do anything!" Michael said harshly. "You'll talk and dream and dance on the edges, but you'll never *do it*. You'll never get it out of you. You'll never put it together. You'll be like a million others." His voice softened into a plea. "Don't throw it away, Paul."

"Tell me you wanted Luis taken," he pleaded, "just tell me the truth."

De Luca recoiled as though a fire had passed between them.

"Jesus, what difference does that make now?"

"It makes a difference."

"What we're trying to do makes a difference."

"Yes, but this . . ." He searched desperately for some way to make him understand. "This is real—it's not a movie."

He realized then that it would not happen, that Michael would not share with him and in the sharing provide a measure of absolution. Instead he held out the glittering promise, something he had seen Michael perform with others but never with him. Or was that true? Had Rennie moved to him so effortlessly because Michael had, unspoken, wished it so? As he had wished Luis gone—and had no need to say that directly. Or left the business of Machado for Sieberling to handle.

"Michael," he said, "it's no good. It's just no good."

It was as though De Luca had taken a blow to the face. His head moved sideways to soften the punch. His skin reddened and his eyes narrowed.

"I should have known you couldn't hack it," he said with contempt. Recovering, his narrowed lids opened wider and wider till they were blazing circles. His jaw thrust out, projecting his beard like an avenging brush. "When you see the picture, don't look for your work, it won't be there."

He turned toward the telephone and, seeing the broad back, Paul knew he no longer existed for him.

Slowly, he returned to the cutting rooms to retrieve his sweater, his notebooks, a blue work shirt. The reels of film whose frames he had meticulously shaped, whose images he had loved, those reels that had cost so much, were stacked in their bins like sleeping soldiers whom he would never again awaken.

He traced a path from the compound to the Zócalo, where the siesta shutters were descending with hollow clangs. As he walked, he saw many eyes upon him, barefoot Indios, white-shirted merchants, tray-bearing women, and he realized that, by now, word of what had happened at Monte Tecla had spread through the town.

CHAPTER

36

×≡×≡×≡×≡× **36** ≡×≡×≡×≡×≡×

At near seven o'clock, the golden Oacala light slanting across the airport murals lent them an almost three-dimensional effect. The stacked, curving bodies of the *campesinos* caught the glare on their machetes, and the Spanish horses reached out from the wall in rearing struggle. There was a small check-in line for the Mexico City flight, and, taking his place at the end, Paul looked toward the large window beyond which the 737 could be seen being attended by ear-padded mechanics. Near the window, seated in one of the reed chairs, he saw Stella, and his blood pressure jacked up.

Moving forward in line, he kept track of her. When he reached the desk, he saw her rise, turn and recognize him. In confusion, he faced the clerk fully and presented his ticket. When he turned back, Stella was nowhere to be seen. He stepped away from the counter, wondering where she had gone and what he would say upon seeing her and where she was sitting, and what she was thinking.

At the rim of the horizon, he caught sight of a helicopter loafing along and wondered if it was one of theirs. In mid-wonder he castigated himself—what did it matter? Yet, as he watched the machine grow smaller and smaller, his agitation grew larger. The picture could have been something so extraordinary—such an achievement. Michael, he said to himself, you shit—you driven shit. If only you could be fine, if only you could be *real*, if only you might possess some hint of a noble side. He almost said the words aloud and jerked his head around to make certain he had not.

But even as the echo of his unsounded words died, he realized that Michael could be no other way—that he could never pursue his desperate inner visions the way others wished he might—that decency would hamper him, consideration bend his talent. The juggernaut rolling everywhere and over everyone was the mainspring of his accomplishment. That ruthlessness was what allowed him, finally, to construct images that moved and shook millions of people. He would, in the end, let no one and nothing stand in his way. He would, surely, start the film up again; surely he would go on, complete. Ixtepan would be a memory. Denny would be a memory. Flo would be a memory. He would be a memory. Standing there, Paul thought he might give years of his life to have Michael's gifts, to own his single-minded vision, but he knew that would never happen. He would never "do it." Michael was right.

He felt a warmth behind him and knew, instantly, that it was Stella. He turned with some trepidation and saw that she, too, was tentative.

"You're on the flight," she said.

"Yes."

She asked him nothing, but he felt he owed her an explanation and added, "He's going to finish the picture."

"Here?" She was incredulous.

"No—someplace else."

"You're not—?"

"No," he assured her, "I'm out of it. Going home." He smiled wryly. "You chose the wrong place for a vacation."

A slight-figured woman carrying an expensive tooled-leather carry-on case moved past them on her way to the check-in counter. Paul glanced at her only cursorily, looked back at Stella and then swung his eyes back to the woman in disbelief. Involuntarily, he grabbed Stella's arm.

"My God," he whispered. "That's Elvira."

She was almost unrecognizable. Only some instinct, some vague total impression, had told him that it was she. She wore a smart white linen dress and blue high-heeled shoes. A lavender silk turban wound, artfully, about her head covered the slashed hair and made her appear much taller at the same time. Her eyes were hidden by fashionably large sunglasses, and there appeared to be hints of crimson on her lips and pink in her cheeks that were not hers naturally. She wore golden hoops in her ears, but there was no other trace of ornament. From a beautiful beige leather shoulder bag she extracted peso notes and extended them toward the clerk. He motioned toward the 737 and, with a smile reserved for only the most important travelers, proceeded to write a ticket.

"She's going. She's on the plane," he said, with wonder.

"Who is she?" Stella wanted to know.

"Michael's girl," he whispered back, "Michael's Indian girl."

Stella stared openly now. "Indian girl? Her?"

As he watched, riveted, the loudspeaker called the passengers for Mexico City to load. Ticket in one hand, leather case in the other, Elvira came toward them, on her way to the gate. High heels rattling the tiles, she came on as Paul stood there, unable to move. She came abreast of them unwaveringly. And passed. With not a look, not a word. As though she had never seen Paul before, climbed a mountain with him to a cave. It was all behind her now. Everything was behind her; she was moving on. She went through the gate first and Stella said, "Are you sure that's the girl?"

"That's Elvira, and I think she's the only person Michael really cares about."

His seat was in the tenth row and Stella's was in the third. Someplace between them Elvira sat; he could see the tip of her turban. The plane started its run and he looked out the window. After the slight thump came and they lifted off, he felt the surge of power in his stomach as the angle of ascent became sharp. The engines pulled them up cleanly, knifing through a low-flying cloud, straining toward the sun. The Sierra Madre were ahead, and already Oacala was behind.

He found the back of Stella's head. For fully five minutes he stared at the free-moving lightness of her hair and the occasional hand that came up to cradle her throat as she read. At one point she arched her back, straightening, fitting herself to the seat, and he caught a glimpse of her profile.

He sat back, next to a plump, well-dressed Mexican man, and, watching the landscape drone by, wondered what Michael was doing at this moment, what feverish schemes were being concocted. The feeling of deprivation, of being locked out so suddenly, attacked him strongly. That son of a bitch. What a carrot he had held out, what a luscious ripe future; it would never happen again.

After ten minutes the seat belt sign went off, and he unbuckled. On sudden impulse, he rose, excused himself and clambered past the Mexican's knees to the aisle. Hesitating a moment to collect himself, he moved forward. There was slight turbulence, and a few rows down he reached out for support as his foot skittered into something under a seat.

Murmuring apologies, he toed the luggage back in place, jingling its contents. Looking up, he saw with surprise that he had grasped Elvira's back rest. She was no longer wearing sunglasses and her blue eyes shone out like beacons.

She moved to place a high-heeled foot protectively on the leather case and, instantly, Paul knew what had jingled inside it, what she would not let leave her side. The gold! All the gold that Michael had given her was in that bag, the bracelets, the necklaces, the hair ornaments, the armbands, the ancient charms and amulets; all the gold. She was free, and Michael had freed her.

She held his eyes with almost hypnotic directness, then she nodded. He nodded too, gravely, and moved on. When he reached the tihrd row Stella looked up at him, puzzled. He leaned down to the bosomy woman in the seat next to hers and talked her into believing there had been some confusion and he belonged where she was. When the woman agreed to the exchange, he slipped into the warm seat.

"Pretty good," Stella said.

"I learned some stuff from Michael."

"I think so," Stella said, "but not too much."

"Oh, yes," he told her. "Limitations."

He looked behind him for the turbaned head. The eyes, he saw, were once again shielded by the oversized sunglasses.

"When he finds out she's gone—" he whispered.

"He'll find some other object to worship."

"I'm not so sure. She had a meaning for him that—"

He found Stella's hand upon his then, and she said, gently, "He's back there; let him stay there."

Off to the right, he saw Monte Tecla in the effulgent sunset glow and felt the strong pull of connection, though from this height he could see no detail, just the sacred mountain itself and a hint of the temple at its peak.

He closed his hand over Stella's, saying softly, "Look there."

She heard the tag end of struggle and sorrow in his voice and moved toward him so that their shoulders touched.

The speck of plane passing overhead pulled De Luca's eyes up with a magnetic power. For ten seconds he held an unwavering connection, then turned to Sieberling who nodded confirmation.

De Luca blinked and slumped against the Mercedes. There was no one to depend upon but himself—as always. To believe otherwise was a chimera. He groaned inwardly. In the days to come there would be so many dislocatioьs, so many forces pulling at him that it would be difficult to maintain his center—but he would.

370

The tragedy that had happened here was the sum of many things. Perhaps, when the boxes of worm-infested chicken were flying about he should have known what he was truly fighting: the misunderstanding, the ignorance, the desperate violence that existed and would exist forever in the hearts of men.

From the open doorway, Rennie beckoned to him. He started toward her thinking, with desperate longing, of Elvira. When night fell he would go, himself, to where she was staying and fetch her. Tonight, of all nights, he needed her calmness, her understanding, her pure and ancient instincts.

He looked up, again, to the plane rising higher and felt, once again, the rage of being bereft and betrayed.

Paul looked down, watching the mound of earth and stone pass from his field of vision. The distance was like time; smoothing the landscape, erasing the scars, covering everything with a protective coating. He tried to spot where the camera had been when it all started, but it was impossible. Already, so much of what had happened was becoming vague, receding with the valley as the sierra loomed up. Stella's shoulder was comforting, and it was incredible how different it all looked from up here, how very different.